I0700510

A VAMPIRE TALE

BEGUILED BY NIGHT BOOK *Two*

NICOLE EIGENER

POLIDORI
PRESS

First Edition: May 2023
Also available in ebook and hardcover
Written, designed, and published in Palm Springs, California

Book and cover design by Nicole Eigener
Cover photograph by Alyssa Thorne Fine Art: alyssathorne.co

ISBN: 979-8-9873802-3-9

Library of Congress Control Number: 2023907272

to Beverley Lee,

mon cœur — our hearts will be in Paris pour toujours.
CITIZENS OF SHADOW *would not exist without you.*

And to all those who feel different …
never stop searching for your people.
You will find them.

Epigraph

> *"There is a loneliness in this world so great that you can see it in the slow movement of the hands of a clock"*
>
> CHARLES BUKOWSKI

> *"What can an eternity of damnation matter to someone who has felt, if only for a second, the infinity of delight?"*
>
> CHARLES BAUDELAIRE

> *"You must go on. I can't go on. I'll go on."*
>
> SAMUEL BECKETT

One

EXORDIUM

There was an unearthly sense of falling

As if one were tumbling from a bridge

Into the fathomless night

Grasping at icy fog and

Trembling in hazard of the strike of one's bones

against the harsh earth

Or on the surface of the deceptive depths

As a million wasps stung their way out of one's veins

And just before the moment of impact

Some demoniac angel swept one up into its terrifying arms and

One was propelled upward again

Bathed in a ghastly protective light...

A light at once familiar and foreign

And one felt at peace,

As if one had at last found the soul's true home.

LOS ANGELES, CALIFORNIA | DECEMBER 1

LAST YEAR

"Listen, honey, you may think you look good now, but just wait another ten years," the duck-lipped blonde slurs, pointing and sloshing her craft cocktail in his direction.

This a hipster trap, a frivolous place where mixologists take thirty minutes to infuse small-batch liqueurs with exotic hardwood smoke, fabricate comically whimsical garnishes, and gently saw pristine, clear cubes off a block of frozen, triple-filtered spring water. And then have the gall to charge $20 for the privilege of a couple sips of their abominations. At least that is how he imagines they would taste: abominable.

But Vauquelin is not here for cocktails tonight ... at least not of the ilk offered on this menu.

He only ever drinks wine, and the mixologists make little attempt to hide their ire when he orders (Hmph. Robbed of their artistry, and forced to merely *pour* something).

The hipsters lap it up.

Vauquelin glares at his bar companion with a stone face, listening (im)patiently as she babbles about Beverly Hills and the very best surgeons and so on, then devotes his attention to twirling his glass around, watching the legs form.

It is a *very* good wine.

He has heard this woman's line hundreds of times before in Los Angeles. In multiple years, decades, settings. It is always the same, only with different clothes and with considerably more elective surgery now than his early years in the city.

But plastic humans taste terrible.

There is something … something *altered* in their blood. If he had to draw a metaphor (because he has no idea, really), he would think this particular type of human is like fast food. A far cry from gourmet. A flipped burger, if you will. Greasy and unsatisfactory, but it will get the job done.

"My darling, let me show you the true secret to living beautifully young, forever," he says, extending his hand in invitation.

The woman laces her fingers into his.

They always do.

Vauquelin licks his Opinel knife clean and folds it back into itself, sauntering back to his car: a luxury rental which, despite being meticulously cleaned between uses, smells of too many drivers and disappointing stag parties.

The woman would no longer register in his mind at all were it not for the chemically-twinged tang of her blood on his tongue — but at least it had taken the treacherous edge off of his hunger.

He left her positioned against a dumpster and not quite dead, not quite emptied, mumbling incoherently in her dirtied dress — with a deep knife gash to obscure the puncture wounds he made in her thigh.

She will live.

He cannot afford the costs of leaving bodies behind.

He had returned only yesterday, just before dawn on a private night flight from the UK, where he had paid a visit to some new friends (imagine that! Vauquelin having friends!). But Los Angeles is vastly different for him now: there is no majestic mansion on West Figueroa to return to … no catacombs, no shelter of his own. Not this time, much to his chagrin … and without those protections, he cannot live in the manner to which he is accustomed.

Instead, he relishes the slight buzz from the gin-infused blood he had consumed, its high plasticine notes tingling on his tongue. Blood which has — well — not quite restored him, but quasi-hushed his body's sanguine cries.

Typing numbers on a keypad, he lets himself into his opulent rental house: a mid-century modern bi-level nestled high in the Hollywood Hills. A bit too modern for his sensibilities, but the views and amenities are splendid.

He unwraps a hefty bouquet of flowers on the bar in the useless kitchen.

He needs their beauty … he craves their inevitable decay.

I will always need it … pour l'éternité.[†]

He fluffs them into a vase and carries it to the bedroom, sniffing the blooms as he walks.

There are far too many windows in this house, but they have all been doubly covered per his request.

The bedroom is pitch black.

Perfect.

Soft, warm light fills the room as he twists the knob on the nightstand lamp and sits on the edge of the bed, hands on his splayed knees.

At once his eyes land on a blood smear across the knee of his trouser leg.

Sloppy work, he admonishes.

[†]- FOR ETERNITY

This nefarious city of Los Angeles — which had once given him hope and love and so much joy — is no longer his home, and once again he is an untethered stranger in an even stranger land.

He has given himself one month here.

Exactly thirty-one days to gather what few things he needs from his futurepast.

Then he will leave modern life behind him for eternity.

Or so he thinks.

Three

LOS ANGELES, CALIFORNIA | SEPTEMBER 1900

Silvery plumes of smoke waft into the early-evening air, coiling into devilish tendrils. Vauquelin sucks them back in and draws his lips into a circle, replacing the plumes with perfect, radiating rings.

A large, blackened scab blights the green lawn. The acrid aroma of destruction poisons the air. He avoids looking at the blemish, although it is expansive enough to consume his view: both in its scope and its significance.

Here he is, in the year 1900 for the second time, sitting on the porch and idly blowing smoke rings over the sooty remains of his decimated future, too numb to do much else.

"Psst."

He watches the rings dissipate, the cigarette immaculately aligned between his middle and forefinger.

"PSST. Mister," says a youthful voice on the other side of his gate.

"Leave me alone," he growls, not deigning to even turn his head toward the sound.

A breeze kicks up, dispatching the black, demoralising odour of despair into his nostrils.

"Why do you look so sad?" a small girl says, pressing her face between the rails. Her arms dangle at her sides.

"Why should you care?" he asks, still gazing blindly into the ether.

With a shrug, she begins to skip up and down the sidewalk. "I just moved in across the street. Mother says I should stay away from you."

"She is correct."

"Mother says you're strange, but you don't look so strange to me. What's your name?"

Vauquelin ignores her.

Another perfect wheel of smoke flutters forth from his lips.

"How long have you lived here? Are you in the moving pictures? My daddy works the camera. Do you know him? Why do you only come outside at night?"

At last he flicks the cigarette to the ground and stands.

"Gosh, you're tall," says the girl. Her jaw falls open as she watches Vauquelin reach his full height.

"And you are rather short for someone with so many questions. Run along home to Mother." He turns his back to walk inside when the creak of the gate rings out into the night, and just like that the child is standing on his front lawn. "Get out," he thunders over his shoulder.

The girl doesn't even flinch.

Oh, god, he thinks, squeezing his eyes shut.

Children are foreign territory for him.

Rarely has he ever been in the vicinity of a child, let alone had one at arm's length. At once he wonders what possessed him to go to the front porch rather than the back garden, as he usually does when he needs to think. Perhaps he required visual confirmation of the fact that his current existence has been incinerated.

Regardless, he never enjoys situations where he must make small talk ... and with a child?

Pfff.

He could snatch her away in an instant, drag her fragile little body down to the cellar. But she would be a mere snack, and he never partakes in his own neighbourhood.

It is too dangerous.

Besides ...

Children are off limits.

Instead, he strides across the lawn and snatches her up by the elbow, marching her across the pavement.

"Ow! You're hurting me!"

"Which is your house?"

She begins to wail, and points to the one directly in front of Vauquelin's.

He strong-arms the squirming girl up the porch and rings the bell. When a woman answers the door, he shoves her inside. "I live just there, across the street," he says, his voice snarled with thorns, pointing to his house. "Should this child enter my property even once more, I shall not be responsible for what happens to her. My home is not a playground."

Vauquelin turns on his heel and stomps across the street, slamming the door so hard it reverberates briefly in the night air.

Los Angeles is not the same since he had reunited with Maeve.

In his first timeline, there had been no children on this street. It is only one of the many differences. How naïve he had been to expect history to behave.

He had been fortunate. It brought him back to Maeve ... yes. But that fortune had run out through his narrow fingers once he turned her.

Vauquelin, born human in the year 1638, sacrificed to darkness in 1668, had survived well into the twenty-first century when his modern life was taken from him. That was his futurepast: his first timeline.

Four hundred years of his history rewound and began again.

He spent three more centuries walking on eggshells, struggling to keep the fragile fabric of history intact so that he might return to her, triumph over her death, and win the restoration of his brilliant former life.

History had been as faithful a mistress to him as he was to her ... until the night he brought Maeve into the folds of his darkness.

The promise of a life together has turned to dust: the fabric frayed faster than he could contain it, and all those meticulous steps amounted to nothing.

Vauquelin could not bear the oppressive serenity inside the house (he had borne it for too long once before) and thus he had gone out of doors for the noise, for the predictable sounds of humanity.

Maeve had been missing for weeks, until this evening.

And now she has left him again.

The dark walls drip with silence.

After her initial disappearance, Vauquelin searched the city for her every night, but now it is as if she has died once more.

He paces the parlour, treading up and down, stopping every few minutes in hopes that the door might open and she will walk through.

That she has changed her mind.

The rug has worn thin from his untiring footsteps upon its weave.

He refuses to go out in search of her again.

It is quite clear she no longer wants him.

It is time for him to face it.

In her human era, Maeve was independent to a fault, headstrong and opinionated: all qualities Vauquelin adored. She was so deliciously rebellious — but in her revenant state she is an outright anarchist. He could not control her before she was vampire, nor did he have the desire.

It is with great regret that Vauquelin reminds himself that all vampires become amplified versions of their human selves: for better or for worse.

He never allowed her to learn the truth about him in his first timeline ... and now Vauquelin can only think Maeve must have been keeping some secrets of her own.

Vauquelin is a reluctant maker; indeed, Maeve is only his third progeny in all his days. He had made her vampire in order to save her life, and to reclaim her love that, in his original journey through time, he let slip through his fingers by concealing from her his true nature.

During his re-traversal of time, Vauquelin feared even stepping on an ant, so great was his apprehension of altering history or making any decision that might revise his future with her. With few exceptions, each step played out just as it had before, due to his meticulous calculations. In reliving his life, he learned that history is astonishingly difficult to re-engineer. It moves through the waters of time like a colossal ship with unrelenting flank speed.

UNLESS —

Unless one makes a decision that throws the ship drastically off its course like an iceberg rising suddenly from the murky, darkened depths.

When Maeve reawakened in the dark blood, history was turned on its ear. She grew petulant and morose.

She rebuked Vauquelin's sage advice and froze when he touched her, until he retreated into himself once again (his only unassailable space).

Once, in their futurepast, he had revelled in the exquisite silence that lay between them. They could while away many hours in the comfort of one another's presence, sans pressure to fill the void with meaningless chatter.

In this hard-earned reunion, however, their silence has become that of strangers — which, in many ways, they are.

At least he is a stranger to her.

Vauquelin once thought he knew Maeve's soul, knew her inside and out: but she does not have the privilege of knowing him as she once did.

Less than a month ago, he appeared on her doorstep, dizzying her with a highly implausible tale of a previous life spent together, of a magnificent love clipped in its prime. He had saved her from the clutches of death and arrived like a dark knight to sweep her into another life she could never have imagined.

She should have been grateful.

But ... like so many times before ...

Vauquelin's hubris has torn him down.

A rosy pink bleeds from the edges of the drapery in the parlour ... the deadly dawn approaches, and still Maeve has not returned.

Vauquelin's feet ache from his relentless pacing and his heart slows: the tell-tale sign that he must go to his rest. He stands at the foot of the staircase and looks up, crippled by the thought of the empty, loveless bed that awaits him.

Each step is haunted for him now.

He manages to land one foot on the first and leans on a knee: he can scarcely imagine scaling the remainder.

This house was once his shelter — for well over one hundred years, though those years were spent in a different timeline. He had borne the grief of Maeve's absence within its walls for decades after her original death, and now he must bear it once more: because she has chosen to leave him.

In the bedroom, he removes his clothing with the steely actions of an automaton, folding each piece mindlessly and placing it on the chaise at the foot of the bed. He slips into the cold, silken sheets and draws the impenetrable velvet bed curtains closed, fighting the slumber that threatens to lock his eyes.

When did he lose her?

LOS ANGELES, CALIFORNIA | AUGUST 1900

They awoke in the protection of Maeve's cellar, then empty of the bones that would soon come to fill this cavernous hollow, encased in one another's arms.

Vauquelin could scarcely believe his own turn of events.

He wrenched a finger down her lower lip, prying her jaws open. Four petite, razor sharp daggers glinted under the gaslight on the ceiling.

She was alive, and vampire — though her heart beat so faintly then.

He had triumphed!

But her face was contorted and drawn, and he recognised that expression at once.

Maeve was starving.

"My love, my love," Vauquelin whispered. He turned his chin to the side and brought her face to his neck. He could hear the punctures her teeth made in his skin, and his own blood vacated his body at an increasingly alarming rate.

He promised himself, just three nights ago (the occasion of her second mortal death) that he would never push her away ... but now, upon her resurrection, panic took his heart in its clutches and his hand fumbled at her elbow: a feeble attempt to dislodge her teeth as they rended his skin.

He wrested her an arm's length away, gasping, "That's quite enough, my darling," and collapsed prostrate on the floor.

Maeve stood, clasping and unclasping her fists, her breath ragged and heaving, red curls in wild abandon about her blood-addled face.

He crawled backwards and practically choked himself, gripping his throat to heal the tatters on his neck, sputtering, "Stay here."

He did not fully expect her to obey him — she had not been fond of taking orders in her human life — but she did.

Vauquelin bolted up the cellar steps and fastened the door behind him, twisting its lock firmly closed, and emerged into the back garden, unbuttoning his collar in desperation as he gulped air.

The night was cool and dusky, the sun having only just made its nightly descent. Vauquelin took to the streets, still busy at this hour. In the windows of the houses he passed, gas lamps came to life one by one like so many flickering fireflies.

It was summertime, and citrus blossoms perfumed the air.

Ruefully, he thought of his futurepast in Los Angeles, where one would rarely smell anything that could be described as lovely.

Automobile exhaust, stale air, and artificial hope was the signature scent of modern L.A., kept imprisoned in the city by its fortress of mountains and canyons. Even the coastline seemed to build barriers to contain the stench of the city of broken dreams.

But in 1900, smog did not yet suffocate the valley ... the few automobiles that rumbled across the crevice-ridden dirt roads were still outnumbered by horse-and-carriage.

He slowed his tempo and turned his glance up to the hills that would, in just two more decades, be covered with glittering homes, crowned by a crooked sign that boasted HOLLYWOODLAND.

Fabricated fancies and happy endings for all.

It would take considerable introspection for him to fully understand the folly of what he had done.

By the time he reached the hills he was too far from home ... the houses drastically decreased in square footage until they were dwarfed in comparison to Maeve's, miles away on Pearl Street: a hulking monument to excess and wealth.

He was so weak.

He had allowed Maeve to come too close to draining him.

Vauquelin crossed over the empty bed of the Los Angeles River to one of his oldest and most steadfast drinking holes: Skid Row. How desperately he wanted to take one of these unfortunate men home, to present him to his beloved, his fledgling, as a gift.

But that could not be.

He would never have been able to make it back in such an enfeebled state, not whilst dragging the weight of a human man under his arm.

Vauquelin did not attempt to be kind or put on an act … not that night. He jumped on the back of the first man he saw and hoisted his head aside, cracking his neck bones as he drank him down, shoving his fingers in the man's filthy mouth to stifle his screams.

Nor did he apologise, as was his custom.

When he was finished, Vauquelin sank to the ground and blood tears gushed down his face in rivulets of crimson.

LOS ANGELES, CALIFORNIA | SEPTEMBER 1900
LATER THAT NIGHT

Vauquelin returned home and looked for a light in the window of the carriage house. It was dark, meaning that Charles, her manservant, had gone to bed. He crept in the side door by the kitchen, which provided easy access to the cellar, and stood for a moment with his hand gripping the doorknob.

Fear plagued his heart: a rarity for him. All he wanted was for Maeve to be waiting in the depths of the cellar, poised to take him into her arms and resume their former life — but he knew it would not be so.

The latch disengaged and he opened the door, bracing himself.

He left it open this time: just in case.

Silence.

One step down, then another.

The stairs had been rarely used — Maeve had never had much use for the cellar — and protested with each determined tread of Vauquelin's feet.

At last he made it to the ground and saw her crumpled in the corner, her head lolled to one side.

Camera flashes of memories assaulted him.

In his first timeline this subterranean room was his catacombs, constructed immediately after Maeve's original, mortal death from the Spanish Flu. It became sacred ground, a resting place for the bones of his victims.

And, perhaps most importantly, it became Maeve's crypt.

But at this juncture it was empty, except for the nightmarish dark shadows of dread spreading down the walls and the corpselike figure of his true love in the corner — not a corpse at all, but very much undead.

She stirred as he tiptoed across the dirt floor and he halted when her eyes rose to meet his.

Her ivory skin had become (was it possible?) even more radiant in death. Her eyes, dark brown in her humanity and now inkier than midnight, were impenetrable. He could not read her thoughts: they were empty, devoid of the vibrant life that had made him love her so.

She rose silently, gliding as if she walked on the very air, and hurled herself toward him.

'Maeve, I — "

But Maeve wouldn't allow him to speak.

She walked him backwards up the stairs with her hand upon his neck, constricting his windpipe — and her voice was gnarled with anger.

"I do not know you! Why are you in my house?"

Vauquelin's eyes widened as she shoved him, making him lose his footing and tumble to the floor of the kitchen. "Maeve! Can you not recall the letter you read, and my most ardent confession?"

Until that moment, he had never before been bested by another vampire.

She wedged her fingertips into her temples and wandered into the parlour, where she dropped onto a sofa like a rag doll. Vauquelin followed and knelt deferentially at her feet, his arms spread wide.

Maeve uttered, in a voice as chilled as ice, "I need something, the source of which I do not know."

Without breaking her gaze, Vauquelin drew his teeth down the vein on his forearm and held it fast to her lips. She drank in greedy gulps, and sip by sip, a bit of life returned to her eyes.

He grasped her to his chest and cradled her head with his hand.

"I shall always protect you, my love," he whispered. "I shall always give you that which you need."

Maeve fell limp in his arms and began to convulse.

Something had gone dreadfully wrong in her transformation.

Help me, Vauquelin prayed — though he knew of no god who would heed prayers uttered forth from the lips of the damned.

She stilled at last, and he carried her back down the stairs, stumbling on the final step and nearly dropping her.

Back in the safety of the cellar they dozed, huddled together on a silk-sheeted mattress. Vauquelin wound tendrils of Maeve's hair between his fingers, stroking her face with his fingertips ... just like he used to do in another lifetime.

She responded with a petite smile and reached up a hand, cupping his neck. "Now I remember you," she whispered.

Her face was serene ... satisfied ... and his fear ebbed.

For now.

LOS ANGELES, CALIFORNIA | SEPTEMBER 1900

THE NEXT EVENING

The cellar was as comfortable as they could make it, but it was damp and bone-chillingly frigid. Vauquelin brought a few necessities downstairs, but in truth, they needed very little.

Their time was spent in conversation and instruction, and in Maeve getting to know Vauquelin again, for now he was a stranger ... a stranger whom she had permitted to completely alter her life — and translate it into undeath.

Vauquelin tucked a blanket up under Maeve's chin.

Her teeth were chattering.

He knew the blanket alone would not cure her chill. The icy fingers of eternity had long ceased to trouble him, but as a fledgling vampire, Maeve was not yet accustomed to the permanent wintertime of not only the bones, but also the soul. Its feathery shadow-frost would never let her go.

Soon — very soon, he hoped — her mind would come to accept it. In the meantime, he enfolded her within his long limbs, desperate to minimise her suffering, and at last, her shudders subsided.

"We must order a bed to protect us, bien-aimée[†] ... we cannot stay in this dismal pit much longer."

Vauquelin fielded her many questions with patience and reverence.

"We can never go outside during the day?" she asked.

"Never."

"Perhaps it won't be so bad," she said. "I have always loved the night. And I burn in the sun so easily ... how nice it will be to never have to use my parasol again!"

Vauquelin steepled his fingers over his lips to disguise his amusement.

Maeve's infallible optimism, one of his most beloved of all her idiosyncrasies, appeared to have survived her violent turning. But his brief moment of euphoria soon turned into dread as he saw her chest begin to heave and her mouth tremble.

The immeasurable reality of Never had submerged into her psyche.

"I shall not see the sunrise again," she said, her voice hiccuping with emotion.

Then came the tears.

She wiped them away and regarded her bloodied hand in horror.

She crumpled to the floor, soiling her pillows with scarlet streaks, and began to wail.

Vauquelin panicked.

The last thing he needed was for Charles to be listening above and think that Vauquelin was hurting her!

"Shhhh ... shh ... you must be the fearless Maeve I once knew you to be. You will need all your strength and courage in the nights to come, my brave one. This will pass. I swear to you," he whispered, his voice honeyed as he enfolded her quaking shoulders in his arms.

She sniffled. "If we get this bed, can we sleep upstairs?"

"Each and every day. This wretched cellar will no longer be our domain."

---

†- BELOVED

"How shall it be constructed?"

Vauquelin crossed to the ewer, their makeshift bath, and soaked a linen cloth, twisting it between his fingers.

He dabbed her swollen face.

And as he absolved her of her bloody outburst, he described the very bed they had once shared, long ago in his futurepast.

"It will be a bed fit for royalty, my love. A bed that any queen would be thrilled to call her own."

It would be a replica of many throughout Vauquelin's history. Lush, inviting mattresses girdled by a massive, intricately carved wood frame. A canopy of heavy, inviolable velvet curtains to keep the spiteful sun at bay, so that they might rest in comfort.

After an unnecessarily lengthy discussion, Maeve rushed up the stairs, and Vauquelin flashed himself to her side, placing his hand over hers on the doorknob.

"No, no ... not just yet," he said, gently. "The sun is not quite down."

"How could you possibly know that? We have no windows, nor a clock!"

"Your body will teach you to tell time. It will know. It is a survival instinct. You must be patient, Maeve."

"ARGH!"

She stamped her foot on the landing and screeched "CHARLES!" at the top of her lungs, making Vauquelin wince as his eardrums vibrated.

Hurried footsteps pounded across the floor beyond and the knob rattled with violence.

"No!" she cried. "You cannot open the door! I am fine, Charles. I just have some orders for you." She slid Vauquelin's sketch of the bed, with an accompanying list of specific materials and instructions, under the door.

"We need this bed built as soon as possible."

"By the end of the week," Vauquelin whispered.

"By Saturday!" she relayed.

"No expense spared," he added.

"I don't care how much it costs, Charles! Please, hurry!"

A heavy sigh was followed by a few moments of awkward silence.

"As you wish, madame," Charles said, dropping his gaze.

Vauquelin held a finger to his lips and they flattened their cheeks against the door, listening for the manservant's departure. He led her gingerly back down the stairs, and she slumped on the mattress.

"The bed will change everything, bien-aimée.[†] Life will return to normal … it is just that everything will be backwards from what you are used to."

And then some, he thought.

She narrowed her eyes.

Vauquelin desperately hoped the bed could be done by Saturday — by then they would need to drink, and coming in and out of the cellar door was proving problematic with Charles always about.

"And we must determine what we will do about Charles."

"Do about him?" she demanded. "Whatever does that mean?"

The prospect of explaining to Maeve that her only steadfast friend must either be turned or killed trussed his stomach into knots.

He thought of Olivier, his lifelong servant turned into his chosen revenant brother … of the bizarre and rare loyalty of humans.

He watched recognition spread across her face, dissolving into an expression Vauquelin could not interpret, until her words sent his flesh crawling.

"We must kill him."

---

† - BELOVED

Charles galloped up and down the stairs all day, directing carpenters and fretting over the dust-ridden footprints they left on Maeve's exquisitely polished walnut floors.

Furthermore, as if Vauquelin's very presence was not enough to upset day-to-day household operations, Charles had to fuss over his burdensome belongings. He was irritated by Maeve's inexplicable acceptance of the peculiar Frenchman, not to mention the delivery of his large crates and trunks in the foyer. In truth, it was not much ... but everyone had to manoeuvre around them — it was making all tasks more difficult.

Now he stood in the foyer as two men hefted armloads of rolled-up velvet up the massive front steps and his eyes bulged as he noticed a golden, silky fringe being dragged upon the sodden flagstones.

'Heavens, man!" Charles rushed over and lifted the delicate trim off the ground, brushing it with his hands and tucking it back into the folds. "Have you any idea the cost of that drape you're dragging in the filth? Take heed!"

He began to follow the labourers upstairs but stiffened when a tumbling clang rang out upon the staircase: a carpenter had dropped a hammer. It pinged down the full flight, gouging the wood on every step it hit before skidding across the landing and coming to a halt at Charles' feet.

He closed his eyes, counting to ten before he stooped to retrieve the destructive tool. With a heaving chest, he extended a hand toward the second floor, refusing to look at the workers, and they hustled up the stairs — afraid of what Charles might do with the wayward, weaponised hammer he gripped in his other hand.

He followed behind them so that he might inspect the new bed Maeve demanded. It was a strange, antiquated concept, quite different from his mistress's usual taste. But he knew better than to question her whims.

Despite the bedroom being a flurry of semi-competent carpenters and in complete disarray, the bed itself seemed suitably constructed. He walked its perimeter as the dense velvet drapes were hung around its crown and sides — his hands laced behind his back, a stern look upon his face.

When the remaining detritus of the bed's fabrication was cleared away, he escorted all the workers down to the front door, slamming it wordlessly behind them.

Charles was not one to suffer fools, especially when it came to Maeve's affairs. He could handle any of her outlandish requests.

But then she was down in the cellar with this Vauquelin, an eccentric, effeminate Frenchman of whom Charles did not approve, and he was confounded by the reasons behind it. For one entire week, she had spent all the daylight hours with him in the wretched, none-too-clean cellar, only to emerge at sunset.

What on earth could they be doing down there all day?

At regular intervals he leaned against the wooden door, listening for clues of their activity, but there was only silence from the other side.

Charles was as protective of her as a father would be ... she was, after all, a single woman of means, with no one else to look after her interests.

He had cared for her since she was seven years old, her avowed servant for life, following her from Pittsburgh to California.

Surely this man was after her money!

Charles was confident that Maeve trusted him implicitly, but his protests about this macabre man who suddenly appeared in their lives fell on deaf ears.

If Maeve wanted something, she would have it: that was how it had always been.

Charles pressed his ear against the door at the exact moment that Vauquelin and Maeve had their own pressed on the reverse. A mere twelve centimetres of solid wood separated the three of them.

Vauquelin wrapped an arm around Maeve's waist and placed his free hand over her lips.

A burly knock rattled their faces, nearly making both of them jump from their skins.

"Maeve? Madam?" Charles waited for a response and cleared his throat. "The workers have finished. I am retiring to my apartment for supper. I bid you a good night."

Vauquelin's face fell as he registered Charles' deliberate omission of him. In his first timeline, they had been quite close.

There had been much respect between them, and Vauquelin adored Charles. Then they both lost Maeve, and not too long after, Vauquelin lost Charles.

But that night the servant's hatred for him practically burned through the door.

So much rebuilding to do.

Vauquelin hung his head.

They waited until they heard Charles' diminishing footsteps as he departed across the wooden floor, followed by the slam of the door that led to the back garden and the carriage house.

"Shall we?" Vauquelin asked, twisting the doorknob.

When they emerged into the kitchen, Maeve surveyed the room as if she had never seen it before.

Vauquelin nibbled the tips of his fingers, reminding himself that he could not expect Maeve to simply fall into an existence he had been familiar with for centuries.

"Maeve, let us sit in the library for a moment."

He took her hand and escorted her in.

If only it were not summer, he thought.

How comforting a fire would be now!

But the fireplace lay dormant in cold repose for the season.

He led her to her favourite chair and she sank into it, reaching for her familiar bottle of cognac.

"Tsst!" Vauquelin exclaimed. "I beg you, don't. The results will be unpleasant, my love."

"But I adore cognac!"

Vauquelin towered over her, dragging a hand down his face.

Oh, dear. Wait until we get to the food.

What a terrible teacher he was! He was unskilled at educating fledgling vampires.

Vauquelin's first progeny was a woman he did not know: Arsinée. His maker, Yvain, coerced Vauquelin to turn her the night of his first resurrection and duped him into believing they were wed. She nearly destroyed his life and he could not get away from her fast enough.

The second was Olivier, who knew him so well and was turned by choice. He looked to the ceiling and began counting on his fingers, mouthing the numbers as he calculated ... *some two hundred-plus-odd-years ago*?

The third was Maeve.

In truth, he despised numbers.

There were far too many in his head at that point.

Still, Vauquelin held great regret for not creating more vampires, if only for the education it would have given him to prepare her.

You are a fool, the voice in his head said.

A vainglorious fool.

He had thought only of having Maeve with him forever, and of retracing his steps so that he might not ruffle a single feather of history. He had not once stopped to consider the aftermath, or what her desires might have been.

Vampires are not so different from mere mortals. They waste their time and focus on the wrong things just as humans do ... but with vastly further-reaching consequences and much, MUCH deeper ennui.

The myriad acts Vauquelin had taken for granted over his fractured timelines and multitude of centuries capitulated into that one moment, as he stood looking at this innocent, damned soul.

Her eyes had regained still more life, holding fast to the merest flickers of expectation, vulnerability, joy.

And now he would have to chip away — one beloved moment by one — at her joie de vivre,[†] at her very essence that had made him fall in love with her in his futurepast.

His shoulders slumped as he fetched her a glass of wine — her least favourite beverage, yet the only liquid aside from blood and water their sensitive revenant systems could tolerate.

When he handed it to her, with fragile hope raising his brows and curling his lips into an optimistic smile, she sniffed it.

In his own experience of her, Maeve was once always up for trying something new.

She took the most minuscule of sips and turned up her nose.

Vauquelin sighed.

---

†- JOY OF BEING ALIVE

Maeve flung the wine in his face and he licked his lips — closing his eyes as the stains bled into his ivory neck stock.

His self-restraint was being put to the test.

He had shown Olivier no such mercy at his turning.

Vauquelin had plunged him immediately into the depths of vampirism, even held his head under its sanguine waters ... and Olivier had thrived. Perhaps that was what Maeve needed, and Vauquelin had been too gentle with her?

"Let us dress and go out into the city," he said, swallowing the unease that began to spread like poison ivy in his psyche.

They drew a bath and sank into the steaming water together.

Vauquelin savoured every moment, mesmerised by the water rushing down her back as he squelched the sponge, intoxicated by the fragrances of the vetiver soap and Maeve's dirty hair.

He dropped the sponge in the bath and dragged the tip of his nose up her spine from mid-back: she stiffened, and turned her chin sharply across her shoulder, her brow creased. He leaned to meet her lips with his own. One hand snaked around her hip, reaching below to her sunken regions, while the other grasped her jaw.

He pierced her water-glistened neck and his back arched inward as her blood hit his throat.

At once she flipped around, obliging him to withdraw — his teeth rended ragged slivers on her skin. She submerged him into the water, biting into his chest.

Vauquelin steeled his jaws through the pain, expecting their bodies to join. Instead, Maeve dug her knee into his burgeoning groin and throttled him, attempting to choke the life out of him.

Fortunately, that was not possible.

Maeve's frenzied movements sent waves of bloodied, pink water cascading across the bathroom floor.

His survival instincts catalysed, and he hurled her off him by her shoulders.

She ran for the bathroom door, but he flashed ahead of her and backed her into it — he caught her elbow, twisting it above her head and holding fast.

"Never attempt to subdue me again," he hissed, exposing his teeth.

Maeve trembled against the door, her eyes bulging.

Vauquelin forced her into a dressing gown and marched her into the bedroom. He himself retreated underground.

They did not leave the house that night.

The next morning, the cellar door once again lay menacingly closed.

Charles rattled the knob — locked.

His brow furrowed.

He abruptly turned on his heel and ventured upstairs.

The bed.

As he approached Maeve's bedroom door, he saw that a note had been slipped underneath, carefully scrawled in Maeve's own, genteel hand:

> *Do not disturb. Please complete your duties,*
> *and meet us in the dining room at 8:00pm.*

At least she was no longer sequestered in the cellar.

Charles cleaned the kitchen, which was a quick job as nothing had been cooked, and proceeded to dust the library and then the parlour. He righted an overturned plant and swept up the spilled soil. Otherwise, nothing was amiss. He went into his mistress's bath, finding the room an unmitigated disaster.

His patience was depleted — this was so unlike her.

Bottles were overturned left and right, the tub was filthy, and there were three bloody towels discarded on the still-wet floor.

Charles' irritation at her secrecy turned into acute distress.

His hands began to shake and he clasped them to his chest, his face turning feverish.

If that man had laid one finger on her ...

When the trembling subsided, he forced himself into action: tidying the room, mopping up the befouled floor, and dropping the towels in a basket.

Distracting himself with his mundane tasks was the only curative for his anger. In the kitchen he prepared Maeve's most-loved dish, a shepherd's pie, periodically glancing at the kitchen clock over his shoulder.

He took up his position in the corner of the dining room with a linen draped across his arm.

Promptly at eight o'clock, they entered.

Charles never took his eyes off Vauquelin, who seated himself at the head of the table (*how very dare he!*).

That strange foreigner had the nerve to behave with such masculine arrogance in a woman's domain, such unmitigated authority and familiarity: as if he hadn't appeared out of nowhere and upended the entire household less than a week ago!

The meal Charles had prepared was laid out on the table, untouched, waiting patiently under Maeve's heirloom sterling silver cloches.

Something rumbled in the back of Charles' throat, and it tasted much like something he was about to regret.

He tried — and failed — to choke it down.

"Madam, I must tender my resignation," he stammered, his voice threatening to break. "I refuse to stand by and watch this unfold."

Vauquelin remained silent, pulling on his cigarette.

He dared not cut his eyes to his prize, who had apologised to him profusely last night.

I do not yet know myself, she had whispered with her chin on her chest, and Vauquelin softened, remembering how he had felt after his first turning.

All is forgiven, my love. We must begin again.

But this particular episode was Maeve's argument ... not his.

Under the table, Vauquelin's foot began to jitter.

He wrapped his fingers around his mouth for another inhale: not only was it his ancient European manner of smoking, but it also served to disguise the nervous smile that threatened his lips, because he knew what was coming.

And there it was.

Maeve's eye began to tic: the tell-tale sign that she was about to explode like a volcano.

"Watch *what* unfold, precisely?" she asked with a sharp tilt of her head.

LOS ANGELES, CALIFORNIA | SEPTEMBER 1900

Vauquelin placed the cigarette in a crystal ashtray and steepled his hands, his elbows perched on the table.

Things had turned quite serious.

Maeve's icy voice echoed in his memory: *We must kill him.*

But Vauquelin did not wish for Charles to die!

He gnawed the inside of his cheek.

Charles was a good human.

He was Maeve's Olivier.

How could she let him go?

She adored him.

At least ... she did *before*.

The hairs on Vauquelin's neck rose as he realised that, if Maeve could so easily lose her love for Charles, she could lose it for him as well: except at this point, he already knew she did not love him as she once had.

Maeve rapped her fingers on the table. "Charles, would you like to live forever?" she asked, her neck quite upright.

Vauquelin spluttered up his mouthful of wine and drew his handkerchief to his lips.

Charles blanched.

Whatever could my mistress mean? he thought, tugging at his starched collar, rapidly turning his head to and fro. The events of the past week had, frankly, been too much for any normal man.

He swallowed hard.

"Madam, I am your faithful servant. But I beg you ... I do not understand what you are asking. I expect to find my eternal reward in Heaven."

Maeve emitted a ghastly laugh. "Heaven! Ha! You daft man. No such place exists. I should know. I have already travelled to the hideous void that awaits us beyond Death. There is nothing on the other side." She raised her voice to a screech and backhanded Vauquelin's carafe of wine, bloodying the pristine, filmy lace tablecloth. "NOTHING!"

Vauquelin darted his eyes from Maeve to Charles.

Not once in his existence had he challenged a potential victim with heaven or hell or naught. He could not even say this with certainty himself. He had circumnavigated the same pits of Death as Maeve (or had his path been a different one? Now he was questioning everything!) but — he had found redemption on the other side.

It was plain that Vauquelin must intervene or Charles would die.

He rushed around the table and jammed his forehead against Maeve's.

My darling ... you must think this through.

His memories of Maeve's stories from his original timeline — what she had told him of her childhood, what she had told him of Charles — these he transferred into her mind.

Charles' devotion to her.

His near-constant presence in her life.

His profound grief at her original death.

She saw it all.

She swooned.

Vauquelin and Charles both leapt up at once to scoop her into their arms — their eyes locked. Together they eased her back down into a chair. And Vauquelin knew what he must do.

Maeve would be fine.

She was vampire.

Charles had to be saved.

Vauquelin drew Charles' elbows into a formidable grip, and whispered, "Stay with me, monsieur," as he wrapped his long fingers around the poor, sweating man's trembling jaw.

What he was about to do was strictly forbidden, at least according to his maker, Yvain, and the rules of his coterie. Vampires were preordained, according to Yvain, to have no sympathy for mortals. But this was where he drew the line against himself and his scruple-less pater.

In the precise manner he had done with Maeve, he clasped Charles' forehead to his own, and shared with him gauzy memories of his mistress' demise in his first timeline.

Charles began to struggle against him, shouting, "Charlatan! How is this possible? How dare you try to deceive me!"

Vauquelin doubled down with his visions.

Charles' face fell as he saw the strange man dressing Maeve's corpse, writing out instructions, standing behind him in deference when the attorneys came.

Vauquelin transmitted the deathly void Maeve left behind in this very house, and how they consoled one another after that horrible event. He closed his grim show with Charles' own death from the influenza epidemic in 1918.

"Perhaps you will understand now why she wanted you to live forever. It is just that she is too hardened now to explain it. Maeve and I ... we are the undead."

Charles' jaw vibrated and his reddened eyes protruded.

For a moment, Vauquelin had convinced him. To his profound regret, however, his visions were too genuine.

Charles recoiled and collapsed on the floor, pulling an astonished Vauquelin down with him. His eyes rolled back in his head until only the whites were visible, and he clawed at his chest.

His lips smacked wildly, grasping for unobtainable words.

Vauquelin loosened Charles' bow tie and collar, prodded his neck … the poor man's pulse dwindled to naught, and with an unceremonious gasp he was gone.

Aghast, Vauquelin sat back on his heels, stunned by disbelief.

But before he could fully absorb what just happened, Vauquelin had to pry a screeching Maeve off of Charles' body, shouting "No, Maeve, no! You cannot drink dead blood!"

It was a lesson he was as-yet unprepared to teach.

Vauquelin dragged Charles into the storage shed in the back garden and sat by his body for several hours holding his hand as it stiffened beneath his grip, while Maeve sat inside reading.

The time had come to rebuild the catacombs.

History had been so predictable going backward: not so much going forward. When Maeve succumbed to her original death in 1918, she left her house to him. Vauquelin created a catacombs in the basement, thieving her coffin from the cemetery and making her own crypt the showpiece. The ossuary served him well for over one hundred years and became his sanctuary — the one place he could be himself, surrounded by Death.

It was his salvation: a safe place to discard bodies, to conceal the regrettably criminal nature of his existence.

The evening after Charles' demise, Vauquelin took a carriage to the home of Monsieur Lavigne, his attorney, with instructions. It was with great regret that Vauquelin had been unable to locate Duclos, his original attorney from his first timeline. That man was a gem.

Lavigne was merely acceptable ... for now.

The next day, as Maeve and Vauquelin slept, a pit was dug in the cellar and lined with concrete, a hinged door placed atop it.

Twelve wooden barrels of nitric acid, each with an ominous skull-and-crossbones and POISON stencilled in black across the panels, were delivered by carriage and painstakingly brought down the stairs to the cellar.

Their contents were emptied into the pit, with one worker seizing from the smell and another succumbing to an atrocious burn across his hand, sizzling his skin down to the bone.

The contractor was livid and complained loudly to Lavigne in the library.

"I regret that your men were injured, but you were duly informed of this dangerous work before you signed on. It is required for my client's occupation," the attorney said. "He is a scientist and needs clean animal bones for his studies. I assure you your men suffer for a good cause."

He wrote out a substantial cheque and passed it across Maeve's desk to the seething contractor.

The man blinked at the more-than-generous amount and swallowed hard, folding the cheque and tucking it into his pocket.

There were no further questions or complaints.

That night, Vauquelin and Maeve lowered Charles' body into the pit. Vauquelin could not bear to watch the acid devour the beloved servant's flesh, and turned his back. His position prevented him from seeing Maeve smiling with a wicked look in her eyes, knitting and unknitting her fingers.

Charles' body was the first addition to the new catacombs.

Maeve scattered Charles' bones with her foot when Vauquelin drew the skeleton out of the vat. Her face bore a shield of frosty indifference. He watched her walk upstairs, and when he heard the door close, he arranged the bones neatly on a shelf. He drew his fingers to his lips, dropping a kiss on them before he departed.

He had truly wanted Charles to live, but alas, it could not be so.

His chest shuddered when he closed the door to the cellar.

Maeve was seated in the library laying out tarot cards — as if nothing had happened.

Vauquelin leaned his long form against the pocket door, and began to roll a cigarette. "You are surprisingly calm about his demise," he said, licking the endpaper and tightening the ends. He drew the cigarette through his lips and lit it.

Maeve did not look up from her cards. "He was nothing to me. Just a servant. You are disturbing my reading."

Vauquelin regarded her coolly through an exhaled blue cloud.

Naturally, he thought of Olivier — who was, at that moment, living free and peacefully in the French Alps: well into his successful third century as a vampire.

The situation was rapidly unravelling, and Vauquelin was desperate to maintain control.

An idea struck him.

"My love, take me to your wardrobe. Show me your loveliest gowns, and we will dress for the evening."

Maeve looked up from the spread of cards, and her face brightened at once. "Yes! Let's!"

They sprinted up the stairs laughing, and Vauquelin felt a little twinge of hopefulness strike a spark in his heart, even as his laughter rang hollow and false in his ears.

Charles' dead eyes still haunted him.

Maeve flung open the doors to her wardrobe, and immediately extracted a dress from the House of Worth, one which Vauquelin remembered vividly.

"You were fitted for this in Paris last year," he said. "It is your favourite. You wore this dress the night we met, in my futurepast."

He touched her cheek, transmitting a memory.

It sent a jolt through her body: she felt his presence that night, saw him sitting next to her in the box at the theatre, saw him fumble with the unlacing of this very dress, right before he threw her on the bed. Remembered how this very man had seemed an answer to her prayers.

A vision forced its way into her consciousness: she was sitting at her long dining table decorated with ostrich plumage and roses, surrounded by elegant guests, a glittering chandelier with real candles, not the gaslit fixture that hung there now, casting its hypnotic warm shadows across their faces.

But he had never told her about a party ... had he?

And she did not remember ever buying a chandelier.

Is this all a figment of my imagination? she wondered. *Is this man deceiving me?*

"Who ARE you?" she wailed.

Her chin went aquiver and her knees buckled. She sank to the ground in a rustling clump, the ripping of her silken dress rending the silence in the room.

Blood tears ran down her cheeks in steady streams and she sobbed, dirtying her beautiful dress with hefty crimson drops.

Vauquelin knelt before her, taking her hand into his. He smoothed her unruly hair back, tilting his head and studying her face with kind eyes.

She unleashed her bottled-up emotions, rocking to and fro, blubbering incomprehensible words.

He gave her his handkerchief, and it occurred to him that Maeve had not yet grieved her own undeath.

So jaded he had been, he had not recognised it.
They leaned against the bed, and Vauquelin held her close.
He let her cry, comforting her until sunrise.
Tonight, things would be different.
They both felt it in their blood.

Nine

LOS ANGELES, CALIFORNIA | SEPTEMBER 1900

THE NEXT NIGHT

When their eyes opened in their velvet tomb at sundown, Vauquelin pondered what they should do next.

There was a vast distance between them in the bed — she consented to have Vauquelin sleep there, but refused to have him closer than an arm's length to her.

He owed her explanations: that much was true.

His thoughts were brawling, and it bestowed upon him the closest a vampire could come to a headache: his facial veins were constricting, and it was painful.

Vauquelin was in desperate need of fresh blood.

He massaged his temples, cultivating a meagre hope that Maeve would ask him what was wrong.

Instead, she lay with her hands folded across her ribcage, staring up into the canopy.

"We must drink," he murmured.

Silence from Maeve.

"And *not* from one another," he emphasised.

They had only been mutually feeding.

The well was running dry.

Without new human blood, Vauquelin could not regenerate his own. Secondhand blood could sustain them for only so long; soon, they would both be in physical distress, and in Maeve's fledgling state he could not allow himself to be anything less than robust.

He was her only protector — she was too newly-resurrected.

She could not be a suckling forever.

Still she said nothing, merely agitating her fingers.

Vauquelin slid out of the bed and stretched, obscured from her eyes by the heavy curtain, and drew himself a bath. He sat in the hot water with his knees splayed, considering whether he had made the greatest mistake of his life in pursuing his own desires.

He had placed all his hopes in reuniting with Maeve, and now that he had, he was devastated by the results.

His malevolent French narrator made an unwelcome interruption to his thoughts.

What if Yvain cursed you when he released you?

Do you truly have the audacity to think there will be no consequences?

« PUTAIN D'ENFER ! »[†] He leapt up in the tub, sending a tsunami of bathwater across the floor.

Maeve's voice echoed through the door. "Vauquelin?"

He tilted his head across his shoulder. "I am fine, I ... slipped."

He towelled himself off and gripped the sink with white-knuckled fists.

And then he put one of those fists through the spiteful, goddamned mirror — splattering shards of glass and his cursed blood across the tile floor.

---

†- FUCKING HELL!

They stood on the front porch, dressed down.

It was Vauquelin's idea: he did not want their appearances to draw attention.

He had done this often at various intervals in his long history, when dressing a certain way was an invitation to disaster.

Thus began the formal lessons.

Just like Vauquelin, Maeve was not one for subtlety ... she struggled that night, as she found it difficult to locate even one understated garment in her closet.

"I am more suited to dig weeds in the garden," she said, glancing down at her drab khaki skirt. She started for a mirror and Vauquelin grasped her elbow, drawing her gently back to face him.

He was not in the frame of mind to be drawn into a discussion about the vampire's absence in mirrors.

Vauquelin forced a smile. "Yet somehow you still manage to beguile."

He made a mental note to destroy all the remaining mirrors as soon as possible.

They stood in silence for several minutes, sniffing the fresh evening air. Neither of them had left the confines of the house in well over a month, since the night he had darkened her door and drawn her into the inescapable depths of his shadows.

Vauquelin tucked her hand into his elbow but she jerked it back at once.

He hefted out a sigh, and headed to the carriage house.

"Soon, my darling, we will have an automobile ... but for now, I will ready the carriage."

During his last time-shift, Vauquelin was greatly hindered by his ignorance in fitting a carriage. It was a skill he had been determined to learn. Upon his return to the seventeenth-century, his stable boys had been much amused by the novelty of their wealthy master offering to work: no nobleman had ever entered their realm, let alone shown any interest in learning their trade.

He gestured to a bench for Maeve to sit, while he hitched her dappled mare Blossom to the carriage and drew the cabriolet top down, as the evening was so fine. When he went to retrieve her, she was besotted by tears again.

He felt sure he knew why.

"Charles always readied the carriage for me," she wailed, worrying her handkerchief between her fingers. "How I mistreated him! I only wish I could have him back. It destroys me that he died thinking I no longer loved him."

She blew her nose violently into the handkerchief and then swooned at the resulting blood.

This brief glimpse of the old Maeve nearly brought Vauquelin to his knees. Something told him to let her live through this moment on her own, so he mounted the driver's seat in silence and drove the carriage to her, hopping down to help her up into the seat.

She refused his assistance, and he stood like a fool with his hand suspended in mid-air, eyes fluttering as she hiked her skirts and seated herself.

As they drove through the porte cochère and out onto the dirt road of Pearl Street, her spirits lifted. It was clear that Maeve needed to get out of the house as much as Vauquelin did.

Blossom's hooves pattering on the road, combined with the cool evening air and promenading people on the sidewalks, slowly eroded the weighty sadness of the past weeks.

They passed a street vendor selling smoked sausages, and the potent fragrance nauseated them both. Vauquelin tossed the whip on Blossom to speed her up, and slowed when they had gone clear of the cart.

"I should have warned you, my sweet ... it is with deep regret I inform you that comestibles are a thing of the past. But do not fear ... soon you will discover a fragrance more delectable than any food you can imagine, a flavour more decadent than the most tender cut of meat, an elixir finer than cognac."

They drove around Los Angeles for several hours, stopping occasionally to let Blossom drink from the horse troughs scattered throughout the city. In the blink of an eye, those troughs would dwindle, and fuelling stations for automobiles would take their place.

Vauquelin was sobered by this thought.

He was in no hurry for the future to arrive. He knew what was coming, that he would once again disdain the changes it would bring.

But for now, he dismissed it.

He had to be optimistic for Maeve.

Whether she realised it or not, she needed all his strength and he would give it freely — as long as he was able — and if she would accept it.

"When will we stop?" Maeve asked. "My veins feel as though they are crawling with spiders."

Vauquelin himself was weakening at a frightening pace.

"We must wait until the majority of humans have gone to sleep. Always remember: caution above everything, even thirst. If I am able to teach you anything, Maeve, the most important lesson must be the fear of discovery. No one must know of our nature."

If they had been together in France at his inception, they could have fed with wild abandon, without consequences. But this was the modern age. News of Jack the Ripper in London and H.H. Holmes in Chicago had ignited fear across the world, causing many citizens of metropolitan areas to lock their doors at night.

Vauquelin stopped the carriage just outside the rail-yard and turned to Maeve. "I cannot tell you the best way for a vampire to behave. I can only tell you of my own methods. And my method is … I endeavour to find those whom no one else will miss. Does this make sense?"

She gave a single, sombre nod.

"I will be right here by your side."

They descended the carriage, and walked towards the rails.

A steam whistle blew, and Maeve jerked with fiery fear.

Vauquelin knew that blood-edginess all too well.

He drew her closer, and whispered in her ear. "Chin up, my darling. Follow my lead."

She stood tall and threw her shoulders back.

There was his brave girl.

They approached a group of three men, isolated from any others.

"Messieurs,[†] could you help us?" Vauquelin pleaded, adding a convincing quiver and an even heavier French accent to his voice. "We are tourists and have lost our way."

The men looked directly at Vauquelin, ignoring Maeve.

He enchanted all three and, taking Maeve by the hand, flung her toward one of them.

"Treat him as you would your favourite meal," Vauquelin said, holding his palms up to the others, who stood frozen in place.

He watched in awe as Maeve folded the man in her arms, heartily sniffing before she punctured his neck. Vauquelin, hands still raised, advanced toward her.

"Yes … yes, you have it … but do not drink it all."

She flung her head back, wild-eyed and gasping, and Vauquelin gently moved her aside and finished him off, knowing the timing of the second-to-last drop.

That lesson would come later for Maeve.

But tonight, he wanted her to feast, to grow strong.

---

†- GENTLEMEN

He drew her bloody chin up and looked into her eyes.

"And is your thirst quenched, bien-aimée?"[†]

"No," she whispered.

He manoeuvred her to the second man and seized the third one by the elbow, locking him into his eyes to reignite his enchantment. "We thank you, monsieur, for giving us your life so that we may live."

Maeve's strength surged with the fresh blood coursing through her veins, and she pushed Vauquelin away.

She ripped her victim's shirt apart, sending buttons scattering across the ground, and bit directly into his carotid, her body quaking as if in orgasm.

Vauquelin watched her, captivated by her fury, and after several minutes passed, he cried, "Stop!"

She obeyed, albeit her eyes were ferine and flickered in the dark.

Watching her drink sent his blood into rhapsody, and he lacerated the third man's jugular, drinking greedily.

Swallow by swallow, Vauquelin's skin softened, rejuvenated by ripe, hot blood, and his erection grew with ferocity.

He whipped out his Opinel and slashed all the men's throats, glancing up to a curious stare from Maeve.

"But they are all dead!" she screeched.

"Quiet ... I will explain later."

He steered her back to the carriage and lifted her skirts, scuttling the wheels across the road and startling Blossom: she huffed and whickered, raising her front hooves in protest.

The blood of their three victims mingled on their tongues.

But then Maeve brought her arms between their chests and shoved him away from her.

"Do not touch me so."

Vauquelin averted his gaze.

---

†- BELOVED

In his previous timeline, she had craved his body ... now she found him abhorrent.

That.

That was the moment he knew he had irretrievably lost her.

And it will be many decades before he comes to understand the reasons behind it.

LOS ANGELES, CALIFORNIA | SEPTEMBER 1900

4:00AM

They lay in bed, freshly bathed, curling their fingers together.

Maeve consented to his touch at last, though she still refused him her body.

She was the happiest he had seen her since their reunion.

Despite the smile on his lips, Vauquelin berated himself for the way events had unfolded. He had forced the life of a vampire on her with no explanation.

But there had been no time ... had there?

He could have lived with her a few more years, and brought the truth out slowly ... instead, he had behaved as a virgin boy would.

Amateur.

A disgusted laugh erupted from his lips.

"What amuses you?" Maeve asked.

"It is just ... I have been alive for hundreds of years and yet I am still so stupid at times."

The French voice dribbled into his head.

Because you ARE *stupid. You have learned nothing. Rien !*[†]

He buried his face in his hands and howled, startling Maeve.

« Arrêtez! Laissez-moi tranquille ! »[‡]

She jerked at his outburst and sat up in the bed, stroking his arm.

"What is the matter? How can I help you?"

He melted in the comfort of her voice, the voice of the original Maeve.

"It is nothing you can help ... my old demons torment me. They will never let me be." He turned his back to her and curled into a foetal position, convinced he would never know peace.

Maeve draped her arm around his abdomen, spooning into him.

Both of their hearts slowed, and they succumbed to their rest.

Nestled in Maeve's comforting embrace, Vauquelin slept more soundly than he had in decades.

In his futurepast, Vauquelin sat alone many nights in movie theatres, watching vampires brought to life on the silver screen, wishing Maeve was next to him. Many a human in Los Angeles has sat near him in the dark of the cinema ... never knowing a vampire was in their presence.

That is his eternal way.

He does not want to be seen.

He does not want to be known.

In his original timeline, by the time movies were common, Maeve was long-dead: due to his inaction.

His fear.

His insecurity (if he is being honest with himself, which he usually is *not*).

[†]- NOTHING!
[‡]- STOP! LEAVE ME ALONE!

Now, he was pacing the parlour and wearing a trail in the weave of Maeve's fine oriental rug, wishing she was with him ... but she was out on her own.

She went against his pleading ... *You are not prepared*, he insisted.

But Maeve was Maeve: a stubborn Celt, made even more stubborn by her transformation into revenancy.

He begrudgingly gave her his Opinel when she left.

"Leave no trace," was all he could muster.

In truth, he begrudged the separation from his beloved Opinel as much as he mourned for her absence.

The blade was a security blanket for him.

This particular Opinel had been purchased in his original timeline, in the year 1890. He had owned it one hundred and thirty years when his time began to unwind, and by his current calendar, the knife had been with him for more than three hundred and fifty years.

He had so desperately wanted to wait for her return, to ensure her safety.

Regardless of the missing knife, he had ignored his own thirst at his peril.

His body was rebelling.

But something else was troubling him.

He had achieved everything he had wanted, but the outcome had left him unsatisfied.

A yearning — unnamed and unidentifiable — churned in his soul ... clenching it, rending it desiccated and dry even as he filled it with blood.

Something was on the horizon ... something he would be unable to predict until it happened, and it would continue to torment him throughout the interminable years of nights ahead.

Maeve no longer wanted him, and his body missed her ... had missed her for centuries.

How desperately Vauquelin longed for her: to be inside her, to merge.

And that night she was out on the roughshod streets of Los Angeles alone, and he had put his full trust in her: because he had no other option.

He wandered to the back garden.

In his futurepast, this garden had a swimming pool and a devil statue overlooking all: his own injection of France into California. Eventually it had remote control lights. Then, in his new timeline, it was just a lawn with a bench and flowerbeds — empty and crass.

Vauquelin took a drag from his cigarette and tucked his thumb into his waistband.

He paced around the lawn, smoking the nub until it singed his fingers and he smelt his own flesh burning. Stubbing it into the turf with the toe of his shoe, he brought his hand up, nonchalantly watching the superficial burn heal.

Maeve was gone ...

Not just that night.

Gone from *him*.

He knew it in his vitals.

It was a cathartic moment, but it did not change anything: not yet.

He fell into his slumber — her side of the bed was achingly empty.

The sun rose, and still she was not where she should be.

Her side of the bed remained unoccupied for well over two weeks.

Eleven

LOS ANGELES, CALIFORNIA | SEPTEMBER 1900

Each and every night in Maeve's absence, Vauquelin hitched Blossom to the carriage and took her out, searching in vain.

The wheels clamoured over the dirt roads of Los Angeles, frequently dipping as they hit potholes, rattling Vauquelin's teeth.

What was he doing here?

He had voluntarily exiled himself in a primitive American wasteland, when he had been living in the bosom of European civility.

New construction was underway at every turn.

The sound of saws, hammering, and horse hooves clopping on dust was his soundtrack on those lonesome nights.

At times, he would stop and look up at the moon, sniffing the air that mutated with every passing night.

The scent of progress, of a city growing.

Of some enigmatic longing taking root in his heart.

Maeve was never anywhere they stopped.

No one he encountered, and dared to ask, had seen a woman in mourning dress with red hair.

In 1900, Los Angeles was not as expansive as it is now ... it was a small town. It took no time at all for Vauquelin, relentlessly driving the carriage with Blossom at the helm, to emerge outside the city boundaries and find himself in dark, dense orange groves.

In truth he loved those solitary journeys ... the California sky was so lovely then, draping slivered wisps of clouds across the moon.

He had always (and will always be, for eternity) a collector of beauty. Nevertheless, he was well aware that not too far into his second future the moon would be blurred, smudged by toxic smog.

Humans were determined to damage the most venerated aspects of their existences.

On those lonesome nights, the moon was pure and clear, yet his thoughts were the polar opposite: muddy and obscure.

The moon mocked him.

> *"As eternal as I*
> *You are,*
> *And yet your shadows*
> *Darken us both,"*

... she seemed to say.

Of course he satisfied his thirst along the way — the luckless humans who crossed him in during these despairing moods felt the full brunt of his anger.

Aside from Maeve's absence, his only problem was that she still had his cherished Opinel, and no American seller had anything to compare. He had to settle for an inferior folding knife meant for gutting a fish.

The new knife left toothy, ugly, jagged gashes upon human flesh: he much preferred clean lines, from an aesthetic point of view.

Most human deaths (not all ... it depended on the circumstances) troubled him: but if they died without a trace of beauty, what was the point?

He had been a *gourmand*[†] in his human life, and those tendencies swelled even greater in his vampire life: it was merely that the source of his sustenance was different.

His thoughts were erratic on those nights, having so newly-reacquired Maeve and so newly-lost her almost simultaneously ... his thoughts flew like flocks of frightened starlings.

Maeve's original death was the only one that gave him a rendezvous with the Reaper, the sole deity he had ever encountered. Her magnificence was painful and disturbing.

He hoped to meet her again.

She, perhaps, was his true match.

The one he could not best.

The one who could conquer him.

In truth, he desperately wanted to see her again.

He had some choice words for her that had built up over his centuries.

When he unlocked the door at Pearl Street and entered, he was met by his wooden-crated belongings, still unpacked and waiting in the parlour. A smattering of seven centuries of existence: the small collection of objets[‡] which were important enough for him to drag across an entire ocean and a continent for a second time.

He was inclined to light a match to the lot: the house and all its contents.

It would be a fitting outcome to what he had wrought.

But even the purity of fire could not cleanse the evil that had blossomed across these wretched walls like so much unheeded mould.

He sat on the floor and leant up against the only object that truly mattered to him: his first portrait, the only surviving glimpse into his life

---

[†]- A PERSON WHO ENJOYS EATING AND OFTEN EATS TOO MUCH
[‡]- TRINKETS

before he was vampire.

His only other portrait, painted after his second creation, hung still on the wall of his manor in Paris, above the fireplace in his bedchamber.

He had not carried it with him this time.

It said much of him that the one he needed with him now was the one of his pre-vampire existence.

A ravenous desire to see it inflamed him.

To see himself as he once was.

Rushing to the kitchen, to a cabinet full of tools, he extracted a pry bar and stomped back to the wooden crate containing the portrait.

Five minutes later, from a mess of splinters and excelsior, he freed the life-sized portrait from its wooden prison and stood looking upon his likeness.

He saw a son of nobility.

A son of France.

A son of the seventeenth century.

He drew an arm around his waist and, with his other arm, wrapped his fingers around his mouth.

Who are you?

Why are you here?

What have you become?

What were you meant to be?

Even after all his centuries, still he could not answer those questions.

The man in the portrait, the man he once was, stared cockily back at him: it was a face full of a confidence he no longer possessed.

He sat on the floor, and leant once more, his back against the frame.

It was a sight to behold: the real, very-much-undead vampire Vauquelin, some seven-hundred-years-old at that time, propped up against the twenty-nine year-old, human Vauquelin.

And the malevolent voice came back with a vengeance.

Perhaps your maker was not so wrong?

Vauquelin snorted.

Well ... can you argue?

He dragged a hand down his face and sank to the ground.

Being vampire is unnatural.

No soul is meant to live this long.

Oh, but they can. And yet you have squandered it.

Vauquelin rubbed his collarbone until it was raw.

He could not deny it.

He had lived in pursuit of self-gratification alone.

He could have died a mortal death in his first 1668, and instead he did not hesitate — he said YES to a cruel vampire.

And then he said yes again, in his second 1668.

He could have been done with all this perpetual torture.

I am a fucking masochist.

But soon — although perhaps not soon enough — he will come to understand why.

All mortals have done it, have they not?

Wished they could live forever?

How wonderful that would be!

But it is the *opposite* of wonderful.

It is a provisional *hell*.

Are vampires truly damned?

The answer is a resounding YES, because it is torture for them to watch:

their loved ones die
the world change and yet somehow not change
society degrade in the name of progress
humanity repeat the same mistakes
over and over and over and over again
because humans learn NOTHING

When one lives forever, one becomes jaded.

Horrific events become less horrific (because — sadly — one becomes accustomed to them). History repeats itself with different names and perhaps different countries and different sensibilities ... if one is lucky, that is.

In Vauquelin's futurepast, he showed this portrait to Maeve and deceived her: she believed it to be his ancestor.

He lied to her and let her believe it. His entire existence has been based on deception. In this timeline, the lies had gotten so deep they threatened to suffocate him.

LOS ANGELES, CALIFORNIA | SEPTEMBER 1900

Vauquelin dreamed he was on a ship, being tossed to and fro by a violent storm with great waves washing over the decks, and his legs lost their purchase ... he was swept out to sea.

Lost.

He opened his eyes and Maeve was sitting astride him, shaking him with great ferocity.

The first words out of his mouth were:

"Do you love me?"

She wrapped her fingers around his neck. "I do not," she said, and manoeuvred off of his hips like a cat: slow and deliberate.

Vauquelin ejected himself from the bed, naked as he always slept, and struggled into his banyan. He reached for her hand.

She took it and led him out to the front lawn, where all his belongings were heaped together in a crude pile. She crossed to his ancient portrait, exposed to the elements, front-and-centre amongst his crates and trunks.

"Then you believe me a fraud?" he asked.

Maeve remained silent for a few moments, regarding the portrait with her black vampire eyes, and then she cut them back to him.

"How can you not see your own fraudulence? You let me die the first time. You do not deserve a reward for saving me. You gave me no say in whether I wanted to live or die! You are the one I blame for Charles' death. And you are a coward, to boot!"

It was not the first time he had been called a coward, and he bristled at the expression.

"How dare you?" Maeve began a methodical traipse to and fro in front of the assemblage, pressing her fingertips to her temples. "This fictitious life you have shown me is a lie, if it is even true! How dare you not have asked me, in our so-called original life, if I wanted to become vampire? Can you not see that I would never have hesitated? We could have had so much together ... but you kept everything from me. So my answer is a resounding NO! I could never love anyone who deceived me so!" Her voice steadily amplified as she spoke, and she ended her tirade with a screech: "You absolute, fucking BASTARD!"

Leaving Vauquelin a blinking, incredulous mess, she strutted behind the pile and re-emerged a moment later, one hand tucked into the elbow of a strange man.

Vauquelin fixed his gaze upon the ground, shaking his head, unable to process what was happening. He covered his ears and screamed, "Maeve? No, no, NO! What is happening? Who is this?" He began to pace.

The man was freakishly tall, even taller than Vauquelin, but brawny, blond, and muscle-bound. His arms looked as though they were dying to burst forth from the seams of his suit jacket. He sported a wax-curled moustache and a beard, the latest fashion. In other words, this man was the unequivocal antithesis of himself: a pale, skeletal, raven-haired ghoul by comparison.

And he was dressed so garishly!

He had no taste, no sense of style!

How could she choose someone like this?

Vauquelin jutted his chin forth.

A vicious, verdigris vein erupted in pulsing fury across his forehead.

Never, ever a good sign.

The stranger wormed himself in front of her, a protective stance that raised Vauquelin's hackles.

"Will this be your dandy monster, then, Maeve?" the man asked, his voice dripping with Irish modulation. He began rolling up his sleeve.

She placed a stern hand over his wrist and drew his arm down with articulated authority.

"Explain to me how it is done, Vauquelin," she said, her voice calm and practiced. "I want him to be like me. He is the one I will choose forever, not you."

Vauquelin's breath vanished.

"You know not what you ask of me," he stuttered. His eyes began to dart back and forth between Maeve, once the love of his life, and this beefy young man with fresh bite wounds on his neck.

He was twenty years old if he was a day!

Vauquelin had been cuckolded.

He would have sworn he heard someone laugh, yet the three faces in this party all bore grim expressions.

"You have deceived me? With this ... this ..." Vauquelin gestured wildly with his hands. His English failed him. "This ... *crétin?*"[†]

"You never once asked me for fidelity. And clearly honesty is not your forté."

He searched her face for even the slightest trace of regret or love for him, but found it lacking. Instead, she regarded him with glacial indifference.

Vauquelin's mind flooded with centuries of memories, of the multiple lifetimes he had relinquished for the (now insubstantial) privilege of being in her presence again.

---

†- IMBECILE, NUMBSKULL

He flashed himself to stand before them, faster than either of them could blink, shoved the brute aside and caged her neck within his fingers, baring his teeth as he enchanted her paramour.

"How could someone once so pure and full of love become the foulest succubus to ever walk the earth?" he bellowed. The question was for Maeve but he directed at the man he had locked in his gaze, who stared back without understanding.

She struggled beneath Vauquelin's deathgrip, but as a fledgling, she was no match for his ancient strength. "You," she struggled to say. "You made me this way. Tell me how to change him!"

He lifted her off the ground by the throat and growled, "You are unworthy of such secrets."

He dropped her and flashed himself to the stranger's side, thrusting his fangs into the man's neck and gulping him down as if he had not nourished himself in weeks. He did not leave the last drop, as decreed by the rules of his maker's twisted coterie ... he took it all.

"One last lesson, chérie,"[†] he said, his voice garbled with blood, "I regret to inform you that vampires cannot raise the dead."

He ran his tongue over his lips with exaggerated extravagance, holding the body away from his own. "I see the appeal. His Celtic flavour is almost as magnificent as yours. A pity you shall never taste it again."

Maeve scrambled to her feet and, her eyes locked into Vauquelin's, extracted a match from her pocket, drawing it through her teeth and casting it into a graceful flight onto the mound of his scant possessions.

It smouldered on the surface of the portrait a fraction of a second before its ancient oils lurched the entire mess into an inferno.

Vauquelin watched with a powerless marble countenance as the flames licked and destroyed his painted face, melting into oblivion the canvas and crazed surface of his ancient portrait.

---

† - DARLING

She tossed Vauquelin's Opinel over her shoulder, embedding its blade into the turf, and laughed.

Her mirth — which once brilliantly illuminated his life — then expelled him into his darkest recesses.

All traces of happiness vacated his soul.

I wish I had never known you, Vauquelin thought, fists clenched at his sides, and promptly damned himself for wishing the unknowing of the one human who had ever brought him true joy.

An army of voices invaded his mind and it would have been far too easy to surrender to their intimidation. Instead he succumbed to his vanity, which has historically not ended well for him.

He picked Maeve up and dragged her kicking and shrieking down the stairs to the cellar. She clawed his face and neck — and as quickly as her fingernails tattered his skin, her marks mended themselves upon his hallowed vampire skin.

Her eyes twitched in terror.

He threw her into a corner and panicked at how to restrain her.

She was still in the feeble state of early vampire life ... but he could no longer trust her to obey him. Any benevolence he had once had for her had vanished like so much mist left behind by a wave.

At once he snapped his fingers and rushed up the stairs two at a time, slamming the door behind him and leaning all his weight against it.

Maeve was a quick study — she was behind the door in a fraction of a second.

Vauquelin wrenched the doorknob out of its base.

He heard the back knob rattle and clunk down the steps, followed by a muffled "Goddamnit!"

He quirked an eyebrow, grinning as he listened to Maeve clatter down the steps in chase of the runaway knob.

It bought him just enough time.

Vauquelin dragged the dead man to the cellar door and kicked the door in, descending the stairs with all the airs of a ballet dancer carrying a dead swan.

He took one last chance.

"My beloved, my Maeve ... it is true that I have delivered you a fanciful tale. Even I doubt it myself at times. But now you know what you are. You cannot deny it, yet you deny me. Still you choose to reject me. You chose a stranger over me. I, who have given you immortality."

He searched her eyes for the love that once existed between them.

It was a bud that had not germinated.

Dead on the vine.

Before him was his love, yet no longer his love.

She sat hunched in the corner, a mere shell of the Maeve that he once adored.

As a vampire, the former fiery, fiercely independent Maeve was now *exponentially* defiant.

She had proven herself to be a formidable opponent to Vauquelin.

Yet now ...

Now he cannot forgive her for cuckolding him.

"So many lessons I had to share with you, my love ... I regret that you did not have the patience to learn them with me."

As the words left his lips, Vauquelin reminded himself that he was none too patient himself. But it was not the time for self-reflection.

He dropped the man into the pit with great violence, not even caring that the acid seared through the thin fabric of his banyan and sizzled his skin.

Superficial burns were truly the least of his worries.

"You did not care that Charles died. Et donc,† Maeve, do you enjoy watching your lover's flesh melt?"

---

† - AND SO

Maeve brought her knees up and leant her chin on her hands.

"Do you mean yours or Cillian's?"

Her face was empty.

Blue eyes blazing, Vauquelin stood and retreated to the front lawn, where his possessions lay obliterated into blackened soot.

He heard the door open behind him, and his heart quickened.

Maeve emerged and sashayed down the steps.

"The sun will rise soon," he warned, his voice rising.

She merely laughed and sauntered out the gates and down the street.

"Get out of my house. You should have little to carry now."

He dove deep into his misery and sank onto the porch.

He had never felt so out of his own mind.

Not with his unwinding time, not with decades of his life being stolen from him, not from entering the obsidian darkness of a vampire existence: twice.

The putrid odour of his scorched antiquities hung heavy in the air.

As he sat, a light breeze kicked up, sending a fragment of the portrait sailing through the breeze, dipping and rising like a feather until it came to a stop upon his knee.

He picked it up with great care.

It was an eye.

His eye, on canvas.

It seemed this eye was judging him for the whole of his incarnation, which was based entirely on half-truths and poor decisions.

He placed it carefully in his pocket, burying his head in his hands.

He begged for forgiveness.

And then stopped.

He lifted his eyes to the night sky.

"For what, precisely, am I asking forgiveness?" he asked aloud.

O, Vauquelin. O, my sweet.

Vauquelin inclined his head to the voice.

You never once listened.

Did you truly believe you would be blessed with this life on your own terms?

He had tried so hard.

He had insisted on doing things his way.

But now, he realised, it was time to pay the piper.

He rocked back and forth on Maeve's front porch, blood tears waterfalling down his face, streaming forth through his nose and sullying the silk of his banyan: at last he admitted defeat.

Please, please help me.

There was only silence.

No voice came to his aid: true to form, they only kicked him when he was down. Yet now they would no longer deign to acknowledge him, so miserable was he.

His suffering was his own.

It was then that the little girl wandered past Maeve's gates.

What timing.

From this moment, this is no longer the past.

It is the present ... at least, it is Vauquelin's present.

Thirteen

LOS ANGELES, CALIFORNIA | OCTOBER 1900

He sits on the stoop until the sun wakes.

Maybe this will be his Final Death?

Please? he begs.

But the voice remains quiet.

The sun's brutal singe upon his skin drives him inside and he drops his smoke-addled banyan on the floor by the bathtub.

He washes and slips into their — her — bed, empty of Maeve.

Slumber evades him: his thoughts are punishing.

I have failed …

I admit it.

I am too vain.

Vauquelin awakens behind the motherly velvet bed curtains the moment the sun dips below the California mountains.

The house is silent.

He is not done for yet but for the first time in his life, all he has is what he can hold in his hands. At least she had not taken his clothes from the closet. He folds his few modern garments with great solemnity into a leather bag, and emerges onto the porch.

Give me my redemption. Why must you continue to punish me? he asks.

He knows not who he is asking, though he suspects it must be Yvain, his maker.

But he had severed ties with him centuries ago!

Yvain should have no control over him now.

I only want for you to be happy

It seems to me that you yourself do not wish to be happy

Whose is this voice?

What is happiness?

What is satisfaction?

Can one find it in a lifetime?

Can one find it in a dozen lifetimes?

The answer is no …

But if one is vampire (who was once human, albeit twice removed) one will ceaselessly scour the earth's surface for it, seeking it in the most unlikely of places, no matter how damned the prospect.

Still, he will respect Maeve's wishes.

Vauquelin walks outside the gates of 2421 Pearl Street — one day it will be known as Figueroa — with his bag slung over his shoulder. His eyes flash to the charred remains of his belongings on the lawn.

The house is immutably closed to him — its memories have evaporated, as if he had never been inside. It mocks him: surely it is glad to be rid of him and his malicious machinations.

The windows are dark.

Its love has vanished without a trace.

He sinks onto his heels and knits his fingers in front of his face, perching his elbows on his knees, and stares at the house.

His eyes close.

I do not accept this outcome, he thinks/prays.

The phrase sends fire up his spine, causing him to open his eyes, and so he repeats it.

I do not accept this outcome.

I do not accept this outcome.

I do not accept this outcome.

I was wrong.

I was selfish.

I failed

I failed

I failed

I ruined her

I cursed her

And, as though out of his own control, his legs rise to standing and propel him away.

As he walks, he considers how many times he had deceived himself by expecting to have something like a human life.

you

are

vampire, the voice says in beat with his steps.

I am vampire

I am vampire

I am vampire, Vauquelin chants in conjunction with his footfall.

Perhaps it is time he starts living like one?

Each footstep grows angrier and more determined.

He walks until his feet are blistered and at the last possible moment finds his shelter in an opium den.

He extracts a twenty dollar bill from his wallet for entry, the equivalent of $650 in present-day currency, and remains awake all day watching humans smoke themselves into oblivion.

What a pathetic vignette, he thinks.

How ironic.

So many illicit substances that humans can pay for, and perhaps be pitied for, yet he must frequently struggle for the blood that keeps him alive. Humans can kill themselves with such substances, yet his kind is denigrated for their "drug," which is merely sustenance.

Even so, his instincts remind him that he is presently surrounded by humans in a comatose state. His fingers begin to agitate.

His tongue drags across his upper lip.

He could feast himself to engorgement on them in this dark space, and no one will be the wiser.

But the cost is too high.

Imbibing chemically-altered blood will decimate him.

It has been proven.

Yet the blood fragrance is so enticing ... it permeates the atmosphere of the airless environs.

The sordid setting disperses a mystical aroma that almost seduces him into abandoning his own cardinal rule.

No.

NO! NO!

He needs only to conjure the memory of that one singular night, far into his futurepast: the drug-addled night that nearly destroyed him. He has no desire to enter that nightmare territory again, and regardless, what he needs most is a clear mind.

He walks to the entrance desk and asks the clerk:

"Allow me fifteen minutes. I will walk across the street to send a telegram, and then I will return. Will you remember me?" He presses a fifty-dollar bill into the clerk's palm, and charms him to be sure.

"Indeed, sir," the clerk replies.

The bill disappears into his pocket.

```
M. FRANÇOIS LAVIGNE
LOS ANGELES, CALIF.


SITUATION HAS DRASTICALLY CHANGED. NEED
REINSTATEMENT OF ORIGINAL HOUSING OR SIMILAR.
DELIVER EMPTY COFFIN AND MEET ME AT 2421 PEARL ST
TOMORROW AT 8:00PM. NO QUESTIONS. DRAW ON ACCOUNT.


M. L DE VAUQUELIN
```

He returns to the opium den and is granted entry with a sly grin from the clerk. He dismisses the pipes that are so generously offered to him all through the night and well into the morning, collapsing into his slumber when his heart can take no more.

That night, a figure comes to him in his opium-fragranced dreams.

The being is ethereal, possessed of an indefinable beauty, and gazes upon him with a serene smile. The comfort they exude — it is like nothing his consciousness can offer up in comparison. They hold out their hand, still bathing him in their luminous smile, and Vauquelin accepts it.

They urge Vauquelin forward and he willingly follows without question, because each step blankets him in warmth and protection. He cries pure, clear human tears in this dream, not bloody vampire ones.

The being looks back over their shoulder from time to time, as if to ensure he is still there, and each time Vauquelin nods, to acknowledge and assure them that he is. That he would follow them anywhere they led.

They turn to him at last and open their arms, and he folds himself into them, enshrouded by love, at the exact moment he is awakened by his body's infallible clock.

Vauquelin squeezes his eyes shut, desperate to hold fast to the tenderness that the mysterious being had shown him. But reality is a cruel slap in the face, and he again has to hold his breath against the toxic perfume of the opium den as his lungs force him back into the dismal certainty of his current state.

As the sun sets, he arises from the filthy, makeshift pallet he had slept on, and shudders when he sees cockroaches rushing from the space he just vacated.

He emerges into the folds of the night.

For the rest of his days ahead, the tranquillity of his dream lover will grasp his mind, bestowing upon him a sense of clarity: even as he wretchedly tries (and fails) to recall the exact lines of their face.

His brain constructs an impenetrable wall to shelter the memory.

He must keep it intact, much as he once kept his hope of reuniting with Maeve, because a soul without hope is a dangerous thing indeed.

He tucks it away in his heart.

He will see them again one day, perhaps sooner than he thinks.

But now, he must bravely face the fallout of what has transpired.

A hired carriage drops Vauquelin at the front gate of Maeve's house, which sits before him with darkened windows.

He just needs one last look.

She is out again ... perhaps it was not only his presence that drove her from its comforting walls.

His eyes flitter around the front, searching for anything amiss.

Even in the dark, the ashy remains of his cauterised earthly existence (at least his *American* existence, he reminds himself) stare back at him like a gaping wound upon the lawn.

He sinks to the ground and strives to gather his scattered thoughts, biting into the muscle below his left thumb.

It is only the bitter iron washing against his tongue that wrenches him into equally bitter consciousness, and he swallows hard, licking the blood from his skin.

As he draws his arm away, the foreign, sickly-sweet odour of smoked opium wafts into his nose.

The suspicious fragrances of the "bed" he slept in during the day have taken up residence in the fibres of his clothing. The odious smell of opiates is secondary, however, to his unwashed self.

His hair is stringy and greasy ... his nails (normally carefully trimmed and manicured in his fastidious habit) are filthy, blackened by smoky grime.

More precisely, he is befouled and very *un*-Vauquelin.

He leans up against the iron balustrade and extracts his pocket watch. The attorney should arrive in twenty minutes.

He spends those minutes pondering his next move.

He has several options now, none of which are appealing.

Firstly, he can beg Maeve for forgiveness.

"Not fucking likely," he whispers aloud, snapping the lid closed on the watch.

Maeve's brutal, elaborately planned rejection would spur any average human man to pursue her.

Plead his case.

Pledge his undying love.

Even beg, perhaps.

But Vauquelin is not an average human man.

He is vampire.

And after centuries of effort to return to her, she has scorned him.

Wasted years are nothing, really, to a revenant.

Still, one can have resentment towards them.

For most mortals, one could easily wager that, if one were able to calculate how many moments of life add up to joy, the quantity (not to mention the quality) would be vastly disappointing.

It is human nature to merely exist, to absorb the moments that really matter: those moments that jostle one's bones and bring one to the point of bursting with absolute elation at being ALIVE.

Alive.

Alive.

Alive.

Like the echo of a beating heart.

All vampires are born human, but the longer they live, the more that humanity erodes.

The further the distance from the joyous moments ... the more hardened they are by their accumulated disappointments and failures.

Vauquelin's fingers twist into coils.

He will —

The attorney's carriage pulls to a stop and the steps fall down.

He ascends, looking over his shoulder one last time.

Mon dieu,[†] *how I loved that house ... and she who was once in it.*

Vauquelin draws the carriage door to a close with a thunk.

He has always loved that sound.

And the driver turns the carriage around on dirt-ridden Pearl Street, the horses' hooves sending impressive clouds of dust up into the air, ferrying Vauquelin back to his first chapter in Los Angeles, so he can begin.

Yet again.

---

†- MY GOD

"May I ask what has transpired, Monsieur?" Lavigne asks.

Bobbing in the carriage, he observes his eccentric client, who had hired him mere months ago in France, and whom he was certainly unaccustomed to seeing so … dishevelled.

Vauquelin withdraws his handkerchief and sneezes violently into it.

"You may not. Have my orders been executed?"

"As you specified."

"When we arrive, I shall ask you inside … and I shall tell you everything."

Fourteen

LOS ANGELES, CALIFORNIA | OCTOBER 1900

Lavigne unlocks a door and welcomes Vauquelin to enter first.

It is the same depressing bungalow he had rented for his client when they first arrived in Los Angeles just over a month ago.

Still vacant.

Its atmosphere is stale and sad. Transitory.

The melancholia of its walls shocks Vauquelin into grim reality as the attorney closes the door behind him. A more appropriate shelter for his rotten state of affairs could scarcely be imagined.

In his first timeline, he had the bungalow next door: same miserable atmosphere, opposite layout. The fact that he could not get the same one this time might have been his first sign that his life was beginning to unravel — but it seemed an insignificant detail at the time.

On his first journey to America, this shabby housing was meant to be temporary: until he could build his own future palace in the burgeoning city of Los Angeles ... the City of Angels (a fallacy for him: perhaps he should never have come here in the first place).

And then he met Maeve.

In his futurepast she visited him at his first bungalow.

His lodgings had severely depressed her, and perhaps even accelerated their relationship: she insisted he move in with her at once, which he did. But in this new timeline, she never saw this particular dismal abode.

Lavigne walks the perimeter lighting the sparse wall-mounted gas lamps, urging out the minuscule available light into the shabby room.

"I hope this will be satisfactory, Monsieur."

Vauquelin has a flash of Olivier … once his valet, now his revenant brother. In his mortal life, Olivier had lighted Vauquelin's candles nightly, had consistently anticipated his thoughts and desires, often before Vauquelin knew them himself.

Olivier cared for him so deeply … as he cares for him still in brotherhood. He would never have dreamed of setting Vauquelin up in such squalor. This attorney cares only for the money that will be handed to him.

Vauquelin's heeled boots ring out on the warped wooden floors. He surveys his bleak surroundings and takes off his black kidskin gloves one finger at a time, seeing it with the eyes Maeve had once seen it with, so many centuries ago in the spiderwebs of his first timeline.

He lifts his chin to the ceiling.

Light ricochets across the walls from the chamberstick held in the trembling hand of his attorney.

There is the exposed beam.

There are the cobwebs.

There is the dusty, hole-ridden sofa.

"Where is the item I requested?" he asks.

The attorney rushes to the bedroom and opens the door, gesturing toward a new, uncrated mahogany coffin.

"It is here per your orders, Monsieur."

Vauquelin lifts the lid to verify that the interior is to his liking, and finding it acceptable, slams it shut with a clamorous ring.

Lavigne quivers in his shoes.

There is something quite changed in the demeanour of his idiosyncratic, affluent client. Lavigne had shepherded the "remains" of Monsieur de Vauquelin's "uncle" from France to San Francisco to Los Angeles — which was most unusual, to be sure — to this day he is unsure what happened with that coffin. And now he has had to procure a vacant one!

It is all very curious!

Even so, for the past month, he has done little aside from living high on the hog with zero communication from his employer. In truth it is not the worst arrangement he has ever had, though there is not a decent baguette to be had in this godforsaken town.

But why does his client need an *empty* coffin?

This is too much!

"Monsieur, I must ask you ..."

« Assiez-vous , Lavigne , »[†] Vauquelin commands, turning his full imposing form to the diminutive attorney.

Lavigne drops hard on the sofa.

"I have already said I would tell you everything. Have you been disappointed in your situation thus far? Have I not upheld my end of our original agreement?"

Lavigne's jittery behaviour on this particular night awakens Vauquelin's thirst, sending it slithering through his dwindling blood supply.

"I could not complain, Monsieur," he stammers.

Vauquelin leans against the wall and narrows his eyes, comparing Lavigne to Duclos, his attorney in the past incarnation of this very situation.

Duclos was a man of old France, a man of steel and resolve.

He briefly considers that Lavigne is a product of a different France: yet another sign that his timeline is no longer reliable. He taps his fingers upon the cracked plaster wall, scrutinising his next steps.

Without the attorney, his life will be that much more difficult:

---

†- SIT DOWN, LAVIGNE

Vauquelin requires a compliant human to assist him with his necessary daylight tasks.

He could tell him the truth, but the attorney would have to be enchanted. He is not in the position, given his current turn of events, to rely on human discretion. Even money is clearly not enough to convince this one.

Vauquelin could turn him, but there are severe ramifications. He neither respects nor values this man enough to be attached to him for eternity.

He shifts his cold eyes to the attorney, who sinks ever deeper into the sofa.

Bloodlust gnaws at Vauquelin's veins — he looks away and gropes his jaw. He should have fed prior to this meeting, but the circumstances have all been wrong.

A memory of Yvain's voice creeps into his consciousness.

Have you not read our lore?

Vauquelin had read fiction of vampires, most of which he found ridiculous ... but lore?

Never.

Why would he?

He lives it.

But the memory sparks an idea.

Could he not experiment?

Make the attorney his thrall?

I could kill Lavigne if things get out of hand, no? he thinks.

Vauquelin has never trifled with Life and Death ... he has always held both in high esteem. But now he must consider his options with care. A deluge of conflicting scenarios assaults his mind, dragging it beneath waves of confusion as his blood need tampers with his brain.

At this moment, he does not know where he is, or when.

His hands begin to tremor.

The passing clatter of a carriage on the street, followed by the sound of a voice speaking in French, intensifies his misperception of his surroundings, and his eyes flicker to and fro.

"Monsieur? Are you unwell?"

Vauquelin snaps his head to Lavigne and takes three long strides.

This man has never once come into contact with Vauquelin's blood: therefore, he will not be turned ... so what *will* happen?

There is only one way to find out.

He pounces on Lavigne and draws his head back with one hand as he bites open a vein on his other wrist, flowing his blood into the human man's mouth.

The man chokes and sputters, and promptly faints away.

Oh.

Oh no.

Could vampire blood itself be deadly?

Vauquelin is baffled. He strikes Lavigne's face over and over.

Nothing.

He panics and drains the man.

And then he runs out into the street, at a loss for what to do with the body.

He could drag it out of the bungalow ... it is late, and only prostitutes are about on his street ... he knows they would not betray him by summoning the police ... but ... but ...

In short, everything is FUCKED.

His mind shifts into emergency mode as he slices a clean line over his puncture marks, revising them with the Opinel. If Lavigne were still alive, Vauquelin could heal his damage. Unfortunately, Death draws the curtains on that skill once she claims her spoils.

Judging by the lightened sky and his slowing heart, it is time for him to go to his rest.

Vauquelin sinks into the coffin and sleeps through the day as the corpse stiffens on his sofa.

He must find another place to live, and fast.

He never thought things out this far, because his life was not supposed to turn out this way. He was meant to have a happily-ever-after, and live with his love. For an all-too-brief moment, he thought he had achieved that.

He has a week — perhaps — in this place until the corpse begins to putrefy.

Prior to this night, he thought his drug-addled decimation in his first timeline was his lowest point.

He was wrong.

Things can always get worse.

Fifteen

LOS ANGELES, CALIFORNIA | OCTOBER 1900

Vauquelin's first thought upon waking is that he cannot just *leave*.

The bungalow is in Lavigne's name, and therefore his movements could be traced. This has never been a problem for Vauquelin ... he has habitually relied on his attorneys' names for centuries, and it has never caused him difficulties.

Until now.

With Los Angeles being a small city at this juncture, he cannot afford to expose his true identity, and self-camouflage is his ingrained tendency.

He must dispose of the body ... but how?

Vauquelin emerges from the coffin and freshens himself as best he can, dressing in his most-unsullied clothing.

Throughout his existence, human and vampire, he has depended on others. Rarely has he had to lift a finger to help himself, yet his distorted timelines have consistently reminded him of his noble failures.

He emerges onto the front stoop and rolls a cigarette.

Lavigne's blood will keep him satiated for at least seven days.

Here he sits in an infant city, in a country in which he has invested all his hope (twice), and what does he have to show for it?

Absolutely nothing.

He had been merely existing, trying to recreate history.

The one being he wanted does not want him.

In times like this, the ghosts manifest.

Had Vauquelin been born into a lower caste, he might have learned the phrase "Do not put all your eggs in one basket." But he had never heard this idiom. He was born, as a human, in the France of l'ancienne régime[†] — during the reign of the Sun King, Louis XIV. The nobility were blissfully unaware of such peasant phrases, because absolutely nothing was closed to them.

It is difficult to shed one's upbringing.

The burdensome weight of a lengthy existence is resting heavy on his shoulders. Imagine having to carry that across centuries.

But on top of that is his own bizarre history/curse: that of bouncing backward and forward through time.

What is the point?

Even now he wonders what he has done to deserve all these attempts to bring him down.

I should not be sitting on this stoop, he thinks. *I should be bones, long dead, forgotten in a crypt in France.*

He sits for hours, legs crossed like a woman as always, watching as the last of the evening merchants parade by … sellers of fruits and vegetables, bolts of cloth, pots and pans. Whenever the prepared food vendors pass by, he draws a bergamot-scented handkerchief to his face, a foppish gesture he retains from old Paris. The last shred of humanity in him, such as it is, longs to inhale the myriad fragrances: but his vampiric nature turns his stomach at the prominent local spices, which, even if he were human, would have been too much for his French sensibilities.

Little by little the merchants and their carts are replaced by strolling

---

† - THE OLD REGIME: PRE-REVOLUTIONARY FRANCE

people of the night: soon, pedestrians, merchants, and families are outnumbered by harlots and con artists.

The evening sky darkens and the air grows salty with the fragrance of the Pacific sea air, bringing to mind his recent journey across the Atlantic.

His thoughts, of course, are punctuated by memories of Maeve. He once believed that letting her die in his first timeline was his life's gravest error, but now it is clear that it was not: it was her failed transformation in his second.

Vauquelin had tampered with history, and the results were devastating.

He should never have come back to America at all, let alone enshroud Maeve in his dark cloak of misery.

I do not belong here

I do not belong anywhere

He folds his head into his hands, and his cigarette sets his hair ablaze.

Putain d'enfer ![†]

He leaps up and pats the flames out. In his distress, he does not notice that a hustler has stopped in front of him.

"Rough night?" he asks.

"Rough lifetimes," Vauquelin replies, sitting once again on the stoop. He kicks the villainous cigarette into the gutter.

"Life*times*?"

"It does not matter," Vauquelin says, holding the young man in his gaze for a moment.

The man is slender with dark circles under his eyes, so dark that they stand out even in the darkness of the evening. Those eyes are violet, shaded by lush, long lashes.

It trips a memory from the depths — and Vauquelin lunges toward him.

The man recoils in defensive alarm, so Vauquelin extends a hand.

"Please do not fear me. I mean you no harm."

---

†- FUCKING HELL!

The man who stands in before him has reminded him of Clément.

In his second past, Vauquelin had briefly considered casting aside his primary objective — reuniting with Maeve — because of a undreamed-of indiscretion with that beguiling, young vampire: who was, unfortunately, the lover of his maker.

It would have been disastrous.

Or would it?

His heart clenches, and regret spreads across his entire body like a fever.

Had he chosen the wrong one?

Vauquelin *could* have let his second history play out as it was meant to, and never attempted to reinsert himself in Maeve's life.

To let her die as she was originally fated, to never know him.

To embrace something new.

Yet he did not. He had been determined to keep his history intact, to repeat it to the letter.

No one has that power ... not even a vampire.

In short, it has taken him nearly eight hundred years to merely *begin* to decipher his raison d'être.[†] Soon, he will come to embrace his nature, to learn that by disavowing it he will only sabotage his own happiness.

He has almost arrived at the brink of understanding — he is not yet prepared.

Soon.

As for now, Vauquelin stands with a crown of singed hair, dressed in uncustomarily dull clothes, in front of a random young man who has brought Vauquelin's assessment of his most recent erroneous decisions to a screeching halt.

Vauquelin remembers his fingers folding into Clément's raven locks.

The fragrance of Clément's body, his as eyes green as a spring meadow.

His own hesitation.

---

†- PURPOSE, REASON FOR BEING

But this man is *not* Clément, and Vauquelin temporarily shelves his reverie. He looks up and down the dirty street, and reminds himself of the place he is in now: a rough corridor of a burgeoning city, choking with desperation, despondence and angst. It is not so different from the modern Los Angeles of his futurepast.

"I find myself in a bit of trouble," Vauquelin says, looking at the ground. "Can you help me?"

"What is it you need, sir?"

Vauquelin opens the door, and gestures invitingly beyond.

The cocksure Abel ascends the steps.

Vauquelin leads Abel inside the shabby bungalow and closes the door behind them. "I need to dispose of a body," he says, gesturing to the ripening corpse on the sofa.

The young man does not even flinch. Corpses, it would seem, are familiar territory for him, and thus he and Vauquelin have something in common right from the start.

As such, Vauquelin breaks one of his own rules.

"What is your name?" he asks.

He never wants to know the names of victims or those he will never encounter again. His brain is already so crowded with centuries of thoughts, knowledge, and memories: he prefers not to add useless clutter, as he can never forget.

"I'm called Abel the Hand," he said, "because I —"

"That's enough," Vauquelin replied, holding up his hands. "Quite enough. I am Michel Baudin. I am only a tourist, and this man tried to rob me. The situation went awry."

Vauquelin also never gives his real name to strangers.

Never.

Abel is one of the smartest hustlers in Los Angeles. He folds his arms and hikes an eyebrow. He may only be seventeen years old, but he cut his teeth on the streets and he knows the man standing before him is lying.

He already has the low-down: 'Michel' is a rich man from Paris and that corpse is his attorney. Everyone knows everything that happens on this street.

He cuts his eyes to the masterful slit on the dead man's throat.

"Hold on, now. Why don't you tell me what really happened? Where's the blood?"

Vauquelin stiffens, lengthening his spine. "I do not owe you any explanations. I will give you five hundred dollars to get rid of him. No more questions."

Without appearing to do so, Abel has already taken stock of the room. "Well, let's use that coffin. That's the easiest way."

« Putain , »[†] Vauquelin mutters under his breath. He had not hidden the coffin before he emerged out-of-doors this evening. "The coffin stays. You may not take it."

"You got another stiff in there, or somethin'?" Abel makes a move to open it.

Faster than he can blink, Vauquelin has a hand around Abel's throat, thrusting him against the wall, drilling his eyes into him.

"I repeat ... no more questions. You will take the money and the corpse, and you will forget you ever laid eyes upon me."

Abel squirms under Vauquelin's grip.

He struggles out a curt, staccato nod.

Vauquelin releases him and snarls, revealing just the slightest tips of his razor-sharp teeth.

Abel averts his eyes. "I'll need that rug," he blurts, pointing to the floor.

---

†- FUCK

"You are welcome to it."

Vauquelin smiles and withdraws a small leather purse.

He extracts five crisp one hundred dollar bills and hands them to Abel.

"Start rolling. He is beginning to smell."

And so Abel the Hand rolls, and Vauquelin hefts the corpse onto Abel's shoulder as easily as one would lift a feather, astonishing Abel with his strength.

How can such a thin man be so strong? Abel marvels.

Vauquelin walks around the room and kills the flames on the gas lamps, smothering the room in utter darkness.

"Good night, and I thank you."

Vauquelin closes the door behind the hustler and locks it, slinking breathlessly against it. When had he become so reckless, so undisciplined?

His behaviour is so uncharacteristic ...

He has lost his self-control, and he must get it back post-haste.

The next evening Vauquelin gathers his scant belongings, lastly dropping the key on the bureau, and walks into the night.

He looks up and down the street.

It has quietened, and Abel is nowhere to be seen.

Vauquelin catches a carriage and asks the driver if there are any general stores still open. He is delivered to one, pays the driver to wait, and emerges with six heavy blankets and a small parcel of tools.

"And now I would like you to drive me to the most luxurious hotel in this hovel of city."

The driver tips his hat and pulls to a stop, some miles away from the shop, in front of the Van Nuys Hotel.

"I thank you."

Vauquelin pays for a single room a full month in advance, leaving strict "never disturb" orders with the concierge.

He requests a case of wine to be brought up at once.

After the bellhop delivers his portmanteau and the wine to his room, he sets to tacking up the blankets over the windows.

He draws a bath in the massive claw foot tub.

He washes — twice — and refills the tub with scalding water, wondering what had ever possessed him to allow a peasant attorney to choose his living space.

Now he is safe, and has the services of a concierge at his disposal.

For the first time in months, he can relax.

He slips between the crisp white sheets of the immaculate bed just as the sun rises, and welcomes his slumber.

A month into his stay at the Van Nuys Hotel, Vauquelin is a little too comfortable. He simply needs to ring the front desk to have anything he needs delivered immediately. It reminds him of his futurepast life in Los Angeles, only without a mobile phone on which to order everything.

Bankers deliver him cash from his account.

Tailors come to his room and bring him bespoke suits and cravats, silk shirts and new leather shoes.

He takes midnight swims in the hotel's opulent indoor pool.

The doorman greets Vauquelin by name when he returns, typically around 4:00am, from his weekly blood walks.

Books arrive several times a week via mail order catalogues. It cannot hold a candle to the convenience of futurepast internet orders, but it is the best option available to him.

In truth, he can see no reason to leave: but once again, he is stagnating.

Each week when he leaves the Van Nuys, he keeps his eyes open for Maeve. Their paths never cross. He is tempted to ride past her house, but can never bring himself to do so.

Vauquelin is unaccustomed to being rejected — he is the one who rejects. And knowing her as he did, he was not confident in any attempt to sway her back. In Maeve's new reality, he had not once been in her good graces ... not really.

One evening, he stops by the desk and sends a telegram to Olivier in Annecy, France.

```
ALL IS LOST.
NEXT STEPS UNSURE.
REPLY VAN NUYS HOTEL
LOS ANGELES, CALIF. USA.
L DE V
```

As he begins the trek to his room, he has immediate regrets. Olivier will be worried — the message is too abrupt. He turns on his heel and returns to the desk to cancel, but is informed the message has regrettably already been transmitted.

"Another, please. Same addressee."

```
DO NOT WORRY. AM SAFE & SOUND.
MAY RETURN FRANCE.
LOOK FOR LETTER W DETAILS.
LOVE TO YOU MY BROTHER.
L DE V
```

Better.

Vauquelin whistles a song from the early 2000s as he ascends to his room in the hotel's gilded, Beaux-Arts lift.

He stops whistling as he inserts the key and an irrational thought seizes him: what if Maeve were inside, sitting on his bed? What would he say to her, what would his reaction be?

His hand rattles the brass key against the lock.

At last, he fumbles the door open and his eyes scan an empty room.

He emits a laugh-snort.

Why would she come looking for you

She does not want you, can you not understand that

But the problem is, he does understand.

He should never have loved, nor have expected to be loved in return.

How could he just walk away?

The short answer is that time is irrelevant to him.

Vauquelin has experienced thousands of little (and quite a few big) deaths and disappointments in his long life.

This loss, though he has poured so many of his years and so much energy into it, is sadly just one of many.

The sum of his time with Maeve, in his original timeline, was a little less than eighteen years.

A long span for human sensibilities, but a brief chapter in the context of eternal life.

Regardless, the life he had with her was so enchanting it compelled him to waste three hundred years on the merest hope he might bask in its light again.

How many people navigate their existences outside of their own realities? How many wish they could be someone they are unable to be, knowing they will die without ever being their truest selves? How many covet a life other than the one they have been given, their hearts burdened by unreciprocated desires?

Yet he must continue on.

He has no choice.

You could not reclaim that life

Because you never deserved it

You lied to yourself

He pours a glass of wine and opens the window, sitting on the sill with one leg draped across the edge. A bottle and three cigarettes later, he is no closer to knowing what he should do next, and the cursed sun is peeking over the mountains.

Tonight.

Tonight, he will write Olivier the promised letter, and he will have a plan.

Louis de Vauquelin
Hotel Van Nuys
Los Angeles, Calif., États-Unis

6 Novembre 1900

My dearest brother,

I hope you are well ... I have not heard your blood call to me,
so I must only assume that you are well and safe. It is with
great regret that I have waited so long to apprise you of my dire
situation here.

All that I had hoped for, all that I endeavoured with such
trepidation to achieve, has been lost. My desires were not
strong enough, it seems, or I was too weak. My incompetence
is astonishing. I allowed myself to be ruled by my own
compulsions, and I have thoroughly ruined her. Life with her
was not meant to be ... my circumstances should have been proof
enough that I was unworthy of my most ardent wish.
So now I find myself free, but adrift in a murky ocean of

*desolation. I am too far from home, in more ways than I care
to count. Shall I return to France with my chin on my chest,
a humbled man?*

*I am no longer convinced France is my home, yet nothing
remains for me in California. For one of the few times in my
life I am fearful, and I ache for familiarity.*

My isolation is infinite and suffocating.

I once believed that I was happy alone.

How wrong I have been, how obstinate.

I am unsure what to do.

Please help me.

*Yours in eternal brotherhood,
Vauquelin*

Vauquelin sets the letter aside and paces the floor with his hands knitted behind his back. It is his steadfast method for thinking. His body must move to get his thoughts circulating. At times, he wonders if it is purely physiological: could the ebb and flow of his blood supply be the cause of his frequent brain malfunctions?

What a pity that no doctors can study the biology of vampires! Vauquelin certainly would never consent to such a study of himself, no more than he can imagine any other vampire doing so.

Regardless, pacing usually opens his mind to thoughts that have been pressurising like a dammed river, but ... not tonight.

The letter to Olivier is too reserved.

It does not communicate, not with any level of accuracy, how desolate he is — because he himself cannot yet define it.

In situations like this, Vauquelin always defers to distraction.

From his nightstand, he retrieves a copy of *Harper's Weekly* and descends in the elevator to the concierge desk. Turning to a dog-eared page, he points to a small advertisement.

"I would like to order this automobile," he says. "I will make the arrangements via telephone and wire transfer, but I will need a place to charge the battery. Do you have such a location?"

"How thrilling, Monsieur de Vauquelin! But regrettably, it is so seldom that we have guests with electric automobiles here. We have no provisions for it, I am afraid."

"I see ..." Vauquelin rolls the magazine up and walks away, tapping it upon his palm as he ponders a solution. As of this moment, he wants nothing in the world as badly as this automobile. He had fallen in love with cars in his futurepast, and frankly, too much of his life has been spent without one — seeing as most of it has been spent in primitive centuries.

He wants it so badly that he considers buying a house for his own electrical source, or departing immediately for France.

No (tap), no (tap), no (tap tap tap) ... relocating is too complicated a decision to hinge on a whim.

Were he to buy a house, he would be required to hire someone else to help him during the day, and his experience with the attorney has soured him on that prospect.

As for returning to France, he is not quite ready to admit defeat.

Despite having to face living here without Maeve, he loves America — though in truth, he knows nothing about it.

Los Angeles is his country.

Even now, in its gritty, unsophisticated era.

Still, he pictures himself driving through the misty, midnight French countryside and parking the automobile in front of his château ... he imagines the sound of rubber tires squelching across the cobblestones in Paris. Perhaps it would be for the best ... at least in France he has magnificent places of his own, though they had grown dull and predictable to his eyes.

Familiarity might be just the balm his soul needs at this stage.

Just as Vauquelin reaches the elevator, the concierge calls out to him.

"Monsieur! A moment of your time?"

"Yes?"

"I've just spoken to the manager, and I have excellent news! I was unaware that the hotel already has plans in place for just such an area. Could you accompany me to the receiving lot?"

Vauquelin smiles and follows the concierge through a service corridor, emerging on a platform where deliveries are made.

The concierge gestures to a small paved area.

"This is it ... not only could you park your automobile here, safe from passers-by, but we will install the charging outlet here. Unfortunately, this could take a month or longer to complete, and I imagine your stay with us is coming to an end."

"On the contrary, I have no immediate plans to leave," Vauquelin replies. "I am most content here. I will place the order for the vehicle."

The news buys him time for deciding what he will do with his life, and perhaps straightens his tilted axis: even just a bit.

Seventeen

LOS ANGELES, CALIFORNIA | NOVEMBER 1900

At sunrise, Vauquelin places a long-distance call to the Baker Motor Vehicle Company in Cleveland, Ohio, and orders a black Stanhope Runabout.

Three weeks later, it arrives at the Van Nuys Hotel. He hurries to see it, dressed in one of his finest new ensembles, for this is an occasion worth celebrating: it will provide him with independent mobility and open the world of Los Angeles to him in ways he has not seen in this era, not to mention while wholly alone.

The car has attracted a small crowd of hotel employees who bustle around it, thrilled by the rare opportunity to see an electric vehicle up close. One of them reaches out to touch it but recoils when Vauquelin delivers him a very stern look.

He walks the perimeter of the automobile, running his hands over its leather fenders and opening and closing the windows, which are designed just like train windows. He presses down on the black tufted seat and climbs in, unhinging the top so that the roof will be open to the night sky, and starts it up.

The silence of the vehicle astonishes him, and for a moment he wonders if it is defective. Though he had owned multiple cars in his first timeline, they had all been gas-powered. A wry grin curls his lips at the notion that electric cars exist in the year 1900, yet they will soon fall out of favour as Americans begin their decades-long love affair with petroleum.

In his futurepast Los Angeles, environmentalists and hipsters fought for electric charging stations to power up their Priuses and Teslas, and here he is, once again ahead of his time.

For now.

The car boasts a maximum speed of fourteen miles per hour: scarcely faster than his ancient coach-and-six! Nevertheless, he is grateful he must no longer rely on hired cabs to move around the city.

Tonight, he plans to put the automobile to the test.

The simple dashboard offers two indicators: one for amperes and one for voltage. He can drive one hundred miles before the batteries will need a charge.

He manoeuvres to the driveway and watches for horse-drawn carriages. The street is still quite busy, and so he eases out into the lane.

Another electric vehicle passes him, tooting an *ah-ooogah* horn.

He declines to *ah-ooga* in return.

Vauquelin is after freedom tonight, not fellowship.

And just like that he is in motion.

Unbound.

Throughout his long years, Vauquelin has been a lover of taking to the road to clear his mind.

The first place he drives is to the beach, to worship the moon.

It is not visible from his hotel room.

For an ancient being who is confined to the dark closeness of the indoors during daylight hours, the light of the moon is a benevolent purification of the senses, giving him a chance to wander — to nightdream, in the same manner as those who are fortunate enough to wander whenever it pleases them.

Hired carriage drivers had always given him curious looks the times he requested it: *who wants to see the ocean at night?*

Vauquelin does — always, any chance he can get.

To vampire eyes, which see with vivid clarity things which humans will never grasp, the ocean is a philosophical reflection of their own existence.

Steadfast.

Unending.

Unconquerable.

The moon casts its soothing beams, rippled by the waves ... and there is nothing but infinity beyond.

He removes his shoes and tucks his socks into them, dropping them on the floor of his new car. He rolls his trouser legs up and trudges through the sand toward the beckoning waves, sinking to the ground.

If he were looking at the Atlantic, he would know that France awaited him across its vast depths, but on the other side of the Pacific are lands he has no hope of ever visiting: Hawaii, Japan, China ... his time is immeasurable but his capabilities are not.

Or are they?

It is feasible that Vauquelin underestimates himself.

He lights a cigarette and draws his knees up, supporting his arms upon them, digging his toes into the sand and taking immense satisfaction from its damp abrasiveness against his skin.

In this age, even in the summer months, no one comes to the beach at night. The water is frigid, and it is extremely dark.

He is well and truly alone.

As you are meant to be, perhaps? the voice mocks.

With all his infinite years to come — and all his back-and-forth through the centuries — there are still so many things he wishes dearly he could do and have.

People and things from his current timeline he can no longer touch.

People and things from his true past he cannot reach.

Another future he can neither envision nor define.

Someone he does not yet know.

But for now he is an unchained anchor, sinking rapidly beneath the depths of his own pathos.

The waves are so soothing, so seductive ...

Would that I could walk out into them and never return, he thinks.

But the sea cannot and will not accept him. He would be expelled from its aqueous mysteries and cast upon the shore.

Alive.

Forever.

He stubs the cigarette into the sand and rises, stretching his long limbs into the darkness. His eyes drift upward — he can see bountiful stars and the Milky Way is bright and prominent in the inky black sky.

In his futurepast Los Angeles, this experience would not have been possible.

This beach will one day be full of humans, loud humans, and the constellations will be erased by the noxious and profuse lights of the City of Angels ... a city that burns so bright, so full of fabricated stars that it douses the literal stars themselves.

Vauquelin knocks the sand from his feet and settles into the leather seats of the car.

Maeve is never far from his mind, and indeed, on this night she is especially present. He imagines her out wandering the same dark streets as he, and he remembers the nights far into his futurepast when he and Maeve would come to the beach and sit for hours. She did not like the water ... she loved the smell and the idea of the seashore, but she had no desire to explore its secrets. He wonders if she, as a vampire now, will come to love the ocean as he does.

The voltage on the car is still impressively high, and so he believes he can drive a bit more and still make it back to the Van Nuys.

He cruises along the dirt roads at a reasonable pace, enjoying the comfort of his own transportation and the fresh air drifting across his face.

Surprisingly, his bloodlust is quiet, though he is at the cusp of his need.

And then it happens.

Vauquelin sees her.

Walking on the street, chilled — desperately alone.

Her titian hair is illuminated like a beacon in the night by the haunting glow of a gas street lamp. Had she not passed under the light at that precise moment, he might not have noticed her.

His heart surges, and he draws the car up beside her.

"Maeve."

She slowly swivels her head toward him and eases her pace.

Vauquelin ejects himself from the car and runs to her, seizing her elbows in his hands, forcing her to look at him.

Her shoulders are hunched — cheeks gaunt, eyes crazed and smeared with black kohl. Her hair is a matted mess of filthy, tangled curls. Her lovely swan neck is blemished by a swath of crusted blood, and she cradles an armful of red roses.

Maeve's cheeks redden and her eyes grow aflame.

"YOU! How dare you approach me! You, the very devil himself!"

Maeve wrenches herself free from Vauquelin's grasp and flings the roses to the ground, clawing at his face and exposed skin, drawing deep, scarlet gashes down his face and neck and across his hands.

Vauquelin nearly loses his footing in his surprise.

Yet he stands and accepts the abuse she heaps upon him, because he believes he has earned it.

Were this a human (or an enemy vampire) attacking him, he would unleash a scorching counter-attack.

Quite the contrary: instead, he humbly lifts his bloodied hands in front of his heart. "Please do not do this," he whispers, and as he speaks, the injuries she inflicted upon him begin to knit themselves together, inspiring amazement from Maeve.

He draws up from his sea of memories an especially tender moment from their futurepast, and touches her cheek. The remembrance rests there like the wing of a butterfly.

She encircles her arms around her abdomen and backs away.

"Please ... I beg you ... keep away from me. You have done quite enough damage for one lifetime."

Vauquelin could never hate Maeve, because he still loves her ... but now he realises he loves only a fantasy. He loves the futurepast Maeve, the one who no longer exists ... whose very soul once embraced his own. The present Maeve who stands before him is a monster of his own creation, no longer the woman he had once known and loved so well, and her transfiguration is his fault.

He destroyed her by making her into something she was not meant to be — if one is a believer in fate.

Yet he never once saw Maeve's turning as an experiment.

He only desired to save her from her mortal death, and to live with her for eternity ... a return of the immense bliss he felt in her presence, of the —

Oh god.
Oh my god.

It dawns on him.

— of the brilliant humanity he had falsified for himself during his first life with her.

Yes, he loved Maeve.

He loved everything about human Maeve ... her independence, her joy, her enthusiasm.

He had effectively erased all of the qualities he loved in Maeve and dragged her behind the mortal world's curtains, extinguishing her exuberant light.

Even so, though he knows she despises him, he worries for her.

Much of his recent time has been consumed by fear that she has been harmed, or incarcerated, or worse: destroyed.

On this night that has turned particularly self-loathing, Vauquelin reminds himself that Maeve is behaving in the precise manner he had after his own turning.

He, too, had rejected his transformation and fled from his maker.

She is *just like him*: which was one of the qualities that drew them together in his futurepast.

They had once found completion in one another (alas, that was long ago, in another lifetime far from their present grasps).

And so he stands on the curb, looking at her with sorrow in his icy blue eyes, consoling himself that Maeve's strength — both as a human and as a being magnificently amplified by her vampire state — will allow her to forge her own path in the shadows, to prevail over the tragedy he had delivered her.

She will find her own way, precisely as he had.

Maeve has always lived by her own rules, and there is no reason to believe she will not continue to do so.

He stands still as a statue watching her walk away, and as she turns a corner, he waits for her to look back.

She never does.

Eighteen

A despondent Vauquelin makes a horseshoe turn and drives in the opposite direction of Maeve. The heaviness of his failures burdens his shoulders so that their weight, combined with his own, seems to slow the car down.

Or perhaps it is that he has nowhere to be (at least for a few hours — the night hours are still open to him), no one to care about him, no one to greet him when he arrives back at his temporary lodgings that are nothing like any sort of home.

As he drives, manipulating the ridiculous lever that serves as the car's steering mechanism, he considers that his entire life has been a profound failure. He has wasted centuries of existence to arrive at a point that has wholly unfulfilled him and destroyed another's existence.

The majority of Vauquelin's experiences have been powered by his own bravado, his own conceit that he can have whatever outcome he desires — if he is just patient enough.

Or kind enough, or forceful enough, or cruel enough.

Nothing has ever been enough.

On the night of his original creation, Yvain, his maker, had offered him refuge, a life among his kind.

A family, of sorts.

But Vauquelin had resoundingly rejected it, and continued to do so throughout his life from then to his futurepast to now, well into his second timeline.

What cost, liberty?

Approximately ninety percent (if not more) of Vauquelin's life has been spent alone.

He had convinced himself that was what he wanted.

And now he sees that he is so viscerally alone — so far removed from any semblance of kinship — that his heart stutters in his chest and snatches his breath away.

He pulls up against the edge of the road and jumps out, untying his neck stock as he leans against the cool steel of the car's body.

How long can this go on? he wonders.

Until you understand, the voice replies at once.

He tilts his chin to the sky, his chest heaving, and jerks his head down as he senses two men approaching.

Vauquelin immediately extracts his Opinel and plunges it into one of the tires facing the road's edge, flattening it to the ground.

He steps in front of the car and waves his hands.

"Gentlemen! I am stranded. Can you help?"

The men rush over, enticed more by the vehicle than by the thought of helping a fellow man.

They come close to Vauquelin, unafraid in the least.

After all, what do men have to fear from other men?

"What a beaut!" one of them exclaims.

"Yessir, a real beauty she is!" The second man runs his hands across the black steel, emitting a sharp whistle. "Sure would like to own one of these myself!"

As the men speak, Vauquelin catches the scent of their breath — they are both profoundly intoxicated, and at once his instincts manifest.

Oh, what a delightful turn of events!

Not just blood, but *alcohol-infused* blood.

Vauquelin can drink a barrel of wine and feel no effect … but consuming boozy human blood will intoxicate him.

Exactly what he needs.

In a flash, his hands are around both men's throats and he backs them up against a wooden fence, widening his frightening eyes.

"Silence," he hisses.

He throttles one of the men while he drains the other, and when his victim is empty, Vauquelin drops the body crumpling to the ground.

He turns panting to the living one, who flails in Vauquelin's grip like a trapped animal, desperate for an escape.

"Shhh …" Vauquelin whispers. "It will all be over soon."

The smell of liquor is practically seeping from the man's pores. Vauquelin draws his nose up his victim's neck before sinking his teeth into his jugular vein. He drinks in greedy gulps, eyes darting about, anxious that someone else might pass by. He cannot seem to break this reckless and impetuous stride he is on …

These qualities do not suit a vampire.

The man's heart dwindles to a stop, and Vauquelin withdraws.

His foot slips when he stands, tumbling him to his knees, and his hands are shredded by broken glass on the walkway.

For the second time, he has been injured tonight.

What an evening, and how extraordinary!

Something is changing.

He extracts the glass shards, shaking his hair out of his face, and as he licks the gore from his fingers he realises that, due to the liquor-infused blood he has consumed, he has ruined himself enough to render him unable to change the damaged tire.

In truth, he does not even know if there is a spare.

It brings to mind an occasion, hundreds of years ago — at the beginning of his current timeline — when he was faced with harnessing horses to a carriage, merely to survive the approaching dawn.

Alas, so much time has been squandered ... so many skills he could have learned.

At that moment, he desperately longs for his futurepast: he could whip out his mobile phone and look up a solution.

How does he keep getting into these ridiculous situations? Could it be that he is suffering the consequences for his corruption of history?

He stands on unsteady legs, stumbling to one knee and bracing himself against the car.

He is exceptionally drunk.

Putain ![†]

He struggles to open the trunk, and his face brightens.

There is a spare tire and a small box of tools.

But how to put it on?

An hour later, he has it figured out.

The Runabout has a new shoe, the men's throats have been artfully slit with the Opinel, and Vauquelin is on his way back to the Van Nuys (he hopes).

The sun is dangerously close to rising when he pulls into the hotel's receiving dock, scraping the side of the car along the wall as he enters. The parking lot is dark, and in his state of extreme intoxication, his sharp vampire vision has dwindled to the paltry levels of a human.

Then things go grey for a while.

He hugs the wall along his way down the service corridor, and believes he has arrived in the lobby. He careens across the floor and his hand lands on something cold and familiar.

It is a button — he *thinks*.

---

† - FUCK!

A ding rings into his consciousness.

"Monsieur! Monsieur!" The concierge runs breathlessly toward him with great animation, waving a letter in his hand, and catches up to Vauquelin just as he collapses his full weight against the elevator door, room key in hand.

"Monsieur, are you unwell?" the concierge asks. He places a hand on Vauquelin's elbow to steady him. "May I assist you to your room?"

Vauquelin turns his weary eyes upon the concierge, and for the first time he notices the name on the helpful man's name tag.

It reads:

CECIL

SAINT PETERSBURG, FLORIDA

"I see you, too, are far from home ... Cecil." Vauquelin says in a low voice. His accent, as so often happens when he is inebriated, is out in full force, and he pronounces the name *Suh-seellll.*

His voice reflects his exhaustion.

Cecil's face is kind ... he is eager to help his esteemed client.

Since the night Vauquelin checked in, he has treated this man with nothing but respect, and has tipped him generously for his unfailing assistance.

Cecil is one of many compassionate humans Vauquelin has encountered across his decades — and vampires treat such rare, helpful mortals with the utmost respect in return.

In his mortal state, Vauquelin was distinguished, respected amongst the nobility — beloved by his peers and servants alike: including his once-servant Olivier, now his brother in dark blood.

Vauquelin is equitable to a fault, a believer in treating everyone as they deserve to be treated.

Like all vampires, Vauquelin's human qualities were augmented in his vampire state.

He became even more aristocratic, cultivated, well-mannered, discerning. But he *is* vampire, and one must never forget that he is all those things AND a discriminate hunter of humans.

Vampires do not feast upon those who help them ... unless the situation becomes desperate. Desperation is a grave state for a vampire, and he hopes against hope that Maeve has already learned this crucial lesson.

Thank god he did not come home hungry, because on a night like this, all bets are off.

"Monsieur?"

Vauquelin's mind has wandered erratically, and he wonders how long he has been standing there with the concierge's arm upon his elbow.

Time for a vampire is volatile: five human minutes could be an hour for a revenant. Ninety days might as well be years.

He meets the patient concierge's eyes and says, "I would be most grateful for your assistance. But only you. No one else."

"It would be my pleasure, Monsieur."

The concierge opens the elevator cage and guides Vauquelin inside. On the journey to the fifth floor, Cecil says, "The letter is from France. I assumed you would want it straightaway, thus my enthusiasm."

A tastefully subtle bell indicates they have arrived, and Cecil meekly extracts the key from Vauquelin's hand, opening a door mere feet from the elevator. He waits until Vauquelin is safely seated on the bed before he hands him the letter.

"Good night, Monsieur."

Cecil does not wait for a tip. He places the key on the night stand and closes the door behind him, locking it from the outside with his own skeleton key.

After three attempts, Vauquelin succeeds in igniting the wall-mounted gas lamp by his bed and fumbles the letter to the floor. He slides down the side of the bed to read it.

For a moment he turns the envelope around and around between his fingers, grateful to know that it had been in Olivier's hands.

It is addressed in Olivier's clean penmanship: an exquisitely antiquated script that Vauquelin recognises at once as a legacy of his blood brother's seventeenth-century origins.

The cancelled French stamps send a longing for home quivering through his bones.

Most of all, he hopes the letter will deliver answers to his predicament.

> *Château du Cavernay*
> *Annecy, Haute-Savoie*
> *France*
>
> *1er Decembre 1900*
>
> *Ah, mon frère de sang,† here we sit across an ocean from each
> another at the end of one year and the first year of a new
> century — and I can do nothing but weep at hearing your
> purpose is unfulfilled.*
>
> *I must admit my heart has been restless since the day you left
> France. I could not explain it to myself — I assumed it must
> only be anxiety at being even further from you. Far from you in
> physical distance has proven to be most unsatisfactory for me.*
>
> *Perhaps I should have released my fears of travel and
> accompanied you ... at least you would not be alone now.*

---

† - MY BROTHER IN BLOOD

*I understand your reasons for wanting a new land, and even
more so your reasons for this last new journey — but perhaps
now is the time to return to your home. You may not need me,
not at first, but I shall travel with a glad heart to Paris to meet
you should you decide to return.*

*My own nights would be soothed by your presence, for though
many years may pass between our meetings, I am always happy
to embrace you. I must admit I am apprehensive knowing
I cannot easily reach you when we need one another.
Whatever your decision, know that my devotion to you knows
no end as always and I remain your*

Olivier

Vauquelin replaces Olivier's letter in its envelope with great care.

The letter has blanketed his heart in serenity, but his senses are still dulled by the great quantities of alcoholic blood moving slowly through his veins.

He nods off to sleep with his chin resting on his chest.

Vauquelin's eyes are level with the ground, his face clammy. He peels his cheek off the wooden floor and, as he heaves himself up, notices a petite blackened puddle where his mouth had been. The edges of Olivier's letter skirts it, sullied with dried blood.

He looks at his hands: there is no blood on his fingers. He must have bitten his cheek or tongue in his slumber and ... drooled.

Disgusting, he thinks. *I have lost myself.*

He cleans his bloody blight from the floor and retrieves the letter, re-reading it several times until he can accurately detect Olivier's true meaning between the lines.

Olivier is in some sort of distress of his own, though he would never admit it openly or detract from Vauquelin's confession.

That alone would be enough to make Vauquelin return to France at once, but Olivier's blatant promise of solidarity is what makes his decision an easy one.

He bathes and dresses in fresh clothing.

In the lobby, Vauquelin is dismayed to learn — from an unfamiliar concierge — that Cecil no longer works at the hotel. His last day was yesterday.

"Has he left a forwarding address, or can you tell me where he has gone? I would like to give him a gift, for being so kind to a foreigner such as myself."

If this were the Los Angeles of today, the new concierge would guard Cecil's privacy with vehemence and refuse to provide any information: but, in 1900, the new man simply says, "Why, certainly!" with mawkish cheer, and writes his predecessor's home address on a slip of paper.

"I am most grateful," Vauquelin says, sliding the note into his coat pocket. "And now, could you assist me with booking passage to France? My stay in America has come to an end."

LOS ANGELES, CALIFORNIA | DECEMBER 1900

Cecil Montgomery arrives at the Van Nuys Hotel and does not enter through the front door, but walks straight into the receiving dock at the back of the building. He approaches Vauquelin's black Runabout, which awaits patiently on its charger. He extracts a key and a brief letter from his pocket:

> *Dear Cecil,*
>
> *I am unexpectedly being recalled to France and thus no longer have a need for this vehicle. I regret that I could not thank you and bid you farewell in person, but as a token of my gratitude for your many kindnesses and the patience you have shown me, the vehicle is now yours. You will find its ownership transferred into your name on the paperwork in the glove box. Enjoy it in good health.*
>
> *Yours sincerely*
> *Louis-Augustin du Cavernay de Vauquelin*

Cecil is mystified by such a gift.

He flips the latch on the glove box, and, sure enough, his name and address are on the paperwork, sitting atop an instruction pamphlet.

He returns to the front desk and confirms that M. de Vauquelin had checked out several days ago, and returns to the car, shaking his head.

With regret he is unsure what to do with the car, as his own home has not yet been electrified.

Nineteen

PORT OF LE HAVRE, FRANCE | JANUARY 1901

Vauquelin's ship arrives at three o'clock on a frigid coastal morning.

By the time the cargo is unloaded and released from customs, it is well past nine o'clock and the sun has risen high in the sky.

In the nearby commune of Deauville, Vauquelin's Paris-based attorney, M. Gagnon (who has been in his service for more than twenty years but had declined to accompany his client to America) signs a paper verifying receipt of a large wooden crate and several trunks.

These items are loaded onto a black hearse, and Gagnon follows behind in a passenger carriage. In a modern automobile, this journey would take two hours. Via carriage in 1900, on primitive French backroads: just over eight. The cortège[†] arrives in Paris at dusk and clatters across damp, icy cobblestones and through iron gates into Vauquelin's courtyard, coming to a stop by a large fountain.

Olivier has risen early and dressed, and now he stands in the dim foyer with a pry bar, pacing the black and white marble-tiled floor. The closer Vauquelin's proximity, the more Olivier's blood pricks his veins, and when

---

†- PROCESSION

it begins to warm his body, he knows that his maker has arrived.

The crates and trunks are unloaded and the attorney is hurriedly dismissed with a girthy stack of franc notes.

Olivier attacks the large crate with the bar, prying apart the nailed wooden lid. Vauquelin slams the top of the coffin off, bursting forth and pulling him into a hearty embrace.

"France has never been so happy to have you on her shores, Vauquelin. You are home where you belong."

It has only been six months since Vauquelin left, a speck of stardust for a vampire, but so much had happened that standing within his own walls in Paris is quite surreal.

Travelling for a vampire is an enormously complicated venture.

The timing must be just so.

And though they may traverse great distances, they are not afforded the natural transition and sense of place that mortals take for granted. He cannot see where he is travelling, and must rely on his senses to know how much time has passed.

It is disorienting in the extreme.

When Vauquelin last went into slumber, he was in Los Angeles, California. When he awoke, he had made two train journeys, crossed an ocean, and been rattled across a small expanse of France — all while trapped inside a wooden box — and now he is … home?

He might as well be an astronaut who has just landed on earth.

He stumbles when Olivier releases him, eyes drinking in his wildly luxuriant surroundings.

Nothing in America can hold a candle to this.

His first thought is that he was a fool to ever want to leave it behind.

Olivier knows Vauquelin well enough to not speak to him, to let him reorient in his own way. Instead, he leads Vauquelin upstairs to his rooms, where an enchanted meal awaits, sprawled across a chaise longue.

Vauquelin falls to his knees and caresses the neck of Olivier's offering, drawing his nose across her cheek: a young woman, likely hired to work in the house just a few days ago, freshly bathed and perfumed. A satin ribbon is tied in a bow around her neck, transmuting her into the gift she is.

In silence, Olivier seats himself and lights a pipe, watching his maker drink. He tilts his head back and discharges a plume of smoke into the air. How delightful it is to have Vauquelin in his presence once more!

Vauquelin devours her blood while she watches him with dreamy spellbound eyes, large and blue. And when her weakened arm falls toward the floor like a rag doll, he lifts her wrist to his lips as if it is a sugared pastry — and withdraws all the crimson cream she has to give.

A quiet rattle emerges from her lips, and her head lolls to the side.

Vauquelin looks away as he urges her eyelids closed.

He *despises* seeing the eyes of the dead.

Olivier opens a bottle of wine and pours a glass for Vauquelin, patting a package of tobacco on the table next to a copper tub, and closes the door behind him.

A fire roars in the fireplace.

The candelabras cast flickering shadows across the walls.

The room is warm and welcoming, familiar, equipped with all Vauquelin craves at this very moment.

He drops his clothes and submerges himself under the steaming water, coming up with a gasp and wildly scratching his head, tousling his hair into a wavy mess of black fronds that cling to his face.

One room over, Olivier plinks out a tune on a three hundred-year-old harpsichord.

The swells of a sea change begin to rise in Vauquelin's subconscious, and though he cannot yet fully define it, he acknowledges one heavy fact.

He may choose to be alone when he needs it, but he cannot exist without kinship — and it cannot be manufactured.

Nor can it be bought.

The man in the next room, whose very presence offers the most security Vauquelin has felt in half a year, is proof.

He hurries his bathing ritual, simply getting clean rather than indulging himself. There is plenty of time for longer, more therapeutic baths.

He slips into the banyan that Olivier has hung on a hook for him and carries the bottle of wine through the door to his sitting room.

Olivier smiles at him, and continues playing.

Vauquelin pours Olivier a glass and stretches out on a chaise, swigging straight from the bottle as the music of their human birth era washes over him. Neither of them have ever lost their love for it.

After the piece is finished, Olivier begins another. For some reason, Vauquelin's reappearance in France has made him shy and reserved.

This new timidity is unfounded, in his mind.

In their human lives, they were born only a few years apart, but their stations — as master and servant — kept them at a great distance emotionally-speaking.

In Vauquelin's social strata, they were not destined to be companions: that was unequivocally forbidden.

Despite this and unending harsh reprimands from his geriatric guardian, Vauquelin made valiant efforts to forge a secret bond with Olivier, who grew to be his dearest friend. In the company of others, all interactions between them were chilly and formal. They saved their genuine camaraderie for when they were alone, which they often were as Olivier rose through the ranks to become his premier valet du chambre[†] and later, head of household.

Olivier knew the depths of the human Vauquelin's soul, knew him

---

†- A prestigious, powerful and lucrative position: duties included looking after a master's clothing and other personal needs as well as being a buffer between the master, the public, and other servants

better than anyone else walking the world had ever been given the chance.

But, in his original timeline, Vauquelin broke the sacred trust they had established: after his turning, he concealed all evidence of his vampirism from Olivier, determined to hide it from his only confidant.

Wise as he was, though, Olivier suspected that Vauquelin was carrying a burdensome shame upon his shoulders.

He never dared inquire.

Prior to this enormous shift in his master's personality, Olivier had always been happy to listen, but he never asked any questions of Vauquelin.

He respected and appreciated their clandestine friendship, but he was a fifth-generation servant of the nobility, and some lines were never crossed.

So Olivier went on doing his duties and making Vauquelin as comfortable as possible, never revealing the slightest hint of his anguish over his master's burgeoning irregularities.

In Vauquelin's first timeline, he ensured his oldest friend never learned the truth about him, that he was vampire. Olivier was the first recipient of Vauquelin's lies, and the last recipient of his full truth.

And then, nearly two decades into his original life of revenancy, Vauquelin was faced with the first great loss of his new era: Olivier was carried away by smallpox, and his death plunged Vauquelin even further into his deepening expanse of misery.

His violence increased threefold.

He lost all his cares, and swiftly constructed his walls of solitude, refusing to make another connection: be it human or vampire. He convinced himself that he did not deserve to exist, that Olivier's death was his fault.

Vauquelin's deception was the cause.

It took more than two centuries for his heart to open even a minuscule fissure, and that was when Maeve slipped in.

Alas, he was by then too practised in deception to relinquish it.

He had become his lies, and they had become him: they were woven into his very psyche.

He let her die rather than telling her the truth.

Now, Vauquelin — listening to Olivier at the harpsichord, very much undead — supposes that he does in fact owe Yvain some gratitude.

Though his maker cruelly ravaged his timeline and threw his existence into chaos, returning him to his human state, Vauquelin can now understand what a gift it was to choose the dark blood a second time... for then he was afforded the chance to turn his dear Olivier and saved him from an early death. Which is precisely what he wanted for Maeve.

The music turns sombre, almost as if on cue, and Vauquelin loses himself a moment in a reverie of Clément ... sadly the one gift Vauquelin could not keep. The memory of the one exquisite night they had together had sustained him on many lonesome occasions, but at that time in his life he could not permit Clément to distract him from his goal: returning to Maeve.

Vauquelin often indulged himself with butterfly thoughts of Clément's verdant eyes, but quickly released them back into the wild. His encounter with Clément was a glitch — it had not happened in his previous timeline, and he feared that it would set him off his determined path. He had no choice but to sever ties with him, though he now knows, in spite of his careful steps, his cautious re-treading of his history was for naught. He had failed spectacularly in his attempt to recreate his previous life.

You were not as careful as you thought

He ignores the voice and tilts his head back to extract the last few drops of the bottle, and with his head in this position, he envisions Clément's lips upon his throat. His eyes close in velvet-clad ecstasy.

Yvain's nasty, condescending laughter echoes in his subconscious.

He leaps up and hurls the bottle into the fireplace, resulting in a violent explosion of glass shards and startling poor Olivier, who stops playing mid-note.

In truth, Olivier is accustomed to such outbursts from Vauquelin, though he tends to fall out of practice during their separations.

Vauquelin cannot catch his breath.

Fuck Yvain, and fuck these repetitions.

"What troubles you?" Olivier asks. "Fear not about the girl. She has already been committed to the catacombs. What is it you need?"

"I need ... I need ..."

Olivier closes the fall board and sighs.

"Let us go and get you dressed."

Vauquelin's bedchamber is in glorious disarray — suits, shirts, and neck-stocks litter the floor. He knocks over a candelabra with a shoe, flinging wax across a four-hundred-year-old table and splattering the hand-cast mouldings on the wall behind.

He is having far too good a time rifling through the many clothes in his armoire, especially after witnessing the obliteration of his possessions in Los Angeles.

But in the room is a glaring absence: his original portrait, now lost to the ages. The spot it had occupied is empty.

He bites his lip.

That portrait was the only way he knew how he looked before he became vampire. It can never be replaced.

But now is not the time to mourn.

Tomorrow night he will move his second portrait into its place.

Olivier is waiting for him downstairs, and they are going out.

When he hits the landing, Olivier nods approvingly. "You look quite ravishing for a man who spent the last month as a corpse."

Vauquelin laughs, clapping him on the back, and the readied carriage takes them out into the city.

They arrive at a tavern and wordlessly separate before entering: Olivier first, and Vauquelin a few minutes behind him.

It has always been their way of hunting together.

The populace is getting smarter, and *Dracula* has caused a sensation on the continent. The cover of night — and gas lights — are their protection, rendering humans unable to discern how perfectly ghastly they would both appear in broad daylight.

Still, they take no chances, and on their own there is a lesser chance of suspicion versus two very odd gentlemen appearing together.

Vauquelin's aims this evening are clear-cut: a kill, followed by a fuck.

He needs both so badly.

The blood of one human is not enough after a long slumber.

He sits at a table and orders a wine from the waiter as he scans the room like a seasoned detective.

Disappointment spreads across his countenance.

The room is populated by couples.

He downs the wine and searches for Olivier, meaning to tell him it is time to move on, but finds him in a corner booth with his mouth on the neck — and his hand very far up the skirt — of an euphoric brunette.

Vauquelin suppresses a smile just as Olivier comes up for air and waves him on.

He begins walking at a slow pace.

How good it is to be back in Paris!

A few miles away the mighty Notre Dame tolls her bells for two o'clock, and the sound fills his heart with ... joy? Confusion? Pride?

Perhaps this disastrous recent turn of events was a lesson he desperately needed to learn: he has a purpose, and he must not stray too far from what he is meant to do.

But what is that, precisely?

You were given orders

« Chuuuut , »[†] Vauquelin hisses.

He is not in the mood for his chastising chorus voice.

He is home!

He is in Paris!

He walks and walks, inhaling the nauseating aromas, sidestepping beggars (yet tossing them his loose coins), revelling in the slightly fishy, earthy fragrance of the Seine, and glancing up at every ornate street lamp and exquisitely constructed building.

He absorbs it all.

The horses' hooves on the cobblestones are music to his ears.

There are no dust clouds here in the City of Light, no muddy roads to navigate. No harsh American accents upon his ears.

And then he stops, high in the Pigalle, in front of the *Cabaret de L'enfer* — The Cabaret of Hell.

Could there ever be a more appropriate nightclub for a vampire?

Certainly not!

Oh, he thinks, *how the goth children of the modern age would love this place!*

He drops a note in the till at the entrance and walks through the mouth of the Devil himself, disappearing into the nightclub's alluring darkness and debauchery.

As he takes in his diabolic surroundings, he considers that he had lost his senses in surrendering turn-of-the-century Paris — twice.

The darksome room is full of late-night revellers. Champagne is flowing, dissonant laughter hurts his ears, and there are couples fornicating onstage, accompanied by a live tango orchestra.

This is Vauquelin's ideal playground, but he has one shot.

[†]- SHH

It is fabricated hedonism: his own brand is genuine.

He walks to the back of the club and tests a door: it opens to an alley. He looks left and then right. It is suitably abandoned for the night, and thus will be his escape route.

The future lies open to Vauquelin, unrestricted, and this is a watershed excursion for him. Tonight he need not measure his steps, nor his missteps.

He merges into the crowd and makes eye contact with multiple people, rejecting his usual subtlety. There is no need for enchantment, for they will not remember him ... this club is a madhouse, full of misfits: everyone is off their heads on absinthe, consumed by the fever of pheromones.

One could become intoxicated and aroused simultaneously from the air alone.

A debonair man pushes his way through the dancing crowd and stops in front of him, cockily tilting his chin up to meet Vauquelin's gaze.

The man smiles and winks, and Vauquelin smiles in return, extending a hand. He leads the man down a corridor and out the back door into the pitch-black alleyway.

"Well?" Vauquelin asks.

The man sinks to his knees, grabbing hold of Vauquelin's trouser button.

"No, no," Vauquelin says, lifting the man up. He brushes a kiss across the man's lips. "That would be wasted effort, I'm afraid. Follow me."

They walk in silence down the alley, occasionally sizing one another up, and emerge into the street.

The Pigalle is a raunchy quarter in turn-of-the-century Paris, and it is quite easy for Vauquelin to locate a hotel that does not question two men checking in.

In the room, which is so filthy Vauquelin does not dare consider using the bed, he bolts the door and pins the man against it, subduing him with his full weight, smothering him with frenzied kisses.

His companion wraps a leg around Vauquelin's waist, grinding their hardening groins together.

Vauquelin moves his mouth to the man's neck, licking, nuzzling his ear, rather tenderly now … until he drives his teeth in, one hand pressed over his victim's mouth to mute his surprised cries.

Vauquelin withdraws after a liberal swallow and unbuttons his trousers — the man mimics him, gasping, "I see you like it rough."

"Turn around," Vauquelin orders, his voice husky with blood, pausing only to stroke the marks he made upon the man's throat, besmirching his fingers with blood and promptly sinking them into his own trousers.

He thrusts brutally into the man, who whimpers in douleur exquise.[†]

He draws his fingertips across the man's lips, and when they part in obeisance Vauquelin slips his fingers inside, tilting his victim's head back as he latches onto his throat and resumes his urgent drinking and thrusting.

The last of the blood trickles down Vauquelin's throat.

He dislodges his teeth, panting heavily as he drops the empty body to the floor.

Vauquelin extracts his Opinel and etches a clean, neat slice over his bite marks. He tidies himself as best he can in this hovel, and climbs out the window.

Ah … how magical it is to be home!

The house is silent when he returns; Olivier has no doubt retired to his own rooms.

He bathes and sits on his stone balcony with only a linen wrapped around his waist, impervious to the chilled air. His breath hangs frost-ridden with each exhale, and thus he sits until the sky begins to turn a blush pink around the edges, threatening to illuminate the slanted slate rooftops of the city.

Even Paris cannot soothe his vacant heart.

---

†- EXQUISITE PAIN, BEAUTIFUL PAIN

Twenty

ÉVREUX, FRANCE | SEPTEMBER 1914

Vauquelin's years are flying by, as they so easily do when one is a revenant. And yet again, he is squandering them.

He has never experienced the twentieth century in Paris, yet he does not belong here — not in this time.

He is unprepared for the resulting desolation of the city. Within weeks of Germany's declaration of war in August, Paris descends into utter chaos. Cattle roam the streets, brought in for emergency sustenance (and Vauquelin himself partakes of several). Businesses are shuttered. Influenza is running rampant. Bombs shake the firmament ... windows are shattered and steeples tumbled.

There are few humans wandering about.

His letters to Olivier in Annecy go unanswered, nor do any arrive for him — lost in transit. The call of Olivier's blood still tingles within his own: his favoured progeny is surviving and well, which alleviates some of Vauquelin's distress.

Moving a continent and an ocean away from Maeve remains his best action of late. Still he can sense her existence, her reality. She, too, is surviving, but not once has her blood beckoned to him ...

Nevertheless, staying in Paris has become unwise.

Of course he had known the Great War was coming — but in his futurepast, he had only seen it via photographs in the newspapers. And during World War II, he had watched newsreels in the Los Angeles cinemas of his futurepast, had seen the gruesome upheaval and distress in his home city.

Now he is witnessing ground warfare with his own eyes, and the reality far exceeds the news reports of the time.

His Paris house was safe from all war — it had never been damaged in his previous timeline, and therefore he does not fear being trapped under rubble in his own home. Nevertheless his sustenance is growing scarce, and so, at the end of August, he evacuates to his château at Évreux.

Vauquelin wanders his provincial gardens, mercifully removed from any military action (though the night skies still illuminate from the relentless bombings, even at this great distance).

The gardens — once lush — are now picked quite bare by the rabbits he brought in to run free across his land, and he reaches down for the one that has the misfortune to sit at his feet, snatching it up and devouring it.

He feasts upon two more on his trek home, carrying the carcasses by the ears, and drops them in a fire pit behind the château.

As it was when he had first had to rely upon the blood of animals, his skin has gone chalky and he moves slowly. Dark circles have emerged below his eyes.

What he wouldn't give for a full measure of human blood!

In his first timeline, in Los Angeles, Vauquelin was poisoned by drug-addled human blood. He swore off the hunt and sustained himself on lapin blood for nearly two decades, until his time began to unwind.

In that era, though, there had been enough time for his body to adapt, and he resumed his original vampiric strength after a year or so. However, minuscule green capillaries rose to the surface of his skin and obliged him to conceal his face and hands with makeup when he went out among humans, as he had done the night of his futurepast museum exhibit.

Without it, he would have looked impossibly macabre.

When he returned to human blood the veinery retracted, returning his skin to its marble-smooth former state.

The rabbits are a sign of utter desperation and once again, he is a shade of his ideal self.

Isolation is ideal: he wants no one to see him, and he hasn't the strength to even protect himself.

He wonders how Yvain — and Clément — are weathering the war.

No doubt Yvain has a legion of human blood slaves in his dungeons, bleeding them just to the point of death, and nursing them back to relative health so he can bleed them again.

Not for the first time, Vauquelin questions whether his liberty is worth it. Right at this moment, he could be deep in the underground bowels of Yvain's château, well-fed, instead of alone and snacking on rabbits, moving like a decrepit nonagenarian human instead of a perpetually thirty-year old one — prying his rusty joints apart merely to stand.

Merely to exist.

All he has to do to shake himself from this fantasy is picture himself in Yvain's den of sin, surrounded by sycophantic, hyper-sexual vampires, with Yvain snapping his fingers and ordering him around.

Absolutely not!

But Clément ... is he still there, with Yvain?

Or has he managed to liberate himself and find his own way?

Vauquelin settles into an overstuffed chair in front of a roaring fire, thrusting his hands out to warm them.

He has no blood ties to Clément: those ties only exist between maker and progeny, and to those revenants who choose to exchange blood on a regular basis. Neither of them had made the slightest attempt to contact one another after they parted in 1668, at the dawning of Vauquelin's second timeline.

His encounter with Clément has never left his mind, as nothing significant ever does.

Many mornings when Vauquelin succumbs to rest, it is not without a small amount of shame he recalls the thoughts of Clément — which never vacated his consciousness even after he reunited with Maeve.

But why is he haunting Vauquelin's mind so often now, after centuries?

For vampires, exceptional moments have no expiration date.

One serendipitous night in 1668 might as well have happened a month ago, and in Vauquelin's unique case, as he sits in a seventeenth-century château in 1915, so could 2020 have been yesterday.

The memories are just as crisp, no matter the centuries between then and now.

In wrestling over and over with what went wrong with Maeve, Vauquelin must admit that only two consequential events were changed in his re-traversal of his past.

One: he turned Olivier, which was a given.

There is no reason to believe Olivier's turning would affect any of Vauquelin's future interactions with Maeve.

Two: he allowed, quite by accident, someone else to divert his attention.

And so now he questions everything.

He had tempted his fate, and now he must deal with the repercussions.

He trudges up the stone staircase to bed and can only think he has cursed himself to be alone.

For who would have him now?

PARIS, FRANCE | NOVEMBER 1918

Three days after Armistice Day, Vauquelin arrives in Paris at midnight. The streets are jammed with celebrating citizens, and Vauquelin commemorates the end of the war in his own way: by feasting upon three humans in the wine cellar of his house. He lies surrounded by their corpses and many, many wine bottles, with two-hundred-year-old, Burgundy-infused human blood coursing through his veins.

His skin reclaims its marble hue, shedding the matte greyness of its wartime death pallor. His bones unfold with ease, his hair recaptures its rightful sheen of the ocean on a starless night.

He kisses the still lips of all his victims, thanking them for restoring his life.

The feathers of Death's black wings brush his cheeks, and by the time he reaches for her she has vanished.

And he will never drink a rabbit again.

Twenty-one

In normal circumstances Vauquelin loves nothing more than a shake-up; a diversion of any sort, anything to tamp down the doldrums of an eternal existence. But ground combat was most unwelcome. Though the war years were tumultuous for Vauquelin, and an altogether new experience, the jazz age in Paris is his reward.

In his original 1920s, Vauquelin was in Los Angeles: grieving Maeve's death from the Spanish flu and embarking on the newborn era of Hollywood glamour. Paris in the twenties was unknown to him. He had missed one of the best eras of Paris, twice — because he ran away.

He is always running to or from something!

Vauquelin becomes a patron of the Grand Guignol, the legendary *théâtre macabre*[†] of Paris. He spends the entirety of the first performance he attends draining the man seated next to him, under cover of the darkness. He slips out the side door, and when the lights come up the audience believes the corpse is just a prop from the show.

Merveilleux ![‡]

[†]- A THEATRE FEATURING PERFORMANCES WITH A GRIM OR GHASTLY ATMOSPHERE
[‡]- MARVELLOUS

But despite the abundant delights of Paris, he misses Los Angeles in a primeval way.

Not the old Los Angeles he had left thirty years ago ... that one is dead to him. There is nothing for him but to wait interminably for his futurepast Los Angeles he had once loved, long ago in another timeline.

Why does this city still beckon to him, after the destruction he had wrought upon Maeve?

There is an unknown magnetism from *modern* Los Angeles, and it refuses to release him.

All he had in futurepast Los Angeles was loneliness, though it had been easier for him to assimilate. He does miss that ... the ability to be around humans. Separate yet together.

Still, thoughts of Clément torture his mind, and Vauquelin cannot fathom the reason.

He has no desire to reignite a fling, for that is all it was.

Something else is afoot.

Indeed, he is tortured by an uninvited phantom.

Vauquelin entertains the idea of writing Clément a letter, and quickly dismisses the idea.

He considers making a surprise appearance at Yvain's château, a few hours outside Paris, and then he begins to seriously question his sanity. He never wants to gaze upon his maker again, as long as he lives: even if that is the *sole* way to reach Clément.

No!

Clément is unavailable to him.

He must accept it, and comfort himself only with memories.

But tonight Vauquelin is on a boat to London, accompanied by his latest human attorney, Renaud.

He is travelling there to withdraw his remaining deposits from a bank. They had been left there in his original 1682 to salvage them from XIV's wrath, and had been lost in the Great Crash. In his current calendar, he is determined to retrieve it just ahead.

They check into a hotel near the bank and part ways; Renaud will extract the deposits in the morning while his client sleeps.

For a bit of entertainment, Vauquelin takes to the streets. His thirst is satisfied, and he has no intention of hunting on this trip: he merely wants to see the city with fresh eyes. In his first timeline, he lived in London for a decade in the early eighteenth century, avoiding Louis XIV's scrutiny of the nobility.

He learned early on how different from Paris is London.

The English vampires did not take kindly to the spawn of Yvain encroaching on their territory. Rumours of his arrival (and his notorious reputation) spread quickly ... vampire eyes watched his every movement. He relied upon his legendary reclusivity — and weekly journeys outside the city boundaries — to take his blood sustenance.

In 1715, on the very night Vauquelin received confirmation of XIV's death, he high-tailed it back to France.

But that was ancient history.

Surely he has nothing to fear now.

All he needs is to complete this one task, and he will be on his way.

He stops at a news-stand and peruses the papers.

Not a single inkling of what is to come in a matter of days.

Guilt deluges him: he could tell multiple people passing him on the dark streets to go to their banks in the morning and take what they can before it is too late — but no one would believe him.

He buys *The London Times* with a twenty-pound note and tells the seller, "Put this straight into your pocket."

The seller eyes him up and down and with a "Pssh!" instead puts it straight into his till.

Oh well, Vauquelin thinks. *I tried.*

He resumes his promenade, eyes on the newspaper, when someone roughly jars his shoulder.

He halts his pace and turns slowly, and just like that he is gazing straight into the eyes of another vampire.

You are not welcome here, the vampire speaks in silence.

You do not know me, Vauquelin replies.

I know who you are, Monsieur de Vauquelin. Believe me when I say you do not belong here. There is unrest amongst those who wield the power in this city. You would be wise to stay off the streets.

Vauquelin narrows his eyes.

How does this man know his name?

Return to France. This is not your place. Heed my words.

Vauquelin brings his fingers to his throat.

He would have assumed this vampire meant him harm: instead, he is being given a warning for his own safety.

Who are you? Vauquelin asks.

The vampire merely inclines his head, draws a finger along the peak of his hat and vanishes into the crowd, leaving Vauquelin speechless.

But these are tumultuous times for many reasons, and Vauquelin knows better than to dawdle. He returns to the hotel straightaway and informs Renaud that they are leaving at sundown the next evening.

Twenty-Two

PARIS, FRANCE | 1935

Vauquelin, his car idling behind him, pushes open the heavy gates of his house, prepared to go on his weekly hunt, but he stops with a foot in mid-air: the smell of the city has changed.

There is something ... *senescent* about it.

A fragrance from centuries ago: old lace, the milky smell of marble, a hint of unwashed flesh feverish from coupling.

The scent of someone from his past.

His heart tingles in his chest, causing his breath to stutter, and he drops his hands from the iron gates, looking up.

Standing directly across the street is a youthful man with thick dark hair cascading across his shoulders. He leans against a stone wall, one heel against it, knee in the air. He twirls a pocket watch by its chain, a sarcastic gaze locked on Vauquelin.

The man is dressed in the current fashion but with much more flair: in fact, his mode is markedly feminine in nature: a black jacket severely nipped with a wasp waist, wide-legged pants — a scarlet ascot tied around his neck, an absurdly large red dahlia tucked in his buttonhole.

Clément.

Without the slightest hesitation Vauquelin begins to sprint across the street, and a mad honking pierces the air as he narrowly misses being clipped by a Peugeot.

He clamps his hand onto his elbow and gestures with his fist at the driver, who immediately pulls the car over and gets out, stomping in his direction.

Vauquelin halts and turns his eyes back to where Clément had been standing but he has vanished into thin air.

It is at that moment, as the driver strides toward him, that Vauquelin realises the car that almost hit him is an early 2000s model.

His head snaps around, and the 1934 Bugatti that had been idling behind him a moment ago is missing.

Modern-day Paris erupts into activity around him.

Unsightly traffic signs rise from the pavement, blighting the space below the antiquated, ornate lamps on every corner.

His once-quiet street is now jammed with cars and Vespas, their horns piercing the atmosphere, and the smell of diesel replaces the phantasmagoric, sensient perfume left behind by Clément.

« PUTAIN D'ENFERRRRR ! »[†] Vauquelin screams, dragging his nails down his face and drawing up vicious bloody stripes upon his cheeks.

The driver stops in front of him, fists up, and Vauquelin clasps the man's throat, lifting him off the ground.

"Listen, connard,[‡] this is the wrong night to come for me," he growls through gritted teeth, fully exposing their points: something he *never* does.

But this is a desperate moment, and, as we speak, Vauquelin is rapidly losing his sense of place in the world.

He releases the driver and in a tearful voice, says, "Walk away. This never happened. Be grateful."

[†]- FUCKING HELL!
[‡]- ASSHOLE

His heart thrums in his chest — his blood sustenance is dwindling at an alarming pace.

He rattles his head to and fro, as if to assure himself he is not dreaming, and notices graffiti marring the ancient stone surrounding the iron gates. An internet influencer is standing in Clément's place, posing this way and that, making kissy faces while holding a clichéd basket of roses and baguettes as someone snaps her picture over and over again.

And to think he had accepted time moving forward naturally again!

You fool, his chorus mocks. *He was so close! You almost had him!*

He pummels the gates, which are now secured behind him, rattling them with all his thundering might, until the electronic lock begins to beep, amplifying into an alarm.

A police officer blows a whistle and runs toward him in a mad dash, yelling « HÉ ! Arrête ! Que fais-tu ? Arrête ! »[†]

This is madness!

"I live here! This is my home!" Vauquelin screams, a vein erupting across his forehead.

"Your home, hein?[‡] Is it now? Input your security code, then. Go on, I'm waiting." The officer taps his nightstick against the lighted keypad, its buttons glowing ominously in the dark.

"I've ... forgotten it," Vauquelin whispers, leaning his head against the cold iron of the gates.

He reaches in his pocket and fingers his Opinel.

But he is in enough trouble at the moment, and the last thing he needs is a dead official in front of his house — if it even *is* his house.

Now, who knows?

Bordel de merde.[§]

[†]- HEY! STOP! WHAT ARE YOU DOING? STOP!
[‡]- EH?
[§]- FOR FUCK'S SAKE

He side-eyes the policeman and ambles down the street, glancing back over his shoulder periodically.

The knife is the only thing he has on him besides his wallet and his passport.

Everything else is (was) in the house.

Vauquelin has gotten lazy. Enough years had passed since his last time-slip — almost three hundred, to be exact — that he is no longer familiar with the horror of finding oneself out of one's own time.

As he passes a news-stand the topmost copy of *Le Monde* catches his eye. *Vendredi, 9 Novembre 20__ .*[†]

His mind switches into survival mode.

He extracts his pocket watch: exactly half-past six.

« Qu'elle heure est-il ? »[‡] he asks the vendor.

"20:15, monsieur."

Time, time … so fickle.

So cruel.

Vauquelin carefully resets the watch and winds it, then opens his wallet: he has about a dozen fifty-franc notes, but all currency is in euros now. These notes are worthless, except maybe to a collector.

He has no credit cards.

No attorney.

He cannot even hire a taxi.

The banks are all closed.

« Je vous remercie . »[§]

[†]- FRIDAY, 9 NOVEMBER 20__
[‡]- WHAT TIME IS IT?
[§]- I THANK YOU

He walks for several blocks, head hung but eyes alert.

For once, among his many time-slips, he does not look *too* out of place: vintage clothes are all the rage.

His first thought is the train station: they have currency exchanges!

He walks twelve long blocks to the Gare du Lyon, which he had to locate on a city kiosk map. It is the closest station.

The teller at the currency exchange laughs wickedly at him when he produces the notes.

"These have not been legal tender since 2012!" She gestures at her co-worker, who comes over to join in the laughter.

Vauquelin's face grows even whiter and he snatches the bills up into his fingers.

« Quel bizarre ! »[†]

They laugh as he walks away.

The station is bustling at this hour, full of tourists and commuters, and he finds himself standing in front of Le Train Bleu, one of the most spectacular restaurants in Paris.

How he would love to go inside and have some wine, and, perhaps, obtain some human advice! But anything he could say now will come off as a con.

He has only one option, that he can see.

He will have to rob someone.

FUCK.

Vauquelin sits on a bench for a good hour, long legs crossed in his perpetually feminine way, watching people pass, and his eyes at last land on an older married couple — American, or possibly Canadian — but regardless, suitably starry-eyed at being in Paris.

He follows them out of the station, until they stop at the rideshare platform.

---

†- WHAT A WEIRDO!

He steps in front of them.

"Bonjour,[†] and welcome to Paris," he says, brightly, his accent deep and utterly endearing. "Is this your first visit?"

"Yes, yes it is!" the wife exclaims. "It's our twentieth wedding anniversary," she adds.

"Ah, what better place to celebrate than the City of Love, the City of Light," Vauquelin says, bowing. "And where are you staying?"

The couple beams at him, and both disclose the name of a chain hotel.

They are so giddy and happy that he almost hates what he is about to do.

He smiles and extends his arms, ensuring their eyes are both locked on his. "You will follow me, oui?[‡] And you will never remember me."

He moves between them, taking their elbows firmly into his hands, and leads them around a corner.

The side street, mercifully, is empty.

He extracts the Opinel and flips it open.

"All my apologies, monsieur et madame.[§] I am desperate. I will not harm you, but I will take your money. Now. Give me everything you have."

The man hands over a wallet with a trembling hand and Vauquelin rifles through. He scans the man's identification, memorising his name, and pockets the majority of the paper bills (Euros, *thank god*), leaving the credit cards in their proper place.

"You will never know my gratitude," Vauquelin says, returning the wallet, and vanishes down the alley.

Three blocks over, he flags down a taxi and quickly counts his spoils in the back seat. €500 in bills and ten €100 traveller's cheques.

That is more than enough for now.

"Car rental? Fast!"

---

† - HELLO
‡ - YES
§ - SIR AND MADAM

The taxi stops at a Europcar, which ironically is just across the street from the Gare du Lyon.

"No! This is no good, keep driving to the next one!"

Then, as the taxi zips back into traffic, Vauquelin's face falls.

He cannot rent a car.

He has no valid driver licence, only his passport: and the last stamp on it is from 1929. He weaves his fingers together, twitching them between his knees in defeat.

"Please take me to a hotel instead ... any hotel will do."

Safely in a spartan room, Vauquelin drags the phone into the bathroom and shuts the door tightly. He could not satisfactorily seal out the sun.

He sits staring at the phone and checking his pocket watch, waiting for the hour to turn to 09:00.

This is his last hope.

If the bank will not cooperate with him, he is fucked.

Royally fucked.

At 08:55, he begins slamming his fist over and over again into the tile of the tub surround, knocking bloody shards of ceramic all over his body and the bathroom floor.

At 09:00 on the nose, he dials.

An automated voice answers.

"Welcome to Banque Courtois. For current balance and account information, press 1. For loans, press 2 ..."

Vauquelin is not in the mood for this nonsense.

He furiously jams all the buttons on the phone at random until he hears a ring, and a human voice answers.

« Banque Courtois . »

"I need to speak to a banker at once."

"Which department do you need, monsieur?"

The level of profanity and anger that erupts from Vauquelin's end of the line warrants an immediate transfer.

« Un moment . »[†]

Bip. Biiiip Biip Biip. Biiip.

"Gilles Beaufort."

"Louis de Vauquelin. Account number [redacted]."

Clicks from a keyboard.

A sharp intake of breath.

Silence.

"Monsieur de Vauquelin … how may I be of assistance?"

"I have been robbed. I have nothing. I need a debit card and some cash immediately. There is only one problem … I need it brought to me. I can show you appropriate identification, but I will not come to the bank. You must come to me. Tonight, after sundown. 18:00."

If this were any normal client, the banker would laugh.

But on M. Beaufort's computer screen, several stunningly large bottom lines glare at him in bold black.

He blinks at the sums in disbelief.

This is uncommon in the extreme.

"Monsieur de Vauquelin, I am afraid you must appear in person for identification purposes. We are open until 17:00."

"Unacceptable. Can you do it personally? I will make it worth your while."

Vampires are charming as *hell*.

With just a glance, they can enchant a mortal in a matter of seconds.

Many humans have met vampires and yet they will never know it … because they have been made to forget.

Vampires (and especially Vauquelin) have no desire to be discovered.

Modern technology has many limitations for vampires.

It is out of their wheelhouse, for the most part.

---

†- ONE MOMENT

A vampire could never enchant a human over a Zoom.

Nor could they do it over the phone.

They need a human's *eyes*.

BUT ... the one thing that has always superseded such modern obstacles is greed. Greed and money will win any human over.

"Is this call being recorded?" Vauquelin asks.

"Absolutely not, Monsieur!" Gilles barks. He clears his throat. "This is a secure financial call with privy information. It is the expressed policy of Banque Courtois never to expose client information."

"Then I have orders for you. I will see you at sundown, in the lobby of Le Meurice. Yes?"

Le Meurice is one of the most expensive hotels in Paris.

Vauquelin cannot ask the banker to deliver the sum he has requested at the tourist trap he is staying in.

He hangs up the phone and sleeps on the floor of the demolished bathroom.

It is not, frankly, the worst situation he has ever been in.

Twenty-Three

PARIS, FRANCE | LAST YEAR

Vauquelin has freshened himself and is waiting in the lobby of Le Meurice at approximately 18:00. He is still wearing his suit from 1935: the only clothing currently in his possession.

He rolls a cigarette and lifts it to his lips, thumb poised on the lighter, when a hotel employee swoops up and wags a finger at him, pointing at the PAS DE FUMER[†] sign just above Vauquelin's head.

Ah, modernity ... not always all it is cracked up to be.

With an exasperated sigh, he tucks the cigarette into his tobacco pouch and rests his chin upon the heel of his hand, waiting for Gilles Beaufort.

The hotel patrons move in hyper-speed, it seems, as Vauquelin waits twitching his foot.

Gilles is late.

Perhaps he will not come.

And then, just then, a red-faced man passes through the brass turnstile door, tugging at his collar.

Vauquelin rises and yells, "Gilles!"

---

†- NO SMOKING

The man rushes to him.

"Monsieur, please," Gilles whispers, his face beading with sweat. "Let us not draw attention. Show me your passport. Now."

A devilish smile twists Vauquelin's lips as he attempts, with one strong finger, to slip the leather strap of the bag from Gilles' shoulder — but Gilles holds it firm.

"Not until I verify your identity."

"Fair enough," Vauquelin says, taking him by the arm. "Follow me."

At the front desk Vauquelin says, "I need a single room. For two nights. I will pay cash in advance."

He turns to Gilles and says, "Pay the woman."

Gilles looks at the clerk and says, "Pardon us a moment," leading Vauquelin out of earshot. "Passport, now," he hisses. "Or we have no deal."

Vauquelin slides it across the counter.

Gilles holds it up, looking back and forth between the photograph and Vauquelin's face.

The photo checks.

Though it was taken in 1925, Vauquelin looks the same as he always has.

"This passport is long expired. If you mean to deceive me, you could have at least forged the dates."

"Look at me, Monsieur Beaufort."

Vauquelin turns on a dazzling smile for the bewildered banker, and now he has him locked in a powerful coup d'œil† — exactly where he needs him.

"You will help me ... won't you, Gilles?"

Held captive by Vauquelin's gaze, Gilles is debilitated by those frightening eyes. They are the blue of the arctic sea and twice as cold, rimmed by a dark ring as azure as the midnight sky. He has never seen such eyes, but looking into them now, he understands he will do anything Vauquelin asks.

----

† - FIRM GLANCE

Absolutely anything.

"Of course, Monsieur de Vauquelin," Gilles whispers.

"There's a good boy."

The clerk interrupts them: "Monsieur? Your credit card, please, for room security."

Vauquelin points to Gilles, who immediately extracts his wallet and produces his own Visa. He unzips the bag and hands over cash for the room fee.

The clerk passes plastic key cards and a map of the hotel to Vauquelin, who heads for the elevator with Gilles trailing him.

Once in the room, Vauquelin determines that Gilles is an ideal human: malleable, impressionable. Weak.

"Sit down," Vauquelin says.

Gilles settles into a chair.

"If I were to give you €10,000, could you disappear from the bank tomorrow? I need assistance, and I will pay for it. As you know, money is of no concern."

Gilles' face is written over with panic and dismay.

"Think carefully, monsieur. I have much to offer you ... more than you could ever imagine. Do not doubt your reward will be great. I know you have seen my account balances. And, seeing as you are a fastidious man, ask me to confirm anything you like."

Gilles has always followed rules. This situation is beyond his pale. He is too close to the edge of sacrificing the safe life he has created for himself.

He is the type of man who craves routine.

This morning, for example, he had the same breakfast he has every day without fail: a croissant with butter and strawberry preserves and an espresso at the café below his apartment. He selected one of his seven identical white shirts and one of his five navy blue suits. He walked through the doors of the same bank he has worked at for the last twenty-five years.

And now he is under the control of a strange man who is hinting — no, not even *hinting* — at criminality.

It's too much!

Perspiration beads on his upper lip.

And still, the strange man stares, stares, stares at him, with those coldly blue eyes like ice.

Vauquelin senses all of Gilles' troubled thoughts. He rises and begins pacing with his hands laced behind his back.

His relentless stride does nothing to ease Gilles' heightening anxiety.

As he paces, he rattles off all of his French addresses —including the year of one property's transfer (1682) — and Gilles frantically matches them to his notes.

Vauquelin provides the exact date his accounts were opened: 6 May, 1760. He even itemises the opening balances, down to the exact value, numbers, and inventory of the original safety deposit boxes.

"Relax yourself, monsieur ... I assure you this has not the slightest twinge of illegality, what I am proposing. Hear me out. I am only an eccentric man with a rare medical condition and an antiquated sensibility. I cannot be exposed to sunlight ... it would be deadly for me. Perhaps you have never encountered a man such as I. It should not surprise you that not all mankind can adapt to modern society ... I am an old soul who carries the burden of my ancestors and their name, a man of old France. The France we can no longer touch. But you needn't fear me. All this means is that I am not a citizen of today." He halts his pacing. "Forgive me my provincial ways. I am a lover of history, not of the present. I live in a house that was built in 1532, and it still has all the same furnishings."

Gilles' face relaxes. "Then why are we not meeting there?"

"My keys were stolen along with my belongings. This is why I need you to help me. You must handle many ancient accounts. I have only a few tasks ... I do not think they are insurmountable ... just to help me modernise a bit. But I am impaired, as I mentioned … otherwise, I would do these things myself. I have no family, no one else to depend upon. I have no reason to deceive you."

Vauquelin is a man of the ages … an ancient Frenchman who would be more comfortable if he were in Los Angeles right now, not pacing in a lavish hotel room in Paris. Trapped in the past and in the future — in his own country which no longer knows him.

He opens his palms. "Please help me."

Gilles sinks even deeper into the chair.

"What …" He struggles to swallow and loosens his bow tie. "What is it I can do for you, Monsieur, beyond what I have already done?"

Vauquelin extracts a piece of paper from his interior jacket pocket.

He unfolds it and passes it to Gilles.

I need an internet plan.
A mobile phone.
A laptop.
Wireless ear buds.
A driver licence.
A credit card.

Vauquelin wraps a hand around his chin and taps his cheek. "And I suppose I must add a new passport to that list."

"That's it? That's all you want?" Gilles asks, his mouth agape.

"That is all I *need*. Can you do this for me? One would be surprised how difficult such things are to obtain in my current state. I am afraid that the driver licence and passport are the only tasks that might be *slightly* illegal, but surely you have connections for such things, no? For reasons already stated, I cannot take a driving test in person, but I assure you … despite my antiquarian ways I have owned multiple automobiles throughout my life.

I am an accomplished driver."

Gilles straightens his back.

Upon his arrival at Le Meurice less than a half hour ago, a million thoughts misfired through his brain.

This client is a crook.

I could lose my job.

I could be killed.

I could be dragged into a life of crime.

I could go to prison.

Before he left the office this evening, Gilles checked Vauquelin's records: the trail dead-ends in 1935. None of this makes sense, not when this odd man appears, in person, to be younger than himself.

Vauquelin tilts his head. "Surely you did not think I was a swindler?"

Gilles is thrown off by his client's manner.

He speaks in outmoded French, which confuses Gilles even further.

"Who *are* you, Monsieur?"

Vauquelin crosses to Gilles and drops into a deep, seventeenth-century bow, thrusting forth a gallant leg. One arm extended, he rests the other upon his heart.

"I am only Vauquelin."

Twenty-four

Vauquelin receives a package at the front desk.

He takes the parcel to his room and opens it neatly with his Opinel.

Inside are all the items he requested, along with a handwritten letter from Gilles.

Monsieur de Vauquelin,

Your requested items are enclosed. I hope you find them to your satisfaction. The phone and the laptop must be charged before using. Also you will find instructions for logging into the accounts I have established for you, and a Visa card in your name. This card can be used internationally as you requested.

I have written this letter by hand since your security as a long-time client of the Banque Courtois is of utmost importance, and your PIN number to extract funds as needed I will give you over the phone.

Your passport and licence will be ready in two weeks.

I hope I have helped you.

*Should you need me further, my mobile number is [redacted].
Please call me to verify you have received this package and I will
provide your* PIN.

Gilles Beaufort

Vauquelin immediately powers on the phone and the laptop, finding
they already have a bit of charge.

The twenty-first century!

Mon dieu ![†] *It came so quickly.*

First thing, he calls Gilles and thanks him, memorising his PIN number.
Next, he sends a text to Olivier at the number he recalled from his
futurepast.

He keeps it vague, in case Olivier no longer has the same number.

I was snatched again.
In case you were wondering.
I am now in Paris and I am going to England SOON.
I will be in touch.
All my love to you.

He immediately sets up an email address and downloads a music app,
and spends the rest of the night searching songs and making playlists.

He cries blood tears when certain songs come through the speakers.

He puts his fingers to his lips, a prayer of sorts.

Please let me stay in this time for a while ... just a little while ...

---

†- MY GOD!

By the time Vauquelin rises the next evening, there has still been no reply from Olivier.

He walks to the Galleries Lafayette.

He purchases a pair of sunglasses (which he immediately rips the tags off of with his teeth and plants on his face), a wristwatch, and several changes of clothing and shoes.

As he heads for the exit laden with many paper bags, a salesgirl stops him to try some cologne.

"No, no ... thank you," he says, but her interruption has made him pause. He removes the sunglasses.

She is glamorous: midnight hair slicked back into a bun, thick brows over long-lashed green eyes. But something else has caught his attention.

"I wish to purchase that lipstick." He points to a backlit advertisement behind the counter: a voluptuous pair of female lips coated in a fetching shade of blood red.

"Of course, monsieur." She moves behind the counter and rummages until she extracts the correct shade, holding it up in triumph. "A gift for a special friend?"

"For me. Put it on."

"On *me?* But monsieur ..."

"No. Put it on *me,*" he purrs, leaning his torso over the counter, and parts his lips ever-so-slightly.

She shrugs and dresses Vauquelin's lips in a bloody matte crimson.

"Does this shade suit me?" he asks.

"Have a look yourself," she says, moving a mirror towards him.

He clasps her wrist tightly.

"I do not care for mirrors ... I only want your opinion."

She panics and twists her arm. The fragrance of her fear supersedes even the heavy French perfumes in the air.

"It makes you look ... like the Devil himself," she mumbles.

Génial ![†]

A grin lifts the corner of his mouth. "Sold," he says.

He drops the lipstick and receipt in one of his bags and vanishes through the doors.

The salesgirl watches him depart, tilting her head, wondering who she had just met, and unable to explain her sudden arousal.

Vauquelin considers walking back to the hotel ... it has only just begun to rain, and the petrichor is captivating. The street lights are hazed by mist, and for just a moment, he is madly in love with modern-day Paris, a city he does not know.

Despite the euphoria emerging in his chest, his arms are full of shopping bags and a walk in the rain is not on his agenda.

Instead, he ducks into a TABAC[‡] where he purchases a quantity of tobacco and rolling papers, and orders a rideshare through his new phone.

He stops at the chain hotel where his robbery victims are staying and leaves an envelope full of cash for them at the front desk, absolving his guilt by paying them back threefold.

At last on his way to Le Meurice, he presses his cheek to the car window and watches the city he had lived in for hundreds of years and yet not at all, as raindrops slither down the glass, the rain morphing the lights into colourful bokeh patterns before his eyes.

He squelches the condensation off the window with his cuff.

Once in his room, he gets to work.

He hires a car.

He books a plane ticket from London Heathrow to LAX, leaving in two weeks' time.

---

†- BRILLIANT!

‡- TOBACCONIST

Then he climbs into bed, naked, and chain smokes — wilfully ignoring another bright orange PAS DE FUMER[†] sign on the nightstand, admiring the vermilion smirch his lips impress upon the cigarette end.

He wishes he could see how his new lipstick looks.

AH !

He has a camera now!

He bites into his lower lip, adding a bead of his own blood to the crimson stain, and snaps a selfie.

He approves.

He rings Olivier.

Voicemail.

No doubt Olivier has evolved into a call-screener. So he calls five more times, and finally Olivier picks up.

"Did you get my text?"

"There you are! I must admit your message sent chills down my spine ... a ghost's breath from the past. I was frantic in 1935, but after a few months plus multiple decades with no contact, I could only assume that was what happened," Olivier laughs.

He never worries about Vauquelin ... he knows better. And regardless, the thrum of Vauquelin's blood runs through his veins. Olivier would know if their bond had been severed, which would only happen in the event of Vauquelin's Final Death.

"Yet you did not reply. Are you too busy for your old friend? I need the gate code for my house. I am locked out."

"1638, of course. I cannot believe you did not try that. There is a keypad on the front door now, too. That one is 1668. I have been meaning to have a similar lock installed at Évreux, but one cannot even find it on a map, so I am not concerned."

Vauquelin drags a hand across his jaw.

---

†- NO SMOKING

The codes are so obvious ... he has to wonder about himself sometimes!

"Oh, for fuck's sake! Thank you. I am leaving again, soon. Could I at long last convince you to travel with me? I am returning to California, via the UK. You would love it."

"What? Why?"

"I cannot explain now. I have not figured things out completely. But it is much more than a pleasure trip, that I can assure you."

"Of course it is," Olivier says.

Vauquelin hears a woman laugh in the background and cocks an eyebrow. "You have a visitor," he says.

"More than a visitor, Vauquelin ... my wife."

A pang shoots through Vauquelin's chest.

He is unsure what emotions the pang manifests.

Olivier deserves this.

The most patient, steadfast man Vauquelin has ever known deserves love, and now he has it.

"Vauquelin ... are you still on the line?"

"Yes, Olivier. I am here."

"Her name is Céline ... she has been with me since 1946. Say hello to Vauquelin."

A muffled clatter as the phone changes hands.

"Vauquelin, allô !† I am anxious to meet you. You must come to see us in Annecy!"

A nervous laugh escapes from his lips. "*Euh* ... put Olivier back on the phone, please," he stammers.

« C'est moi , »‡ Olivier says. "She is delightful, Vauquelin. Come to Annecy first. You can straighten your head. Then you can go on your adventure."

---

†- HELLO
‡- IT'S ME

Vauquelin rubs his eyes with his free hand. "You know quite well I will never come there, my brother."

Olivier keeps an apartment in Paris, but has long preferred living in the quiet provinces, in Vauquelin's ancestral estate.

Vauquelin has always despised the provinces: even Évreux is too quiet for him.

As a child, he had been frequently dragged from Paris to one estate or another. His mother's childhood home, which fell under his father's ownership upon their marriage, is the Château du Cavernay in Annecy: a medieval manor keeping watch across the ages over a pristine lake, crowned by the French Alps.

Situated mere kilometres from the Swiss border, the winters are brutal. Vauquelin cannot tolerate it. Furthermore, he vehemently dislikes hunting in small towns.

He often wonders how Olivier manages, and why he loves it so.

But the true reason Vauquelin cannot/will not go there is that he was born in that house: and that house is where his mother died, bringing him into the world.

Death was imprinted on his soul at his first breath.

"Vauquelin?"

His chin trembles as he pictures Olivier sitting up in bed, extending a hand in concern. The only man who had truly cared for him during his brief human era and continued to do so beyond — the only one who had loved him unconditionally, even in darkness, so much that he joined him in its depths without question.

Vauquelin knows that he and Olivier will always love each other, as long as their feet tread upon the earth. But now Olivier has someone else to care for, and deep-seated conflicts are warring in Vauquelin's mind.

"Vauquelin. Speak to me."

"Are you content?"

"I am most content, my brother … I am loved forever, and thus I love. I cannot ask for more. Except that you would come to us. You have solace here with us, if you will accept it."

Us. Us. Us.

Vauquelin has no us.

His Us has been shattered, gone screaming up to the sky in flames in Los Angeles.

He agitates his lips between his fingers, smearing them with lipstick, and stares at his fingers … blood on his hands.

So much blood.

"Vauquelin … are you there?"

"I am … I will always be here." Another laugh erupts, half-disgusted. At himself. "You know better than anyone, my dear Olivier, that chaos seems to soothe my soul. I leave for London in two weeks."

"But why? What is there for you?"

"All I can say is that I will find what I am looking for when I find it. Good night, my brother, and I promise you I will meet Céline sooner or later. Give her my love. If only for putting up with you as long as she has."

Olivier can hear devotion and approval in Vauquelin's voice, and this makes him smile and dig a hand into Céline's hair, drawing her to his side. She has heard many tales of the legendary Vauquelin.

"*Bon voyage.*† I love you."

"I love you, Olivier."

Vauquelin ends the call.

And then he gets out of bed, puts all his new devices on their chargers, and packs his things — because he's going home.

---

† - SAFE TRAVELS

Twenty-five

Vauquelin arrives at the gates of his house and approaches the nefarious security keypad, gleaming ominously green in the night air.

He carries a perpetual fear of confrontations with the police.

He casts his eyes about, ensuring no one is watching him.

With a quivering finger he punches in *1-6-3-8*.

Nothing happens.

The lock does not release.

He inputs the numbers again, and then his modern knowledge kicks in.

He adds a #.

The lock beeps and disengages at last — he pushes on the gates, passing through and shouldering them back into place once he is inside.

His skin prickles as he rightfully walks onto his property.

The last time he was here, it was 1935.

He knows it will be clean and tidy inside, that Olivier will have hired someone to maintain the property in his absence.

But what will remain?

What might he have lost?

He reaches the front door and another odious fucking keypad glows green in the night.

1-6-6-8-#.

The lock whispers open and Vauquelin is annoyed.

This is underwhelming, to say the least.

Nothing can compare to opening a door the traditional way.

The key to this house is weighty, made of solid brass ... longer than his hand and topped with elegant scroll work: it was the original one from when the dwelling was constructed in 1532. The mere act of opening this door was always an event in itself. He hopes Olivier has saved the key — his progeny is not in thrall to history as is Vauquelin.

He emerges into the foyer, comforted by the fact that the house looks precisely as it did only a few nights ago, when he was in 1935 and his time slipped, and wanders his hallways: grounded and ungrounded at once.

In only two weeks, he will embark on one of the most ambitious endeavours of his existence.

For now, he wants only to relax and have some sense of stability.

Even if just for a moment.

This manor, *L'hôtel de Coquillages,* is a part of his legacy.

It is the birthplace of his self-awareness.

In his first timeline, he lost this property.

Because of his rebellion, his refusal to cave to royal demands, it became a government building: owned first by Louis XIV and then by the Crown of France and eventually the Republic. He managed to turn the tides in his second one. The weight of this sits upon his shoulders now, and he sinks to his knees on the marble floor of the foyer in gratitude.

It is his grand intention to never lose it again.

He is alive.

Sort of.

No ... you are undead, he reminds himself.

This time-slip has caused a significant disruption in Vauquelin's thinking. No longer will he accept the erratic twists of his fate.

Vauquelin will be the master of his own destiny.

Despite having told himself this before and failing miserably, still he has hope, tattered and time-worn as it is.

He strolls the floors of his ancient house, reminiscing the times when it was fully staffed.

Its chimerical sounds provide a haunting soundtrack to his steps.

The floors, both marble and wood, were once polished by hand.

Horses were maintained in the stable.

Wine was delivered, many casks and bottles at a time, in the back of the manor.

The chandeliers were lowered by pulley ... the beeswax tapers were lit one-by-one, by hand.

Each prism was polished individually with a soft cloth, so that its luminance might not be suffocated by the offensive appearance of dust and blackened soot.

The clinking of the crystals is so clear in his ears that he lifts his eyes, expecting them to be dancing above his head.

They are immobile.

Each corner and hidden passageway carries the tread of Vauquelin's feet, from his human infancy to his childhood and growth into ... whatever it is he has become.

A miracle?

An abomination?

A demon?

He has read every single book in the library, held each one lovingly in his palms, absorbing its secrets word by word.

All of the many paintings of his ancestors have been gazed upon, often for hours, by his eyes. He knows each crazed line in the paint, knows every nook and cranny of the gilded, carved frames.

He walks up the imposing staircase and stops at one particular spot: a fault in the stone that still fits his middle fingertip to perfection.

He had worn it smooth in his childhood, pondering his future.

This is where he is meant to be.

And as he does all these things, a dream has been achieved: he is meandering his ancient hallways with the music of his futurepast in his ears, courtesy of Bluetooth ear buds.

Now ... how to make this permanent?

Yet something is still missing.

The emptiness churns in his spirit, desperate to be filled but coming up short.

He makes his way to his bedchamber.

There is his incomparable bed, the one that he had never been able to successfully recreate in his futurepast, the one in which he awoke to discover he was human once more: if only for one night.

Now he has no record of how he looked as a human. He only has his memory. The only remaining visual is this portrait — and it screams VOUS ÊTES VAMPIRE ![†]

Seeing it fills him with a bizarre pride.

The entire house is a shrine to his vampiric benefaction.

He owes himself something, surely?

Perhaps what he owes is self-acceptance ... a lesson that can never be purchased or taught.

Yvain, in his crude way, had told Vauquelin as much after his first turning, but his personality could not abide by such advice.

He would live on his own terms, regardless.

And now, now that he had done so for centuries, where is he?

What has he gained?

Nothing.

Nothing.

Nothing.

---

† - YOU ARE VAMPIRE!

Twenty-six

ENGLISH CHANNEL | 30 NOVEMBER | LAST YEAR

The train is packed bumper to bumper with cars in the Eurotunnel, but Vauquelin is ecstatic.

It is an altogether new experience! For a vampire, doing something one has never done before is a pinnacle high.

He is sitting in a car that is on a train, travelling beneath the waters of the English Channel!

What a world.

The lost modern music he had lamented for centuries is once again available at the touch of a button: or even by the command of his voice.

It assumes ownership over the atmosphere in the car, and he maximises the volume, smothering himself in it.

Mere weeks ago, he was in 1935 Paris, on the brink of another world war. Evidently, fate does not wish for him to witness the Nazis taking over his fair city ... fine by him.

He leans his chin against his hand and stretches his legs out ... still disorienting, being in the driver's seat of a car that is moving beyond his control.

It is a reminder that soon he must be alert, for the instant he emerges on

English soil he will drive on the left side of the road: something else he has never done.

As he rides through the tunnel, a memory strikes as viciously as if it had happened yesterday: his maiden kill — some eight hundred years ago — to this night the guilt still terrorises his soul. His first victim's deathly open eyes embedded within him a horror which has never abated.

Open-eye deaths happen more frequently than Vauquelin would prefer ... he cannot help but think they are judging him, exposing the tar-blackness of his soul. Such deaths chip away at his spirit, and he agonises that one night he will wake and find there is nothing left.

He knocks his head against the seat and chases those murky ruminations away, replacing them with the satisfying thought of hot, metallic blood sliding down his throat. No eyes.

Still, even after all these lifetimes, the merest sense of that iron tang soothes his savage beast, and awakens another.

He moves his hand between his legs, gripping his erection, and sighs.

Loneliness is cruel.

It is even crueller when one is a revenant.

When one is human, one has lifelines: they are there for the taking.

One can venture into the daylight, where there are other humans, someone to return a smile and maybe even say hello.

One can eat a meal alone, and perhaps some other human will come up and ask to join.

Human beings often offer their assistance willingly.

One can approach another human at any moment and say, "Nice weather we're having!" and the other human will say "Yes! But it's supposed to turn bad this week!" And then they'll laugh together and go on about their days.

But if one is a revenant ... one is restricted to sundown hours, and humans get especially cagey in the dark.

Courtesy is not so abundant in the midnight hours.

Humans are taught from a young age that no decent people are out at night: it is the playground of miscreants and con artists.

And this is true: especially so of vampires ... because they are, by their very natures, untrustworthy.

The darkness is their arena.

But not all vampires are satisfied with their lot in life, and this is certainly the case for Vauquelin.

They must accept it, though — because they have no choice.

Despite Vauquelin being born in France ... despite his rebirth in darkness ... to the French vampire coteries he has no alliance.

They require unquestioning obedience in exchange for their protection.

They are cruel and self-serving.

His destiny was to create more vampires.

Fuck that.

He will take his own fate by the throat.

Ninety or so years ago (according to Vauquelin's literal timetable: five by his improbable one), he travelled to England to extract his funds: and a vampire was kind to him ... that vampire's face is irrevocably etched into his mind.

Vampires have eidetic memories.

True ... some events are more memorable than others, but every experience is a mental photograph.

It is *torture*.

Absolute, bloody torture.

Centuries ago, Olivier was attacked by a rogue band of French vampires on the streets of Paris. Vauquelin heard his progeny's dire bloodcall and rushed to find him cowering in an alleyway, desperate and bloodied. At the end of the passage Vauquelin caught the slightest glimpse of another vampire, looking back over his shoulder. He vanished into the shadows, his long black coat catching briefly on the corner of the stone wall.

Vauquelin launched forward, fangs out for counter-attack, and Olivier grabbed his ankle.

"No, Vauquelin … he ran them off. I heard his voice… he is English."

Olivier did not catch his name. In such chaotic circumstances, he had been unable to obtain any information out of his mystery defender.

But the thought of an English vampire interfering in a violent conflict outside his own territory, sacrificing his own safety, never left Vauquelin's mind, and he carried a debt of gratitude to the stranger who rescued his brother, Olivier.

After the attack, Olivier retreated to Vauquelin's château in Annecy.

He had had quite enough of city life for the time being.

Weeks later, Olivier wrote to Vauquelin with news. He had done a bit of detective work, against his maker's caution, reaching out to an Italian vampire he frequently visited — a female who sometimes offered her bodily comfort and blood to him. And she also knew exactly who had saved Olivier: there was no mistaking the vampire he described in such vivid detail.

> *25 August 1790*
> *Annecy*
>
> *My brother— the dark one who assisted me … his name is Clove. Please do not prompt me on how I obtained this information. I must ask you to trust me and leave it at that. All I can say is his strength was admirable, and I am grateful for his appearance. Had he not been there to assist me, I would no longer be your*
>
> *Olivier*

Vauquelin has never been one to renege on debts.

He took Olivier at his word, as he had always done.

This indelible memory is the primary reason Vauquelin is now travelling to London: he wants to find others who are like him ... cruel by nature but not by intent.

He needs answers ... he needs confirmation.

He aims to find Clove, to learn from him. And the only key Vauquelin has to locate him is through that random encounter with an English vampire in 1929.

Liberty has always been Vauquelin's cream: the thing he is most unwilling to sacrifice. But now, having been alive for over eight hundred years, a new cream has risen to the top for Vauquelin: kinship. *Us.*

His classical loneliness has devastated him and left him barren.

He can still count his progeny on one hand.

On that thought, the tunnel opens into the night sky of Folkestone and just like that, he is in the United Kingdom.

The act of driving the car out of a train, tempered by his slight panic at avoiding a crash, is a bit underwhelming. In truth, this journey has not been much different from a plane trip, but vastly more comfortable.

He pulls into a parking spot and has to catch his breath.

He has travelled often: on planes, on ships, and on trains.

But never before has he been *under* the ocean!

He extracts his phone, and says "Directions to London."

The AI voice guides him to the inner city, though she cannot locate the hotel where he stayed in 1929.

It must be closed.

But then again, how could he dare hope that The Vampire would be in the same area again, almost one hundred years later?

"Directions to closest five-star hotel."

A week into his London trip, Vauquelin is getting bored.

He has not seen The Vampire, let alone any vampires at all, since he set foot in the UK.

Still, he walks the streets every night.

And he stops in nightclubs, exuding his French charms, feasting from human wrists under the guise of silver-tongued kisses, healing his bite marks and sustaining himself just enough to avoid a kill.

Two weeks of this — and then, one night, while Vauquelin feeds his credit card into a parking meter, a black tingle twitches up his spine: the mark of a vampire's presence.

He lifts his gaze.

It is the one he seeks, standing across the street with his arms laced behind his back. The vampire inclines his head and extends a hand, beckoning Vauquelin to come.

And then they are standing face to face, with no ill will between them.

"Good evening," Vauquelin says. He might not have this opportunity again, and he cannot afford to vacillate. "Clove?"

"Sorry to disappoint you," the vampire replies. "Flynn Frenière."

The French name ignites a flame in Vauquelin's heart, and it reflects in his eyes.

"My name surprises you? I don't offer my surname readily, but I knew it would be important to you. There's both French and Irish blood in my veins, but I've embraced what the night has to offer here. You're half Sicilian, I believe."

Vauquelin hikes an eyebrow. "How do you know this?"

"Our method of communication here is ... extremely trustworthy."

Flynn's lips quirk into a grin, the tip of one fang visible.

Trustworthy vampires?

Should Vauquelin dare to believe this?

"If you know me so well, you must know that my timeline is fluid, and that I have no faith in my revenant countrymen. I must rely only on myself ... to the dubious extent that I am able, of course."

Flynn studies Vauquelin's face.

"That's regrettable. I've heard about your maker."

"Then you must not have a high opinion of me," Vauquelin mutters, jutting his chin out. "Why would you be so courteous?"

"I'm an excellent judge of character. And I've helped many a vampire out of ... let's say ... a *predicament*. But I only offer my help to those I think deserve it, those with kindness in their souls. I see your loneliness, Vauquelin. And I see your sincerity. If it's Clove you seek, maybe I can help you?"

Vauquelin's expression is the answer.

He has never felt so accepted.

He might as well disintegrate into a puddle of water.

No one has ever described him as *kind*.

And this validates his purpose in coming here: he knew he could not be alone in his thinking.

"I just ... I need ..." Vauquelin conceals his eyes behind his hand. "I have travelled here solely in hopes of securing a meeting with Clove," he stutters.

Flynn extracts a box of matches from his pocket, twirling it around in his fingers before extracting a stick and planting it between his lips. He knows Clove. Knows he doesn't accept callers. "He keeps himself guarded because of his situation. But I can contact him."

"I understand your hesitation to trust me, but I assure you ... I have no allegiance to my French vampire coterie. I barely have allegiance to myself, though that is what I am seeking. You have been good to me, Flynn. I am unaccustomed to compassion amongst my kind." His voice breaks.

Flynn cocks a brow. "Clove has vampire youth in his charge." He pauses, his gaze landing on Vauquelin's face again. "The Bloody Little Prophets. Surely I needn't explain further." The trio has a reputation on these shores: he wonders whether news of their exploits has travelled to the continent. Flynn eases back into the shadows and folds his arms, waiting to see if the phrase resonates with Vauquelin.

Vampire youth?

Vauquelin's jaw falls open.

In Vauquelin's revenant world, the turning of youth is forbidden.

He lets his gaze drift away from Flynn, mulling over the implications of the name. *Bloody Little Prophets?*

"There's more you should know, monsieur … but surely you understand his need for secrecy and confidence." He holds up three fingers. "Give me three nights and I'll meet you with an answer … same time, in this spot."

Flynn vanishes down the darkened street.

Vauquelin returns to his lodgings, his mind befuddled by thoughts of young vampires.

His eyes do not close that morning … nor for the next two.

Instead he spends all his hours online, searching in vain for dark knowledge that no mortals have been able to uncover, let alone accurately present.

How fascinating that so many of them seem to think they have the key to defining vampires!

True darkness can never be seen by mortal eyes.

Those few books that have been written are hidden in dusty, underground libraries, held steadfastly in the possession of those who can truly respect their power — under a deep need to keep their secrets out of the wrong hands.

Unsurprisingly, there is nothing online to help him.

For the first time in his life, he regrets not heeding his maker's advice to study their lore.

Flynn is waiting for him three nights later, just as he promised, and bows his head as Vauquelin emerges from his car.

"Let's take a ride ... I'd rather not speak where we might be overheard."

"Of course."

They drive in silence until Vauquelin pulls into a car park and kills the engine.

Flynn turns to him.

"Clove will see you, but I can't give you precise directions to his location. He'll take things from there. You've got to go alone ... no exception."

Vauquelin looks down, agitating a button on his jacket.

"My friend, that is never a problem. I am always alone."

The meeting is established: tomorrow night.

Flynn tells Vauquelin which roads to take and gives him a rough, hand-sketched map.

"You'll need to leave your car at this bridge." He points to a space on the map. "There's no accessible inroad, nor are there any pathways," Flynn explains. "May I suggest comfortable footwear?" he says, a wry smile curling his lip. He had noticed the fashionable yet highly impractical shoes Vauquelin is wearing tonight.

Like most vampires, Flynn registers all details.

"You can drop me just there," Flynn says, pointing to an intersection.

"Could I not buy you a drink?"

"No, thank you, Vauquelin ... we were destined to meet, and that purpose has been fulfilled. If you don't arrive at the appointed time, there won't be another chance to meet with Clove. Good night."

Vauquelin watches Flynn until he rounds a corner. He folds the map carefully and places it in the glove box.

He has never driven into the English countryside: his time has always been spent in London.

This is a bizarre journey for Vauquelin to even consider embarking upon, but regardless of what happens, he knows one thing: his life will not move forward unless he opens his mind.

And it starts opening now.

Twenty-seven

WEST COUNTRY, UNITED KINGDOM | THE NEXT NIGHT

The late autumn English chill increases with every kilometre, and by the time Vauquelin arrives at the bridge Flynn designated, the car's heater is running at full blast.

The trip has taken a little over three hours from London, and he is loath to leave the cocoon of the warm car and trudge out across the pitch-black field that lies ahead of him, as dark and obscure as his future.

At this moment, Vauquelin has no means of knowing how drastically this meeting will change his life.

How it will change *everything*.

Vauquelin is a lifelong misanthrope — and this extends to his own revenant kind as well, with a handful of exceptions.

The few times he has lowered his impenetrable walls, disaster has ensued — which is why he has chosen to be alone for much of his immortal existence. He is fond of his own company (one would have to be!), and prefers it over guaranteed disappointment. But chronic seclusion has finally taken its toll on him, and recent events have brought his dependence on others to light.

Not merely to accomplish ordinary tasks ... no, no.

Such assistance can easily be gotten.

Though it is true that his condition renders him virtually helpless in daylight hours, and closes the door to convenience, most chores can be schemed one way or another.

Nor does he seek mere companionship: what he desires is a depth of understanding.

Acceptance. Not that of others, but his own: of himself.

It may have taken him roughly eight hundred years to realise this, but at long last he is prepared.

He *thinks*.

So his feet carry him across an English plain, and each step brings him closer to a momentous tête-à-tête[†] that will alter not only his self-perception, but initiate the bending away of the steely, cold fortress of his heart.

The loam sucks at his feet, threatening to draw him down into its depths.

The remains of a crumbling Roman amphitheatre — modest in size, carved into the hillside and overrun with weeds — come into his view, and looming in front, the shadowy silhouette of a man: but this is no ordinary man. This is a vampire.

"Vauquelin."

"Clove."

Three slight figures — the so-called Bloody Little Prophets, Vauquelin presumes — stand behind Clove, manoeuvring so that they might get a better glimpse of their strange visitor.

Vauquelin is astonished that Clove has brought these young, teenage vampires into his presence.

It must mean that Clove trusts him... that Flynn had deemed him deserving of this meeting.

---

†- HEAD TO HEAD MEETING. READ THE FULL ENCOUNTER IN *CRIMSON IS THE NIGHT* BY BEVERLEY LEE AND NICOLE EIGENER, AVAILABLE AT THEVAMPIRE.ORG

Emotions surge in Vauquelin's chest — *honour?* — and an abject loneliness creeps into his bones. Even from this distance, Vauquelin senses their impassioned kinship. He would have expected such young boys to be wild and restless, not so well-behaved and reverent. Flynn's assessment of Clove's disposition as a devoted guardian was, then, grounded in truth. What would it be like to have someone to rely upon him, someone to safeguard?

Is this envy? he wonders. The sentiment is unfamiliar to him, not to mention confusing: never once during his human life had he desired dependants, and his reluctance to create vampire progeny remains as steadfast.

Clove turns to face him and at last Vauquelin finds his courage to speak.

"It has been quite some time since I desired to be near other vampires," Vauquelin says, his voice low and subdued. "I thank you for heeding my invitation, because seeing them now, I understand your great desire to protect them."

"I came immediately upon your request. Flynn impressed upon me your urgent desire to meet." Clove steps forward, opening his hands in a gesture Vauquelin recognises from his mortal youth, one that shows he carries no weapons. "I will admit it was a surprise. Your reputation for solitude is legendary. As was mine ... but times change." Clove lets his meaning drift into the stillness, the presence of his boys a repressed thrum of energy coiled within the night. "I will save the introductions until we are somewhere less public."

And then Clove invites Vauquelin to visit their home. Their home!

Vauquelin appraises the trio as Clove speaks, puzzling over the tangled emotions knotting within his psyche. At last he moves forward, a hand extended — he stumbles. They are only youths — yet with all that he has seen and endured by travelling back and forth through four centuries, he could never have anticipated the pivotal effect their presence would have on him.

Clove reaches out with a stiff arm to steady him, and Vauquelin prepares a whispered lie.

"My apologies ... how weak I must appear to you all! It is just that I am wearied from my travels here. I would be delighted to visit your home.' He drops his voice to a low whisper. 'I do not wish for the boys to be frightened of me."

As they walk, the only sound that of their feet imprinting the marshy earth, Vauquelin considers the benevolence Clove has offered. He had not known how desperately he yearned for this communion, and the nearness of four unknown vampires — vampires he needn't fear or face down — provides him with an immense comfort he had not known in decades. His unease begins to melt away. Here is an established family, one that welcomes him.

His chest shudders: joy and disbelief mingle and flutter his heart.

The ancient stones of Gehenna come into view. The mythical structure would strike even the most steadfast of hearts, mortal and immortal alike, with black dread, but Vauquelin knows that behind these walls is safety. Protection.

Vauquelin is so unaccustomed to being near youth that their presence rattles him: in fact, he is a nervous wreck. Their earnest faces, their curiosity — it is almost too much for him to bear.

But now they have vanished, and Clove leads him to a window.

There are intruders below ... reckless mortals who believe they have nothing to fear from shadows, when in fact they are on the verge of drowning in their disputable bravado beneath a bloody tide.

Under cover of darkness, in the courtyard below, Vauquelin watches the boys make their kill, watches their seemingly innocent grace explode into violence.

Vauquelin turns to Clove, standing so steeled and confident beside him.

He wants so badly to touch him, to close ranks with him, but something in Clove's demeanour tells him to keep his distance. His fingers begin to agitate and he folds back into himself, withdrawing a few paces behind.

It is a delicate reminder that this is Clove's domain, not his ... that he is not a part of what is transpiring within these saturnine walls.

He has let himself be undone by his longing — for what, exactly, he still does not know.

A slight touch on Vauquelin's shoulder jars him out of his slack-jawed reverie, and he cuts his eyes to Clove's inquiring face. Language fails him.

Instead, he tucks a hand into Clove's elbow and returns his gaze to the magnificently chilling events unfolding in the ancient courtyard.

So few times had Vauquelin ever fed with another vampire ... so few times had he witnessed such kinship among his kind. He had been viscerally alone for most of his existence: both by choice and circumstance. The distance between him and Olivier is now deeper than the bottom of the sea. Vauquelin had made a sharp descent into solitude, crushed by the obscurity of the only other person in existence who truly knew his soul — inside and out.

Before him he sees everything he has ever wanted: love, lust, blood ... kith and kin. So much of it all, perfuming the very air, and still so far beyond his reach. How had these young vampires learned by heart what he had struggled to grasp for all his centuries, only to find it amongst each other?

The sight of them nearly makes him come apart at the seams.

The fabled Vauquelin ... shattered by the spectacle of youthful bloodlust. A disdainful groan erupts from his throat. "Nothing could have prepared me for this. I thought I had lost my capacity for marvel amongst my travels."

They all — Clove and the boys — have opened a hidden corridor deep in his soul that, before tonight, he was unsure existed.

Life, it seems, can still offer delicious surprises, and to a vampire, that is worth more than the richest sanguine fluid.

He watches the boys standing huddled in the chilly courtyard, their arms around each others' waists and shoulders, their faces upturned to his shadowy figure behind the window. "May they come back up now? I should like to talk to them, if you will allow it. After all, are we not gathered here to learn about one another?"

He cocks an eyebrow at Clove as he turns his back to the stone sill.

Clove lets the slightest smile hover on his lips as he mirrors Vauquelin's arched brow. His guest has all the properties of a rubber ball, his disposition bouncing capriciously. Clove had expected a character reserved in nature. This particular version holds his interest far more.

'Indeed, we are. And we both understand that education in all matters is of profound importance, especially to those of us who have surpassed many lifetimes."

When the boys return, satiated and triumphant from their kill, Vauquelin sees them in a completely different light. Their impressive show has eroded their initial hesitation.

Vauquelin falls silent as he watches them assemble, wondering if they had ever encountered a vampire as old as he. An immeasurable sea of years spans between them — a vastness between their wide-eyed modernity and his jaded antiquity. His countenance is eternally youthful, especially here in this dimly-lit tower, but his skin bears the sheen of a marble sepulchre and his eyes have grown even colder: such a jarring contrast to the freshly-fed bloom of the boys who stand before him.

The shadows are his home, wherever they might be ... in the shadows, he is beautiful in perpetuity.

He reaches into his bag for a bottle, and as his hand passes under the dripping candelabra, the verdigris veinery of his hands almost appears to glow in the illusory light.

'Bravo! Quite a show, mes petits,'[†] he says, taking a long pull of wine. He runs his tongue across his upper lip and conjures a devilish grin, leaning back in the chair. 'It brought me to mind of my own fledgling days, though that was many moons ago.' He winks at Clove, and waggles his spindly fingers at the boys. 'Come now, I am all yours. You may ask me anything you like.'

His braggadocio is slowly returning; still, he avoids meeting the boys' eyes. They are too spirited, too earnest.

And the ethereal Teal — Teal's ocean eyes are harrowing to behold. They are dazzling, mesmerising: deep, illuminated pools holding fast to memories of terror.

Vauquelin sends a silent question to Clove:

Are they aware of my time slips?

He does not want to further complicate the evening by breaching the topic of time travel, yet it is a part of his existence he must accept. He is oblivious as to whether other vampires are able to manoeuvre back and forth through time as he can.

Clove gives a single, curt nod.

Such freedom to discuss himself, his struggles — prior to this night, only Olivier had heard such candour from Vauquelin. He takes his turn to speak, and he divulges his plans. He has never spoken them aloud prior to this moment.

He settles into a chair and gathers his scattered thoughts.

"I am back in this time to gather what I can," Vauquelin begins, "because I am done with the future, with what I call my futurepast. I am no longer convinced it is a welcoming place for a vampire such as I. You are all quite privileged to have Clove to guide you, and your struggles will be different from mine. You have the benefit of youth to help you adapt to events which lie ahead."

---

†- MY LITTLE ONES

Were these ordinary human teenagers, Vauquelin feels sure this little speech would go unappreciated, as the advice of elders inevitably does — but he sees the words settle into their hearts, sees the meaning behind them flicker in the phosphorus seas of their eyes.

"Please do not ever take his wisdom and experience for granted."

For a moment Vauquelin's countenance grows hollow as he drifts away into the depths of his own ether. He is so far gone that he does not hear Gabriel's question, and shakes his head with a start when the fledgling touches his hand, whispering, "Monsieur de Vauquelin?"

Vauquelin trails his gaze from their hands to Gabriel's face. Those dark blue eyes stir him: they hold a depth of wisdom uncommon in one so young, especially of the present era. An inexplicable affinity for Gabriel surges in his soul, and it inspires him to gift the young vampire with something unique, something that will belong to only them.

"You may call me V ... it shall be your own special moniker for me."

Clove watches as Gabriel kneels before Vauquelin, knowing it is partly in honour of one so revered, partly so he would not be taller so as to seem a threat. Vampires are always aware of such things.

Moth steps back so he is hidden in shadow, but a split second away if Gabriel needs him. Teal comes to Clove's side, seating himself on the edge of the desk, hands clasped upon his thighs.

Gabriel repeats his question.

"How have you done this alone?" He lets his gaze meet Vauquelin's, holds it there for a few brief seconds, as Clove had taught him, then lets it drop as a mark of respect.

"Ah, Gabriel," Vauquelin begins, the name rumbling across his tongue in silky French. He reaches out to tenderly smooth back Gabriel's dark hair — he does not recoil as Vauquelin half-expects him to. This small gesture blankets his heart in warmth.

In the shadows, Moth stiffens.

Vauquelin shoots him a sideward glance, allowing a subtle grin to curl the edge of his lip. Then, his focus drills back into Gabriel. It might as well only be the two of them in the damp, bone-chilling room.

"It was my choice from the beginning. At the time of my turning I was offered a family, a coterie as we call orders of our kind in France, but I was not so fortunate as you," he says, gesturing with an upturned hand to Clove, Moth, and Teal. "This coterie was ... how shall I say ... conceited, disloyal. It was a facile decision to leave them behind. I lived unbound, yet I had to teach myself everything I know. There have been pockets of time where I had companionship, but the corridors of the heart — vampire or human — can be dark and treacherous, my young friend. In the end, I came to learn that there is only one person I can trust, and that person is me."

His face darkens as the words tumble, and he drops his chin to his chest.

Admitting his own truths always drowns him in despair.

Teal leans across, placing his hand over Clove's, turning his bright-eyed gaze towards the vampire who had saved him on more than one occasion, and adds another question, softly, earnestly, as he turns to Vauquelin.

"If one like us came to you for help, would you protect them?"

Vauquelin inclines his head. After the display in the courtyard, his view of them as mere boys has dissipated: these young vampires can certainly hold their own. Their assailants were human, and mortals are easily toppled. But there are stronger, much more malevolent forces which could bring them harm.

As he looks into the hauntingly bright eyes of the fair-haired vampire before him, the reality of their existence settles into his heart. He recognises the suffering behind those eyes, more than one so young should ever have known. Their youthful faces belie their experiences, yet they would be such for eternity. It could prove to be dangerous for them: their physical prowess might be subverted by their innocent appearance.

"My young friend," Vauquelin says at last, "were I so fortunate to be needed by one such as you, it would be my honour and duty to shield you."

So seldom had anyone ever *needed* Vauquelin. It is something he had wished for many times throughout all his days, but he has built the walls of his heart so high: few have ever managed to scale them. Yet the four vampires in this room have done so this very night, and he knows he will be unable to forget them when he departs.

But ... like so many times before ... will they want him to be a part of their lives?

He doubts it.

At last there is the one called Moth.

The only one who has not yet interrogated him.

Moth skulks in the shadows, his head lowered, the toe of his boot scuffing the dusty floor.

Clove inclines his head as he studies his young ward.

"Moth? You have a question?"

"It doesn't matter." Moth shrugs, his hands in his jacket pockets.

Clove strides across, lifting Moth's chin with one long finger. He sees the struggle in Moth's mismatched eyes, sees the shield ready to slam shut.

"It always matters."

Moth sighs and Clove steps back, opening his arm to include Vauquelin in the conversation.

"How can you be done with the future?" Moth pauses. "Sounds to me like running away." His tongue flickers out, as though he's testing the air. Testing what Vauquelin's reaction might be. "Taking the fucking safest option." Moth's question is out there, and, much like the originator, it refuses to stay cowed.

Storm clouds of anger briefly shadow Vauquelin's face. He emits an exasperated sigh to blow them away and glowers at Moth — but there is a twinkle in his eye.

"Safest, you say?" Vauquelin stands to his full, imposing height and begins to pace the perimeter of the room. "Safety, my young friend, is an illusion. A vampire is never truly invincible. Were it so, we could walk freely amongst humans, bringing our sanguine habits to the forefront. Do you believe the humans would be happy to welcome us? Would they take pity on us for our condition? I think not."

He halts his pacing and jabs a finger at Moth. "A vampire should never be faulted for doing what he must for self-preservation." Vauquelin resumes his pounding tread, lacing his hands behind his back. "I am not, as you say, 'taking the fucking safest option.' I am retreating to times which are more palatable for me, the times of my origin. I am weary of struggling to hide from police and curiosity-seekers ... of chasing down blood. I am bone-tired. It is not a matter of mere safety. We will never be safe. Surely you boys know that by now."

Vauquelin buries his face in his hands. But after the events of this night, as those words tumble forth, he considers whether Moth might be right.

After this heated exchange, Clove sagely begins to urge them all off to bed. Dawn is chasing the moon away, and there does not seem enough time in the world left for all the unanswered questions hovering on their tongues.

Moth remains, leaning against the wall, his thumbs through the belt loops of his dirty jeans ... his face in a scowl.

This *enfant vampire*[†] is full of piss and vinegar, and for a fleeting moment Vauquelin could be looking at his own nearly-grown, rebellious self.

Though he was twice Moth's age at the time of his turning, Vauquelin has always spoken his mind, even in the folly of his human youth.

He can only admire Moth.

"We are kindred spirits, Moth," he whispers.

The boys retreat into the shadows.

---

†- VAMPIRE CHILD

Suffice it to say that hard-held theories were undone and undead existences were irrevocably altered for all of them.

How envious Vauquelin is of Clove and his wards! They are of a bloodline far-removed from his own ... daybreak will take them into death sleep regardless of their unquiet minds, whereas his own respite is at best a dubious possibility. At intervals, his cruel thoughts pummel him, and his eyes refuse to close no matter the status of the sun.

Vauquelin tosses and turns in the chamber provided for him.

He attempts to picture them, enfolded in Death's sweet embrace, though he does not know where they lay.

Oh, oh ... so exquisitely beautiful, the lot of them.

Seldom has he felt so violently alone.

Vauquelin springs from the bed and spends the remainder of the daylight hours pacing the perimeter of the room, running his hands over its cold, stone walls, raking his fingers through his hair, banking the fire, clenching and unclenching his hands.

This sojourn has been cathartic, and as he senses the sun dipping below the horizon, he knows at once that he cannot stay here a moment longer. He will embrace the night, his only true companion, inviting its velvety expanse to fill the emptiness inside him as it has so many times before.

He navigates the immeasurable corridors thinking of Clove and the boys: still, he hopes, enfolded in Death's sweet embrace deep beneath his feet. He kneels at the entrance, extracting a thick, wax-sealed letter from his satchel. The folded pages bear all his words which had been unable to find their way to the surface last night, words carrying the weight of the impact of this transcendent rendezvous.

He props the letter up next to the door.

Vauquelin steals away under cover of the late hour, and sits in a moonlit frosted field with his head in his hands, so vastly far from home — wherever and whenever that is — knowing that all he wants is *Someone*.

Someone to whom he matters more than anything else, who can see him and love him as he is, despite his imperfections and flaws.

As he sits on the hard ground, with hoarfrost dampening his trousers and shimmying into the marrow of his bones, stripping heather flowers from their stems, sharp howls rip through the veiled silence, startling him.

The boys!

He takes a deep breath and a broad smile widens his lips: he bites them to stand his ground against the emotion sweeping across his heart.

Vauquelin stands and raises his hand.

« Allons-y ! »[†] he shouts into the night.

The car beeps when Vauquelin presses the fob, and it is a startling reminder of his reality — a closing of the curtains on the surreal and transformative events of last night.

He retains an exhilarating contact high. But now he knows what is next and there is no time to waste.

How incredibly lucky they all are to have one another.

The boys' haunted faces — and Clove's penetrating eyes — are etched into his soul, and will reside there for all time to come.

Vauquelin motors across the English countryside, his rampant desire to merge into his new consciousness fuelling his resolve ... and his lead foot.

But it will take time: something he mercifully has a great deal of at his disposal (he hopes).

It will also require patience.

And patience is his least favourite virtue.

---

†- LET'S GO!

Twenty-eight

LOS ANGELES, CALIFORNIA | DECEMBER 2 | LAST YEAR

Vauquelin lands at LAX in a private jet.

The departure from Heathrow is at 17:00, and, in order to protect himself from any scheduling mishaps with continental time changes, he has no choice but to arrive at the hanger dressed in black from head to toe: all skin covered, sunglasses in place.

His mysterious ensemble does not raise any eyebrows … private airlines are quite accustomed to eccentric clients wanting to conceal their identities and having bizarre demands.

The flight is eleven-plus hours.

This is a colossally risky way for a vampire to travel, rendering most continental journeys impossible. It is precisely why vampires tend to cluster in one region, why they congregate in certain cities.

In all honesty, travelling through time is much simpler!

The cabin of the jet, at the client's request, is completely dark while airborne, and the client is not to be disturbed under any circumstances: not even for refreshments or arrival information.

He spends the entire flight listening to music and recreating the playlists he lost in his Great Time-Slip.

The time-slips have happened so frequently at this point: he must name the first one, like one names wars.

He has a playlist for every mood.

There is a baroque playlist.

A vampire playlist.

Lully. Lots of Lully.

Rameau, the punk of the eighteenth century.

Another unique playlist that combines the genres of all of his eras.

Upon arrival, he is rushed into a blacked-out SUV and driven to a house he has leased high in the Hollywood Hills, just off Mulholland Drive.

Once inside Vauquelin runs a bath and, as soon as he is freshly cleaned, the doorbell chimes.

It is one of the things he loves about modern L.A. — if you have the funds, you can get absolutely anything you want.

Anything.

As long as the cash is there, no one will question it.

The next evening, a car is delivered to him.

Oh, how he wanted his Pagani back.

Another possession that had been stolen from him in his Great Time-Slip. But it would be foolish to purchase such an extravagant automobile now, when he does not intend to be here for long.

Instead, he has leased a black Ferrari 488.

And this he drives just outside Little Tokyo, to the bar where he meets the Plastic Woman who Satisfies His Thirst, if Only Temporarily.

Vauquelin adores (well ... once adored) Los Angeles.

In his first timeline, many years into his futurepast, he was at his peak in this city. He had finally achieved peace with himself, and his existence.

UNTIL.

Until his existence was ripped from beneath his feet like a rug, and he found himself robbed of all his comforts, dropped without explanation in the year 1959, and further and further back.

Again and again, until he arrived at his origins.

In 1668: where he truly belongs.

Vauquelin has one aim: to decipher the enigma of the manipulation of his time. If Yvain can do it, so can he.

In his second 1668 he was awestricken to learn that it was Yvain, his maker, who was mauling his time, toying with his creature Vauquelin as if he were a marionette. He rewound Vauquelin's time to his last day as a human, forcing him to choose again. As if he could say no!

After his second resurrection, he inherited his maker's unique skill for healing (an ability he had long coveted) and much of his power — but the secrets of time travel did not pass through his blood. Vauquelin intends to harness that power for himself.

There is only one question: why did this recent time-slip happen?

And who is at the helm?

Vauquelin is supremely exhausted by having his timeline altered.

There he was, minding his own business, just trying to go out for some blood, and ... *wait.*

C'est quoi ce bordel ?[†]

CLÉMENT.

There is no denying he saw Clément with his own eyes, standing across the street in 1935 Paris: the man who had undone Vauquelin with his celadon devil eyes, with his velvety dream soul trapped in the body of a revenant, hands twirling a pocket watch ... hands with a shockingly strong grip that had never vacated Vauquelin's senses.

The man who, quite possibly, might have derailed Vauquelin's

[†]- WHAT THE FUCK?

(self-anointed) fate.

Could Clément be complicit in this most recent time slip?

Vauquelin's thoughts begin to pirouette, spiralling into madness.

He walks onto the back terrace. There is a magnificent view of the sprawling Los Angeles metropolis below: lights twinkle, spotlights scan the sky, and it is unearthly quiet up here in the hills. He cannot hear the mad traffic below, only an occasional jet engine.

It is December. The temperature is 45°F/7°C.

He strips off his clothes and plunges into the pool.

The icy cold water does not affect him, not really: but the one thing it can do is clear his mind.

He leans his head against the edge, and above him are towering Italian cypresses and palm trees, crowned by a muddy amber sky.

No stars. One cannot truly see the stars in Los Angeles.

The only "stars" one can see are on the red carpets.

His thoughts war in his brain as he deconstructs the recent turns of events. At Vauquelin's first making, Clément was present: he had been a vampire for only twelve moons, turned in 1667, one year before Vauquelin. He was an extra in Vauquelin's early days, not a leading actor.

In his second timeline, Vauquelin made the choice to become a revenant again for one reason — to divert Maeve from a cruel death, to have her alive. Clément forced himself into Vauquelin's erratic, altered timeline, and emerged in the forefront as an unexpected and significant divergence in the way things were *supposed to be*.

Despite Vauquelin's determination to repeat his history to the letter, Clément had appeared and disrupted everything, becoming quite an important figure. How could he have not recognised the implications of his joining with Clément, despite its brevity?

So many of Vauquelin's choices have been misguided.

Clément's shadow has been following him all these centuries despite his refusal to acknowledge it.

How is Clément faring in his twenty-first century life?

Is he still with Yvain?

Vauquelin sinks under the water, adrift in his turmoil. He forces his head to stay under, under, under as his brain explodes with memories ... the extraordinary events he has witnessed ... the unique things he has seen ... the horrors he has inflicted ... the lives he has destroyed.

Maeve, Clément, Olivier ... no, not Olivier, he is so happy, he deserves that happiness ... Clove and the boys, oh how I envy them ... but do I not deserve happiness? What have I done that is so bad, aside from just trying to stay alive and unnoticed?

His ears thrum below the surface.

He has been underwater for at least fifteen minutes.

I am lost ...

I am lost ...

He sinks to the bottom of the pool.

His chorus murmurs in his ears:

> *The answers have been before you all along.*
> *You are not LOST, you fool ...*
> *You only need to learn to SEE.*
> *To embrace.*
> *To surrender.*
> *You have lived far too long*
> *under the depths of your own self-deception.*

Vauquelin rises to the surface and slithers out of the pool up onto the concrete edge, gasping like a fish in the air. His lungs do not struggle ... after all, he is undead. He is simply aghast at his own idiocy.

Clouds whisk along the horizon at an alarming speed, laying themselves to rest upon the mountaintops. In the morning, while he sleeps, a blanket of snow will drape itself across their peaks.

The sky grows violet, and Vauquelin is exhausted by his revelations.

He wakes with a heightened vigour and alarm bells sounding in his mind: *don't get too comfortable.*

Vauquelin's Great Time-Slip delivered him back to his origins but it was a bumpy ride, dropping him carelessly into the receding depths of history, decades at a time. And none of this had been his choice.

The concept of homesickness is an insufficient word to describe his longing. In his native French, to miss something is for the thing to be missing from you.

Ça me manques ... "it is missing from me."

France is missing from him.

His existence is missing from him.

Something he cannot identify — something which only manifests as a painful emptiness, a tender bruise upon his soul — is missing from him.

The missings had been bulking up across his many centuries, until he can no longer bear the burden of all that is missing.

Vauquelin must go back. He can see no other way.

From the moment he conceived of this scheme, his mind has not allowed him the luxury of knowing *how* he will make this happen: he only knows it *must* happen.

There is no denying it: he is too old for this world.

It is unnatural for a man to live beyond his allotted years.

In the first half of the seventeenth century, when Vauquelin was born as a human, the average lifespan was thirty-five years. For the aristocracy, it was considerably longer: spared the woes of physical labour, and with access to regular medical care — primitive though it was — many a noble lived well into their eighties.

Louis XIV, his namesake, was seventy-six when he took his last breath.

Had Vauquelin remained a human he might have lived as long as Louis, which would have been feasible given their similar high-bred standings.

He would have died as any other noble died, and his properties would have transferred to some distant relative as he has no direct heir.

In truth, prior to his turning, he had no expectations of living past the age of thirty-five. His human lifestyle was hedonistic, rife with rich food, wine, orgiastic escapades, and manufactured substances.

Though it is unlikely he would have taken up arms and been killed in battle, it is highly likely that he would have died of a lover's disease or the top killer of the era: smallpox.

At the very least, he might have met his demise in a duel (although his swordsmanship was quite legendary in that era).

Despite his countless privileges, Vauquelin's human path would not have afforded him a long life like Louis — he would have been dead within five years had he not been turned.

But Vauquelin the vampire has lived multiple human lifetimes.

It is too much.

It is normal and acceptable for aging humans to buck the strain of societal change and feebly revolt against the unstoppable train of progress. Imagine what that must be like for a revenant whose mind is eternally thirty years old!

Though the vampire body is frozen in time, their mind is subjected to perpetual change. Instinct — and instinct alone — leads the vampire to transmogrify their brain to survive. To blend, to remain in the shadows, to arouse no suspicion: it is the only way to stay alive.

In his futurepast modern existence, he was thoroughly exhausted by the adaptation to and evolution of humanity. And now he is facing doing it a third time. In truth he cannot fathom it, given that absolutely nothing ever turns out the way he plans.

The twenty-first century had been convenient for him. Even so, the consequences of that convenience wrecked his ancient sensibilities: still he could not fully integrate into human society, and found his kind being mocked in popular culture.

When his pages first began turning backward in his futurepast, it was a shock to his system. But the further he retreated in time, the more and more relaxed he felt.

Who among us ever expects time to move backward?

NO ONE.

No one.

But for this vampire, it was sweet, sweet relief.

Familiarity.

Comfort.

Ease.

Survival.

And most importantly, less surveillance and forensics. The modern world is laden with challenges for a vampire, and history (his once-faithful mistress) had turned her back on him.

Now he has to face an awful truth: that his unwavering desire to edit his futurepast mistakes led him down the wrong path.

But Vauquelin was given a choice: twice.

There were some foils along the way, but at that time of his life, he had blinders on. And there is one important lesson he never seems to learn.

Fais attention à ce que vous souhaitez.
BE CAREFUL WHAT YOU WISH FOR.

Twenty-nine

Vauquelin sits naked in the middle of the enormous king-sized bed of his rented house, legs splayed, tapping out searches on the laptop between his knees.

There is not much he wants from the future.

A handful of books, but mostly music.

All these things are digital, and therefore weightless. Whether this technology will survive his fantastic journey, only time will tell.

For everything else, his eidetic memory will suffice.

He is going back where he belongs, and he will conquer his chaotic timelines once and for all.

His chest caves as he chokes back a sob, the breath sucked from his lungs by the weight of realisation, and his heart stops as if he were asleep.

A few days later several parcels arrive.

Deliver after 5:00pm, his note said.

He tips the young man who brings the packages up the ridiculously steep stairs from the ground level, barely casting an eye at him, and locks the door behind him. He slices the tape on each one with his Opinel, and takes inventory of the contents, checking each item off on the list he made on his phone:

- One large leather bag with interior pockets and locks
- Five power banks with solar chargers
- Three sets of ear buds
- A packet of nylon-wrapped phone chargers

He places his hands on his hips with satisfaction.

That is the sum of what he wants from the future.

Music and digital text.

True, he could have saved himself the trouble of travelling all this way under such trepidatious conditions. He could have obtained these very same things in Europe.

But Vauquelin had to come back to Los Angeles.

He once loved this city, tarnished though it is for him now.

Visiting L.A. provides him with a new visual postcard: after all, he had lived here for a century and a quarter. He watched it rise out of the dust into a gleaming beacon of shattered hopes and dreams.

One last look: that is the last item he needs.

He did not mark it on his list because it was a given.

There is still one more ... it is just that he does not know about it.

Yet.

Vauquelin parks at 2721 South Figueroa.

The last time he was here Figueroa was Pearl Street, and the year was 1900. In his first timeline, Maeve left this house to him after her death in 1918, and he lived in it until the twenty-first century.

He has always adored it.

He kills the engine and sits awhile, staring.

Its appearance has changed: drastically.

His instincts say: *let it go.*

Drive on.

As if he could do that!

He opens the car door and looks over both shoulders, at last unfolding his long legs out onto the pavement.

The street is devoid of cars, and certainly of foot traffic: pedestrians in this part of town are rare ... it is off any main drags.

Besides: nobody walks in L.A.

Just at that moment the relative silence (*Los Angeles* silence, that is ... sirens, car horns, helicopters, and the constant hum of tires are ever-present L.A. white noise) is shattered by a clattering cascade of aluminium cans: a homeless person is digging in the dumpster of the Catholic church next door.

His ears tune into the sound of cars zipping along the freeway above his head, and he casts his eyes upward, recalling the moment his time was first corrupted — resulting in the closure of his first timeline.

That night, he was standing on the porch of the very house in front of him — which was once his own — attempting to go out and live his life.

Instead, he witnessed his timeline unravel before his eyes.

But now he turns his attention back to the house, which seems to have been converted into a business of some sort ... he notices a darkened sign mounted just to the left of the door.

A human could not read it: there is no illumination.

But there it is, in steadfast engraved brass:

GREATER LOS ANGELES

PAN-AMERICAN CULTURAL CENTER

Many years ago, there was a copper doorbell in the shape of a satyr's head, covered over in verdigris patina, in the exact spot where that sign now rests.

In 1918 (in his first timeline) there was a large, menacing QUARANTINE poster, warning off any visitors against the Spanish Influenza.

The lawn has been paved over and is defiantly empty, neat white stripes designating parking spaces.

What has Maeve done?

How could she ever have let it go?

Vauquelin imagines the interior as it had been during their glory days together in his first timeline. The memory fills him with a short-lived joy.

He leaps effortlessly over the iron gate and security lights immediately engage. He creeps along the perimeter of the yard and up the front steps.

His eyes land first on the green glow of a key pad, and then dart to multiple cameras, each flashing with insidious red judgement. He presses his face to the window, and his fears are confirmed at once.

The historic house has been brutally stripped of its mahogany wood panelling and hand-cut herringboned floors ... made over into the American twenty-first century (un)ideal: flat grey walls, concrete floors, obtuse furniture that looks comfortable but is not.

Dimly illuminated Edison bulbs hang from industrial ceiling fixtures.

An obscene, overblown floral mural blights one wall and Maeve's endless hardwood bookshelves have been replaced by plain pine plywood shelves, held up by black iron plumbing pipes.

Cold LED track lights.

Soulless hip, the latest thing.

Why humans insist on buying historic properties and lobotomising them, he will never understand.

No doubt the stacks of bones in the cellar rattled the renovators a bit, and for that he is glad.

Still, his heart sinks.

The death of this house sends his resolve into overdrive.

At least his home in Paris is intact: untouched for centuries.

That is where — and when — he belongs.

He cannot bear the sight of the house any longer.

He trudges to the car and pauses a moment, his breath coming in relentless spurts, and kicks a dent in the side.

It is the only way he can keep the blood tears at bay.

Back in his hotel room, he pops the lid on his laptop and an idea strikes him: he browses to a video site and types in "abandoned French château." Hundreds of thumbnails populate the screen, and he scrolls endlessly.

The architecture of storied, monied France is the exact balm his soul needs at this moment, and he watches a few minutes of perhaps twenty videos, until one in particular gives him pause: the rooms look *mighty familiar.*

True, many châteaux share design traits, but ...

He scrubs the video back to the beginning and watches in disbelief as a crew of young men squeeze through an iron fence and make their way across a slightly overgrown lawn, until they reach the front door, so distinguished, yet delightfully decrepit ... and they break the lock.

If it were possible for Vauquelin to get any paler, he does: because they are now standing in the foyer of his château in Évreux.

His breathing stops.

"Look at this valuable antique furniture, left here to rot," the host says. "It looks as if someone left here in a hurry."

It isn't abandoned! I just haven't been home in a while!

(A while ... poor Vauquelin doesn't realise that a hundred years isn't a while for humans!)

They clumsily pull linen drapes off a chaise.

"This is where the master of the castle would have come to meet his guests."

Vauquelin snorts — *Guests, indeed!*

Ha!

He is riveted, and amused!

Until, that is, they begin wandering through his château, room by room, touching his antiques, roughly handling them (although they talk about respecting the property and the objects ... thank god they had the decency to not disclose the precise location).

It's not fucking ABANDONED, *you assholes ...*

Vauquelin's anxiety skyrockets.

If he *had* blood pressure, it would be off the charts.

Instead his heart goes staccato, weakening him.

When the crew reaches his library and begins rifling through the books, ripping pages, he bites his knuckles until they bleed.

They pull the books from the tops of their spines, breaking their fragile leather bindings.

« Ferme ta gueule ... »[†] he whispers, cringing wide-eyed at this roughshod treatment of HIS PRECIOUS THINGS.

They strip the linen off the portrait of his mother on the wall of the library and knock it crooked: one of them straightens it, and a piece of the gilded frame crumbles into dust.

« Oups ! »[‡] Laughter erupts off-camera.

That is the moment Vauquelin truly loses his shit. His eyes dart to the upload date below the video: two months ago.

And five hundred thousand views!

Salaud ![§] *Five hundred thousand humans have eyeballed my interiors?*

---

†- SHUT THE FUCK UP...

‡- OOPS!

§- SON OF A BITCH!

He grabs fistfuls of his hair, nearly tearing it from the roots (it would grow back overnight, but *still*) … and then, with a deep breath, he fires up an email to the channel owner.

> Dear urbafranxe: that magnificent château you rifled through at Évreux is most certainly not abandoned — it is my home! I am proud that it is untouched, and you are unmistakably wrong: the sole descendant (that would be me) is quite appreciative of its contents and has not left it to ROT. If you would care to meet me there, I would be happy to give you a full tour and unlock all the doorknobs you rattled and for which you could not gain entry — I can ease your disappointment.
>
> But know this: if I find even one solitary thing missing, I know where to look, and how to find you: I have memorised every single object in this château, and I will know if anything has been moved even a fraction of a millimetre … so I do hope you left everything precisely as you found it. If not, you are being given the opportunity to make it right.
>
> Meet me there on 31 January at 19:00.
>
> I am yours warmly, etc.,
> Louis dCdV
> Los Angeles, Calif.

He thinks a moment and types in his mobile number as a P.S., adding "ok to text" and hits SEND.

The insidious digital clock on the nightstand catches his eye as it turns: 03:15. He instantly calculates that it is 12:15 in Paris.

Centuries of life are no match for a foolish clock. No matter where (or when) he lands, his vampire body will remain faithful to him.

It is the only aspect of his existence he can rely on at this point.

He lies on the bed and flips through the cable channels, stopping on a yoga program.

How *very* Los Angeles.

But what could it hurt?

He follows the poses: downward dog and warrior.

Ridiculous.

To his surprise, his muscles respond: his agitated heart steadies into its slow, comforting vampire rhythm. It slowly dissipates the anger the video had unleashed within him, and the practitioner's voice soothes him.

When the practice ends, he flicks over to the 24-hour news channel. This promptly erases the peace and calm he achieved from the yoga poses.

He has an advantage over humans who sleep through the night: all the stories that really matter are aired while they slumber away.

In the span of thirty minutes, he is so sufficiently depressed by humanity that his intention to return to his origin era is steeled even more. At least, in his more ancient and backward times, people were upfront about their biases and bigotry.

Here, in modern times, the human commerce machine uses advertising to show their support for various causes du jour,[†] while in the back alleys of capitalism, they feed money to politicians to legislate people's rights away.

Perhaps, he thinks, things are easier when one knows where one stands and is not given lip service by shiny media faces and influencers.

And in his vampire reality, he grows ever more jaded by what the future will yield. Progress is a malignant joke and comes in a riptide, sucking back into itself and coughing up the dredges in broken shells and seaweed.

The past cannot come fast enough.

He belongs nowhere except seventeenth-century France, in his own time: and he aims to stay there.

Bring it on, he whispers.

I am ready.

---

†- CAUSES OF THE DAY

Part
Two

LOS ANGELES, CALIFORNIA | DECEMBER 31

LAST YEAR

Vauquelin's hourglass is down to the dregs, depositing its last granules on his time in Los Angeles: or so he thinks.

The city is in the throes of celebration ... the death of one year, the birth of another. So many years ... but their passage bears little meaning to an immortal predator.

Vauquelin has kept mostly to the confines of his lodgings on this trip, writing notes and planning for his imminent return to Paris: and to his past. But its walls, magnificent night views aside, make him claustrophobic: the house is not very large. It does not matter ... only two more nights remain until he returns to Paris.

On the spur of the moment he decides to take himself out on the town.

A quick scan of the maps app on his phone yields an upscale nightclub on Sunset — he chooses it simply because it is a fairly quick, uncomplicated drive from his temporary house.

He is in pursuit, but not of blood: he cannot yet identify that which he chases, nor can he know he is on the verge of finding it — or, rather, that it is about to find him.

It won't be long now.

Vauquelin cuts a rather modernised version of how he used to look at his origin: he is wearing new black lambskin trousers which fit him as if they were painted on his body, and a cropped magenta jacket — with an innocently sinister peek of ivory lace emerging from its cuffs. On his feet: sharply pointed black boots. They remind him of a pair of shoes he had worn in the late seventeenth century. His hair cascades in smooth obsidian waves, coming to a rest upon his shoulders.

As he slinks through the crowd he delivers devastating grins to those who knock into him, dragging his icy gaze up and down bodies, searching for that something. Whatever it is, he doubts he will find it in this space — nevertheless, his eyes are open.

He has been here for an hour, still no closer to any revelations.

His theft of *petit* blood snacks all evening has polished the edges of his bloodlust smooth. A bit of enchantment here, neck nip there, and no one is the wiser.

A sweet alcoholic haze medicates the melancholy in his veins.

He twists his wrist.

It is 23:15.

Less than an hour to go until everyone loses their collective minds.

Humans are besotted with this annual ritual: the proverbial turning of the page, the freshness of a brand-new year ... an opportunity to change things for the better.

Even knowing, deep down, their lives will remain the same.

And he knows his will, too.

Unless —

A woman writhes under his arm as he checks his watch.

"Well ... hello there," he says, lifting only his heavy-lidded eyes.

"Helloooooo." She sips her drink through a tiny cocktail straw, sucking the remainder down, and serendipitously pops an ice cube into

Vauquelin's mouth.

His eyes widen and he smiles in surprise, working his tongue to melt it.

A quick survey of his unanticipated prey reveals a specific species: the Edgy Los Angeles Girl. An electric blue streak in her hair, ballsy, hot body ... and she knows it.

Dressed in black.

Goth is all the rage, you know.

But she has flipped a hidden switch in Vauquelin, arousing his drowsy hunger with her capricious act.

Potential victims do not typically fall in his lap in this manner, and he ponders what fantastical flavours he might discover in her blood cascading down his throat.

Even so, he must be cautious.

He cannot consume a full quantity of drugged blood.

He bends down and murmurs, "What are you on?" as he brushes her neck with the tip of his nose.

A sexual little grunt escapes her throat.

He *loves* it when they do that.

"Vodka tonics," she purrs.

"Nothing else? Can you get me something?"

It is a little trial of his own ... his means for determining whether a human's blood is clean. In his first timeline, he had been decimated by unknowingly drinking a human's ecstasy-laden blood.

It took him down for weeks: he thought he had achieved his Final Death.

Now he takes no chances.

She struggles under his grip.

"No-uhhhhh! I don't do that shit. Fuck off."

She attempts to pry his fingers from her arm.

"No, no ... that's good. I was only verifying." He releases her and folds his arms. "As a matter of fact, I despise drugs."

She stops struggling.

"You do? Well, aren't you original."

"Everyone in L.A. seems to love them. But not me."

"Yeah? Well, what's your kink, then?"

"My ... *kink*?" His face contorts.

"You said everyone in L.A. loves drugs. True. But if they aren't into that, then they definitely have some other kink. So what's yours?"

Vauquelin grasps his jaw.

My kink, he thinks ... *is that what one could call my nature?*

She runs a hand down his abdomen, and he follows her movement with his eyes.

He wraps a finger and thumb around her wrist when she reaches his belt buckle, poking the tip of his tongue out and shaking his head.

"Uh oh ... are you gay? Or bi or something?" she asks.

This is an extremely personal question and it pisses him off.

He is unaccustomed to the candour of modern youth.

"Why do you ask me this?"

"I mean, I have a whole table full of hot male friends." She gestures to a table, and Vauquelin turns his head. "And none of them do fucking *drugs,* if that's what you're worried about. Like, maybe some edibles now and then, but that's not —"

"Or something," he interrupts.

"Come on," she says, taking him by the hand. "I know just who you need to meet."

Vauquelin hesitates as she tugs.

But perhaps he just needs to relax.

Isn't he entitled to a little fun?

He slackens his arm and permits the girl to lead him across the dance floor to the other side of the club. By the time they arrive at a circular corner booth, Vauquelin has already troubled his mind with myriad second thoughts — wondering why he has put himself in this ungraceful situation — and teeters on the verge of flight: until he glimpses the faces of her friends.

They are all gorgeous.

Extraordinarily so.

The combined fragrance of their blood intoxicates him and his ankle buckles, prompting him to lean on the table — though he does his best to make it look intentional — with an awkward, close-lipped smile plastered across his face.

"Who's your friend, Megs?"

She tucks a hand under Vauquelin's elbow, and he is grateful for the support. He uprights himself and flattens her close against his ribcage, absorbing her warmth.

Hoisting onto her tiptoes, she whispers in his ear.

"Go on. Introduce yourself."

"Clément," he says.

Of all the false names to conjure! Why that one?

Simultaneous questions pepper him, and each occupant of the booth looks up at him with an expectant expression.

He looks like he must be Somebody, but then again, so do many in Los Angeles. Everyone has an angle here.

"What do you do?"

"Are you in a band?"

"Badass jacket!"

"Where are you from?"

His eyes dart from question to question.

The only answer he can manage is "I am from France."

Their focused attention overwhelms him.

They reach out to touch him.

He jerks his hands back, extending his spine, and everyone flinches.

"Dude, relax. We won't bite."

Vauquelin huffs out a laugh, keeping his lips tight.

But I might.

It is another moment that makes him realise how ill-equipped he is to exist among mortals. He will never be one of them, no matter how desperately he wants it … no matter how accepting they seem to be on the surface.

"Come on, join us!"

The humans compress their bodies in the booth, making room for him on the edge, and he sits with his arms folded on the table, his body rigid as a mannequin.

One of the guys reaches across the table and taps his forearm, startling him. He had been so quiet that Vauquelin had scarcely registered his presence.

"Hi. I'm Eric."

Eric's lopsided grin, and the subsequent curly lock of dark hair which drops over his eye, makes Vauquelin's heart do a little somersault.

But he has no time to react, as a server has approached the table.

"Another round," the girl says, pointing at the bottles and glasses littering the table. "… and what are you having, Claymont?"

"Red wine, please."

He scrutinises the group intently, saying nothing.

They are affectionate with one another, laughing, whispering.

They seem to be old friends.

Eric glances at him repeatedly, pretending not to, but the girl notices.

The corners of her mouth curl into an impish grin and she quirks her brows, looking back and forth between the two of them — which makes Vauquelin even more uncomfortable.

Are they playing some kind of joke on me?

He tamps down the spark of anger that flares within him and narrows his eyes. Beneath the table, his foot begins to twitch.

With each passing second, Vauquelin's self-consciousness intensifies, despite their attempts to draw him in.

What the hell is he doing here?

He understands nothing of their chatter, the music is far too loud for him to grasp their nuances, and his patience is wearing thin.

Ça fout tout[†] ... why did I think this was a good idea?

The clock is ticking, the wine still has not arrived, and he finds himself unsure what to do with his hands. In bars, a glass of wine is a reliable lifeline for him, a crutch to give him a somewhat ordinary appearance.

He caresses his chin with his thumb, draping his forefinger across his upper lip, and considers his next move.

The mirthful, boisterous conversations battling across the table hurt his sensitive ears and threaten to send him into mayhem.

He slides out of the booth and reaches into his pocket, dropping several large bills on the table.

"It is time for me to go. Your drinks are on me. Enchanted to meet you all," he says, avoiding eye contact, and strides out of the club.

He stops just outside the door and lights a cigarette, tapping his fingers on the car keys in his pocket. Perhaps it was impolite that he did not wish them a good year, but at this moment Vauquelin has nothing to feel good about. All he has is his familiar solitude, always upon his back like a favourite coat.

Few cars pass ... everyone is indoors celebrating.

The dull, bass-laden thump of the club music bleeds out into the night air, percussed by sporadic neighbourhood fireworks: a long-time tradition on New Year's Eve in the City of Angels.

"Hello, again." Eric appears by Vauquelin's side and points to his

----

† - EVERYTHING IS FUCKED

cigarette. "Could I have one of those?"

Vauquelin hesitates, biting the inside of his cheek, filling his mouth with the soothing taste of iron, his salve.

He had been mere seconds away from leaving.

He cuts his gaze to his car — it is just there, right across the street.

But then he looks back to Eric, whose handsome, friendly face reminds him that he must begin tearing down his walls. There is no time like the present ... and it is much easier to do with one human versus a group.

He shrugs and places the cigarette between his lips, rolling a fresh one for Eric, and lights it for him — surreptitiously making an assessment.

Slender. Thick, loose curls shining under the street light, not quite as dark as Vauquelin's own, stopping just above his jawline. Half-inch silver hoops adorn each earlobe, accenting his strong jaws.

Smartly dressed, in all black like the girl who had introduced them.

Vauquelin allows his eyes to travel down.

Eric ...

There is something about him.

Something a vampire cannot readily dismiss.

Their eyes are level. They are almost exactly the same height.

Vauquelin's heartbeat revs.

"Thanks! Was the noise too much for you?" Eric shoves his free hand in his pocket and begins to babble, covertly studying Vauquelin. "I know how it is. They had to drag me out tonight — I wanted to stay in. I don't really like going clubbing, especially on New Year's Eve. It's way too peopley. So how do you know Megan?"

"Who?"

Eric's hand trembles as he lifts the cigarette to his lips, belying his initial confidence, and it bewilders Vauquelin.

Is this young man afraid of him?

"My friend, Megan. The girl who brought you over."

"Ah. I do not know her … I just met her tonight."

"Oh, okay. So you're just out by yourself? That's kind of sad."

Vauquelin cringes. "Is it?"

"Well, yeah. Luckily Megan found you! Do you live here?"

"I am only in town for a few more nights, then I will return to Paris."

And then it happens.

The countdown.

10 …

9 …

"Do you not wish to return to your friends?" Vauquelin whispers.

8 …

7 …

"No." Eric expels an emphatic blue plume of smoke.

6 …

5 …

Their eyes lock.

4 …

3 …

Silence enshrouds Vauquelin's ears as Eric flicks his stub to the curb.

2 …

1 …

Eric sneaks an arm around Vauquelin's waist and kisses him deeply.

"Happy New Year," he whispers.

Vauquelin leans back like an offended cat and juts out his chin, searching Eric's face.

No human has ever just … spontaneously *kissed* him.

Not in the entire span of his bloody interminable life.

Eric's wholesome bravery charms him: and it also widens a crevice deep in the hollow caverns of Vauquelin's spirit … the one that had been recently fissured by Clove and the boys.

By their unity.

Their *us*.

Occasionally, life still delivers him unexpected delights, and when they occur, they become indispensable.

Like this one.

He curls his long fingers around Eric's elbow and guides him across the street, unlocking the Ferrari with his key fob on the way.

Its lights flash, punctuating the darkness on the street.

Eric claps his hands to his head. "Are you fucking kidding me right now? This is like my favourite car ever! I always wanted to ride in one!"

Vauquelin smiles broadly, though he keeps his lips closed, and opens the passenger door, gesturing with his hand.

"Well, then ... get in. Let's take that ride. Come have a drink with me."

"Hell yeah."

Vauquelin retracts the electronic top on the car, and soon the motor howls as they speed across the 101 to his exit.

Thirty-one

The car heroically handles the twisted hairpin turns on Mulholland as they wind higher and higher up into the Hollywood Hills, the night sky illuminated by thousands of fireworks — constant excruciating whistles and rumbles bounce off the canyons in repeated raucous echoes.

Halfway into the drive, Eric's phone blows up with messages, chiming in rapid succession.

> Where did u run off to
> We're leaving
> Meet us at the car

"Ha! They're all wondering where I am," Eric says.
"Tell them you will be just fine."

> the hills.
> i left with that french guy

> You did NOT! I KNEW IT!
> I called this! He's hot.
> Weird, but hot.
> You're welcome ;)
> Where r u guys, can we come?

"They want to join us."

Vauquelin parks the car in front of the garage, stiffly shifting his body to face Eric.

"Would you like to invite them?" His jacket falls open and Eric's eyes travel across his collarbone.

Eric types a reply quickly with his thumbs:

not telling
muting my phone now ;)

"Nope." Eric stretches his legs out on the floorboard and tucks the phone in his pocket.

The driveway is at ground-level and the house is half-built up into a hill. They walk up a steep cement staircase to the front door, which Vauquelin opens with a keypad, inviting Eric to walk inside first.

He drops his car keys on a table.

"I have wine, if you would like," he says from the kitchen. "I have no other drink except water."

"Wine's good." Eric beelines to the patio door. "Wow, this view is badass! You can see everything up here. Do you own this place?"

Vauquelin returns with a bottle and two glasses. "Leasing. I do not like this unimaginative modern decor, it is not my style. I lived in Los Angeles for many years ... I once owned a Victorian house downtown. But this time, I am only visiting."

He passes one to Eric, and sprawls back across the red sofa.

"Damn, there's a lot of flowers in here ... did someone die?" As the words leave Eric's lips, a bright crimson steals across his cheeks. "Oh god, I'm sorry ... that was so rude. Sometimes I have zero filter."

A glimmer of amusement crinkles Vauquelin's eyes. "No. It so happens that I adore flowers. They are a necessity for me. Come closer," he says, patting the spot next to him.

Eric flops down and scoots over.

Vauquelin leans toward him, resting his elbows on his knees.

His eyes are exceptionally bright blue tonight.

"My name is not really Clément," he says. "It is Louis-Augustin de Vauquelin."

And the walls come tumbling down.

"Then why did you say that?"

"I do not really know," Vauquelin says, rolling his shoulders and leaning back into the sofa. That one small truth lifted so much weight. "Tonight, maybe I just wished to be someone else."

"I get it. L.A. has that effect on people. It's an easy place to reinvent yourself for sure. I was born in Mexico but I've lived here since I was a baby. Sometimes it feels like I'm one of maybe five people in this city who actually grew up here. My last name is Castañeda. So there." He strokes Vauquelin's knee with a fingertip. "Now we aren't strangers."

Vauquelin shivers.

The heat of Eric's small gesture careens up his leg, and he unwinds a fraction. "I am honoured to know you, Eric Castañeda."

Crumbling stone by ancient stone.

Eric's easy-going air takes him unawares.

Vauquelin is not approachable by any stretch of the imagination, nor is he accustomed to making humans comfortable.

But Eric is treating him as though he is — normal.

It is a bizarre observation.

Still, Vauquelin makes no move toward him in return.

The thought of it petrifies him, because if he touches Eric his self-control will completely evaporate.

Only twice before have humans responded to him in this manner, and both of those affairs ended in misery.

Centuries ago, Vauquelin's maker had criticised him repeatedly about his sympathy for mortals.

But this is now ... a brand-new year, according to the calendar.

Humans love the opportunity for a fresh start.

Maybe the universe is telling him something.

Maybe he should listen.

Maybe ...

He inches his knee toward Eric, stopping himself just short.

He retrieves his glass from the table, agitating his fingers on the stem and then bringing the rim to his lips.

"Okay," Eric huffs, bringing his hand to the back of his neck. "You need to chill. I'm nervous as fuck and you aren't helping. Please tell me this isn't your first time with a guy."

Vauquelin almost chokes on his sip of wine. "Oh, my sweet. That is hardly the issue. Are you truly that unaware of the effect you're having on me?"

Eric blinks rapidly. "How old are you?" he asks.

Vauquelin purses his lips.

He despises this mortal question.

"I am thirty. I will always be thirty." Fingers straight back to the glass.

"Forever young, huh? That's cool. Maybe you should stay in L.A. — we've got plenty of plastic surgeons to make that possible for you!"

"I don't need help." Vauquelin downs the last of the wine and pours another, fixating on a fallen petal from the vase of ranunculus on the table. He cannot avert his gaze from it: for if he does he will meet Eric's eyes again, and now he is unsure if he can bear it.

They are too earnest, too open.

He can see far too much in them.

But Vauquelin does not have to look ... because suddenly Eric's hands are buried in his hair, Eric is kissing his eyelids, his temples, and he fades away into oblivion.

A small sigh trembles in Vauquelin's throat as Eric's warm hand roams beneath his jacket, as Eric's mortal lips caress his undead ones.

Vauquelin allows his fingertips to trip up Eric's rib bones, coming to rest on his heart, absorbing the reverberation of its healthy, heavy beats through his hand and into his own body.

He seizes Eric's wrist, drawing their hands behind his own back.

Their eyes drill into one another and all hell breaks loose.

Limbs and tongues are intertwined, shoes are kicked off, shirts and belts are flying ... the bottle is knocked over and bleeding merlot all over the white shag rug.

This is where Vauquelin must stop, and he does — paralysed by want and bereft from it at the same time.

He braces his arm against Eric's breastbone.

"Wait, Eric. Please."

His blood is tingling.

Something uncoils within him.

It slithers through his marrow.

This is a test of his will ... of his very being.

Sex is kindred with Death for Vauquelin ... she waits eternally in the wings for her spoils.

There is only one precedent for this exact situation: Maeve.

Not in this timeline of course — but the first night he met her, hundreds of years ago in the murky recesses of his futurepast. His anima demands something that the human in him finds abhorrent. He must forbid that instinct, lock it away — if he can.

That remains to be seen.

"You're so cold," Eric says. "Do you want to turn on the fire?" But as he speaks his eyes tick to the electric fireplace, which is already blazing, and he realises he himself is sweaty. "What's going on?" Eric asks, his voice heightening in urgency. "Are you okay?"

Vauquelin parts his lips, resisting an escalating urge to tell Eric the truth. But does it matter?

Right now, the truth of their mutual attraction, evident by their hips smashed together in tightening pants, seems more urgent.

"I am always cold. Follow me."

Vauquelin disentangles himself and leads Eric down the hall to his bedroom, flinging the duvet back. He stretches his arms across the edge of the bed, crossing his ankles, peering across the expanse of the mattress.

I should not be doing this.

His heart thrums in his ribcage.

Nevertheless he sucks in his breath, strips off his leather trousers and lies down, closing his eyes.

They fly open when the bed dips and the torrid length of Eric's body skims along his own.

Their skins electrify upon contact.

Delicate kisses escalate into fiery ones as their hands explore.

Oh, how well their lips fit together!

Vauquelin draws his nose across Eric's chest to his armpit.

Ummmph.

He extends Eric's arm over his head and buries his face there, momentarily debilitated by his maleness, by his heady human scent.

Here and now Vauquelin rejects his darkness, pretends he is just an ordinary person losing himself in pleasure without purpose: without a kill waiting for him at the end.

He reaches over and opens the nightstand drawer, yet he does not take anything from inside.

Your move, he says — in his silent, clandestine vampire way.

The very human Eric is incapable of hearing that voice.

But he does know what is usually kept obscured in bedside drawers.

His gaze drifts from the nightstand to Vauquelin and back.

He reaches in and extracts a bottle — raking nervous eyes to Vauquelin, verifying his unspoken meaning.

In answer Vauquelin does something he has never once done in bed. He releases everything, making himself completely vulnerable, surrenders what remains of his self-restraint.

Vauquelin gets on his hands and knees.

Pleasure ripples across his senses as Eric kisses the smooth small of his back and taunts him with slippery fingers. Vauquelin unfurls slowly like a repressed flower half-starved for sunlight at Eric's touch.

Eric's other hand trembles as he draws it over his own cock.

He's not usually the one in this position.

What if he's no good?

His courage fluctuates — but then it amplifies the moment Vauquelin accepts him into his body.

Stars of pain flood Vauquelin's eyes, quickly extinguished by a blissful energy — an escalating euphoria he never knew existed within him. Mesmerising emotion courses through his body, dizzying him, caressing every nerve ending, enrapturing his plasma.

Vauquelin has given Eric carte blanche[†] into an unspoiled region in his body, an immaculate location for which only he holds the key. But Eric has no way of realising the significance of this: at this moment, only Vauquelin knows.

Eric grasps Vauquelin's waist: his skin is so cold, yet inside he's blazing — embracing Eric in a dizzying, cathartic heat.

All of a sudden ownership of his own body dissipates. His hips move in a motion foreign to him, and he surrenders to this unreality, losing his sense of where he ends and Vauquelin begins.

Vauquelin bites his lower lip, scattering bloody droplets onto the sheets with every thrust, and grinds his teeth as the splendourous sensation peaks

---

†- A BLANK PAGE: COMPLETE FREEDOM TO ACT AS ONE WISHES

and begins to wane.

He does not want it to ever stop — his spirit panics, frightened by this unanticipated euphoria and desperate to conserve it. That when it ends he might disappear along with it.

He is unaware that, behind him, Eric is having his own transfigurative experience ... for Vauquelin cannot see the expression of mystified exhilaration that has taken over Eric's face.

Eric's head lolls back and a guttural growl escapes from his throat as he withdraws and spurts hot, silky streams across Vauquelin's spine.

Vauquelin draws a finger across his lower back and promptly plunges it into his mouth. The flavour disrupts his reality — it sends a shiver racing through his veins.

They both collapse on their backs, panting.

"Fuck," Eric gasps, dragging his hands through his hair. "*Fuuuuck.*"

The only sound in the room is their staccato breathing.

Vauquelin hopes Eric will not notice the blood spots on the sheets.

That would be difficult to explain, and he has not yet decided what the outcome of this night will be.

Vauquelin cannot understand the panicked emptiness of his body without Eric inside it.

He turns on his side and drapes an arm across Eric's chest, trying — and failing — to disguise his tremulous hands and hold fast to the sensation. His breath refuses to calm.

He draws his eyes down their clinging bodies.

His chilled porcelain skin is a marked contrast to Eric's blood-warm, olive complexion.

Eric caresses Vauquelin's foot with his own ... this unbearably delicate and intimate endearment rockets new splinters of rapture across Vauquelin's flesh.

Both of them lie still as statues, breath slowing, eyes widened in the dark, wondering what the hell just transpired between them.

"I am always the top," Vauquelin struggles out.

"Yeah?" Eric whispers. "Well, pretty sure you just turned me into a vers."

Vauquelin does not know this term. *Vers?* He translates it into something that makes sense, nuzzling Eric's face. "That can only mean something miraculous," he says, glancing at the clock on the nightstand. It is half-past two. "Stay with me a while?"

Eric cannot get any words to his tongue — he can only nod in wonder.

When Vauquelin places his feet on the floor and attempts to stand, the muscles in his legs vibrate like overwrought violin strings.

Now his intentions have become even more obscure.

"Give me a moment," he whispers. "I'll meet you out there."

Eric slips out the bedroom door.

The moment the door latch catches, Vauquelin drops his face to the sheets and drags his nose and lips across the sullied surface, drawing in the earthy, seawater perfume of Eric's ejaculation, his own blood, and the magical scent of their united bodies ... the resulting humanity, something he had come close to so seldom in his life. He lies prostrate on the deliciously filthy results of their joining, indelibly imprinting it into his senses.

Vauquelin emerges a few moments later and takes another bottle of wine from the kitchen, nodding toward the terrace door.

Eric follows him out to the jacuzzi and they sink down side-by-side, the steaming water jetting around their bodies.

A shy silence settles between them and Eric is the one to break it.

"So do you go by Louis?"

"No. I have only ever been Vauquelin." He leans to the edge and rolls two immaculate cigarettes. He places both between his lips and lights them, passing one to Eric, still struggling to meet his pointed glance.

Eric accepts it, agitating it in his fingers, nervously ashing on the sill of the jacuzzi. He whispers "*Vauquelin, Vauquelin,*" rolling it around in his mouth like a piece of exotic, luxurious candy.

The sound of the name hangs heavy in the air between them, ensnared in riotous clouds of cigarette smoke and steam.

It is a night of new beginnings and firsts.

Vauquelin continues obliterating his rules, trying on this unfamiliar cloak of honesty. His walls have already been compromised: now he aims to demolish them, fists out.

An unquenchable urgency skyrockets in his chest and before he realises it, the sacred revelation he has always fought so vehemently to conceal bursts from his lips.

"I am vampire."

Eric's resulting incredulous stare evolves into an eruption of unbridled laughter. He draws his chin down, still laughing — until he glances up again to meet Vauquelin's humourless expression.

His smile vanishes.

"Oh my GAWD. You seriously believe that?" Eric drags his hands down his face. "I knew you were too good to be true. Why does everyone in this town have to be a fucking weirdo?" he asks the sky.

"You felt my teeth, no? Allow me to prove it. Give me your hand."

"Uh, yeah, *obviously*. But I just figured you've got a goth thing going on." Eric hesitates, then flings out an arm.

What could it hurt?

He's seen these fake fang guys in the clubs before.

So not a big deal.

"It was actually kinda hot, if I'm honest."

Vauquelin taps the thick vein below Eric's thumb, bringing it to the surface. He drives in his teeth — and oh, is that blood delectable!

His eyes flutter as it slides down his throat like hot honey, and he sighs as he drinks: his chin vibrates.

Eric freaks when he sees the indescribable delirium on Vauquelin's face.

What the FUCK *is going on right now?*

"Owowow!" Eric tries to pull his hand back but Vauquelin's teeth are embedded in his flesh, and he groans from the pain.

"Regard," Vauquelin says, caressing the marks. He lifts his fingertips to his lips and quells the blood away with a flick of his tongue.

The wounds fold back into Eric's skin, disappearing before their eyes.

"Holy fucking shit!" Eric vaults out of the jacuzzi, slamming his back against the glass patio door and rattling its panes. "Are you gonna kill me?"

"Absolutely not. If I were, we would not be having this extremely awkward conversation. You would already be dead. Come back."

Eric's breath catches in his throat.

His eyes scurry as he searches his muddled brain for where he left his phone — it's probably buried under the pile of clothes on the living room floor.

He plots his escape route, preparing to bolt. But then he stops cold and fumbles at the door, gripping the handle.

His body is still quivering with aftershocks of the bizarre magnetism he felt inside this strange man's body and throughout his own.

He recalls the uncommon ease he had felt in Vauquelin's presence all night. Not for one single moment had he been frightened of him — except for now.

He tilts his head and a puzzled expression settles on his face.

"Eric ... I promise you are not going to die. Come back. Please."

Eric takes reluctant steps back into the jacuzzi and sinks down opposite Vauquelin. With his hands between his knees, he stares vacantly into the furious bubbles, subtly rocking back and forth.

Vauquelin reaches for his shoulder but Eric hoists a decisive palm up.

"Dude, just give me a minute. This is a lot to process."

"I never admit this to anyone. *Never*," Vauquelin says.

Eric glowers. "Is that supposed to make me feel special?"

"Well ... yes! I do not make a habit of broadcasting this fact about myself. Think about it. I could have killed you already, easily. Or I could have just sent you on your way, and never made this confession. But you cannot deny it — something significant has occurred between us tonight, Eric." Vauquelin slumps back in the water and gnaws on his thumb.

Just that one slight, minuscule sampling of Eric's blood is sending Vauquelin's mind into a frenzy and his back arches in discomfort.

The unnatural blue lights in the jacuzzi, broken in increments by its rollicking jets, cast an eerie, dancing glow upon both of their skins — but they make Vauquelin look thoroughly transcendental.

Eric has to admit he's intrigued by Vauquelin's manner: he doesn't behave or speak like anyone he's ever met, but then again, he hasn't been around that many Europeans. Or vampires, for that matter!

But god, the way their bodies moved together ... he's still not over it.

Besides all that — he's completely addicted to the way his name sounds when Vauquelin says it ... *Air-eek*, with a barely-audible *uh* at the end.

At last Eric locks Vauquelin's eyes into his own. "No, I can't."

He holds out his hand and Vauquelin pulls him closer. He leans his head on Vauquelin's shoulder. "Not much has happened to me in my life. But in my guts I know this is big. Maybe the biggest."

Vauquelin smooths Eric's curls back and drops a series of kisses across his forehead.

"I was born in 1638. I was made vampire thirty years later, and so I will always be thirty years old. I must consume blood to stay alive. I am caught in a ceaseless vortex of beauty and horror. That is my reality. I have lived through countless years, Eric, and I have had many lovers — but they rarely survive a night with me. I do not fall easily."

At the mention of falling, Eric swerves his head in a dramatic arc to look up at Vauquelin.

This is fucking insane, Eric thinks, drawing his brows together.

Even so, he wants to drink it up, to bathe in this unanticipated deadly seduction — he wants all of it.

Now.

To let it destroy him, if that's what it takes.

Vauquelin misinterprets Eric's reaction and looks away, drifting his eyes across the expanse of twinkling lights on the hills. "Still you think I am lying to you."

It appears that, even in the midst of pure sincerity, Vauquelin is incapable of escaping his shackles of lies.

He is eternally restrained by deception.

Perhaps that is the true curse of the vampire — and he cannot break loose from it any more than he could shed his own skin.

"No," Eric says. "I have proof." He holds up his perfect, unharmed wrist, and draws a fingertip down the violet-green path of the vein Vauquelin had bitten.

He swivels, landing between Vauquelin's legs, drawing a hand up through the water. "Take me back inside. I need more."

Even with Eric fast asleep in his bed, Vauquelin fights his slumber: especially since Eric's phone, now parked on the bedside table, vibrates repeatedly.

Vauquelin glances at it:

r u ok?
u better answer, Eric! >:(
if u don't answer soon i'm calling police!

On that note Vauquelin retrieves the phone and swipes up, holding it in front of Eric's face to unlock it, and replies: mimicking (accurately, he hopes) Eric's manner of speech.

I'm totally fine!
I'm hanging out in the Hills.
This house is badass.
Don't worry
Just be happy for me <3

Then he powers off the phone and drifts off to sleep himself, one leg intertwined with Eric's.

Thirty-two

LOS ANGELES, CALIFORNIA | JANUARY 1
THIS YEAR

Vauquelin has been sitting in a chair for several hours, wide awake in the protective bedroom, safe behind the thick, doubled-up blackout curtains which banish the deadly rays of the sun. He grazes his knuckles back and forth against his jaw, psychoanalysing himself and watching Eric dream.

His frenetic mind refuses to surrender him to his much-needed rest.

The night before last, his plans had been transparent ... he had accomplished what he set out for in Los Angeles and was prepared to return home, and — if he could ever manage to decipher the mystery of time travel — back to his origins.

To the seventeenth century.

In truth he has been chastising himself since the moment Eric first sat down in his car.

Vauquelin's extraordinary longevity affords him a unique skill: he can read any human soul like a book.

Despite this, you have often been wrong.

ARRÊTE ÇA ![†] he admonishes the voice, slamming his hands to his ears.

---

†- STOP IT!

This ... this is not the same.

It all sounds very romantic, no? But Vauquelin has often tasted regret in the blood of his victims, regret that was his alone: for ending a promising life. Many times he has chosen poorly, and he has to live with this wretchedness.

Those are the ones that haunt him still.

In his first timeline, he never once partook of Maeve's blood: not even a pinprick as he had done with Eric. He locked her away from ever learning he was vampire. But in this one, in which he turned her, his tongue was tainted with regret — only he had not admitted it to himself until now.

In Eric's blood, he discovered a quite unexpected essence: strength in solitude. And Eric's solitude is so similar to his own it illuminates Vauquelin's very soul.

What remains of it, that is.

Some humans believe in fate ... others, not so much. Be that as it may, Vauquelin has every reason to be its slave — he must acknowledge that there is a purpose for his and Eric's paths crossing last night.

Now all his prior plans ring hollow in his ears and his strategy has been thwarted: his eternally enigmatic puzzle is slipping into its destined order, piece by piece.

Vauquelin was not destined to be with Maeve. Had he been, he would have been truthful with her from the very beginning. He had deceived them both. And in turn, he blighted Maeve's life — nearly taking himself down with her. Turning her was an unforgivable transgression, fuelled by his own arrogance.

He should never have attempted to toy with history. He learned this when he saw her that night on the street — but the lesson came far too late.

Lying to oneself is perhaps the greatest sin of all — for there may be innumerable casualties in the wake of such sin.

Eric had accomplished something monumental, without even knowing it: he inspired Vauquelin to bring his truth to the forefront and question his disdain for the present — subverting his belief that modern times mean nothing to him. Forced him to consider that maybe he needn't run away from his current reality ... that he should embrace it, in the same manner he has now embraced his own authenticity.

That he must no longer hide from himself.

There is only one problem: it could all be taken away from him in an instant.

Eric's sudden appearance in Vauquelin's life has cracked his firmament like an earthquake, and brought another fear to the surface: that he will leave today and Vauquelin will never see him again.

How could he possibly expect Eric to feel the same?

Vampires cannot survive on capricious decisions. There have been few instances in his life where Vauquelin threw caution to the wind.

This is one of those times and he will not hesitate — despite the fact that happiness terrifies him ... because, unlike Death, it never, ever lasts.

All these concepts war in his brain until they are interrupted by Eric propping himself on his elbows.

"Oh my god, what time is it? Did I sleep the whole day?"

Eric is still here.

Despite my fantastic tales, despite everything.

Vauquelin rises tall in the chair.

"It is not yet noon." Vauquelin crosses and sits on the edge of the bed, taking Eric's hand. "I have a question to ask you. I cannot let you leave me without knowing the answer."

And Vauquelin ponders what he will do if —

Just then Eric laces his fingers into Vauquelin's, bringing their hands to his lips. "I need coffee." His stomach growls. "And, like, a burrito the size of my head."

Coffee? Food? The kitchen is empty!

So human. So very human, this boy.

Vauquelin had the forethought to bring Eric a glass of water ... but he had not exactly planned to have a living guest, and he cannot possibly be expected to remember that mortals have such basic needs.

"Later. How old are you? I have not yet asked." Vauquelin asks.

"Guess," Eric yawns.

"Twenty ... six?"

"Close. Twenty four. Twenty five on May eleventh."

Vauquelin grasps the nape of Eric's neck and holds him fast.

Eric snuggles into Vauquelin's deathgrip with a drowsy smile and he does not break the gaze, which sends Vauquelin plummeting even deeper.

For eight hundred years — across the span of fractured timelines — he has walked the earth, dancing back and forth across the pages of history.

He has seen ...

Capitals fall.

Generations of deaths.

Countries severed like limbs and renamed, reattached ... their citizens scattered to the broad corners of the earth. Sometimes those limbs fester and must be removed again. Buildings come up and down, styles fall in and out of favour, technology emerges, becomes obsolete, and evolves.

Loved ones die, or turn their backs to him.

Betrayal.

Indiscretion.

Disloyalty.

He has felt great love but it has always been temporary.

He has made substantial errors in judgement, as all who are born human will. Yet the vast majority of his existence has been just that: merely existing, in self-imposed exile, hidden safely behind his impenetrable walls — which were erected upon a fraudulent foundation.

Alone.

Protected.

And now he is on the verge of shattering that steeled safety he has relied upon for aeons — of discarding his (frankly) dubious plans to the four winds.

It all distils into this moment.

His consciousness swirls with the events of this extraordinary turn of a year, events which would have not occurred had he jumped in his car and left instead of having that one last cigarette — had Eric not fearlessly lifted his enigmatic veil.

Eric is a gift.

I do not deserve him.

Even so, he proceeds.

"Are you happy with your age?" As soon as the words leave his mouth, Vauquelin drags his hands through his hair — mussing it like a wild man, sending it into a savage mess, criticising himself for his regrettable choice of words.

What a preposterous question to ask a young man in his prime!

Vauquelin has only been back in the twenty-first century for a month and a half ... and he had been speaking little but French for the prior thirty-five years. When he is agitated, his tongue perpetually betrays him.

Eric's face contorts. "Huh?"

"How to say it ... could you imagine being twenty four forever?"

"What are you asking me, exactly? Oh. Ohhhhhhh. Oh my god." Eric leaps out of bed. "You mean, to make me like you?"

"Yes, but even more importantly, I am asking for you to belong to me. I would protect you forever, or for as long as you want me to. But I must be very clear about something. You would only be the fourth vampire I have ever created in my existence. It is *crucial* to me that you understand the enormity of this offering. Many have begged me for it, and I refuse. It is an eternal bond that few have inspired me to make. My life is hard,

Eric, and nothing like the movies. There are serious and very, very dark consequences to being vampire. But the rewards outweigh the sacrifices. That I can assure you."

Vauquelin recounts the loneliness, the torment ...

The toll that living under the shroud of night takes on a soul.

The horror of watching the world change and realising that you are not fully capable of changing along with it.

The despair that results from each termination of a human life, so that you might live on. The relinquishment of so many comforts ... the small, seemingly insignificant joys that humans take for granted until they become locked away forever, such as food. The blood whisperings of maker and progeny. Eternal condemnation as a criminal: the (unfortunately) organic consequence of a vampire's nature.

Steep, sinister prices which a mortal cannot possibly comprehend.

"This is a *sacrement du sang* ... a blood oath. There are many things you enjoy that will be eternally forbidden to you. You will no longer be human. Your body will change. My shadows will smother your world in infinite darkness. I am deeply ashamed of attempting to steal the sun from a California boy." A frown darkens his face as he squeezes Eric's shoulder. "This may be too heavy a decision for someone of your age. You do not know me. I could turn you, and you may still come to despise me ... it has happened before." With downcast eyes Vauquelin hugs himself, the plausibility of someone like Eric hating him dragging him into his blackened depths like an anchor.

Eric sidesteps Vauquelin and slips into his boxers. He gulps the water, and the glass rattles against his teeth.

Yesterday, he was just an aimless kid, unsure of where his life was headed. He had just been coasting, letting one day fall into another. His friends had to force him out of the apartment, to go out and party when he had planned to stay home and play the video games he got for Christmas.

Now, he has slept with a vampire — who is offering him a forever, a life he could never have dreamed up or dared to hope for — and on top of that, Eric has allowed Vauquelin to pry his heart open, when it had been indefinitely and firmly closed.

"Then tell me who you are, and I'll do the same," Eric murmurs, mindlessly tugging on one of his ear loops.

"I regret that I am not that interesting, even after all these years. I have spent most of my life alone, because I find my own company to be the most reliable."

"Me too. I'm an only child. I used to get so lonely, but I'd rather be happy by myself than miserable with someone else. Do you like being alone?"

"In a way, yes. I, too, was an only child. It is rare for me to find affinity with another, Eric. I read. I love music. Sometimes I paint, though I have no talent for it. I buy many ridiculous things. I have far too much money and I often waste it, just like I waste my time. Old habits are difficult to break. It is easy to while away the years, much easier than one would imagine. Most of that time has been spent in my own head — which is truly the darkest place to be. It took ages for me to understand that I soothe my longings with objects when what I truly need is love, someone to belong to and who belongs to me. And I want that someone to be you."

Eric sits on the bed. He attempts to draw his leg across his knee, but his nerves are shot and he ends up crossing his feet, holding his hands up in a baffled plea.

"Why, though? Why me? There's literally *nothing* special about me. I'm just a slacker from L.A. — I barely graduated from college!"

Vauquelin tilts his head, studying Eric's face.

It *would* seem insanity to a mortal, to one who had not lived long enough to see through the foibles of humanity, to the importance they place on status and achievement. But to a revenant, such things do not matter.

At some point in history, humans lost their sense of urgent connection to another soul — now it is tied to one-night stands and what one can do for another.

Vauquelin wants to simply say, *My eyes have seen you now. And I can no longer imagine life without seeing you.*

But Vauquelin could not say this to Eric ... could he? How could he say this in a way that would not frighten a modern, twenty-four-year-old man?

Instead, he says, "I disagree. You are a rare being, Eric. I could not always see myself as such, and you have made me realise I still don't. Even my centuries of existence cannot convince me that I am worthy of anything."

Especially not you.

"Did you ever have a job?"

"A job?" Vauquelin breathes a tense laugh. "No, Eric, I have never had a job. I had a title from the moment I was born. It would not have been allowed."

"Why not?"

"My ancestors owned vast amounts of land, estates ... we were landlords and breeders of horses. The only job for me was doing whatever I felt, whenever I felt like doing it."

Eric quirks an eyebrow. "It's hard for me to imagine that kind of privilege. I didn't even have my own bedroom growing up. I've slept on couches more than I've ever slept in beds." He can scarcely believe these words have come out of his mouth, and he abruptly looks away.

And now Vauquelin is watching him, not with pity, but with something else. Something much more valuable than fucking *pity*.

"I do not admit this with pride. It was just the way of my world at the time of my human birth. This was hundreds of years ago, Eric ... I cannot help my origins anymore than you can. Even now there are few ideal jobs for a vampire. Could you see me going each night to work in an office, for example?"

"Ha! No. But what about me ... how would I make money?"

"This will never be a concern ... I assure you."

Eric shakes his head. "No way. I've always looked after myself. I started working when I was fifteen."

"Money is the least of the worry here. There is a lot of it. Okay? More than either of us could spend in multiple lifetimes. That is absolutely irrelevant. What is important to me is that you opened something within me, something that no one has ever touched. And I can only hope I have done the same for you. Surely you can see that I am no ordinary man, Eric. I am not some random stranger feeding you a line of nonsense to get you into bed. I can see inside your mind. And the truth is our souls have intertwined, whether we accept it or not. No amount of wealth can purchase that. There is a reason we are still here together at this moment."

The brunt of Vauquelin's revelations drapes a suffocating silence upon the room — its danger threatens to scorch them both.

Eric's skin prickles. "I can't explain what's going on in my head right now. Like ... words won't even form. Did you hypnotise me or something? Can't vampires do that?" he asks, a hint of mockery edging his lips.

Vauquelin leaps up with exaggerated violence, making Eric flinch, and begins pacing in indignant strides. "NO! I absolutely did NOT! Please, Eric! I may be vampire, but I do have *some* morals!" He collapses back into the chair. "You are hearing words from my soul that no other human has ever before heard."

That.

That was the moment they both felt what their confessions to each other meant, when they felt the enormity of *everything* that had happened.

"Did you choose to become a vampire?"

"Yes ... but also no." He folds his hands in his lap and absent-mindedly traces a heart over and over again on his palm with his thumb.

"Had I not, I would have been killed, which in retrospect might have been more merciful."

He sounds weak — he must rectify this. He turns his head back to Eric.

"But in fact I did choose it — twice — and I have no regrets. For if I had not chosen it the second time, I would never have met you. I am exceptional among my kind, my sweet ... I have been tossed back and forth in time against my will. But that is a long, complicated story for another night. All that matters now is that, by some miracle, time has placed me at your feet."

Vauquelin banishes the ambiguous knowledge he cannot share with Eric — that he could turn him and disappear from his life forever without warning. Not just yet ... because he does not want to believe his time will shift. Not anymore.

Eric fixes his gaze on the wall above Vauquelin's head, lost in thought.

Vauquelin remains silent.

"And you said you weren't interesting. Come on ... how can I top all that? I hate talking about myself. But here goes," Eric says, lying back down on the bed with a heavy sigh. He tilts his head down to his belly and fiddles with the waistband of his shorts. "I'm a loner. I've never related to other people, and they never seem to get me. All my life, I've never fit in anywhere, not really ... I have to put on a fake cheerful face at work. I never even had that many friends until recently, when I fell in with Megan and her crew. For a long time, no one even knew that I'm gay. I'm not fully out ... I like to keep things about myself private. Megan knows. I've been crashing on her couch in Los Feliz. I literally only have like a couple of boxes of stuff to my name. I lost almost everything I had when my ex left. But that's a boring story."

Eric stops fidgeting and sits upright, at last looking up at Vauquelin.

He's admitting things to this man that he's never told anyone, laying himself bare ... his shoulders fold in. Shame is something one carries deep down, like a dirty secret. Yet he's pouring it all out willingly, and he can't imagine where this tsunami of trust is coming from: maybe it's because Vauquelin will not judge him, because he has given him his dirty secrets, too. This alone gives Eric the strength to continue.

"I had no idea that coming home with you would change my life. I don't understand how a total stranger could make me feel seen and cared for, but somehow you do. Something crazy happened to me when you sat down at our table — I knew in a second I'd never meet anyone like you again. That's why, when you left, I came outside and kissed you ... even though I was completely freaking out. One night isn't enough to form a lifelong bond on, but ..." His breath quickens as he darts his tongue across his lips, and that damned lock of curls tumbles across his brow, catching on his eyelashes.

Vauquelin bows his head, knocking his clasped hands against his crown. Eric, this beautiful boy, is already unable to live out in the open ... and if he is turned, he will be yoked with an additional burden of shadows.

It could break his spirit ... corrupt him.

How could Vauquelin desire to bring Eric under the wings of his darkness, when someday soon human society might accept him as he is?

He could live in the light in more ways than one.

The saddest thing humans can ever do is be untrue to themselves, to live a life that can only be labelled as inauthentic.

Even sadder for vampire to do this to themselves, because they are capable of making decisions that may take lifetimes to emerge: and the aftermath is exponentially devastating. The ripple effects cast across the infinite nights like a hidden earthquake under the sea, taking days or weeks or — in the case of a revenant — centuries to reach the shore.

"You are correct, Eric," he breathes. "It is not enough. And it is cruel of me to ask it of you." He stands and backs up to the wall, his eyes darting to and fro across the ceiling as he desperately searches his skittish mind for the words that will convince Eric — none are adequate.

The conversation is spinning out of his control, pulling Eric away from his grasp second by terrifying second.

Vauquelin cannot expect a young man in his twenties to accept his wild stories at face value — to comprehend the depths of his revenant knowledge, his capacity for the recognition of a rare human being.

To there and then achieve his level of comfort in the shadows.

To embrace him and walk their saturnine corridors beside him, caring nothing about the opinions of ignorant humans.

There are many aspects of Vauquelin's life he takes for granted.

He must acknowledge that Eric is not obligated to surrender his life to him merely because *it is all he wants in the world*.

A sigh of defeat threatens Vauquelin's lips and he rams it shuddering back into his chest.

"You are safe now, Eric. I give you my word. If you do not want me, you can walk away. I will return to Paris and you will never have to see me again. Please ... all I can say, now that I know of your existence, is whatever remains of my sunless life would be even darker without you in it."

Vauquelin clamours to the side of the bed, kneeling before it as if it were a prie-dieu.[†] « Putain d'enfer , »[‡] he says, worrying his forehead with his fingertips. "This is lunacy. What have you done to me? I never beg!"

"Are you sure you want me?"

Vauquelin looks up, and light washes over his face.

"I have made many misjudgements across the expanse of my life, but I will never believe this is one of them."

"Then yes."

Vauquelin rises, holding out a hand.

---

†- A PIECE OF FURNITURE FOR USE DURING PRAYER, CONSISTING OF A KNEELING SURFACE AND A NARROW UPRIGHT FRONT WITH A REST FOR THE ELBOWS OR FOR BOOKS
‡- FUCKING HELL

Eric inverts it and brings Vauquelin's palm to his lips.

Thirty-Three

Vauquelin can rest now.

"Stay as long as you like, and make yourself at home," he says, dragging a thumb across Eric's jaw.

Vauquelin closes the bedroom door behind him and calls the charter jet service. "My return has been delayed," he says in a hushed voice. "Could you change my flight to two weeks from tonight, departing at the same hour? Louis de Vauquelin. V-A-U. Yes, I'll hold ... fine, *merci*. Thank you."

Two weeks?

He can only hope his time holds.

He surrenders quickly to his slumber, with something like hope embracing his heart for the first time he can remember.

Eric stands outside the door for a minute as he considers getting a rideshare and heading home. He could freshen up, change, and come back later. He isn't sleepy ... he usually only gets three or four hours a night anyway. But he's afraid if he does, he'll wake up and discover that none of this is real. That it's just a dream. He can no more leave this house than he can stop breathing.

He meanders, snooping around the remaining rooms he hasn't seen yet. The house is coldly impersonal: he can't identify a single thing, aside from the flowers, that sheds any light on the enigma of Vauquelin.

He ends up in the kitchen with his head in the empty refrigerator, puffing out his cheeks. He opens all the cabinets.

Nothing, not even a crumb.

His stomach protests with boisterous violence — he hasn't had anything to eat in almost twenty four hours.

So he orders delivery on his phone, walking out to the front to get the street number. He certainly hadn't been paying attention to any addresses last night!

He skips down the steep stairs to wait for the driver.

Eric's world is different now.

He sees everything with revolutionary eyes.

He knows his old ones will never, ever see things the same way.

An hour later he has a SoCal burrito big enough to feed three people, an iced coffee, and a new toothbrush.

Gotta love L.A., he thinks — *anything you want, anytime.*

It is now 4:30pm and the sky is darkening as the sun slips behind the mountains, draping a rosy, violet-tinged canopy over the canyon. The lights below begin to flicker on one by one.

He eats by the pool on a chaise lounge, feet propped up, thumbing through his phone.

His last message is from Megan, replying to Vauquelin's impostor text.

Huh. Totally don't remember sending her that.

He shrugs it off.

Who knows? He had sex brain last night.

ok <3
be safe and have fun

Eric bites his lip and replies.

i am. it's all good :)
really, really good, actually.
later.

He tosses his clothes in the washing machine and takes a shower in the hall bathroom, tying a towel around his waist.

The house is deathly silent.

He doesn't want to disturb Vauquelin, so he reclines on the couch and kills a couple hours scrolling videos with the volume muted.

The sound of water rumbling through the pipes makes his heart stutter.

It means Vauquelin is awake.

And now that heart is attempting to fight its way out of Eric's chest as he waits for him to come out.

A door creaks open down the hall.

Pattering steps echo on the wooden floor, and Vauquelin rounds the corner. He is barefoot, wearing only black silk pyjama pants, towelling his wet hair — it clings in dense, coal-black rivulets against his pale cheeks.

He halts and regards Eric with an uninterpretable expression.

"*Euh* ... I felt certain you would have given up on me by now," Vauquelin whispers, wrenching the towel in his fists.

"Is it okay that I stayed?" Eric whispers back.

"Okay is an insufficient word." He sits next to Eric. "Seeing you here is an answer to an obscure prayer I did not know I had uttered aloud."

Eric's resulting crooked grin undoes Vauquelin, but also reminds him that this is a human man sitting on his furniture, one who is here by choice.

"You must be starving."

"I ordered in," Eric laughs. "I told you ... I can take care of myself. But what about you?" He shifts on the sofa, hooking an arm around Vauquelin's neck, and the vampire's eyes drift to the heavy vein pulsing on his bicep.

He moves Eric's arm away. "No. I thank you, but no."

"Why not? Can't I help you?" His shoulders sag. "I really want to."

Vauquelin's refusal confuses Eric.

He doesn't get it.

Vauquelin smiles: a genuine, large smile, exposing his teeth because of joy and not a threat ... something that happens so infrequently in his life it is almost painful.

He covers his mouth and glances away.

And then he loosens Eric's towel.

Thirty-four

JANUARY 4

On this, their fifth night, to look at Vauquelin and Eric one would never think they had not been together forever. Their placid asylum in one another's presence delights and frightens them both, but in vastly different ways. Vauquelin lights the fireplace on the terrace, and they shove the outdoor sofa in front of it.

"Tell me something in French," Eric says.

Vauquelin draws his knuckles to his chin, assuming a comically seductive stance, and says, « Quelque chose . »

"What does that mean?"

"Something."

Eric gives him a teasing punch.

« Aïe ! »[†] Vauquelin laughs. "You told me to say 'something,' so that is what I delivered."

"Come on! Please? I just want to listen to you talk. Longer than that."

Vauquelin thinks for a moment, drawing his fingers to his lips. And then he begins reciting a poem from his vast eidetic memory banks — one he

---

† - OUCH!

could never have uttered with such authenticity prior to this night.

Mère des souvenirs, amant des amants,

Ô toi, tous mes plaisirs! ô toi, tous mes devoirs!

Tu te rappelleras la beauté des caresses,

La douceur du foyer et le charme des soirs,

Les soirs illuminés par l'ardeur du charbon,

Et les soirs au balcon, voilés de vapeurs roses.

Que ton sein m'était doux! que ton cœur m'était bon!

Nous avons dit souvent d'impérissables choses ...

Que l'espace est profond! que le cœur est puissant!

En me penchant vers toi, reine des adorées,

Je croyais respirer le parfum de ton sang.

Eric writhes next to him, pressing the heel of his hand into his groin.

"Oof," he breathes, adjusting himself.

Vauquelin hikes an eyebrow and grins. "Shall I stop?"

Eric mouths *Ohh no*, shaking his head. "Sorry ... keep going."

Vauquelin drapes himself on the armrest, resting his chin on the palm of his hand as he continues his recitation.

La nuit s'épaississait ainsi qu'une cloison,

Et mes yeux dans le noir devinaient tes prunelles,

Et je buvais ton souffle, ô douceur! ô poison!

Je sais l'art d'évoquer les minutes heureuses,

Et revis mon passé blotti dans tes genoux.

Car à quoi bon chercher tes beautés langoureuses

Ailleurs qu'en ton cher corps et qu'en ton cœur si doux?

Ces serments, ces parfums, ces baisers infinis,
Renaîtront-ils d'un gouffre interdit à nos sondes,
Comme montent au ciel les soleils rajeunis
Après s'être lavés au fond des mers profondes?
— Ô serments! ô parfums! ô baisers infinis!

« Ça va. Satisfait ? »[†]
"So hot. What was that?"
"A poem by Charles Baudelaire."
"Huh. Never heard of him."
"Do you know Edgar Allen Poe?"
"Oh, yeah ... The Raven, The Tell-Tale Heart ... good stuff. I love horror stories. And movies."
"Baudelaire was France's Poe."
"What did it mean?"
Vauquelin takes Eric's hand and locks him in his unblinking gaze: inclining his head from time to time on certain important phrases.

Source of my memories, lover beyond compare,
O you, who are all my pleasures! O you, all my hopes!
You will remember the beauty of our caresses,
The sweetness of the fire and the charm of the evenings,

The evenings lighted by the hushed flame of the coal,
And the evenings on the balcony, veiled in pink vapours,
How sweet was your soul! how good your heart was to me!
To each other we have said imperishable things ...
How deep the world appeared to us! How powerful the heart!

---

† - THERE. SATISFIED?

When I leaned close to you, prince of lovers,
I believed I could breathe the perfume of your blood.

The night closed around us like a wall,
And my eyes detected the darkness of yours,
And I drank in your breath: oh sweetness! Oh poison!

I know the art of evoking happy moments
And relive my past nestled in your lap.
For what use to search for your languorous beauties
Elsewhere than in your dear body and in your heart so sweet?

Those cries, those perfumes, those endless kisses,
Will they be reborn from an abyss forbidden to our touch?
Will they not rise like suns,
After washing themselves at the bottom of the deep seas?
— O oaths! O perfumes! O endless kisses!

"I changed a few words in translation," Vauquelin says, "but there you have it."

Eric melts.

Speechless.

Vauquelin sucks in his breath and rises.

The poem has made everything clear.

"Eric, you must leave this house. Tonight. Right this minute, in fact."

"What?" The word shudders from Eric's lips in a sigh. His face falls, and tears swiftly well in the corners of his eyes. He bites his fingers to stop them from coming forth.

Don't you dare fucking cry, he tells himself.

Eric has been in three relationships.

The longest one lasted two years, and ended just six months ago when the other left for graduate school in Vermont. He stomped Eric's heart into the ground. At their parting, he told Eric that it had been fun, but he was actually bi ... it had just been an experiment and it wasn't working.

They should see other people.

Girls too.

Figure things out on their own.

A huge fight resulted, and Eric's boyfriend kicked him out.

The next day, he was gone, and their apartment was empty.

Eric was devastated.

Megan took him in, and he made out with her one night.

It just left him empty and sad.

"Aw, sweetie ... it's okay," Megan said.

She knew right away.

Even though his body didn't respond, their friendship survived that awkward night.

Eric rapid-fire replays all his conversations with Vauquelin.

Did he say something stupid?

He probably fucked everything up, like possibly the greatest thing he's ever had in his life, just like he always does.

Was he just some out-of-towner's fling?

He should have played it cooler, not been so available.

He's been fawning over Vauquelin since the moment they met: *of course* he decided he's not good enough, or sophisticated enough.

Why would he think otherwise?

Vauquelin's heart shrivels as he watches the bewildering range of emotions battling upon Eric's face. Still, he remains steadfast in his conviction to set Eric free — though the thought of it destroys him.

"Why?" Eric whispers. "Did I do something wrong? I thought ... that poem, I mean ... I thought we ..."

Eric clamps the back of his hand across his mouth and he can't hold it together any longer. He hunches over as if an invisible fist has punched him in the gut, and a strangled sob escapes his throat.

Vauquelin can smell Eric's blood, fragranced by his despair, and the sight of the boy's clear, pure human tears splashing down on the wooden deck nearly makes him crumble.

He could stop all this at once

He could strong-arm Eric inside, and turn him right now.

But he will not.

Love cannot exist without pain.

They must miss each other, must learn how much it will hurt for them to be apart: or this will never, ever work.

Vauquelin turns his back to Eric and saunters to the terrace railing, staring across the Hollywood Hills, up to the muddy crescent moon struggling its way through a gloomy winter haze.

Eric starts to follow him but something tells him to stop.

This sweet American boy ... Vauquelin senses his nearness as much as if Eric is drawing a hand up his backbone — though he is several meters away, whimpering quietly behind him.

Vauquelin grips the rails until the bones of his fingers rise to the surface of his skin, and his heart constricts under a tight fist of grief.

But it is the only way he can be sure ... for both of their sakes.

That *Eric* can be sure, which is of ultimate importance to Vauquelin.

He refuses to perpetuate the mistakes of his past. It all ends now.

"You must go and do all your favourite things. Bask in the sun. Think long and hard on what I have asked of you. I want you to have clarity when you make your decision."

Vauquelin turns to face him and something rips apart inside Eric.

He doesn't know it now, but it's his old life being torn to shreds.

Even if Vauquelin is lying, all he wants is to believe it.

"Oh god," Eric sniffles. "I thought you were kicking me to the curb, that I disappointed you somehow. But can't you understand how I feel? How can you do this to me? How can you show me this side of you and just snatch it away? Now I can't imagine ever being away from you, Vauquelin, not even for a minute. Please ... don't." His lips quiver.

Vauquelin pulls Eric into a tight embrace and kisses him as though he might never see him again — because that could very well be the case.

"I regret there is no other option," Vauquelin says, gently guiding him to the front door.

The atmosphere in the car is grim ... the silence of the journey is interrupted only by Eric's intermittent sniffles.

They arrive at Megan's apartment building and Vauquelin leaves the car idling. "Eric. Please. Can you not look at me?"

Eric's chest heaves. He gazes out his window a moment before turning back to Vauquelin.

He caresses Eric's jaw. "Your friends have seen me. They know something is different about me, that much is evident. But you must tell no one of my true nature. Absolutely no one. Or everything could be lost."

"I swear I won't," Eric murmurs. "I'll protect us."

"I will be waiting for you when — or if — you are ready."

Vauquelin pulls away from the curb, his spirits utterly wasted and desolate, watching Eric in his rear-view mirror until he disappears from sight.

Now that he has tasted happiness again, he is bereft by his want of it.

Please, please, please ... let him find his way back to me, Vauquelin implores, bracing himself for the chastising voice to laugh at him, to call him a fool ... but they are curiously silent.

Thirty-five

LATER THAT NIGHT

The streets of Los Angeles are drastically foreign to him without Eric, and Vauquelin beats a fist against his empty passenger seat.

Parking in the first deserted lot he finds, he rips open the top buttons of his shirt, sending them clattering to the floorboards.

His lungs deflate and refuse to fill with air, paralysing him with breathless despair.

All his precious material possessions ... he would gladly surrender everything right this second. He would set this stupidly expensive car on fire if it would rejuvenate his barren life and deliver him back to Eric.

Nothing else matters to him now.

He drapes his arms over the steering wheel, knocking his head against it, and nods off: exceptionally rare for him to do so during the night hours, but he hasn't slept well since his first night with Eric and without him his spirit is drained. His blood levels are frighteningly low — he has absolutely nothing left to sustain him.

Sometimes, in moments of utter desolation, the universe hears our pitiful implorations, even when we cannot hear them ourselves. It might be an answer to our prayers ... or it might be a reckoning.

A resounding boom convulses the car, thrashing Vauquelin into consciousness.

He whips his head to the epicentre of the sound.

A young man pummels the window, a gun in his fist.

"Out of the car, motherfucker!" The glass muffles his violent voice.

Vauquelin opens the door, unfolding his legs to the ground and closing his eyes as the man jams the gun into his temple.

His only emotion is regret for placing himself in such a vulnerable situation. He licks his lips and brings his hands to the air.

"NOW!"

The man smashes the butt of the gun into the bridge of Vauquelin's nose. The slow splintering of his nasal bones echoes through his ears, delivering him lucidity.

Blood cascades down his face and pain blossoms across his nerve endings — it was just what he didn't know he needed: a physical manifestation of his anguish.

God, that felt good.

His assailant screams "Give me the goddamn keys!" — spraying Vauquelin's face with spittle.

In a span of seconds Vauquelin sheds the tender self he has been with Eric for the past week, and assumes the role of indignant, seasoned predator.

He stands, dangling the keyring on his forefinger, taunting his foe.

"You have made the greatest error of your pathetic life tonight."

The hoodlum makes a swipe for the fob, still jamming the gun into Vauquelin's temple.

He neatly snaps the man's forearm as if it were a matchstick — the gun clatters to the ground as he howls in pain.

Vauquelin leisurely stoops to retrieve the firearm and cocks the trigger, pointing it at the man's forehead.

"On your knees," Vauquelin commands.

His assailant craters to the pavement, cradling his wrecked arm.

"I am afraid you selected the wrong victim. You cannot frighten me ... nor can you kill me. But in truth I am most grateful to you."

The hoodlum's face contorts wildly as Vauquelin's vicious wounds vanish, leaving only nasty streaks of gore in their wake.

"What the fuck?" he mutters.

Vauquelin steels his jaws and digs into the man's throat.

His fingernails flay the skin, exposing the windpipe.

He coils his hand around its girth, crushing it as he uproots it — stepping back to observe his work as the punk writhes and collapses to the pavement.

Vauquelin touches the heart.

Still beating strong (enough).

He dips a fingertip into the blood and tastes it. Finding it unaltered — perhaps a trace of marijuana but nothing else — he drops to his knees and laps it up from the ghastly, spurting neck, further sullying his ivory jacket.

Regrettably the majority of the blood is ruined, having oozed out onto the asphalt.

Vauquelin stands and shoots the man in the face and again in the neck, editing his own inflicted damage into close-range, bullet-ridden annihilation.

He kicks the mangled throat-meat to the side of the body. He washes his hands, face, and boots with a bottle of water, slips on his driving gloves, and places the gun in the glove box. He retrieves a blanket from the trunk, spreading it out across the driver's seat.

This unanticipated violence was just the balm he needed, and he did not even have to go looking for it — it was delivered to him.

Vauquelin returns to the empty house, aroused by the adrenaline pumping through his veins.

He incinerates his bloodied clothes in the fire pit on the terrace, Eric's absence tearing him down like Death.

Thirty-six

Eric stands on the sidewalk a moment, hands sunk in his pockets.

When Vauquelin's car turns the corner, his shoulders drop and he lets himself into Megan's apartment.

He sits on her sofa and the atmosphere now appears numbingly surreal to him, even though he's been living here for almost six months.

He fights the urge to call Vauquelin and tell him to come back right this minute, that he doesn't need time to think about it.

That he's already made up his mind.

He takes his phone out of his pocket and suspends his thumb above Vauquelin's name, just shy of tapping the screen.

But he knows Vauquelin is right … this is too massive of a decision.

So he gets down to business.

It's 8:00pm.

He drives to the clothing shop on Melrose where he's worked for the past four years, and announces he's quitting.

All his former co-workers hug him, and the manager cries.

They all love him and are sad to see him go.

While he's there, he buys a few new clothes.

They follow him around the shop, asking him if he got another job, what his plans are.

He says he finally figured out what he wants to do with his life, and he just needs some time to plot his next steps.

When they prod him further, he simply smiles.

He stops to pick up a massive to-go bag and takes it back to Megan's.

Her key rattles in the lock as he sits on the couch stuffing his face, idly channel surfing — having no idea that at this very moment Vauquelin is in the throes of a bloodthirsty car-jacking less than a mile away.

"Hey. I got a shit ton of tacos," he mumbles. "Want some?"

"Well, well, well! Look who finally came up for air. Welcome back from Ooh La La Land." She sits down next to him and helps herself to some chips and guacamole. "So, what's he like? Are you gonna see him again?"

"There's no way I could even begin to describe him, Megs. I've never met anyone like him! But yes, fuck yes. He's busy the next few days. Anyway … I've fallen pretty hard."

"Uh … sudden much? What the fuck, Eric? You don't even know him! He doesn't know you! What does he do for a living?"

"Nothing," he says. "He's independently wealthy."

"So you're just gonna take up with some rich, freaky French guy — who you just met in a bar? Okay … it's your life. And wow, you're still wearing the same clothes you had on the last time I saw you. Nice."

Eric scowls. "Hello … I *washed* them at his house. And don't call him freaky. That's really fucking uncool, Megan."

"Whatever. I'm gonna go take a shower. I just hope you know what you're getting into."

He stops chewing and watches her walk away.

Her voice rings out from the bedroom: "Jesus, Eric! I only wanted you to get out of this apartment and get laid!"

Damn … when she puts it that way, it makes his plans sound *completely* ridiculous.

Is that all it was meant to be?

The crumpled, greasy paper bags on the table, the half-eaten container of rapidly-browning guac, the styrofoam: after Vauquelin, everything from his ordinary life before looks so ... *wrong*.

A wave of nausea clenches Eric's stomach — provoked not by the food, but by his own unsure thoughts and Megan's blunt assessment.

Less than a week ago, he thought vampires were only in books and movies, and now he knows it isn't fiction.

It troubles him that he can't explain why this particular man is so exceptional: but it doesn't really matter, does it? She'd never believe it anyway. Eric has a secret, and he will protect it as if it were a priceless gemstone.

He works hard to avoid betraying himself, but he's good at that. He's been a master of disguise for most of his life, since the first time someone noticed he was different. He can flit in and out of normality, slamming the doors on any threat that the soft parts of himself might be exposed to the wrong person — the parts he can't bear for anyone to touch or see.

He sleeps on Megan's couch for the next three nights, but tells her little — only that he's perfectly okay, just having fun, seeing where things go. And that he's feeling pretty optimistic for the first time in a long time.

"Don't worry. It's not that serious," he lies.

Megan finally comes around, because she has to admit there's truly something different about Eric since he came back.

He's brighter, more sure of himself.

It's the first time in months she's seen him without a cranky expression on his face. Now he seems ... joyful.

She doesn't want to take this away from him. He deserves it, after what he's been through.

"Just don't go getting your heart crushed again. You're like my little brother. Your text said I should be happy for you, and I am. Seriously.

Even though now I kinda regret bringing him over to the table the other night." She ruffles his hair and hugs him. "Love you."

He gives her his lopsided grin, the one which not so long ago made her heart shiver and wish he liked girls, not guys.

Over the next few days, Eric eats all the food he wants, and lots of it.

He gets a haircut.

He pleasures himself passionately in the shower — the only place he has any degree of privacy. Eric pictures Vauquelin's face, lusciously ecstatic as he swallowed.

No one else had ever done that for Eric.

They always spit, or didn't even let him finish.

Vauquelin had done it with enthusiasm, tilting his head back and licking his lips like it was a fine wine.

Every hour that passes heightens his resolve, then the next one sucks him under an abyss of despair. He rides it like a wave, adrenaline spiking his veins and vanishing with no notice.

But isn't love supposed to feel this way? he thinks. *Like it will wreck you and slam you against the rocks?*

And if it doesn't, is it even worth it?

He hadn't felt this way with his ex.

It wasn't him leaving, exactly, that shut down Eric's heart — it was the gaping hole that remained when he left. And now that hole is filling up, overflowing. He tries to pinpoint the moment he allowed Vauquelin to slip in there, before he realised it was too late ... but it's everything.

All of it.

And he can't separate the moments now, because they're part of him.

There's a tide rising and if he stops to think about it everything will be torn to shreds.

So he keeps going.

He goes to the bank and closes his accounts, getting everything in cash.

He visits his grandmother and tells her he's thinking about using the money he has saved to do some traveling.

He caves and texts Vauquelin several times, sending him selfies: but he never gets an answer. All his messages are left on read.

He starts to worry that maybe he typed in the number wrong (to be fair, it's a really long, weird, French number), or ...

OR!

What if it was a fake one?

What if it's all bullshit and he's built this up into something it's not?

Megan is right ... he's just obsessed.

FUCK! he *always* does this.

There's no way this is gonna happen.

He's always been a dreamer, and imagined things in ways others never seem to see. Everything that happened was so surreal, so unbelievable — and it still is. Maybe Vauquelin really doesn't want him to come back, and sent him away to let him down easy.

Maybe he's just a smooth talker.

But then he thinks about the intensity of the time he spent with Vauquelin, and beats himself up more for even questioning that their connection was anything less than magic.

He reminds himself that Vauquelin felt it, too.

That poem ... it put everything that happened between them into words. Words Eric would never have come across on his own.

Why would Vauquelin tell him all that if he didn't mean it?

It was *proof* they both felt it.

On the last day, Eric drives down to Dana Point and surfs by himself, though the water is frigid this time of year, and sits on the beach in the light of day, changing out of his wetsuit and letting the rays kiss him all over.

People pass him on the beach.

Sometimes they look at him, and he looks back.

You don't know, he thinks. *You don't know about him ... only I do.*

It makes him feel singular, chosen.

Real.

He sends another selfie of his final day in the sun ... it's his last hope that Vauquelin will be able to see how he looks in the daytime.

Still no replies.

Eric's heart contracts a little more with every unanswered text.

He doesn't know that Vauquelin has saved each photograph, and looks at them over and over again — that he remains silent only because he does not want to influence Eric further.

He has sequestered himself deep into his shadow life, where he is safest.

Eric watches the sunset on the Pacific and when it dips below the horizon, he locks his car door and hurls the keys into the ocean.

He loses sight of them in the waves.

He orders a rideshare to take him back to Los Feliz.

He packs his stuff and sits stiffly on the couch, hoping Megan doesn't come home early.

He composes another text, but pauses before hitting send.

He makes a vow to himself.

This is the last one.

If Vauquelin doesn't answer this time ...

Then.

Then he'll admit it's really over.

He hits SEND.

I'm ready <3

Bring on the night

Eric's phone chimes with Vauquelin's immediate reply:

On my way.

BUTTERFLIES!

Eric races downstairs and waits on the sidewalk.

Megan is at work tonight, blissfully unaware her friend is leaving — and she'll never see him again.

His suitcase is at his feet, his skateboard propped up against it, his game console shoved in a duffel bag. He practises a cool and relaxed stance despite the fact that every nerve in his body is reverberating.

Still, even as he postures, he manages to convince himself that Vauquelin won't show up.

This is all a sick tease.

He's gonna ghost me.

I'm a fucking idiot.

Vauquelin's car stops at the red light up the street and Eric trips over an untied shoelace.

He gets out and sweeps Eric into his arms, pressing his lips to his neck, mumbling, "Are you sure?"

And Eric's answer is muffled by Vauquelin's hair.

"I'm more than sure."

During his brief exile from Vauquelin, Eric discovered that his normal daylight activities are things he can easily surrender, or transfer to the night hours.

He's a natural night owl anyway — he'll be perfectly happy going to sleep at dawn.

But he couldn't live with himself if he didn't at least try to see what a life with this extraordinary man could be.

If he could never look into Vauquelin's piercing blue eyes again, the ones that can look right inside him, they'll haunt him forever.

He doesn't understand it all but it doesn't make any difference — meeting Vauquelin has permanently altered him.

He can't veer away.

The way Eric sees it, he has nothing to lose.

If it all goes to hell, he can start again.

It's one thing he definitely doesn't suck at, because he's done it over and over again ... so many times.

"No turning back?" Vauquelin cautions, holding Eric at arm's length.

They stand there staring at one another, just breathing — the enormity of their next step flashes in Eric's mind like a nuclear bomb and Vauquelin's presence bathes him in a deadly divine light.

If this is madness, then so be it.

"Never."

They load Eric's things in the trunk and Vauquelin hands Eric the keys. He speeds them under the uplit, towering palms, the night air growing chillier as they rise up the hills to the house on Mulholland Drive.

Vauquelin leads Eric into the bathroom and runs a bath in the spectacular, oversized tub. Behind it is a ceiling-high wall of glass, looking out over the terrace and the canyon beyond.

While the water fills Eric undresses, balling up his clothes and flinging them to the floor, and Vauquelin's eyes are drawn to Eric's waist.

Eric is plainly happy to be back in his presence.

« *Mon dieu.* »[†] He laces his fingers on top of his head and hefts a deep breath through his lips, "Man to man, Eric … I remember the ways of my own human body at your age. I must confess to you … vampires cannot ejaculate."

Of all the vampiric wisdom Vauquelin has imparted, this bit brings Eric to a screeching halt. His feet slip on the tile and he grabs Vauquelin's arm for support.

"EXCUSEMEWHAT?"

He's only twenty four — he gets off multiple times a week … if not *per day*. His mouth tightens.

"I know. It sounds horrible … but vampires find their release in myriad other ways, far exceeding any human response. Do not worry: you will never be starved for pleasure. Vampire delights will put all your human ones to shame. There are no words in any language to describe this … you must experience it yourself. You will not miss it, but I did not want you to be surprised once it is too late. Does this change your mind?"

Eric backs Vauquelin to the wall, grinding their hips together, digging his fingers into Vauquelin's backside.

"Ummph," Vauquelin hums, arching his back and biting his lip.

"So *that's* why I can't make you come."

---

† - MY GOD

Vauquelin clasps Eric's shoulders and locks him in an intense gaze.

Eric quivers, unable to suss out the expression: he can't decide if Vauquelin wants to kiss him, hit him … or kill him.

"You are wrong, my sweet … you did."

"What? But you … didn't."

God, Eric thinks, swallowing hard. *This is so fucking confusing.*

Vauquelin's eyes metamorphose into a warm, deep blue, as deep as the ocean and twice as mysterious. "Yes. I absolutely did. This has never happened for me, not once during my whole existence. As I told you, vampire delights are different from human ones. It is a different plane. I cannot prove it to you now, not until …" He drops his gaze. "I only hope I can return it to you."

Eric crumples under his grasp.

"Well … I deserve another human one for the road … don't you think?"

"Say no more." Vauquelin immediately pulls the drain lever in the tub. "As many as you can manage, bien-aimé."[†]

He freezes as the special pet name he once had for Maeve leaves his lips. But she had emptied his heart, crushed it beneath her feet, and cast him aside: even so, it beats softly in his chest now, waiting to surrender its ownership to a new beloved.

Vauquelin extracts his Opinel. "Allow me to shave you."

He had done this for Olivier, turning the tables and assuming the role of his future progeny's servant, though there had not been even the slightest of romantic inklings on that occasion. Olivier is his chosen brother.

Yet he remembers the ritual with great fondness, and he intends to repeat it tonight: with Eric.

[†]- BELOVED

Perhaps to assuage his guilt for the horror he will momentarily unleash?

Eric's Adam's apple bobs and a sceptical look sprawls across his face. "You want to shave me with a *pocket knife*?"

"This is no ordinary knife, *mon bijou.*[†] It has been with me for centuries. This blade is so finely honed I could slice through tendons with it, if I wished." He strokes it along the contours of Eric's throat. "Do you trust me?"

Eric blanches. For the second time tonight, fear thrashes his heart.

But if he didn't trust Vauquelin, would he even be here right now?

Eric's expression alarms Vauquelin — what was he thinking, taunting Eric with his crude, excessively morbid brand of humour? It will never be his intention to frighten him. He kneels at Eric's feet, dropping the knife to the floor.

It was an unforgivable feral reflex.

"Take this," he says, retrieving the Opinel, pressing it handle-first into Eric's hand. "I wish for you to hold it, for you to understand that you could hurt me, too."

Eric folds the blade back into itself, clutching the Opinel in his fist.

"I do trust you. I'm giving you everything."

Vauquelin's chest caves. "My beauty. Forgive me my untamed ways." He stands and careens into the bedroom, mystified by his own behaviour.

Eric does not follow him.

Vauquelin sits on the bedside in a daze, fully expecting Eric to dress and walk out the front door ... but he does not.

Instead, Eric emerges after a few minutes and sits next to him.

He rests his chin on Vauquelin's shoulder.

"You're absolute shit at joking around ... you know that, right?"

Vauquelin collapses on his back, covering his face with his hands.

Eric tackles him, smothering him with kisses.

---

† - MY JEWEL

"Let's start over."

He pulls Vauquelin up and drags him back into the bathroom, snatching the Opinel off the counter and pressing it back into his hands.

"Now. Try again. You've got this."

Vauquelin glowers, but *this* expression is one Eric can interpret.

It means he won: this time.

"So," Vauquelin begins with a sheepish grin. "I noticed your face was smooth the night we met. Do I correctly assume you do not ever want to have to shave again?"

"Seriously? Hell no."

"I am fortunate that I was in the habit of having myself waxed before my first turning."

"No way! They did that back then? I thought you were just naturally hairless."

Vauquelin shakes his head in disbelief and laughs, ending in a kiss on Eric's neck.

"What's so funny?" Eric asks.

He's still a little shaken up and testy.

"Nothing. You are just ... je ne sais quoi."

Vauquelin is testing his patience. Eric gives him a Look.

"I cannot translate that, my sweet. It is French for something that cannot be defined and therefore it is the perfect phrase to describe you. But back to what I was saying. Modern humanity assumes that people of the past were backward prudes, yet they would blush at the things I have seen. You will discover this in your own time, Eric, but there is truly nothing new under the sun ... nor under the moon. Everything is only repackaged. Beeswax and honey have been available since the dawn of time."

There is a wireless speaker in the bathroom, and Vauquelin has planned music for this occasion. He pauses to press play on his phone.

"What is this?" Eric asks, as the sombre music fills the atmosphere.

"Do you not like it?"

He lathers Eric's face and smooths the razor across, relieving it of its slight, soft stubble, dipping the blade in the basin and drawing it languidly back and forth.

"No, I do. It's oddly soothing. I've never heard music like this before. It sounds ... really old."

"It is," Vauquelin replies. "The composer is Marin Marais. This is one of my favourite pieces from my early years as vampire. I used to bathe while my house musician played music like this in the next room. It seemed appropriate for this momentous night. My past lives ... merging with our future life."

"I kind of love it. But I feel like I should whisper during it." He drops his voice. "What if I cut my hair short?"

"It will grow back while you sleep."

"Hmm. Okay. What if I get a tattoo?"

"It will disappear while you sleep."

"Wow, interesting." Eric puckers his lips.

Vauquelin taps them to still him, then guides Eric's head back to get his neck.

"So, no food, huh? What happens if I eat something?"

"You do not want to know. If you wish to try, I will not stop you. However, I may point and laugh at you."

Eric scowls and immediately his face turns hopeful as he thinks of another topic. "Mirrors?"

"That, regrettably, is true. Mirrors cannot reflect our metaphysical nature."

"Crucifixes?"

"I adore crucifixes. Such an impotent object cannot subdue a vampire. Someday I will show you my collection of rosaries."

"Can vampires really die? I mean, if you're immortal it doesn't seem like something as simple as a stake could take you down."

Vauquelin halts the blade, casting his eyes across the wall.

Can they?

There have been a few times in Vauquelin's life in which he wished to die, or thought he was on the verge of his Final Death. He had been tired, full of existential dread, wondering if he could continue.

How long is too long to live?

He has not yet discovered the answer to that question.

But he has promised Eric the truth.

"Yes, Eric. We can die. But a mere stake will not do the job. You must take off a vampire's head, or remove the heart from their body. Otherwise, they will regenerate. We are immortal, yes — but we are not invulnerable. Even so we must protect ourselves. And you must never, ever go out into daylight — the sun is perhaps our greatest foe. The night shadows are our sanctuary."

Vauquelin wipes the shaving cream remnants off Eric's jaws with a towel. He does not want to think about dying.

He only wants to think about Eric's resurrection. He embraces Eric from behind and draws their cheeks together, whispering, "How I loved seeing your photographs ... the sun worshipping your lovely skin, kissing my beloved with its rays."

"I was worried you hadn't seen them."

But things have gotten far too melancholy.

"I thank you for that priceless gift. So ... anything else you'd like me to shave?" Vauquelin cocks an eyebrow and twirls the Opinel.

Eric snorts. "Take it all! I almost got waxed once but I totally chickened out. Make me as smooth as you."

Soon Eric's body, cheekbones to toes, is as slick and immaculate as marble, except for a narrow, sparse trail leading from Eric's navel to his cock.

"Shall we keep this?" Vauquelin asks, running a fingertip down. "My lips love its path too well."

Eric drops his chin, and then lifts his heavy, desirous eyes.

"Whew." Gooseflesh ripples across his skin and he arches his shoulders, delivering that seductive, twisted grin. "How could I say no to that?"

Vauquelin nudges him toward the mirror, keeping his distance.

"Are you happy with your appearance? This is how you will look forever. Last chance. Last glance."

Eric spins on his heels and holds his arms out.

"You tell me."

"Flawless."

They sink into the tub and soak for a while, their slippery bodies tussling against each other. Vauquelin wraps his legs around Eric's waist and draws him back against his chest, running his fingers through Eric's damp curls, nestling their jawbones together.

"This is literally all I've ever wanted," Eric whispers.

Vauquelin lets his head fall back against the back of the tub.

"Me too, bien-aimé[†] ... me too."

Seldom has Vauquelin ever felt so content.

Despite this his eyes darken, and he pushes his dread to his deepest recesses.

[†]- BELOVED

Thirty-eight

JANUARY 8

Vauquelin folds his fingers to his lips, as if in prayer.

"I am going to hurt you now. But I will never hurt you again, will you please remember that? I am escorting you through hell, but I will be beside you always. And I will be here waiting when you emerge on the other side. This I swear to you."

"I know you will." Eric trembles, and the bed registers his fear. He clasps Vauquelin's shoulders to steady his arms.

"I am deeply anguished by what you must endure," Vauquelin whispers, "but I am not sorry that you will emerge free from pain and death, the beauty and kindness you possess now forever preserved."

Icy fingers trickle notes across his spine as he recalls the similar words that were spoken at his own first making, by Yvain.

Regardless, Eric is not a plaything, as Vauquelin had been for Yvain: unlike his maker, Vauquelin respects the magnitude of what he is about to do, and he makes a silent vow never to abandon Eric.

What about Maeve? his chorus taunts.

How dare she enter his subconscious at this crucial moment!

No. This is different.

Vauquelin has pushed his truth to the forefront, delivering it with an unapologetically open heart.

"Now close your eyes, my love."

He kisses Eric with great tenderness then pushes his head to the side, drawing in all his breath — he plunges his teeth into Eric's neck, one hand clamped over his mouth to mute his screams.

The neighbours will not hear Eric's agony — it is just that Vauquelin cannot bear to hear it himself.

Prior to this moment, he has only had a negligible taste of Eric's blood — Vauquelin is not prepared for its crescendo, nor its finale.

Its hymn enraptures his veinery, knocking him to his back.

But he cannot interrupt the rite.

He swerves his body and pierces Eric's femoral artery, his fangs drawing out every drop of life this boy has to give.

Eric's essence fuses into the full sum of Vauquelin's existence — all those bloody meaningless years, syphoning down his throat, and he is full at last.

At last.

No other can satisfy your longing
This is your zenith

Vauquelin makes an incision in his own throat with the Opinel and feeds his cursed sang down Eric's tongue, then waits with euphoric adrenaline throttling his heart, praying that he has not destroyed this precious one.

One that he hopes will remain his for all time to come.

And then Eric's heart stops.

Thirty-nine

Vauquelin watches Eric's skin turn grey and waxy as Death takes him in her clutches, yet she cannot steal the sun from inside his golden boy.

For the next three days and nights, Vauquelin cannot sleep.

He paces in despair, horrified by the cruel transformation and the tragedy of Eric's suffering.

He will never be complacent about this ritual.

He will never not find it devastating.

He will never overcome his doubt that this will be the time he fails, and that his intended will not rise again, but instead be stolen from him.

Yet, for both of his own revenancies, he navigated the labyrinths of damnation alone, with no one to care what happened to him during or after.

Throughout the metamorphosis, he sits by Eric's side, dabbing his brow with warm cloths, soothing his flailing limbs, stifling his spine-chilling shrieks, holding him in his arms, absorbing the convulsions rattling Eric's exquisite body.

And Vauquelin is there when Eric resurrects — a vampire.

On the third night Eric's eyelids flutter open, and Vauquelin chokes back a cry, exuding a deep sigh of redemption, solaced at seeing his treasure's chocolate irises alchemize into a surreal mystical copper.

"My arcane angel," he breathes, urging Eric's lips apart: his canines and premolars have elongated into four daggers, the hallmark of Vauquelin's bloodline, and he runs the tips of his fingers over each one, admiring them, pricking his skin on their deadly sharpness.

He extends his neck and offers his jugular to Eric, blood of his blood, embracing the divine, rapturous pain of nourishing his resurrected fledgling, humbled by his own lifeforce vacating his body to sustain another.

Vauquelin lifts himself on unsteady arms and rises to his knees.

I beg you ... just let me stay here with him.

The sun is due to rise.

They both collapse into slumber, one quenched ... one parched.

Both entirely reborn.

Forty

JANUARY 11

THE FOLLOWING NIGHT

Vauquelin brings Eric an offering: a tourist he lured away from a wine store. The man is enchanted — his wife is buttressed against the back wall of a coffee shop down the road: alive, but drained to the point of incoherency. He says nothing as Vauquelin guides him into the house.

Eric panics.

"What's wrong with him?"

His first vampiric test is staring at him with hollow eyes.

"What am I supposed to do? Holy shit, I can't believe I'm about to fucking kill someone." He paces relentlessly across the floor, already adopting Vauquelin's habit, digging his hands into his curls.

"Hush. You are not going to kill him." Vauquelin eases the man to the floor, arranging him on his back.

"I'm not?" Eric halts.

"No. Not this time, mon amour.[†] But you must drink, or you will fall ill." Vauquelin beckons Eric to sit next to him on the floor. "Come."

He takes the first swallow in demonstration and gives Eric the rest,

---

† - MY LOVE

watching in fascination as his new fledgling parts his lips and approaches the victim's neck in fits and starts.

Eric grimaces in disgust when the metallic saltiness of the blood hits his throat. It cascades from his lips as he tilts his chin up to look at Vauquelin with desperate, bulging eyes, uttering small, pitiful grunts in his despair.

There it is.

The hideous side of being vampire.

"The nausea is like the revulsion, my love ... you only feel it once."

Vauquelin gently urges Eric's head back to the source. Sip by wretched sip, rhapsody overwrites his fledgling's horror ... greed and confidence take over, and Eric bears down, gulping, driving his teeth even deeper into the man's throat.

Vauquelin could not be prouder.

Still, after several minutes pass, he pulls him away.

"I'm not done yet," Eric gurgles, his voice dulled by blood, his eyes wild, head quaking. Scarlet rivulets stream down his chin.

"Yes, my darling ... you are." Vauquelin palliates the wounds on the man's neck and turns to Eric.

"I wanted your first taste of a human to be here, in safety. I know this is all quite overwhelming for you, but the first one is always the hardest. The horror of it all will ease. Then you will love it ... you will crave it. You will seek it out and wallow in it. But now we must get this man out of our house. Immediately. I shall return shortly."

Vauquelin carries the man to the car and takes off.

Eric stumbles to the bathroom. The blood on his face and trembling hands, resulting in rosy water swirls in the sink, makes him dry-heave. He scrubs his mouth and neck hard ... twice.

Sprawling on the sofa, he clutches a pillow to his chest.

His stomach grumbles at its still-unfamiliar contents.

This is so fucked, he thinks. *I just drank a stranger's blood.*

He doesn't remember the taste of Vauquelin. He had been delirious, washed away in newborn vampire stupor, and Vauquelin has not offered his blood again.

But now he's starting to feel fantastic.

Really, really fantastic.

Before Vauquelin brought the man tonight, Eric's body felt so grotesque — like it no longer belonged to him. His veins itched and burned as if they were frostbitten, and his brain buzzed as if there were a million wasps flying through it.

After the blood sustenance his body is somewhat ... *normal?*

No, not normal.

He searches for the right word.

Transcendent.

Eric wonders if Vauquelin ever felt this lost and confused when he was turned ... he's so confident, like this is what he was born to do.

Maybe I'm not cut out for this life, Eric thinks. *Well ... it's far too late to walk it back now, isn't it?*

His phone chimes, startling him.

A text from Megan:

Hey! Just checking in
Haven't heard from u in awhile
Everything ok? xoxo

The message is so unspeakably ordinary, a voice from another life — his dead life. How can he pretend to act normal, like anything is the same as it was? It isn't possible anymore. He's lost his ability to code-switch. Megan's Eric no longer exists ... he can't answer her ever again.

He panics and blocks her number, powering down the phone.

He wanders through the dark house hugging himself, rubbing his arms to chase his body chills away (it doesn't work), and he can see everything with vivid clarity.

He walks barefoot onto the terrace, marvelling that the cold wood doesn't freeze his feet. The air is vastly different than it had been a few days ago, when it was typical Los Angeles air: flat, dull, and fairly odourless up here in the hills. Now, the scent of every sprig of grass, each palm frond, every leaf — even the soil itself finds its way into his senses.

And though Vauquelin is away, his blood manifests within Eric: a frighteningly delicious, wet-black silk, clinging to his flesh.

He never wants this sensation to leave him.

It never will.

Though he does not yet understand, it is Vauquelin's ancient blood coursing through his veinery, claiming him as his own.

In the bedroom Eric catches the perfume of Vauquelin's essence infused on the sheets — the distinctive musky-alabaster fragrance of his maker's skin and hair. He lies prostrate on the bed and buries his face in Vauquelin's pillows, overcome with a profound longing.

"Come home to me soon," he whispers into the dark.

The front door slams and he rushes into the living room, leaping up and wrapping his legs around Vauquelin's hips, nearly knocking him over.

"What's all this?" Vauquelin smiles, stroking Eric's back. "I was only gone a minute."

"Felt like years." Eric lets himself down to the floor, and Vauquelin leads him by the hand to the sofa — all business, which alarms him.

"No, no. Everything is fine. More than fine. It is just … there are some things we must think about for our future. I have delayed my return home but I must go back soon. We do not belong in Los Angeles, not right now. We must come to Paris. I have much to teach you, and I cannot do it here.

Do you have a passport?"

"Yes, I go back to Mexico once a year to see my cousins," Eric replies. "It's in my suitcase."

At Eric's mention of family, Vauquelin's heart drops.

He was orphaned at the age of five.

He has always had only himself.

He has never known that depth of kinship.

What was he thinking, snatching this young man away from his sun-addled life and the humans who care about him?

"You cannot tell your people that you are running off to Europe with someone you met a week ago."

"They have no say in what I do with my life. I want to be with you, wherever you are. I'll tell my grandma I'm going on a trip. If I just disappear, she'll worry. She'll call the cops."

Panic spreads across Vauquelin's face and he begins to pace, cradling his head in his arms.

Oh god. Cops! That thought had not crossed his mind.

Things are no longer so clear as they had been a few minutes ago.

"That *cannot happen*, okay? We will have to think of something else to tell her. Putain!"† Pace. Pace. Pace. A finger snap. "You could say you're going to Palm Springs. That wouldn't be too strange, correct?"

"Yeah, totally not. My friends and I go to Palm Springs and Joshua Tree all the time."

"Okay ... then call her."

"No, I better text ... she'll know I'm lying if she hears my voice. I suck at lying." Eric's thumbs begin flying across the screen.

"What are you saying to her?" Vauquelin demands, looking over Eric's shoulder.

Eric stops tapping and gestures to Vauquelin to calm down.

---

†- FUCK!

"I've got this."

For some reason, the thought of texting a grandmother strikes Vauquelin as funny, and he laughs.

"What?" Eric says, pausing again.

"Your grandmother has a mobile phone?"

"What's the big deal?" Eric shrugs. "She's only sixty. Everyone has them now."

Eric places the phone on the coffee table and it dawns on him that he'll probably never see her again — he sucks back a sob.

She raised him: he never knew his parents. "Okay. Okay, okay. I can do this. Whew." He shakes his palms and rubs his eyes with the heels of his hands. "But I don't speak French! And I only took one year of Spanish in high school!"

"That is a start. There will be plenty of time for you to learn. And we can study Spanish together, if you would like. Perhaps we could travel to Madrid or Barcelona. I have never stopped in Spain, and it will be something new for both of us."

The next night, two vampires — one ancient, one fledgling — leave the United States and Los Angeles far, far behind.

Eric's first words when they step onto the tarmac at Orly: "Well, this is great. Just great. I can't believe I moved to fucking France and I can't eat anything."

Forty-one

PARIS, FRANCE | JANUARY 13

A rainy winter night greets them at Aéroport de Paris-Orly, and the journey to Vauquelin's house in the centre of Paris is another hour's drive. When they reach the edges of the city, Éric presses his face against the car window, occasionally rubbing it with his cuff so he can glimpse Paris whizzing by.

"The Eiffel Tower! Can we come back?"

"Of course we can. We will see everything you want, and things you do not yet know you want to see. We will go to the top, and you can see the whole of Paris."

The car arrives at the entrance and he hops out to enter the code.

The gates open like skeletal arms, inviting them into their own obscured, new world.

The house is set back roughly three hundred metres from the street, and Éric's eyes widen when they emerge from the car.

Really? This is his house? he thinks. *It looks like a fucking museum!*

"Holy shit! Has it been in your family a long time?"

"Yes. My father acquired it in 1601. It was one hundred and seventy years old at the time and quite dilapidated. He spent many years to restore it.

I grew into adulthood within these walls."

Vauquelin keys in the door code and turns to Éric.

"Welcome home, my love."

Éric kisses him, and whips his phone out. "Smile." He hangs on Vauquelin's shoulder and snaps a selfie. "A memory of our first night in Paris."

Éric glances around the black and white marble-floored foyer — bisected by gargantuan curved staircases and a hallway stretching infinitely beyond. A colossal unlit crystal chandelier is suspended above his head.

He peers back over his shoulder at Vauquelin, starry-eyed.

"Well ... what do you think?" Vauquelin asks.

Snatching his skateboard, Éric rockets straight down the length of the hallway beyond, shouting "Woohoooooooo!"

Vauquelin claps his hands over his mouth and shakes his head.

Oh, how I needed him. Merci.

Hundreds of years spent in this house had left Vauquelin rather blasé about it, but now — Éric's spirited astonishment allows him to see it with fresh eyes. Its ancient beauty, to which he had become immune, takes on a new splendour through his progeny's innocent — and genuine — excitement. The cold walls seem to glow with warmth and *home*.

Vauquelin wanders the first floor, lighting candles along his path, and shouts, "Éric? Where are you?"

There is no answer, and Vauquelin panics.

He races down the hallways, flinging every door open.

"Éric?"

He takes the stairs two at a time, and finds his fledgling in the library, mesmerised by its contents.

His shoulders slump and he claps a hand to his chest, exhaling deeply.

"I could not find you. I was yelling for you."

"I'm sorry! I wandered off. Jesus, V, this place is huge. I couldn't hear you! I should've waited for you ... I just got so excited."

Vauquelin stops cold.

"V?" he asks.

His breath leaves his lungs and he wrings his hands.

He had always disdained nicknames for himself until the night he invited one of Clove's boys to call him V.

It is a special moniker.

Unique to an experience in England ... yet Éric knows nothing of that night. He had conceived of this all on his own.

It is kismet.

Suddenly Vauquelin's world seems secure ... at least for a moment.

He desperately wants to hold onto it, with all his might.

"Is it okay if I call you that? I mean, Vauquelin is kind of a mouthful. Not that I'm complaining," Éric adds with a devilish smirk.

Éric's humour defuses everything — it always does.

Vauquelin rubs his eyes, unsure how he has come to deserve this.

"You honour me," he says.

And now only two vampires in the world will be privileged to use it. Not even Olivier.

"How many books are in here? This is amazing!"

"Oh, I do not know exactly ... somewhere around sixteen thousand, give or take a few. Read whatever you like. Everything I have is yours."

"I can definitely get used to this!"

Éric is a book lover: magnificent!

But they still have so much to learn about one another.

"Show me around! I promise I won't wander off this time."

In the bedchamber, while Vauquelin flits around lighting about a million candlesticks, Éric reclines on a cheetah-skin chaise, edged in carved, gold-leafed wood.

"So now I get why you said the house in L.A. wasn't your style.

This, though … this is totally you." He tilts his head to and fro, periodically shaking it in disbelief.

The walls are dark as midnight — gilded panel frames burst forth across their expanse. Thick, deep purple curtains enshroud every window, golden fringe and tassels spilling down their edges.

The ceiling is so elevated that Éric can't begin to imagine its height.

His eyes travel up to the carved, golden trim bordering its cornices.

It culminates in an octagonal fresco of a blue sky: the devil battling an angel in pink-and-orange tinted clouds.

In the centre of the room, directly below the fresco, is Vauquelin's bed.

It must be twenty feet tall — at least. It's huge. Like, ten people could sleep comfortably in it. Thick, lush emerald green velvet curtains surround it, with even more golden fringe and silky little pompons.

Vauquelin crouches at the fireplace and ignites the logs, blowing out the match with a puff. Then he stands upright, and over his head is his second life-size portrait: the only one left in his possession.

Éric draws his gaze from Vauquelin's feet up to the painting in crushing awe. The ancient, untouchable Vauquelin above: his own, very tangible Vauquelin below.

He leaps up from the chaise and embraces him. "I can't believe this is real," he says, mumbling into Vauquelin's shoulder. "Make it real."

Since he met Éric, Vauquelin's mind has frequently drifted to that fateful night with Clove and his boys, and the envy that had taken up residence in his psyche. He wonders how different his life might have been had he not clung so tightly to his reclusive nature.

He still cringes at the thought of the dressing-down he had gotten from one of Clove's boys. Scarcely younger than his own fledgling, and very much of his time, Moth had accused Vauquelin of taking the easy way out … of running away.

But that night, Vauquelin had been exhausted by his lifetime of travails, and unaware that his future was executing intricate plans to place Éric in his path.

Nonetheless, if all those years of solitude — and the resulting heartache from his failed attempts at attachment — were necessary for him to merit this beauty he is holding in his arms now, it is all worth its weight in gold.

Now, everything is new.

"The fire will warm up this room for us. I have much more to show you." He takes Éric by the hand.

Their tour ends in a dark corridor off the former larder, in front of a large set of mahogany doors. A cast iron fleur de lys and filigreed leaves spiral into the centre, framing an intricate, serpentine lock.

He turns to his fledgling with raised eyebrows.

"Whoa, this door looks serious."

"It is," Vauquelin says solemnly. He lifts a section of wood from the parquet floor and holds up his index finger. "Please, Éric. Always remember the location of this panel."

Underneath is a ring bearing a solitary skeleton key, which Vauquelin uses to unlock the door. He creaks it open. "Follow me."

They walk down a dim stone staircase, the steps severely concave in their centres. Éric stumbles and Vauquelin flings an arm out to steady him.

"I should have warned you. I apologise. This passage is quite ancient, worn down over time by many footsteps. This chamber was originally a wine cellar."

They have reached the subterranean level.

Vauquelin extracts a lighter from his pocket, igniting a torch on the wall and lifting it from its brace. He offers his elbow to Éric and guides him along the pathway. It culminates in a vast room, boundaried by wooden shelves stacked with thousands of bottles.

"What is it now?"

"This is our protection ... our salvation."

"Wine?"

"No. You must learn to look beyond what your eyes show you, Éric."

He lifts the torch high above his head and Éric's lips part.

As they move forward, the shelves of wine transition to shelves of bones. Hundreds upon thousands of human bones and skulls, stacked neatly, organised by shape and size.

An archive of Death.

"Besides you, my brother Olivier is the only one who knows of my ossuary. I clean them here." Vauquelin stoops to a stone door in the floor with an embedded iron lock, which he unlocks with the same key and hefts open.

The acrid odour of acid strikes Éric, and he clamps a hand over his nose and mouth.

"Wow ... just — oh my god. Wow." He wanders among the shelves, trying to add up how many lives these bones represent. "How long have you had this?"

"*This* collection?" Vauquelin calculates on his fingers and looks to the ceiling. "Some three hundred and fifty years ... since my second turning in 1668. Remember, I told you I have travelled back and forth through time. The acid pit, however ... I got that idea in my futurepast, from a 1950s movie. It is the perfect solution, really. Long ago, vampires did not concern themselves with discarding bodies. Death was so common. In the modern age, with detectives and forensics, it has become more challenging for us to survive."

"But we don't have to kill ... right? You've shown me that. We can just take their blood and let them live."

Vauquelin leans back against the wall of bones ... he glowers and scratches his neck, sucking air in through his teeth. This is a delicate topic, and Éric's innocent question is symptomatic of his modern mindset.

"I wish it could be so," he says, "but we are reapers, Éric. Without Death, our bodies will degrade over time. Blood alone will sustain you, but only the death of a human will keep you strong. I subsisted on rabbits for decades, but it changed my body. Over time, it made me move like a ninety year old man ... it dulled my hair and made my skin shrink. It is not a sustainable existence. I wish I could explain why this is so, but I cannot. I do not know all the mysteries of the vampire, but I will endeavour to tell you the truth as I understand it. I doubt you would find me so attractive were I not devoted to Death. She is our only god. Without her, we will wither."

Vauquelin's explanation simmers within Éric's psyche.

Sometimes he can't help but wonder whether Vauquelin is really hundreds of years old. How could that possibly be true? But so far he hasn't seen any evidence to doubt it. This house ... V's portrait ... his very own, highly altered existence.

"Would you like to go out into the city?" Vauquelin asks. "Add to our collection?"

"Not tonight ... tonight I just want to get to know the house, okay?" Éric tugs Vauquelin's hand, and they leave the catacombs behind them for now.

Later, Éric lies wide awake on his side in the enormous bed facing the sleeping Vauquelin, curling a strand of his long hair in his fingers, drawing it to his cheek and inhaling its mysterious fragrance. He can't pinpoint exactly what V's hair smells like ... maybe it's a combination of all the essential oils V obsessively dabs on himself. They mingle with the unique musk of his skin and Éric finds it enthralling.

He studies Vauquelin in the dark — face bathed with startling innocence in his slumber, buried under the blankets which barely keep them warm during the day. He almost looks human as he sleeps, yet Eric imagines the multitude of memories and experiences that are locked away behind his closed eyes. Éric is fully aware he has only scratched the surface of him ... Vauquelin will never be able to tell him everything he has endured, all that he has seen.

For a moment he's wracked by an insane jealousy, envious of every person that Vauquelin has seen or touched, of everyone that had the honour of dying beneath his fangs.

But Éric is the one who is here now ... he is the one lying next to Vauquelin, who will wake up next to him every night.

That's all he needs.

He caresses Vauquelin's chest — and immediately jerks his hand away.

V isn't breathing!

His heart is deathly still!

All of a sudden Éric is terrifyingly lost.

Until this morning he has always fallen asleep before V.

This means that Éric's heart doesn't beat during slumber either.

Undead.

Whew.

So many ghastly discoveries for one night.

He clasps his hands behind his head and tumbles onto his back.

Those infinite stacks of bones are etched into his mind: a dreadful glimpse into his own future.

He truly had not wanted to go out, because he knew what it meant: that it would have been the occasion of his first kill, and he isn't mentally prepared for that yet.

"Almost," he whispers, burrowing closer to V.

If V's heart isn't beating, Éric doesn't want his own to beat either.

But despite the thick blankets he can't get warm. The top one is a silky, white animal skin with small black spots scattered throughout the fur, and he can't stop stroking it with his fingertips.

Its softness entrances him.

His veins are icy, wriggling as though insects are crawling inside them, their bristled legs dragging and tearing. He tosses and turns, until exhaustion pulls him beneath the black swells of sleep, plying him with blood-soaked dreams.

He has a human on their back, crushing them under the weight of his body, ... their face is ripped to shreds. In his hand is a still-beating heart, dribbling blood on his bare legs. He holds the heart high above his head and squeezes, extending his tongue to lap it up.

And then Vauquelin is shaking him awake.

"You were dreaming ... and kicking me. Quite violently, I might add."

For a second, Éric doesn't know where he is, until Vauquelin strokes his face: then his eyes focus.

"Sorry ... I'm sorry. I just feel really weird right now." His face is drawn and his lips are dry. He licks them to no avail and struggles to swallow.

"Because the thirst is upon you." Vauquelin urges him into a sitting position. He traces his own jugular with his fingers and brings Éric's head to his neck.

Éric thrusts a hand against Vauquelin's chest.

"No ... I can't hurt you, V. I won't."

"I insist you drink from me."

Éric knows that tone.

It isn't one he can argue with.

So he exhales, squinting, then flings his leg across Vauquelin so that they face each other, their bodies close. He grasps Vauquelin's jaw in one hand and circles an arm around his torso, searching his maker's face.

Éric's unvoiced fears flow into Vauquelin, and he wants to absolve his fledging of all worry. He will gladly carry Éric's burdens, bringing them to roost with his own.

The silence is interrupted by the sound of his skin popping beneath

Éric's teeth and a luminous pain radiates across his shoulder, writhing into his musculature.

He intensifies his grip on Éric — who withdraws with a jerk.

"No. Don't stop," Vauquelin hisses, stiffening his jaw. "You need more." Vauquelin stiffens his jaw.

His ancient blood rushes from his body, feeding Éric, protecting him. Owning him.

Éric moans against his neck, and his cock thickens along the inside of Vauquelin's thigh.

"Enough ... enough," Vauquelin whispers. He slumps back against the pillows with ruby ribbons cascading down his neck.

He brings Éric's hand to his wounds, and caresses his own neck with the tips of his fledgling's fingers.

Éric's touch erases the damage, and his mouth falls agape.

"What is the matter?" Vauquelin asks.

"I healed you."

"In more ways than one, mon cœur,"[†] Vauquelin breathes.

And Éric licks away the remainder of the blood.

---

†- MY LOVE, MY HEART

Forty-two

ÉVREUX, FRANCE | JANUARY 30

Vauquelin has brought Éric to the château because they have an appointment tomorrow night: with the urban explorers who exposed his property on the video site. He is beyond giddy about serving them some karma, and it provides a golden opportunity for Eric to flex his newborn vampire gifts.

It takes almost fifteen minutes for them to reach the château from the gates at the end of the road.

"Come ON," Éric exclaims when they pull up. "Seriously? How many gorgeous houses does one person need? When you said 'country house' I was picturing something like a little cottage retreat. It didn't look this big in the video!"

"What do you mean? Surely you can see it is smaller than the one in Paris. This is the least interesting of our houses."

"There are *more*? Has this one been in your family for a long time, too?"

"Not exactly ... I acquired it in my second 1682. It is a long, tedious story. Being in the countryside is quite tedious as well, which you will discover in no time. After growing up in L.A. I cannot imagine you enjoying its pastoral silence. And it is impossible to have things delivered here. I do not come here often. I have yet another château, in the French Alps. Olivier and his wife live there."

"Can we go? I bet it's beautiful in the wintertime! I've never seen snow!"

Vauquelin's breath catches sharply in his throat.

Truth, he cautions himself.

"In fact, I never wish to visit that house. I will not sell it, because it belonged to my mother ... she lost her life giving birth to me there. I cannot bear it." His lips tighten and he clears his throat.

Éric slips an arm around V's waist, remaining quiet.

"We will go elsewhere for you to see snow, mon cœur.[†] Perhaps Switzerland."

Aside from Éric's imminent lesson, Vauquelin must focus on ensuring his fledgling develops into a consummate vampire. And to help him with that, he has invited Olivier and Céline to join them.

Olivier was outraged by Vauquelin's news of the urban explorers, and he immediately installed security — apologising to Vauquelin so profusely that he was finally told to shut up. Regardless, Vauquelin insisted upon Olivier's presence for this meeting.

A church bell chimes.

Many years ago, Vauquelin installed the bell, along with a pulley, in the sky-reaching tower above the front doors.

He suspects the château was at one time a monastery, though the bell was long gone when he purchased the property.

"What's that bell?" Éric gasps. He has been edgy since their arrival.

"Olivier and Céline have arrived," Vauquelin says, starting for the door.

"I'm scared," Éric says, clinging to Vauquelin's arm. "What if they don't like me?"

Vauquelin kisses Éric's forehead. "You have nothing to worry about. They will love you." He adds one of Éric's favourite words: "Chill."

---

†- MY LOVE

With a wry smile Vauquelin heaves open the doors, and soon there is much embracing.

His lips tremble with emotion.

"May I present ... Éric Castañeda de Vauquelin."

Olivier scowls. "*Pardon*? You never gave me your name."

Éric's eyes widen in alarm.

The last thing he needs is to offend Vauquelin's brother!

This isn't off to a good start.

He nibbles his fingertips.

Vauquelin shoots Olivier a consolatory look, and everyone — with the exception of Éric — erupts into uproarious laughter. He draws Éric's hand through his elbow, and only then does his fledgling relax.

"Vauquelin, Éric, je vous présente ma femme,[†] Céline de Rochefort Boucher."

"Gah, so many names," Éric mutters, lost in the lingual shuffle.

Vauquelin kisses her cheeks. "At last. Enchantée,[‡] Madame, my sister. Éric does not yet know French ... please, let us all use English."

Olivier and Céline cannot stop touching and embracing Éric, welcoming him into their family. Céline is thrilled by the fresh, young vampire. Olivier is her maker: and though she has been vampire for almost eighty years, she has not yet created one of her own.

She leads Éric to the salon and pummels him with questions.

Vauquelin drapes an affectionate arm across Olivier's shoulders as they follow. "It appears our little family is growing," he beams.

"This takes me quite by surprise, Vauquelin. I did not anticipate such a souvenir from your travels."

"Nor did I. Yet my life feels complete."

They pause at the entrance to the salon.

---

†- MAY I PRESENT MY WIFE
‡- PLEASED TO MEET YOU

Does he know? Olivier asks in silence.

Not yet. The right time will come.

Olivier barricades Vauquelin against hearing his next thought:

Let us hope your confidence is justified.

Vauquelin watches with pride as they all gather in the salon ... Olivier strides to Céline's side where a spellbound Éric hangs on her every word.

Vauquelin has never known this wholesome experience of having a family.

He places his hands on his waist and searches his mind to locate the perfect word for the queer emotion washing over him.

Oh, yes ... *there* is the word: bliss.

"I can't believe this is my LIFE now!" Éric shouts, laughing.

Vauquelin laughs, too, but his eyes are haunted and his smile slowly degrades into an expression of dread.

He turns his back to conceal his face from Éric.

Everything is too perfect.

Surely, this cannot last.

In the middle of the next day Vauquelin awakens in a panic, followed by relief when he sees Éric spread-eagled in the bed next to him, his dark mop of curls scattered across the pillows.

He wonders if he will ever shake this unease, yet he is grateful his fledgling sleeps hard, his nightmares having subsided — though he does take up far more than his share of the bed.

Even so, Vauquelin would not trade him for the world.

Éric has excelled in his transformative state.

He is exceptionally kind and polite, his human warmth and enthusiasm amplified by vampiric grace.

And this makes Vauquelin fear for Éric's safety more than anything else, even more so if he ends up alone.

He is too trusting for his own good.

Forty-three

ÉVREUX

THE NEXT NIGHT

They are all seated in the foyer, waiting for the arrival of the urban explorers at the appointed time.

All are bored.

The crew is late.

Unfashionably late.

Éric is cuddled up to Vauquelin, their hands tangled.

Their fingertips slide and brush against each other, sending delicate waves of delight through both their bodies. Their hands struggle for domination, until they both surrender into caresses of thighs, and gentle knockings of their foreheads.

« Bordel de merde ! »[†] Olivier mutters under his breath, rolling his eyes. "We should send them back upstairs."

Céline nudges him.

"Let them be. Why should they hide their magnificent love away? You once spoiled me with such adoration," she chides.

The clock is ticking.

[†]- FOR FUCK'S SAKE

"I bet they don't show up," Éric says.

"Oh, they will show up," Olivier counters. "And they will film it all."

The deep, resonating tone of the church bell interrupts their thoughts.

"Wait here," Vauquelin says, rising. "I will play the gracious host."

He flings the heavy doors open, and there they are: a group of four young people waiting on the steps, burdened with camera equipment.

"Welcome," Vauquelin says, extending an arm, smiling broadly with his lips closed.

The crew gawks at him.

He is shirtless, wearing an eighteenth century frock coat and jeans.

His feet are bare, despite the chill of the January air.

This unique mash-up of centuries was all Éric's idea.

The crew scans the other occupants of the foyer.

The vibrations of a pocketed mobile phone echo in the cavernous foyer: no one makes a move until one of the crew drops her bag with a thunk, and quickly stooping to retrieve it. While she is down, she takes a sly peek at her phone.

Something is off here

Stay alert

The young man standing in front, whom Vauquelin recognises as the host of the Fateful Upload, steps forward and bows.

He speaks in French.

"Thank you for inviting us, Monsieur. Upfront, we would like to apologise for intruding on your property ... there are so many abandoned châteaux in France, you understand. It was our mistake. We are grateful for your invitation."

"Oh, on the contrary," Vauquelin says with feigned enthusiasm in English, always mindful of Eric. "*We* are grateful that you found our home worthy of sharing with the *entire fucking world*. Allow me to introduce you to my family. I am Louis du Cavernay de Vauquelin. This is my lover, Éric ... my brother, Olivier ... his wife, Céline." He delights in hearing his voice deliver all their given names. There is no need for concern, because half of the occupants in this chamber will take these names to their graves.

The vampires have rehearsed this moment. They all bow in the manner of the Sun King, with the exception of Céline, who curtsies.

"We would adore giving you a tour of this magnificent château, and explain some things you got ... how shall we say... quite *incorrect*."

A crew member extracts a video camera and hoists it onto his shoulder.

"I'm sorry ... may we film?"

"Oh, but of course," Vauquelin says. "It would be our honour to have footage of this night. Please. Let us commence." Vauquelin takes Éric's hand, inclining his head to Olivier and Céline.

The tour begins in the library.

Vauquelin walks straight to the portrait of his mother.

"Do you remember this? You damaged the frame in the video."

"I am deeply sorry, Monsieur," the host says.

Vauquelin begins to pace with an index finger pressed against his lips.

"Do you know the value of this portrait? It was painted in 1620. Its frame was gilded by hand. Artisans carved this wood, and laid twenty-four karat gold leaf upon its intricate secrets in onion skin layers. Have you any idea how fragile is such a frame?"

"Monsieur de Vauquelin ... with all due respect ... the frame was quite dilapidated by the time we found it."

Vauquelin squints. "I see ... when *you* found it."

"When were you last here?" the camera operator asks.

"Is that important?" Vauquelin turns on his heel.

"Actually, yes. Can't you see the château is in urgent need of repair?"

Vauquelin leans up against a wall, stretching his arms above his head, and says, "Ancient houses carry their own disreputable charm. Since I bought this estate in 1682 ..."

The host interrupts him with a sneering laugh. "Surely you're joking?"

"I did not stutter. I said 1682. Sixteen hundred eighty two." Vauquelin repeats, drawing out the words.

Éric leers at Vauquelin in captivated astonishment ... he's never seen this sarcastic, witty side of Vauquelin and he is *into* it.

Fuck yeah, he thinks.

Another mobile phone vibration buzzes, and its owner shamelessly extracts his phone.

1682? This guy is fucked in the head!

We should leave.
Now.

Vauquelin has no reason to doubt their messages are about him.

He flashes himself to the door, shocking them all with his speed, and locks it.

Audible gulps rend the silence.

"No. No one will be leaving tonight," Vauquelin says, crossing to the bookshelves. "Look at me, and listen. Another thing. Never remove a book from its resting place by the top of the spine. Most of these books are five hundred years old or more. Watch and learn." He drapes his long fingers over the top of a large book and withdraws it from its back edge. "There. See? This way, the leather is not torn at the top. I am only trying to educate you. You must understand ... a house may be abandoned, or so you think, but its contents still have worth. And they have a story. Would you all like to hear the story of le Château de la Musse?"

One nods, dumbstruck.

The others are sceptical, fidgeting in place.

Vauquelin resumes pacing, bringing one fingertip back to his lips, his other hand on the small of his back.

"As I was saying, in 1682 I bought this estate. Because Louis the Fourteenth stole my title, Monsieur Le Duc de Vauquelin, and my ancestral château. Are you bored yet?" He stops, taking in the room. "No? During the Revolution I saw many a noble with their chin draped over the neck of Madame Guillotine, and that changed everything, as you can imagine. Olivier, do you recall how our shoes were soiled by the blood of the aristocracy flowing down the gutters of Paris?"

"Oh, *indeed*," Olivier nods solemnly. "I lost many favourite pairs, while they only lost their heads."

"The nineteenth century was quite tedious, to be honest. Europe began to bore me. And so I ended up in the United States in 1900. Suffice it to say a lot has happened between then and this very moment. But all that withstanding, I assure you that this château has been quite owned and occupied — by me — for a very, *very* long time. So you see your mistake now, I trust."

Vauquelin crosses to the camera operator and lifts the gear off his shoulder, placing it on the floor and leaving it running. He issues a silent, hypnotic command.

Do not move a muscle.

He turns his gaze like an automaton to each of the others, delivering the same order. They still like sculptures under his spell, and Vauquelin crosses to the host, curling his fingers into a deathgrip around his neck.

"And now," Vauquelin whispers, "I have a famished one who has been waiting for this moment."

He twitches his head to his vampires.

Go.

Vauquelin draws the host's collar aside with a fingertip and sniffs from his clavicle up to his ear. "Do you still think me a ghost? I assure you I am quite real." He lacerates the skin on the young man's neck, dragging his fangs and ripping a jagged line in the skin before he impales him.

As the doomed mortal's blood hits his throat he darts his eyes to Éric and smiles against his victim's neck. Then crimson fluid begins to flow in earnest and Vauquelin forgets about his beloved, just for a few, volatile minutes of ecstasy — for now he is involuntarily intoxicated by his sanguine bounty and he closes himself to anything but blood.

Éric's eyelids flutter. For a fraction of a second he's unhinged by his jealousy at seeing Vauquelin's lips on another man's neck, not to mention the groans coming from the guy's throat that sound a little too close to someone getting off instead of being killed. But then the bloodlust hits him hard and fast, and, like his maker, he abandons all thoughts except for its satisfaction.

He bites into his lower lip and a thin line of scarlet scurries down his chin as he scans the immobilised prey in front of him. His bright copper eyes flick to Olivier and Céline.

They each extend a hand, and a mind-whisper from Oliver caresses Éric's fledgling brain.

The second choice is yours, Éric.

Holy fucking shit, Éric thinks, swallowing hard. His hands begin to tremble. *I can't fucking do this.* But just then he catches a scent from the only female crew member. She smells like Megan and he falls on her, knocking her to the floor. Her eyes are vacant, but she caresses a gentle finger down Éric's cheek as if she wants him to kiss her.

"Please don't scream," he whispers.

A shudder runs down Éric's back and he flings his head back, fixating on the chandelier above him. One deep breath and his head falls once more, his eyes glaze over ... he plunges his fangs into her neck with such force that blood splatters a metre across the marble floor. He jerks away when he hears it splash but the fragrance focusses him again, and he suckles her as if he's starving.

Vauquelin stoops next to Éric, strokes the back of his fledgling's head. "Is this night as difficult as you imagined, bien-aimé?"[†]

"After that epic intro? No way." Éric's voice is garbled by blood.

A crooked grin and he dives right back in.

Vauquelin admires Éric's style, despite the fact that he is making a mess. "Remember, do not drink past the last beat," he whispers into Éric's hair. "Never drink the last."

Éric places a hand against her heart. It's so, so faint now.

"I think I've had enough." He stands tall and licks the remaining blood from his lips, surveying the room.

Bodies are scattered across the floor.

Olivier and Céline have already retired, backing one another up with violent kisses into their bedchamber.

The air is fragranced with iron, accented with the piquant top notes of vampire pheromones after a kill.

"What'll we do with them?" Éric whispers.

"We will dispose of them tomorrow night. They can wait."

Vauquelin stoops to retrieve the video camera, flipping the power off.

He gives it to Éric. "A souvenir for you."

Éric's desire stirs. He sets the camera on a table and takes Vauquelin's hand, sending his own silent message.

It's my turn to be in control.

The smell of a man is vastly different from the smell of a woman: pepperier, muskier ... although they both carry their secret olfactory delights.

The female body is slippery, soft and welcoming — the male body is war:

---

rigid, aggressive, ready for battle at a moment's notice.

Éric yelps in bittersweet pain when their close-to-the-skin hip bones collide, and the bravado he brought into this room rapidly slips away. Even so, he pushes Vauquelin's head down the trail below his abdomen.

I need your mouth on me. I need it.

Vauquelin brushes his cheekbone along Éric's cock, intoxicated by its aromatic fragrance, its silken texture ... he looks directly into Éric's eyes as he snakes his tongue up its veined length, grazing the velvety surface with the tips of his teeth.

Éric shudders as Vauquelin licks the blood away.

Vauquelin rises to his knees and leans over at a drastic angle — reaching for a vessel on the night-table — and takes Éric's hands in his, coating them in vetiver-scented lanolin. Their eyes grow heavy with desire ... their cheeks are warm from their kill, their alabaster skin flushed scarlet with the blood of the victims they had consumed.

Éric swerves behind him, chest-to-back, encircling an arm around Vauquelin's waist, gracefully upthrusting. He holds fast to Vauquelin's bicep, punctuating his skin with petite love bites, losing himself in his maker's body.

Vauquelin casts an arm back, bringing his hand behind Éric's head — they groan in unison with each rapturous surge of Éric's hips.

Afterward, they lie breathlessly tangled together, both their skins glistening with lanolin streaks and the slightest blood sweat, the bedsheets spattered with tinges of pink. Vauquelin bites the fleshy mound of Éric's shoulder, urging out his honeyed blood and savouring its dense roll like nectar across his tongue.

Éric nuzzles him, silently enquiring, and Vauquelin turns his head to the side, inviting his lover to drink from him with a contented sigh. He latches onto Éric's exposed neck and the struggle begins.

What happens when two male vampires, with their shared blood pumping at its height, tangle against one another for domination?

War ensues.

A war that cannot be won, not when their desire is on such equal footing.

All fangs now subdermal, their bodies push and pull — knocking into one other as their blood merges.

They both withdraw simultaneously — gasping — sucking the blood from their teeth.

Vauquelin crumbles on the bed, clutching at Éric, desperate to keep him close. How can he be so strong and yet so weak at once?

A battle indeed.

Until Éric, everything in Vauquelin's life has been unpredictable.

But he hopes against hope that this will endure, that it will remain as true as it is in this moment.

Is that too much to ask?

Their skirmish ebbs, overtaken by a hastening urge to rejoin, succumbing to tender kisses. To give one another sweet apologies for the primal aggression they can never tame.

« Je t'aime,[†] Éric , » Vauquelin breathes. He heaves his fledgling onto his stomach, bringing Éric's hips up to join his own.

"I'll love you forever," Éric gasps.

He rocks into Éric's body, sending them both into ecstasy ... and possibly oblivion.

---

†- I LOVE YOU

Forty-four

Olivier notices Éric sitting alone at a table in the library, reading.

"Ah, more studying! Good boy. What are you looking at?" he asks.

"Fashion plates from the seventeenth century." Éric bristles. He doesn't actually appreciate being called a *good boy*. What is he, a fucking puppy? "Just trying to picture V wearing all this stuff."

"V, hmmm?" Olivier grimaces ... he knows how deeply their maker despises sobriquets. "Wondering how Vauquelin used to look? I can tell you all about that. Once upon a time, I dressed him daily ... and then nightly. I was his servant. For many decades."

Olivier slides into the chair next to Éric.

"His portrait in Paris is the only way to see how he looked during that era. That is where you will truly understand him. He commissioned it after his second turning. It hangs above the fireplace in his bedchamber."

"I know," Éric says with a smug grin. "It's the first thing he showed me the night we arrived from the States."

They lock one another into a narrow-eyed stare down.

"Do not dare assume you know him as deeply I do," Olivier hisses through gritted teeth.

"Oh yeah?" Éric huffs. "Trust ..." He hikes a defiant eyebrow. "I *know* him. Better than you do." He folds his arms and rocks back in the chair.

At first, Olivier had been relieved that Vauquelin found a companion, but now the reality of it disturbs him. He has known Vauquelin for centuries, but his maker's cocky young fledgling is getting under his skin.

"Do you then? Well, let me tell you something you do not know. If one night you cannot find Vauquelin, do not worry. He disappears sometimes without warning. But rest assured, it will not be your fault."

As soon as the words leave his mouth, Olivier bites his inner lip.

He has made an unjustifiable error ... but it is too late to take it back.

The words float in the atmosphere like the fragrance of blood.

The gravity of Olivier's revelation bottoms Éric out, stealing the breath from his lungs, defusing his insolence.

"Where would he go without telling me?" he murmurs.

Despite Éric's onset vulnerability, the damage is done.

Olivier doubles down.

"It is less a matter of where than *when*. How curious... has he not yet explained this to you?"

Vauquelin appears in the doorway, just in time to overhear that last question: he glances from Olivier to Éric and back again.

Éric's hands are tucked into his armpits, his torso deeply bent at his waist — his face bears the countenance of one who has just been slapped. Vauquelin's tall, towering beloved has somehow made himself smaller, diminishing as if he wants to disappear: and the sight of Éric in this humiliated condition raises all of Vauquelin's hackles.

Profound hostility permeates the air.

"That I have not yet explained *what*, Olivier?" Vauquelin's voice rises in panic with each syllable, culminating in a shout.

Olivier averts his eyes.

"V? What's going on, what have you not told me?" Éric demands.

He runs to Vauquelin and grasps the lapels of his jacket.

A vein erupts on Vauquelin's forehead as he sends a silent message to Olivier: *Thank you for ruining this for me.*

Olivier has seldom seen his maker so flustered — nor has Éric.

Vauquelin had been thinking for weeks on how to broach the fragile topic of his improbable timeline to Éric, who has already been inundated with oceans of information as it is. He was awaiting the perfect time, the one definitive moment when Éric's ears would be prepared to hear it, for the time when both of their souls were strong enough to carry its heaviness together.

And now Olivier has crossed a line for the first time in their long history together: yet another betrayal for Vauquelin's ever-growing list.

"This is not the proper setting for this subject," Vauquelin growls.

Éric's face is written over with panic. "Fuck that! You have to tell me *now*! You said you'd never abandon me!"

"And I never will." Vauquelin delivers a death glare to Olivier, who prudently rises and leaves the room, slamming the doors behind him.

He flickers his gaze back to Éric, softening his expression.

"Where will you go? Why can't I go with you, wherever it is?"

Vauquelin turns his back. "I cannot answer that, my love. Because I do not know, and this is only my burden to bear."

"No, it isn't, V. Now it's mine, too." Éric's chin quivers, and he whispers, "You lied to me."

"I most certainly did not! I had yet to find the right words to explain!"

"Lying by omission, then. Why should I believe you? The first word I heard out of your mouth was a lie!" Éric jabs a finger into Vauquelin's breastbone. "A fake name!" Bloody tears well in the corners of his eyes. "So what else have you lied about? You made me this way. You brought me to France. I gave up my entire life for you. You're responsible for me!"

"You think I do not realise that?" Vauquelin bellows. "Your existence is my greatest treasure! Your creation was not by whim or accident. It should come as no surprise to you that I have an enemy, Éric. My darling, my love …

I am no saint. I have existed the entirety of my life upon a bedrock of lies. That stopped with you. I only offer you my truth ... always."

Olivier crouches outside the door, eavesdropping, beating a fist against his forehead. He has jeopardised his epochs-long relationship with Vauquelin ... for a *fledgling*.

"Then explain it! Don't I deserve that?"

Vauquelin sinks into a chair, resting his elbows on his knees.

"Where can I even start? My life is a multi-volume history."

Éric sits at his feet. "I want to know everything. Every little detail. From the beginning."

The mere thought of recounting his history envelops Vauquelin in a shroud of exhaustion, and for a flash of a second, he looks ancient — not thirty. Deep shadows sweep across his face, but in a flutter of a moth's wing he is Vauquelin again.

First he must extinguish his rage at Olivier, at his desire to make him pay for his blunder. Despite the fracture, Vauquelin understands that Olivier is one of only two beings he can trust with Éric's welfare should his time shift again.

Regardless ... Vauquelin must own this: he should have already informed Éric. He cannot blame Olivier for his own failures.

« Bien-aimé , »[†] he begins, cupping Éric's chin in his hand. Speech strangles on his tongue.

Had Yvain ever once felt this way about him?

He doubts it, for he was only ever Yvain's creature.

As he so adored addressing Vauquelin.

But when Vauquelin looks at Éric he does not see a creature, a mere product of his own curse — he sees a future, a boundless wealth of love ... a love which is unfortunately shadowed by their very nature.

Yvain never loved Vauquelin.

---

†- BELOVED

Vauquelin was an object.

A collectible.

Éric is far beyond that ... Vauquelin's passion for him has surpassed anything he has ever known, has escalated into an almost religious fervour.

And now his beloved is staring up at him, his face distorted by concern and expectations, waiting to hear his history: a history so dark, bloody, and mind-bending that Vauquelin hates to let it leave his lips. He wishes to protect Éric from such horror.

But he cannot.

His truth is the *very* least he owes Éric, and his debts to him are incalculable.

Éric, who had surrendered his humanity to be with him.

Vauquelin refuses to be the Yvain in his fledgling's life.

And so he tells him everything.

Forty-five

"How is it possible that you could just be snatched up and dropped into another era? What, like you're just cut and pasted? I don't get it. Sorry, but it totally doesn't seem like something that could actually happen."

"Our very *existence* does not seem possible, Éric. I do not understand it myself. In my first timeline, I survived until the same year I met you. I lived in Los Angeles. Perhaps our paths crossed then, and we never knew it. It was not destined for us to meet at that time. And then my history began to unwind, bringing me back to 1668 yet again, to the night I was first made vampire. From there, time marched forward."

"So what happens to everyone else if your time slips? They just have to go on without you?"

The verbalised prospect sends them both into a tailspin and they frantically cling to one another.

Vauquelin cradles Éric's head against his shoulder, preventing his fledgling from witnessing the expression of profound desolation that has settled on his face.

"Do you know why you had to go back?"

"Yvain brought me there, to answer for my alleged mistakes."

"He sounds like a total fucking douchebag."

The word throws Vauquelin for a loop, but he gets the gist ... it is such a very modern, very Éric thing to say, and despite the gravity of the topic, he erupts into peals of laughter. Just as quickly though, his countenance grows grim once again.

"He is savage and capricious, and I am just a toy to him. He never cared for me. A month before I met you I was in Paris, only in the year 1935. I thought I recognised someone from my past standing on the sidewalk opposite my house. By the time I reached the middle of the street my time shifted to this past year. I returned to Los Angeles because I once loved that city, and I missed it. I was making plans to return to my origins, to learn how to get myself back, because I thought that was where I truly belonged. But then you walked into my life, my darling one, and turned my world upside down."

"Oh my god ... it happened that recently?" Éric whispers, his voice breaking. "But ... do you still want to go back?"

His mind is drowning in the extraordinary chronicle Vauquelin has recounted, struggling under its depths.

It's so hard to believe, but he's trying.

"Never ... because you do not exist in my past. I could no longer survive a life without you in it. You are my present and future, Éric, and that is where I belong. By your side, for always ... forward, not back."

"But you just admitted you can't control it! What if it happens again? What'll we do?" Éric buries his head in Vauquelin's lap.

Vauquelin stares straight ahead into the fireplace, his long fingers massaging Éric's shoulder.

Despite the warmth of the room, ice bleeds across his heart like overnight frost on a window.

He asked for this.

And now he can only wait for the bottom to fall out of their sublime life.

The storytelling and interrogations have drained Vauquelin and slumber falls upon him quickly, but Éric is restless.

Each time Vauquelin's eyes close, Éric pokes him with another question or statement.

"So ... about what's-her-name." Éric refuses to say it out loud.

"Please go to sleep, Éric," Vauquelin yawns.

His heart is slowing ... he cannot remain awake much longer.

"I beg you. We will talk more tomorrow night."

"I still can't wrap my head around the fact that you lived with a woman for so long."

"Does this trouble you?"

"I'm not sure yet."

Vauquelin drags a hand down his face and sucks his teeth.

"Here's the thing, Éric ... you are not allowed to be bothered by my past, nor am I allowed to be bothered by yours. We cannot be expected to apologise for the things we have done or people we have known before we met. All that aside ... jealousy is unbecoming in a vampire, my love."

"I guess I just don't understand."

Vauquelin hoists himself onto his side. "What is there to understand, my love? I am an ancient being. Surely you realise I have not been an angel all these years. My sexuality is fluid: I love minds first, then I come to love the bodies that hold them. I truly do not regard attraction in terms of men or women. In fact, at times I find it hard to think of myself as one or the other."

Eric sulks with his arms folded.

"Come now. Am I to believe you have never slept with a woman?"

"NO! Not even once! I love girls, but I have zero interest in fucking them. So what happens when you get bored with me and decide you need to go get some pussy? It wouldn't be the first time I've been screwed over by someone who only thought he was gay."

Vauquelin shoulders slump.

How could anyone break Éric's heart?

But then another memory washes over him, a pre-vampire memory that he had long buried away. He, too, had been discarded by such a duplicitous lover.

"Then we must consider ourselves fortunate. If he had not left you, perhaps we would not be together." He pauses, swallowing back a lump in his throat as he realises the same could be said for Maeve. So much truth... he is unaccustomed to its sharp, implacable edges. "However, I do not love labels, my sweet, and I never will."

He secretly adores seeing Éric's sudden jealous streak. But he dares not let his face betray it — he is determined to take Éric seriously at all times, despite his occasional naïveté. Éric deserves to work through every confusing emotion that comes his way, and there are many yet ahead.

"What is it you infer, Éric?" he asks, splaying his hands. "Are you asking me to be faithful to you?"

"YES."

Vauquelin drags a thumb across Eric's pouty bottom lip.

"You did not have to ask, my love. I gave you my name. You are the only one, my constant. My eyes will never wander ... no other could ever compare to you."

Éric's rage subsides, but he isn't done having his say.

"What if she tries to find you? Was she ever here in this house?"

"No, I never brought her to France. Believe me, she has no interest in me, nor I in her," Vauquelin says. "I do not even know where she is now."

"The thought of anyone else touching you like I do makes me sick."

"No one will ever have that privilege. And I would destroy anyone who dared to touch you. This goes both ways, you realise. I am *yours*, Éric ...

we belong to each other, and nothing, not even time, will ever change that. My life is no longer mine. I have ceased to be me without you."

He kisses Éric, running his hand down his fledgling's silky thigh.

Then he turns over and sails a pillow at Éric's face.

"Now go to sleep."

"UGH!"

"Éric …"

Forty-six

PARIS, FRANCE | APRIL

Prior to leaving Évreux, Éric had plaintively asked Vauquelin if he still wanted to return to the seventeenth century — and he answered with an emphatic no.

Never again.

He had lived in limbo for so long, prior to the unexpected reward of Éric's presence — he did not believe he truly belonged anywhere.

Not in the past, nor in the future.

He desired to return to his birth era for one reason: it was the closest he could come to genuine comfort.

He dreamed only of retrieving the tattered remnants of what he once loved in his futurepast, of finding a way to carry them with him to the only time in which he truly felt at peace.

But then Éric manifested in his life like so much urgently needed sunlight, and everything changed.

His fledgling has been scampering around the house since sundown. The sound of power tools (and occasional profanity) reverberates across the walls. Vauquelin's anxiety is at its peak and he recoils from the unfamiliar racket, hoping Éric is not damaging ancient surfaces.

But then again — Vauquelin reminds himself — after their little show at the château, he must trust Éric to have respect.

At last the unnerving electrical din stops, and Vauquelin knocks on the library doors. "May I come in now?"

Éric opens them with a flourish and a big smile.

"I can't wait for you to hear this!" He takes Vauquelin's hand. "Sit down ... lean back."

Éric fiddles with Vauquelin's phone, and the silence in the room is eradicated by one of Vauquelin's reclaimed digital playlists.

"So there are wireless speakers all over the place now, in every room. Even the bathroom. We can play whatever you want, and it'll broadcast on all the speakers. We can even put on different music in different parts of the house. I'll show you how to do it."

Vauquelin shakes his head in wondrous disbelief.

Now he has exactly what he intended to achieve in the first place: to be surrounded by the epochal objets[†] that make him who he is, to immerse himself in his ancientness with souvenirs of his other, modern life.

Only one thing was missing from that list: something he did not know he not only wanted, but desperately *needed*.

And now that something is stretched out on the chaise alongside him, his head in his lap. Vauquelin dips a hand in Éric's curls, leaning forward to rest his lips upon his beloved's forehead.

"I'll be right back. I'm gonna run down to the TABAC,"[‡] Éric says, picking up his board.

"No!" Vauquelin knocks his laptop over and it clatters to the floor.

---

† - TRINKETS
‡ - TOBACCONIST

He yanks it up, inspecting it for damage. "Absolutely not."

Éric stops with one arm jacketed, the other hanging at his side.

"Why not?"

"I forbid it, that is why *not*. How could you ask this, Éric, after everything I've told you?"

Éric flops down in a chair. "We're out of tobacco. I don't understand why I can't go out by myself. I grew up in L.A. — I told you I can handle it. I promise I won't get into any trouble."

"When you grew up in L.A. you were not mine. I am busy. Have some delivered."

Éric's heart twitters at hearing *mine*, but he really wants to go out.

"I just wanted to get some fresh air," he mumbles, his face sullen as he picks at a loose thread on the ripped knees of his jeans.

"You have heard my history. You are my bloodline, Éric. It is not that I do not trust *you*. You already know there are things at play in our life that give me great fear for our safety, and I could not bear it if someone were to harm you. So no. You cannot go out alone. In fact, I do not want you opening the door or going outside the gates without me."

"But I can heal ... and I'm immortal!" Éric's eyes flash with just the slightest hint of defiance — he's a little bruised by V's patriarchal tone. But then he recognises the serious expression on Vauquelin's face. It reminds him that V could vanish at any moment, and his fragile swagger fades away.

Our safety.

Ours.

His throat tightens.

In fact Vauquelin had given him very few rules, and when he thinks about it those rules are all pretty practical. Éric reminds himself he still has a lot to learn, that he has to take his new life seriously.

Things are not the same as they were when he was human ... they never will be again.

"Wait. Would Yvain ever come after *me*?"

Hearing that cursed name cross Éric's tongue, combined with the thought of Yvain laying a finger on him, makes Vauquelin woozy and his shoulders cave.

Yvain has a rotten soul.

Despite the fact that Yvain released him centuries ago, Vauquelin has never shaken the shackles of paranoia that grip his psyche. Still, someone is always watching him, and he is convinced Yvain is behind it. The French vampire kindred is a delicate filigree — their numbers are small.

They talk.

Granted, Vauquelin does not associate with them, but he suspects they are aware of his every move, reporting everything back to Yvain.

Éric's pitiful, confused countenance moves Vauquelin.

"My darling, come. Please. Let us have the tobacco delivered."

They order from an app.

"I will take you anywhere you want to go, show you anything you would like to see," Vauquelin says. "You are not a prisoner. But I love you, Éric, and I must ask you to trust me if anything I demand seems unreasonable, just for a while. Please. I cannot lose you." His eyes redden, and he makes no attempt to disguise his emotions.

Vauquelin draws their foreheads together, delivers his beloved a snippet of darkness ... undefinable but severe and devastating. "You must let me at least try to protect what we have."

"Okay, V. I promise," Éric whispers.

But Vauquelin's shared vision deposits dread deep in the pits of Éric's psyche. He was raised on superstition. If someone could harm him, what about V?

What would he do without him?

Don't think about it, Éric consoles himself. *Just listen to him.*

When the bell rings at the gate Vauquelin answers, returning with a plastic bag laden with tobacco and rolling papers.

He spends a while showing Éric how to roll cigarettes like a champion.

"Damn it! How do you get them so perfect every single time?"

"Centuries of practice," Vauquelin says with a smile, but it aches on his lips. "You will have it down in no time. Now I will ask you to excuse me ... I will return soon." He plunges his hands in his pockets, kissing the crown of Éric's head, and vanishes deep into the bowels of the house.

Just a few months into his vampiric state, time has already begun to lose its meaning for Éric ... soon, dawn is approaching, he's rolled thirty impeccable cigarettes, and Vauquelin still isn't back.

Éric ambles through the hallways, searching for him.

He finds him at last in the catacombs, sitting in a corner, framed by bones ... his face streaked with blood.

Éric crouches in front of him and takes one of Vauquelin's hands, kissing each finger. "How can I make it better?"

Vauquelin begins weeping in earnest and hangs his head.

"Oh god ..."

"Tell me." Eric sinks next to him, wrapping an arm around Vauquelin's shoulders. "I have all the time in the world." With his gentle, asymmetric smile, and a tilt of his head, he smooths Vauquelin's hair behind his ears.

Words are inadequate to explain Vauquelin's distress, but his face is wretched with his terror of losing this life they are building together.

Things are too good, too open, and he has never had that, even though he thought he did ... once. But it was never like this. Éric now knows everything about him, every gory, ugly detail, and Vauquelin's own blood runs through his veins.

He dove head-first into Éric's waters with his heart on his sleeve.

In his entire multi-century life, Vauquelin has never been as close to another being as he is to Éric: not even Maeve, because he had never allowed her to truly know him ... and by the time he was ready, it was too late.

Éric knows Vauquelin's body ... he knows his mind: he has caressed the interiors of his soul.

How can Vauquelin admit that he has laid himself bare, accurately describe the nakedness that cripples him without his steely fortress walls to insulate him?

Yet he must find the strength to confess it, or he will slip directly back into his existence of lies.

And he must acknowledge that Éric has done the same for him.

"Don't you know I adore you?" Éric asks.

"I do know," Vauquelin whispers, "and that is why I am crying."

Éric coaxes him up and leads him upstairs to bed.

Vauquelin falls asleep cradled in Éric's arms.

Forty-seven

PARIS, FRANCE | APRIL

"Can we buy at least one mirror?" Éric asks out of the blue. "Just one?"

"Why? What would be the point?"

"I want to do an experiment."

Vauquelin finds it difficult to say no to Éric, at least when his safety is not in question. He knows full well what the results will be: regardless, he surrenders. Éric deserves his own experiences, his own disappointments — he cannot be expected to robotically follow esoteric rules.

Two nights later, a herculean mirror arrives and Éric hauls it into their bedchamber, shutting the door behind him and locking Vauquelin out.

Éric takes his phone and positions himself in front of the mirror.

From his perspective, it looks as though the phone is floating in mid-air. Still unsettling ... still freaky.

Whew.

His first time confronting his absence in a mirror ... how could anyone ever get used to that?

He turns the phone backward, holding it beside his face, and snaps a photo. He blows air through his lips, turning it around to see the results, and — *nothing*.

Éric shuffles out of the room and into the library, where Vauquelin is stretched out reading.

He's been reading so much lately.

Éric wonders why, but he doesn't want to pry.

He drops to the ground and shows Vauquelin the selfie he took in the mirror.

"My idea didn't work," he says, his eyes downcast.

"I am so sorry, Éric. Regrettably some lessons can only be learned the hard way." Vauquelin tilts his head and strokes Éric's hair. It hurts him to see him so disappointed.

"I just wanted a photo of us together," Éric sighs. "Our full bodies, not just selfies. I thought maybe the camera could outsmart the mirror."

"Then we shall have it."

A week later Vauquelin's salon is swarming with photography equipment and hair and makeup people, and a photographer barks orders while assistants set up the gear.

Prior to their arrival, Éric spent considerable time planning a special ensemble for their final set. He made a checklist on his phone, gathered all the pieces, and pushed them to the back of his own closet — concealing it from Vauquelin.

Tonight, Éric is well-fed: Vauquelin has warned him repeatedly about mingling with humans when one has the thirst. And there would be far too many tantalising mortals in this house to expect a famished young vampire to control himself.

The crew had arrived in the afternoon while Éric and Vauquelin were sleeping, admitted by Vauquelin's attorney, and they remain there through the night, photographing the lovers through multiple wardrobe changes.

These photographs will just be for Vauquelin and Éric: no one else will see them. Ever. It seems shameful that this overwhelming beauty, this bountiful love they possess, cannot be shared with the world — that it must be hidden away from others' eyes. Even so, Vauquelin remains vigilant about protecting his fledgling, and he refuses to expose their identity to these mortal strangers.

"No showing of teeth and no biting tonight," Vauquelin warns Éric before they enter.

"Bummer. I guess we'll have to leave that to selfies." Éric thrusts out a petulant lower lip. But he gets it — the truth about them must remain concealed in the shadows. He's lucky V even agreed in the first place.

Éric is a natural … the camera adores him.

He is wholly in his element.

He had participated in fashion shows before at his old job, and had demonstrated an affinity for styling and working with cameras — however, he had never before attended a full-scale fashion shoot. The equipment and the process fascinates him.

He even made a playlist for this night: a sexy, energetic soundtrack.

"How do you manage this?" Vauquelin asks, tilting his head as he marvels at the sight of Éric moving and posturing in a solo set: his fledgling contorts his body into some truly improbable angles. "I believe you have done this professionally before, no?"

"Ha! No way!" Éric steps out of his pose and twirls. "I've just had a lifelong obsession with fashion magazines. This is so fucking cool! Thanks for doing this for me, my love."

This is a lot of pressure for Vauquelin. He wrings his hands and watches Éric, befuddled by the sight of him in the midst of so many humans. He considers whether he had lost his senses in allowing this spectacle — there is no pleasure to be gained from having so many eyes directed upon himself and Éric, nor does he appreciate having strangers in their domain.

The music, the inane chattering of mortals, the very modern modishness of his fledgling pirouetting in the backdrop of the ancient artefacts of his centuries ... it all floods his heart with a complicated deluge of emotions. He suddenly wants to whisk Éric away, to hide him from anyone else's scrutiny — he feels so exposed and so in love that he wants to burst into flames.

But he tamps those thoughts down. It is, after all, only one night, and he must acknowledge that Éric desperately needs this adventure.

"Where did you find this French music? Even I have never heard this!"

"Easy. I'll always be younger than you." Éric dances up to Vauquelin, gyrating their hips together and gently urging his maker's lower lip out, grazing their tongues together before he grooves his way back in front of the cameras.

So much life ... so much vibrancy.

"Last set," the photographer calls. The crew is wilting ... it is almost three in the morning, and they've been here nearly twelve hours.

"Hang on," Éric says, holding up a finger and backing out of the room. "I'm gonna change in another room. V ... wear whatever you want. Think about it. I'll be right back."

Vauquelin cocks a questioning brow, curious to know what Éric is scheming. While he is gone, he slips behind the screen and listlessly flips through the portable racks they bought for this event.

He knots his hair atop his head and emerges in a black tuxedo jacket with tails lined in crimson ... the tails graze the floor. He is shirtless, as Éric always seems to prefer, and wearing black, wide-legged trousers with red velvet embroidered slippers.

Vauquelin brings forth an antique box of mouches[†] from his pocket and selects a heart, dampening it on his tongue, and pats it expertly onto his cheekbone, just below his left eye.

---

†- ARTIFICIAL BEAUTY MARKS FASHIONABLE IN EUROPE IN THE 16TH- 18TH CENTURIES

He hands a lipstick to the makeup artist and pouts while she dresses his lips. When she finishes she produces a mirror — he grasps her wrist and gives her a stern shake of his head.

"How are these guys still going?" the photographer's assistant whispers to a technician. "I'm exhausted!"

The technician shrugs.

"Cocaine?" he mouths.

The doors creak, opening a crack.

One could hear a pin drop, yet the sound of Éric's whispered voice takes ownership over the room.

"Everybody ready?"

"We're only waiting on you, Éric," Vauquelin says, a bit more impatiently than he intended. In truth, he is more than a little bored, and Éric's confidence and body movements have shifted his mind to more private activities with his fledgling.

"Here I am ..." Éric flings the doors wide.

Vauquelin's jaw drops.

He has become somewhat accustomed to the serendipitous surprises Éric delivers on a regular basis, but he could never have prepared himself for this.

Éric emerges through the tall gilded doors to the salon in head-to-toe seventeenth-century costume. Down to a sword in its hilt, down to the silk stockings and red-heeled shoes upon his feet.

Unfortunately, Éric has made a lamentable choice: he is wearing the infamous pink *justaucorps* — the jacket Vauquelin had worn at both of his turnings, and the sight of his beloved in this evil relic upsets him.

« Pardonnez-moi , »[†] Vauquelin mutters. He strides out of the room, brusquely brushing Éric's shoulder aside as he passes. He props himself

---

†- PARDON ME

against the wall just outside, rubbing his eyes and clamouring out of his jacket, letting it fall to the floor as Éric rushes to him.

"Oh no! Are you mad? Please don't be mad. I know, I snooped. I'm sorry —" Éric clamps his hands over his mouth.

"No, mon amour,[†] you have done nothing wrong. You could not have known. I just … I must put myself back together." His body is hunched over … his eyes are bloodshot. "Please tell them we need a minute."

He marches upstairs to the bathroom and splashes his face, unconvinced he has sufficiently regained his composure. His chin quivers as he rifles through his armoire, dressing himself in clothing he has not worn in ages. All crimson and silver and diamonds. He lets his hair back down to its full length and leans on his ebony, devil's-head walking stick. The weight of his centuries — now adorning his fledgling's divine body — submerges him in the depths of his pathos.

But he refuses to ruin Éric's splendid evening.

He meets Éric in the hallway outside the salon and gallantly kisses his hand. "I must apologise for my outburst, Éric. I only wish you had been with me from the beginning … but since you have not, you have given me the greatest gift I have ever received: the pleasure of seeing you as you might have looked."

Éric stops breathing for a second.

Vauquelin is magnificent.

He looks … *correct*.

Like his portrait.

The sight of him sends Éric's blood vibrating to the thrum of his heart. Of all the fantastical, unbelievable experiences he's had since becoming vampire, this one almost brings him to his knees.

"Don't be sorry, V. I just wanted to surprise you," Éric whispers, "but it turns out I'm the one whose breath is taken away."

---

†- MY LOVE

"You give me so much euphoria, so much beauty, and to think I believed life could no longer delight me. How wrong I was. Shall we return?"

Yet his feet do not move forward.

It is a benchmark for Vauquelin, another cataclysmic point in his eldritch history. Now he has learned it is impossible for one to repeat it, nor can one recreate it — one must be open to change, and embrace all the wonderful things that new life has to offer.

He had been blind to this throughout his ages.

And his successful turning of Éric, with candour and fidelity emulsifying their mutual blood, is his benediction.

His eyes grow vacant as he parts the threadbare curtains of his backstory.

His heart sinks for Maeve.

He had destroyed her.

She still owns a piece of him.

She always will.

"They're waiting for us," Éric says, but then he notices Vauquelin's long face. "V... are you okay?"

Vauquelin clutches Éric's hands, bringing their chests together.

His past is his past — and Éric deserves his here and now.

"Just the whisperings of ghosts. You have unfortunately raised some spectres with your escapade. It is bound to happen. Please be patient with me?" A weary smile lifts a corner of his mouth.

"Always."

They make their entrance arm-in-arm, striding across the parquet floor, both astonishingly tall — the heels of their shoes hammering the parquet, the clanging steel of their swords interrupting the collectively stunned silence of the crew.

Their phantasmal appearance — under the auspices of Éric's very contemporary playlist — ignites a devilishly postmodern mood across the salon.

Ancient history — merging with the present.

Intoxicating.

The photographer immediately begins shooting when they pass through the doors. "My god," he breathes. "Look at you two. Absolutely ravishing. These costumes are priceless, Monsieur de Vauquelin. How did you come to own them?"

Vauquelin turns to Éric and winks. "They've been in my family for generations."

That morning, after the crew has long gone and Éric has fallen asleep, Vauquelin feeds the ominous pink *justaucorps* into the bedroom fireplace with a poker.

He rejoices in watching it burn.

Forty-eight

PARIS, FRANCE | APRIL

Éric is not in bed next to him when the sun sets, but Vauquelin is slowly learning to ease his worry about that (somewhat).

No doubt Éric is in the room he has chosen for himself: he had created a lair of sorts, turning one of Vauquelin's many unused spaces into a game lounge. His console would emit a cacophony of bizarre noises blasting in surround sound — crashing cars, revving engines, ear-splitting music, automatic weapons, screams — all tripping and echoing off the six metre ceiling, the unfamiliar sounds misunderstood by the ancient walls of the room.

Vauquelin cannot quite grasp the appeal of these games — nevertheless he loves to lean against the open doors, watching Éric twitch on the seventeenth-century sofa, working his controller and shouting obscenities at the flat screen mounted on the wall.

He adores his fledgling and all his enigmatic, thoroughly modern ways.

But tonight the house is quiet.

Éric had warned Vauquelin, only a few nights ago, that he was letting his constant worries rob them both of living in the moment.

Of enjoying and loving each other as they are, NOW.

That V needs to chill.

But as Vauquelin wanders the halls searching for him, he realises that Éric's scent has evaporated, and panic spirals through his veins.

Perhaps he had become *too* chill.

Éric is not in the library.

Nor is his skateboard propped next to the front door, as had become his habit.

His first fear is that Éric has gone out alone, against his advice.

But then he flings open the doors to Éric's lair, and finds the room devoid of equipment.

No television screen.

No gaming console.

No speakers.

No Éric.

Vauquelin sprints outside.

The street beyond his courtyard is bustling with carriages and night merchants.

Blood tears flood his eyes and he falls forward on the cobblestone drive, punching it with his fists and wrecking the skin on his knuckles.

He pushes himself up in his wrath, and through the gates he sees Clément leering at him, shaking his head in pity. And dressed in the height of seventeenth-century fashion.

They approach one another on their opposite sides, and Vauquelin grips the bars with his long, cold fingers.

His face is streaked with blood, boldly displaying his desperation.

"Why?" He pounds on the gate. "Why, why, WHY?"

"Please let me in." Clément's expression softens.

He had once felt something akin to love for Vauquelin, and though he is complicit in this particular time-slip, he takes no pleasure in seeing Vauquelin suffer.

"I will explain."

"I cannot let you in, I cannot reach the ..." Vauquelin swallows his next word: *keypad*. He drops his hand into the pocket of his banyan and, instead of the remote that should be there, his fingers graze the unmistakable heaviness of a brass key.

Fuck.

His eyes go blank as he wrestles the key into the lock and creaks the gates open.

Clément lifts his walking stick and bends his torso in the slightest bow as he saunters in. "*Merci*. It has been quite a while, Vauquelin."

Vauquelin refuses to look at him. He opens the door and thrusts an arm to the interior. The house seems altogether wrong and surreal, disenchanted by Éric's glaring absence.

Clément removes his gauntlet gloves, one slow finger at a time, as he surveys the foyer. "I remember your home well, Vauquelin. That exquisite night of our flight here, and how we found refuge from Yvain."

Vauquelin turns his head. His chest heaves.

"Yvain released me. Yet each morsel of happiness I manage to hold in my grasp is stolen by him. Your presence confirms it. So why are you here? What do you have against me?"

"It is not my doing. It is Yvain. He wishes to see you, to make amends. That is why I appeared to you before your last slip. You were not meant to return to the future in 1935, Vauquelin. You were meant to be here, in this era. Something went awry. I am unsure what happened that night, what caused you to be whisked forward instead. But ..." Clément folds his hands. "It no longer matters. Here we are. Together again."

Vauquelin jams his tongue against his teeth and his jaw muscles begin to twitch. Without Yvain's miscalculation, then, Vauquelin would never have met Éric ... it was an accident. "I suppose I should be grateful?"

"I have indeed missed you."

The vainglorious Clément assumes Vauquelin is talking about him!

Clément was an anomaly in Vauquelin's re-traversal of time, and in fact, Vauquelin had often had his thoughts disrupted by memories of Clément, and the tectonic night they spent together.

But Clément belongs to Yvain, and that fact necessitated their parting.

Vauquelin is different now ... they are both different.

The last thing in the world Vauquelin wants is to lay eyes upon his wretched maker. Yet he must, and he cannot deny it.

"Where is he?"

"At the château, of course." Clément slaps the gloves against his palm. "Dress yourself. I will wait. Then I will accompany you there."

Yvain's cruel laughter echoes in Vauquelin ears — he muffles it with his hands, releasing an ear-piercing scream borne from the anguish of his tormented ages.

Clément hunches over, wincing.

At Vauquelin's uproar Olivier sprints down the staircase into the foyer, perplexed by his maker having a visitor. This is most uncommon.

He looks back and forth between Clément and Vauquelin.

"What is the meaning of this?" Olivier exclaims in a rising voice. "Vauquelin, did you invite this man here?"

Vauquelin's mind stutters.

He does not know the exact year in which he has landed.

Perhaps, in this new timeline, Olivier is not yet vampire.

Vauquelin cannot fathom turning him again in the midst of this chaos.

But as Olivier bellows his questions, Vauquelin realises that his teeth are down and he has called him Vauquelin — not Monsieur, as he insisted upon when he was mortal.

"That is an emphatic no, my brother. Nevertheless, he is here, and I have this under control." He is nonplussed by his own confidence.

Vauquelin squeezes Olivier's shoulder and retreats to his bedchamber, taking the steps two at a time.

While he dresses, he thinks only of Éric, who at this point in time is centuries away from being born. And now he cannot even look at the beautiful photographs they had taken: they are locked away in Vauquelin's filmy, newly-forged futurepast.

« Tu me manques, mon cœur … »[†] he whispers.

His life is incomplete once more, as if a limb has been severed, and his stolen love echoes in his ears.

How dare he have had the audacity to attempt a life for himself and Éric?

The devastating premise of enduring yet another timeline unfurls in his mind like an unending bolt of disintegrating, dust-ridden black velvet.

He knows how the story will end if he must do it again — Éric will be lost to him for eternity.

He cannot recreate their history …

And he will not survive without him.

Vauquelin flings open the doors to his armoire.

Only a few weeks ago, Éric had rifled through this closet, making his stealthy selections for their beautiful photoshoot, the results of which now exist solely in Vauquelin's ineradicable memory.

He grazes his fingers over the ancient garments and an electrical shock runs up his fingers, sparking briefly in the darkness — the still-close voltage of his fledgling's touch.

He takes his sweet time and emerges some time later, having floundered at the thought of dressing himself once again in his complicated ancient garments, which now seem so foreign and unwelcome to his sensibilities.

He has chosen head-to-toe black: not considered the colour of mourning

---

[†]- I MISS YOU, MY LOVE

in this era, but for Vauquelin it most certainly is.

He descends with leaden steps.

Only five months ago, it had been his avowed intention to return to his past ... but never in this manner. And now he wants no part of it.

Let us get this over with.

"Soon," Clément laughs. "Soon. Yvain always says patience has never been your strong point."

The city of Paris dwindles in Vauquelin's eyes as they ride into the countryside, and his heart empties with every creak of the carriage wheels.

Forty-nine

Éric wakes, and Vauquelin is not there beside him.

Probably reading in the library again, Eric thinks, stretching his long limbs under the duvet.

Vauquelin's side of the bed is mussed — his scent emanates into the expanse of the room. Éric turns on his stomach and wallows in the bewitching fragrance, rubbing his face on the sheets and hugging V's pillows.

He snatches his phone from the bedside table and rolls onto his back, scrolling through their photos. He smiles ... he never tires of looking at them, especially his favourite one, which was actually an out-take: V is looking right into the camera and Éric is kissing his neck.

He can just feel V's arm around his waist, and he adores the look of triumph on V's face.

Mine.

Éric rises and brushes his teeth.

Gonna make him *mine right this minute,* he thinks.

As soon as I find him.

A dull thump reverberates from the hallway outside their bedroom and he stops mid-stroke.

"V?"

Nothing.

He spits and wipes his mouth, checking his phone.

19:00.

He still isn't good at telling when the sun is setting or rising.

One of these nights he'll know it by heart …

It is only a matter of time, bien-aimé, V promised him.

He showers and dresses, and begins scouting the house.

The vastness of it scares him tonight.

It's too quiet.

Too full of dread.

Éric's steps grow increasingly frantic as he reaches the third story. Vauquelin never comes to the top floor … why would he be up there now? But Éric won't stop until he has covered every space.

He flings open a wide set of doors at the top of the stairs.

Behind them is a vast, long-abandoned ballroom.

Candleless chandeliers hang from the ceiling, slathered in dangling cobwebs — a solitary chaise sits shrouded under a linen cover by a jib door. But there are no footprints on the expansive, dusty parquet floor, which can only mean one thing: Vauquelin has not been in this room.

He hears uninvited snippets in his head.

I have an enemy …

Vauquelin disappears sometimes without warning …

I will never abandon you …

He walks out to the gardens behind the house.

Vauquelin is not there, either.

Éric sprints back upstairs to their bedchamber and extracts a wax-sealed packet from a dresser drawer.

He recalls the exact moment V pressed it into his hands.

"Promise me you will open this only if you cannot find me," V had said, his voice low and grave. And that you will obey every word."

Éric had nodded solemnly, a knot clenching in his throat.

"I swear it."

He cracks the seal.

If I should vanish from your life, my love, you must understand that it is not my choice. I love you ... I would never choose to leave you. My life no longer belongs to me because of you, who will forever be the best part of me. If I am gone, please know that I am withering without you, my precious one, and that I am doing everything in my power to return to you. Call Olivier first. If he does not respond, go at once to Gehenna in England. Directions are below. Clove will know to expect you.

Never forget that I am thinking of you always, no matter where (or when) I am.

sois fort, mon amour
jusqu'à ce qu'on se retrouve
toutes mes nuits sont à toi pour l'éternité[†]
v

Éric's trembling hands lose their strength and the pages full of V's elegant, ancient handwriting waterfall to the floor.

He doubles over, heaving — stumbles to the bathroom and vomits up all the blood they consumed last night. He and Vauquelin had brought two Italian tourists back to the house from a nightclub.

---

†- BE STRONG, MY LOVE...ONLY UNTIL WE FIND EACH OTHER AGAIN — ALL MY NIGHTS ARE YOURS FOR ETERNITY

He drags himself over to the bathtub and wets a wash cloth, swabbing his bloody, swollen face.

His breath comes in spurts, and his skin seems even colder than usual.

He crawls on all fours back to the pages and flips to the next — a legal document, notarised and embossed — nearly ripping it in his urgency.

The following properties:

L'hôtel du Coquillage
13 quai Malaquais, 75006 Paris

Château de la Musse
27930 Évreux

and all contents within are hereby transferred, with full indemnity, to the ownership of Éric Castañeda de Vauquelin.

Signed
Louis-Augustin du Cavernay de Vauquelin

Notarised
Adrienne Blanchet

"Oh no … no, no, NO!"

His stomach lurches again.

A third page lists Vauquelin's many bank account numbers, with several small safety deposit keys taped to the bottom.

There's a lump remaining in the envelope, and Éric turns it upside down. Vauquelin's trusted Opinel tumbles to the floor.

Shitshitshit

Éric frantically extracts his phone and taps Olivier's number ... it goes straight to voicemail.

He rings Céline.

Voicemail.

Fuckfuckfuck

He taps again.

"Olivier, it's Éric. Vauquelin is missing. I need help! Please help me!"

His throat is raw from his upheaval of bile and blood.

He calls Céline again and leaves the same message, only his now-wrecked voice breaks — and his incoherent pleas, tearful and desperate, are cut off midway.

He paces for what seems like hours, hands dug in his hair, and neither of them call him back.

It's almost midnight.

It's too late to go to England tonight.

He's lost all his blood, he's starving, and he's afraid to go out alone.

Éric stumbles out into the garden and looks at the full moon above.

Where are you, V?

And when?

Can you feel me there, wherever you are?

Since the night he first met Vauquelin, he's been floating on a blissed-out sea of surreality. Now no one's at the helm, and he's adrift.

Nothing makes sense without V, and Éric is so far from home.

No, this IS my home, he corrects himself.

V would want me to be strong.

Éric has never experienced the death of a loved one: he was only a baby when his parents died. But this is what it must feel like ... empty and desolate, as if his chest is about to crater.

The limestone walls of the house tower over his head.

Knowing V won't be inside — well, Éric's feet might as well be made of iron. His breath stutters as a tidal wave of sorrow crashes over him, knocking him to the ground. He curls into the foetal position and rocks himself slowly until he is empty of tears.

A discordant chorus of frantic ambulance sirens bleats through the silence, disrupting his thoughts, and he lurches up.

His grief erodes, morphing into a burgeoning outrage.

The once-pleasant fragrance of Vauquelin's night garden, blooming with wild abandon in the springtime temperatures, redefines itself — to Éric's senses — into a sickly odour of death and decay.

He grabs hold of a potted plant and smashes it on the ground.

That felt good ... *really* good.

Right now he wants to destroy everything he sees around him, to make something pay for his profound despair.

Fresh indignation propels Éric up and he strides back inside.

His phone remains silent as a sphinx in his pocket.

Still nothing from Olivier or Céline ... it infuriates him.

What the actual FUCK? *They're supposed to protect me!*

Éric never wanted to believe this could actually happen.

But it did.

And now he can only rely on himself, just like he's always done ... on what he's been taught.

He scrolls through his map app for a delivery service.

He orders a pizza, and then he waits.

A half-hour later, the bell rings at the gate, and he dashes out to greet the delivery person.

"Come on in," Éric says as a young male wheels a bicycle into the entrance, bearing an insulated bag.

Éric drags the gates closed and reaches into his pocket. "Crap, I wanted to tip you but I left my cash in the house. Can you come up to the door? I'll grab it. Dude — I wasn't even thinking. Do you speak English?"

The guy laughs. "Yes. Thank you, that's fine."

Éric invites him in, and he props the bicycle against the vestibule wall, discreetly locking the door behind them.

Ha. Vampire takeout, Éric thinks, smiling brightly for the first time all night. Once upon a time, he could have devoured an entire pizza in one sitting. Now the smell of it is making him want to hurl but he swallows the nausea down.

"It's just here on the table ... one sec."

But Éric makes no move to retrieve anything.

Still smiling, he stares at the guy, and mind-whispers a command.

Don't move. Don't make a sound.

He backs him up to the wall by the shoulders.

The man's face contorts. At first, he assumes Éric is coming on to him and he hefts his palms against Éric's chest, a futile attempt to put some space between them. "No, no ... I'm not —"

Éric laughs, baring his teeth. It's exhilarating to reveal the truth about himself to someone else. To show that he's a fucking vampire and he belongs to Vauquelin, that this is really real, even if no one else knows about them. "You thought I was gonna kiss you, huh? That's hilarious."

But then innate violence erases his smile.

He drives a knee into the guy's groin, simultaneously disabling him and nailing him to the wall, and latches onto his neck, bringing him down to the floor as he drinks.

When the blood flow slackens, Éric sits back on his heels, huffing for air, and does a double-take: the guy is staring at him.

Judging him.

A dismal squeak escapes from Éric's lips and he vaults backward.

His victim isn't moving, though: his head sags to the side.

Éric gulps and reaches out a shaking hand to close the man's eyes.

"I'm so, so sorry," he whispers. But then his guilt just ... fizzles out like a spent candle.

In the end, Éric is kind of shocked at how easy it was, at how he feels absolutely nothing except full.

It's no longer a human ... it's just an empty wrapper.

Still, those dead eyes were creepy as fuck.

He drags the corpse to the cellar, releasing it with a careless thud, and lifts the panel in the floor to retrieve the key. He heaves open the pit door and slides it in, a little too enthusiastically: a rivulet of acid tsunamis up and sizzles his arm.

"Ow! Owwww! FUCK!"

He sucks in air through his teeth and watches in amazement as his blistered skin begins to mend before his eyes. Then he sits and turns his eyes to the body fizzing and thrashing in the acid, its meat slowly melting away.

It's really fucking sick, and not in a good way.

But as the flesh sizzles into oblivion, offering up spotless white bones to the surface, he glances around his shoulder to Vauquelin's collection.

The victims cannot be tracked here.

Now he gets it.

He finally gets what Vauquelin had meant when he said this is our salvation.

Leave no trace.

He sprints back upstairs to retrieve the pizza box and the bicycle, and drops those in too ... much more carefully this time.

He brings the lid down and returns to his phone.

Olivier still hasn't called him back.

That FUCKER!

He taps the restaurant number again and complains profusely that his order was never delivered.

They apologise and dispatch another which Eric accepts with impressive feigned normalcy, sending the employee safely on her way with a very generous tip.

"Always be smart, my love," Vauquelin had told Éric often, *"always protect yourself from all sides."*

He returns to the cellar and extracts the bones with an enormous set of iron tongs, stacking them neatly to dry just as V had shown him.

Later, he places them on an empty shelf.

His shelf.

Éric sits at the desk in the library and takes up V's quill.

He spends an hour practicing with it, eventually catching on to its foreign scratch and flow. He has never felt this alone.

But he must do something to stay close to Vauquelin.

> *April 20*
> *Night One*
>
> *I know you can't help it but my heart seems irreparably broken. I don't know how I can be whole again without you.*

He taps the quill against his lips: he sucks at writing letters.

> *I made my first solo kill tonight. I think you'd be proud of how I handled it. I was starving. Don't worry, I did everything the way you told me, and I used the pit. I wasn't sure I'd be able to do it alone, but I think I did okay. I started my own shelf :)*

When he finishes the smiley face the tip of the quill snaps off, bleeding a gnarly ink blob on the paper.

godDAMNit

He opens the desk drawer and tilts his head. Of *course*: there are at least a dozen more quills ready and waiting, their tips carefully whittled.

Vauquelin always thinks ahead.

He inhales deeply, and dips a new one into the inkwell.

I'm so mad, V. I'm so fucking mad that you're not here with me, where you belong.

Everything is empty. The universe put us together and then tore everything to shreds.

I love you. I miss you. There's a hole in my heart.

Please come back.

Éric signs it with a great flourish and places it in the drawer.

He ambles upstairs to bed.

When his head hits the pillow, he takes a deep breath and immediately freezes, because he realises something.

It doesn't smell like V anymore.

Fifty

ÉPINAY-SUR-SEINE, FRANCE | 1680

The carriage rumbles to a stop outside Yvain's wretched château.

The driver descends and opens the door ... for Clément.

Vauquelin thrusts his chin out.

He has to open his own door and carefully slide out, mindful of keeping his leg as straight as possible. For this encounter, he has come armed.

He casts his eyes up the deteriorating façade, and the thought of entering almost disables him.

An inexplicable shudder rips up Vauquelin's vertebrae.

If only he knew that Éric was looking up the height of his own beautiful walls in Paris at that exact moment — except Éric is three-and-a-half centuries into the future.

But behind these particular walls is a treacherous fiend, a brutish master who has trifled with Vauquelin's existence one too many times.

Vauquelin shuffles just ahead of Clément to the entrance.

He will not bow down.

He refuses to be inferior, simply because Clément is determined to align himself with a monster.

Clément accompanies him deep into the recesses of the château, an ancient stone structure that has stood since the Renaissance.

Torches line the walls.

The steps end in a dark chamber, and in the middle Yvain is seated upon a decrepit throne, the king of nothing.

Not even of shadows.

Hateful knots strangle Vauquelin's stomach at the sight of him.

Perpetually out of fashion, and unclean to boot, Yvain is always dressed a century behind. On his neck is a dingy ruff, on his back a threadbare velvet *justaucorps* — a conflicting cocktail of centuries. His grey hair hangs stringy and dull upon his shoulders. His dirty fingers are weighted by gaudy rings. Yvain is considerably wealthier than Vauquelin, but one would never know this by looking at him.

He has no grace.

Time is at a standstill within Yvain's walls, and within his shrivelled heart. He is imprisoned in a mental fortress of his own making: barricaded against the passage of time. He squanders his waking hours in this dank, dusty cavern, drinking wine, fucking his thralls into a stupor, and forcing them to sleep in coffins ... locking them in this chamber while he goes to his rest upstairs.

They are forbidden from leaving the grounds, and yet Yvain relies on them to deliver his blood rations to his feet.

This is the fate Yvain intended for Vauquelin, who will never understand how Yvain manages to elicit such unfaltering esteem from his pitiful creatures.

Can they not see through his flimsy façade?

On the night of his first resurrection, Vauquelin fled. He refused to join Yvain's sordid coterie, despite his maker's insistence. Even as a newly cursed revenant, he valued himself — and his liberty — too highly to resign his life to such squalor and blind submission.

"Welcome back, Vauquelin. I heard your plea. You so desperately desired to return to your origins, I thought it only kind of me to help you along. Still so fetching ... still naïve, and so simple after all these years. I have a revelation for you: makers cannot release their progeny. That was all artifice for your benefit, just to pacify you. At least you believed in something for a little while. Still you are mine, and so you will always be. A shame about your poor little fledgling, however, left on his own ... and still wet behind the ears, to boot. Whatever will he do without his beloved maker?" Yvain clicks his tongue. "The *justaucorps* was a grave mistake, Vauquelin. Still you have not learned to protect your heritage. How could you allow a baby to wear that cursed masterpiece? And then you had the gall to destroy it."

Vauquelin's blood surges through his veins like a burning thread: this is his love for Éric warming his senses. Now he knows all his suffering, and his travels, were shaping him for the golden, sun-kissed reward of Éric — he would never have been worthy of him without these trials.

He lunges toward Yvain, fangs out, but is quickly subdued by his maker's revenant minions. The short, sharp rapier hidden beneath his breeches punctures his leg and he groans, gritting his teeth against the pain.

A spot of blood spreads on the black fabric of his breeches, but it cannot be seen: only smelt.

His captors jerk their heads toward his leg, sniffing the air like beasts.

Fuck.

"Back off," Yvain barks. "Let him be. I am the only one who may drink from Vauquelin."

Their shoulders sink, hands falling to their sides. Satisfied by their obedience, Yvain wheels his eyes back to his most-prized progeny.

Vauquelin clenches his hands into fists. There is no chance he will allow Yvain the privilege of tasting even one drop of his blood, which is now fortified with Éric's.

"Did you think Maeve's failed transfiguration was your own doing?

So self-righteous. *It will always be me,*" he growls. "Rest assured, my pet — I will spend eternity making sure every single being you dare to love is destroyed unless you return to my folds."

"You wanted me to make vampires, and I have," Vauquelin hisses. "That rarely turns out well for me, or for them. I've done what you asked, so why have you disrupted my life yet again?"

A vision caresses his consciousness, a portrait of Éric in the depths of his immortal sleep ... Vauquelin watches his miracle of a love, draws his curls from his closed eyes, and with his next breath the petals fall from his mind — and he locks the memory away. It must be protected in this house of misery: such a flower will wither under its black embrace.

Yvain coughs out a callous laugh.

"Ah, Vauquelin, Vauquelin. Your perennial optimism is astonishing. I fail to understand how you have maintained it across all these centuries, and yet still ignore one crucial fact: your fate is to be a perpetual puppet on my own strings."

"When will this torture end, Yvain?" Vauquelin drops to his knees at his maker's feet. "I am rebellious, I will admit ... but why must that fact alone condemn me to eternal anguish?"

"Leave us!" Yvain bellows. "Yes, Clément. Even you. My words are for Vauquelin alone."

Vauquelin flicks his eyes to Clément, who slinks out the door.

A key engages in the elaborate iron lock, and it quietly reappears under the base, baffling Vauquelin.

He glances at Yvain, but his maker's expression betrays no knowledge of the key's sudden return.

Yvain, settled back into his throne, worries the bridge of his nose between his fingers. "I have long dreaded this night. Yet I suppose I have invited it by obscuring the truth from you."

"What?" Vauquelin's voice breaks with despair. "What is it you mean to tell me?"

The sum of his bravado evaporates in the presence of Yvain.

Despite his bountiful conceit, it always has.

By bringing Vauquelin back to his origins the first time, creating a second timeline for him, Yvain made a grave error. In forcing Vauquelin to relive his history, he irrevocably damaged the time continuum.

In the first timeline, Yvain, in a moment of weakness, made himself vulnerable to a lesser vampire and his body was destroyed. He did not die: his spirit lived on, and he watched Vauquelin survive into the twenty-first century.

Just when Vauquelin became content, and established a comfortable existence for himself, Yvain began systematically turning Vauquelin's pages backward. He brought him back to the night of his first creation, so that Vauquelin was human once more ... to a night that pre-dated Yvain's destruction. And Yvain gave him no option but to choose it again — by dangling the possibility of Vauquelin reclaiming his life with Maeve.

Of course Vauquelin said yes.

When Yvain realised the folly of this act, it was too late. He had fucked up history, given Vauquelin his power and, by virtue of time, effectively made him the elder. It was only then that he backed off: until he could stand it no longer and unwound Vauquelin's life once more, reverting him through his epochal corridors and creating his second timeline.

But nothing will ever change the fact that Yvain is Vauquelin's maker, despite the defiled timelines.

Yvain carries a secret he has never told his progeny: a dark and twisted secret that would make even the fiercest vampire cringe. He stands and begins pacing with his hands behind his back.

For the first time, Vauquelin sees himself in his maker, sees that he had inherited more than the power to heal, which was once the only trait he had desired.

Now, Vauquelin only covets Yvain's ability to manipulate time — though his reasons for it have changed drastically. How wrong he had been, convincing himself that he wanted to return to this era, that the seventeenth century is his only proper place.

Where he belongs is with Éric: without him he has no purpose.

No worth.

No reason for the earth to bear his tread a moment longer.

"In my human life, I had a son," Yvain begins. "I was raised in the aristocracy of the Renaissance, you will recall ..."

Vauquelin tucks his legs in and rests his elbows on his knees.

"Yes, yes," he sighs. "Get on with it." While Yvain has his back turned, Vauquelin flings an arm out and pockets the key.

"After the birth of my son, I learned that I was a bastard. The son of a stable boy. I developed a hatred for the noble man who raised me, despite his kindness. I despised my mother for lying with a peasant. I rejected my so-called heritage. I left my wife and son and went to war. I took out my anger in battle, on the fronts for France. And upon my return, I realised that I had my own family. The ones who had raised me meant nothing. I fell in love once more with my own flesh and blood."

Yvain stops and turns forward to Vauquelin, whose face is unmoved.

"I became a devoted father. I vowed to never leave them. And then, one fateful night in a tavern, I had the great misfortune to encounter a vampire. My own maker, whose blood runs through your veins as well, Vauquelin. He took everything from me. He drove me underground, forbade me to see my beloved family, even to bid them farewell."

Does he expect pity? Vauquelin wonders.

His face is cold: his jaws are tight.

He thinks of Éric, alone and scared, and he can only pray that he is safe under the protection of Olivier or with Clove and his boys at Gehenna. They have only been apart for the three days of their exile from one another, and the pain of their separation opens within Vauquelin like an immense, gaping wound.

His soul brims with hatred for his sorry excuse for a maker.

Yvain looks away and continues his relentless pace.

"But still I would watch them from afar, even though my wretched nature prevented me from approaching them. My son had a son, who had a son, who had a son. I watched them all … I watched them all grow into strong men. And then, one night, I lost myself. That was the first night I saw you."

Vauquelin braces himself against the floor.

"You were just a small boy then," Yvain says, stopping to face his most-prized progeny. "but I knew you were mine."

"You have pursued me since I was a *child?*" Vauquelin implores, extending his spine. "This is insanity! You are more depraved than my worst nightmares!"

Yvain steeples his fingers against his lips and continues pacing.

"I knew you were mine, Vauquelin, because I watched you grow into a man, as well. You are my blood in more ways than you think."

Vauquelin leaps up. "No. No. This is not possible. My father was Édouard de Vauquelin." It dawns on him that Yvain had never given his surname … there had been no need.

He was always just Yvain.

That was all he had ever offered, and Vauquelin had never cared to ask — even though he himself gave his own full name at their formal introduction: the night of his first turning.

"Yes, Vauquelin. He was indeed your father. And he was my great-grandson, my heir."

Vauquelin's vision blurs. His blood begins to tingle in his veins, stealing all the strength in his musculature. Yvain's insidious revelation swirls in his brain until the cold stones of the floor rise to meet his burning cheeks.

Fifty-one

He plummets under his own black seas, drowning in the depths of time.

"WAKE UP!"

Yvain slaps Vauquelin, sending fireworks of violent, starbright pain spangling through his eyes.

At first, Vauquelin is bathed in the sweet, gossamer haze of dreams.

It was only a nightmare.

I will reach out for my beloved, my Éric, and be comforted by him ... everything will be as it should.

But another harsh strike knocks him into consciousness.

"Wake. UP!"

Vauquelin brings a hand to his cheek and gazes upon Yvain as if he has never laid eyes upon him before.

And then he is lucid, scorched by Yvain's leering, rapt stare.

"Your cruelty knows no limit," Vauquelin whispers.

It is not the first time these words have left his lips.

Once before he had pleaded with Yvain to return him to his natural time, and he was unequivocally denied.

Now, Vauquelin's timeline is far removed from natural — Yvain has disrupted it so often his trust is obliterated.

Vauquelin's heart stutters: it ceases beating a moment, and then a tranquil glow settles across it, surging it back into its pulsing thrum.

ÉRIC.

Éric. Do not despair. I am fighting for you.

Vauquelin propels himself forward, knocking Yvain from his perch. He sinks onto Yvain's hips, pinning him to the floor, and strokes his cheek.

"Eh bien, grand-père,[†] you have always been mistaken about me. You never understood who I am. Your bedeviled sang[‡] may pollute my veins for eternity, but you cannot own me."

Yvain clasps Vauquelin by the throat and hurls him off, sending him skidding across the floor. "Never forget! You are powerless to subdue me!"

They face off, chest to chest, their breaths heavy and ragged.

A million thoughts scatter through Vauquelin's mind.

He cannot predict the end result of this horrifying encounter, or what his next move should be.

But it matters not, for Yvain makes the decision for him.

He jerks his progeny to his feet and up against the wall, pinning his arms.

"At last, my creature," Yvain breathes. "... I have long dreamed of our bodies uniting, to truly own you at last. To bring our blood full circle, to find completion. For you are the last of my once-human bloodline."

Yvain reaches down to Vauquelin's waist — hastening to unbutton his breeches — and his hands encircle Vauquelin's cock.

A hideous moan bursts from his lips.

Revulsion ripples and boils in Vauquelin's abdomen, threatening to peak in his throat.

Everything flashes at lightning speed.

His breeches drop to his ankles and he manages to clutch the rapier just before it falls, drawing a deep gash along his leg.

He allows himself a fraction of joy from the pain before he seizes the

---

[†]- WELL, THEN, GRANDFATHER
[‡]- BLOOD

rapier and drives it between Yvain's rib cage, aiming for his heart.

Vauquelin retracts it with great speed and retreats a few steps, drawing his breeches back to their proper location.

His maker's eyes protrude, and a vein erupts on his forehead.

Another family trait.

"You would dare betray me, to spill our hallowed blood?" Yvain screams. He lunges toward Vauquelin, clasping a hand to his wound, which is already beginning to rejuvenate.

Raucous poundings echo off the heavy wooden doors as Yvain's coterie responds to its master's distress call.

"BEGONE!" Yvain bellows, turning his head to the sound. "This is none of your concern!"

"You are the fool, not I. Blood of your blood, indeed," Vauquelin sneers, clamping his fingers on Yvain's chin. "And now are you proud of me?"

He yanks Yvain's head aside and sinks his teeth, piggishly gulping his maker's blood. It is rotten, wasted — spiced with centuries of betrayal and falsehood — yet its power bolsters him sip by sip.

Yvain falters under Vauquelin's grip, the chosen one, the last remaining sprig on his fiendish family tree.

Vauquelin knows this now yet still he gulps, suckling with all his might, each passing second rendering Yvain more and more impotent to fight him off.

His demise is of his own making.

But this time, Vauquelin aims to demolish Yvain's spirit, to erase him from existence, so that he need never fear his maker's obsessive eye again.

Never drink the last drop.

Yvain had taught him and he had taught Éric ... *The last drop is a tribute to our ancestors, to those who gave us the sacred privilege of eternal life.*

Yvain's heartbeat terminates: nevertheless Vauquelin heightens the intensity of his syphoning, pulling everything he can, splaying his knees across the stone floor for leverage.

Yvain's throat shrivels and dessicates beneath Vauquelin's fingers, and still he does not stop.

He arches his back. His chin vibrates, and still his suction does not cease. At last there is nothing left to drink: Vauquelin's teeth can draw no more.

He stands and lifts his depleted maker by the hair of his ratty head, pausing as Yvain's noxious blood energy surges through his body, nearly causing him to lose his footing.

The steel of the rapier reverberates as he wrenches it from the stone floor. He hacks off Yvain's head, letting it fall to the floor, sending it skittering across with his foot.

It is the only way to ensure neither his body or spirit ever rises again.

His chorus whispers to him: *You have earned this trophy.*

Preserve him in your catacombs, in your eternal collection.

Remember him.

As if Vauquelin could forget!

Vauquelin skulks into a corner. His body quivers, quaking with the powerful blood coursing through his veins.

I have destroyed everything…

He has conquered his maker, once his human grandsire, who took his secrets of bending time with him. Now Vauquelin will never learn the paradox of his cross-century time travels — and Éric will be locked away from him forever.

He cowers in a corner, a fist pressed against his lips.

How can he return to the future now, the future that only months ago he had not known he wanted?

Vauquelin rises on unsteady legs like a newborn foal, and as he rises, an uncanny strength fuses into his bones, bolstering his heart.

He retrieves Yvain's atrocious head by its hair and extracts the key from his pocket, opening the heavy doors.

Fifty-two

PARIS, FRANCE | MAY | THIS YEAR

Night 30

I still haven't gone to the UK. I know you wanted me to, but V ... Olivier and Céline won't answer me. I don't know why. What have I done to make them hate me? I can't stop worrying about it and it's making me feel a little crazy. I thought about going to Annecy, to their house, but I don't know where it is exactly, and I didn't want to put myself in harm's way in a strange city. I think it's safer for me to stay here in Paris, in <u>our</u> house.

I haven't washed our sheets since the night you left. I keep hoping that somehow I can smell you again, but it's gone. I can't forget it though ... that — and remembering the times I'd lean on you, just us touching each other even if we weren't talking, but there, together, just being US — is the only thing keeping me going if I'm honest.

I got a job. That photographer called me. He wanted you, too, but I told him you were ... away. I was bored, so I said yes. Don't worry, I deleted all my socials like you said. No one can track me down. I turned off geolocation on my phone.

But I'm in a magazine, V! I hope you'd be proud. I didn't smile. I look super sultry. Check it out:

He smears glue on a picture he cut out from the magazine and pastes it onto the letter. And then he continues.

I'm super proud of these pictures. I love working with that photographer. He's so cool, and he's been really good to me. I made a little money. I haven't been to your bank ... it just feels wrong.

Everything is wrong.

There's no joy left.

Éric drops the quill and squeezes his eyes shut, dropping a blood tear on the word *left*. He watches it fall, almost in slow motion, and his chest begins to heave. He rests his chin on his hand.

He sniffles and picks up the quill again, starting a second page.

Sometimes I regret ever meeting you.

NO.
No, no, no. Fuck that!

Éric immediately crumples the paper and holds it over the candle flame, because that isn't fucking TRUE! He holds it in his fingers and lets it burn until it scorches his fingertips. He licks them and begins again.

Sometimes I wonder why I went out that night, why I let my friends drag me out, and now I know there was a bigger reason at play. So we could meet. Even if I was only allowed to have a few months with you, and that's all I'll ever get, I'll always think it was worth it. Always.

Every morning when I go to bed I stare at your portrait, because it's the only way I know that you were real and that I can see you looking at me. I need that, V. I still need you to look at me, to see me , because you're the only one who's ever seen the real me. Sometimes I walk down to the catacombs just to look at your bone collection, because I know they fed you ... they kept you alive so you could come to me.

We were robbed. In the worst way. Because it wasn't a thing that was stolen from us. It was OUR LIFE.

And you've left me by myself in this fancy-ass fucking house and it means NOTHING *to me, because you're not here. And I have no way of knowing if you'll <u>ever</u> come back. I still can't get my head around life without you but I guess I have to accept it, because by now I'm pretty sure I'll never get to see you again.*

Éric loses it on the last line and collapses on the rug, soiling it with his bloody tears.

Fifty-Three

ÉPINAY-SUR-SEINE, FRANCE | 1680

Clément, eyes wide, jaw slack, is the first face Vauquelin sees on the other side of the threshold.

Vauquelin looks past him to the thirty-some-odd vampires behind him: Yvain's coterie.

"You made no attempt to stop me, Clément. You encouraged this. Why?" Vauquelin asks in a ragged voice.

Each member of the coterie falls into deep bows and curtsies, with the exception of Clément: he merely inclines his head. "We could only hope for this night. You are not the only one he tormented, Vauquelin. But I am pleased to see your audacious ego has remained intact over the centuries."

Vauquelin rolls his shoulders, paying no heed to Clément's insult.

As he moves forward, the coterie cleaves left and right, allowing him passage.

At last, Clément falls in behind him. "Vauquelin, please listen to me."

Vauquelin, swinging Yvain's head by the hair, swerves his torso to face Clément. "You have no words that could soothe me now."

Clément at last succumbs to a deep bow. "I believe I do. I can show you how to return to your desired time."

Vauquelin drops Yvain's head in shock and quickly retrieves it.

What a pathetic trophy.

"But first we must address the fact that you are the rightful heir to this coterie, and they look to you for guidance. You are now their sovereign." He gestures to the gathering of vampires behind him, watching Vauquelin and Clément expectantly.

"No one here is of my blood. I am beholden to only one, and he is not among you."

He focuses his mind on Clément.

Speak to me in private.

Follow me, Clément replies.

Clément leads Vauquelin up the dank stone stairway to the second floor of the château. He lifts a key from his châtelaine[†] and opens the door to a bedchamber. Smothered in opulence, the room belies the decrepit state of the remainder of the house.

"These are Yvain's private quarters. I do not believe you have ever seen them ... am I wrong?"

"Mercifully, he never brought me here."

He drops the head with a thunk on a wooden caquetoire[‡] chair.

"But I am confident you have spent a considerable amount of time on your knees in this room."

Clément stiffens, blinking in fury. "I am attempting to help you. I see no call for you to insult me."

Vauquelin studies Clément and a glimpse of their former affinity flashes over him, dulling the edges of his rage. But more importantly, he reminds

---

himself that Clément is possibly his only hope of returning to his life —
to Éric.

"I apologise. I am not myself after this night's unexpected turn of events."

"Quite understandable. Please," he extends his arm toward a sofa, and
they sit. "Vauquelin ... I told you long ago that Yvain offered me refuge
in my early days as a revenant. He treated me with nothing but kindness:
with love. That never changed."

"Consider yourself fortunate. He only treated me with disdain and
frivolity. All the more bewildering, considering what I learned tonight."

Vauquelin's pained expression cripples Clément's confidence, and he
turns his face away. "I suspected his relation to you from the beginning.
None of the others knew, yet they were all mad with jealousy over the
attention he lavished upon you. And was I, for a time ... until I met you at
last. I was determined to seduce you that night because I wanted to take
something from Yvain, to punish him ... to sully his precious one. But you
were nothing like I expected, Vauquelin. You opened my eyes to other
possibilities, and after many years with him, I began to despise him."

"This explains your lack of tears tonight, no?"

Clément relaxes against the backrest and crosses his legs.

"Indeed. You have done us all a colossal blessing. I must confess it to
you now, Vauquelin ... I abhorred witnessing Yvain's perpetually cruel
treatment of you."

"Why did you never once speak up for me, then? Why?"

Clément laughs. "Come now, Vauquelin ... we are speaking of Yvain.
Please. You know he could never be swayed. He was a scoundrel. And a
reckless one, at that. A more miserable, vengeful man — even before he was
made vampire — could scarcely be found in all of Europe. I can tell you in
full honesty that there were many in this coterie who wished Arsinée had
finished him off that night, and were, in fact, waiting with bated breath,
hoping she would succeed."

He reaches out to Vauquelin's cheek.

Vauquelin clasps Clément's wrist mid-air.

"No one must touch me. No one will drink from me. I made a vow to my beloved ... I refuse to break it."

Clément folds his hands in his lap.

"You have changed, Vauquelin, and not merely because you have eradicated your maker. I can see that something much more significant has happened to you."

Vauquelin's blood comes alive and surges within his veins.

But still he will not utter Éric's name in this godforsaken place — he will not betray their connection.

It is theirs ... it belongs to no one else.

"What do you desire in return for your assistance?"

"Must it come down to that?"

Vauquelin searches Clément's face for some trace of sincerity, but finds it lacking. This vampire would not have sacrificed the better part of his life rolling over for a wretch like Yvain if he did not expect some sort of gain.

"I'm afraid it must. If you aid me, then I will owe you a debt ... and I do not wish to be obligated to you under any circumstances."

Clément rises and knits his hands behind his back, bowing slightly. "If you insist. There is a way you could repay me, and I would be most grateful." He walks to a large, ornate cabinet and fiddles again with his *châtelaine*, producing another key.

"Yvain was not some vampiric genius, as he desired for everyone in his thrall to believe. Behold."

Clément gestures to shelves of books.

"This is the revenant lore of France. And it can all be yours."

He steps aside, inviting Vauquelin to look.

Lining the shelves are volumes of leather-bound, ancient books.

Blood history.

Ancestral records.

Alchemy, necromancy, black masses.

Dark magic.

The origins of the vampire.

Disease and revenancy.

The Black Plague.

Vauquelin scans all the titles, unimpressed, until his eyes land on a wrinkled, vellum pamphlet lying on top of a stack of others ...

EPOCHAL CORRUPTION.

Vauquelin lunges for the pamphlet — and Clément clamps his elbow.

"Tsssst, tsst ... not yet. Let us discuss terms. Give me what I desire and you may leave with every single volume in this cabinet. I no longer have a need for them. I will even send an escort behind you on your journey back to Paris to ensure their safe arrival. These are exceedingly rare, Vauquelin. Many are the only copies in existence, most importantly the one that has captured your interest ... none can be found in any library. I want to emphasise to you their inestimable value. Yvain said you never cared to study the lore. It is a shame, really ... had you been more curious, perhaps you would not be in this unfortunate quandary, nor separated from your beloved."

Vauquelin's teeth begin to chatter, so badly does he want this pamphlet. Not the books ... he could give fuckall for black magic and the miserable sanguine history of the vampire. But he covets them nonetheless.

"What do you want from me?"

"It is a simple request that will cost you nothing. I want you to return with me to the chamber below and declare me the successor of this coterie. That I am now their elder, and they must obey me and all my decrees."

Vauquelin extends his hand. "I cannot conceive of a more worthy leader for this coterie, Clément."

Vauquelin has always disdained the very concept of a coterie, especially

Yvain's: he wanted no part of it in his past, and he wants no part of it now.

His decision is — as Éric had been fond of saying — a no-brainer.

The carriage rolls away from the château, burdened by two wooden trunks full of ancient tomes, and Vauquelin smiles at last, clutching the only paper he wanted in his lap.

Fifty-four

PARIS, FRANCE | JUNE | THIS YEAR

Éric skates to a shoot one night instead of ridesharing or taking the Métro, since it's less than five kilometres from the house.

There's a vintage car in Vauquelin's former stables, but Éric can't find the keys. It's just sitting there, next to some dusty, ancient carriages.

It's a Bugatti, and probably super rare. He doesn't want to mess with it.

He's never driven such an old car ... what if he crashed it? How would he explain that?

Besides, Parisian drivers are fucking INSANE.

Calling a rideshare is so much easier but skating is *a million times* better.

When he arrives at the atelier they immediately start poking and prodding him, repositioning him like a plastic mannequin for hours, and he wonders how long he'll keep this up ... but at least it's something to do.

Every single time he looks into the camera ... and even when he looks away ... he's looking for V.

Searching.

Beseeching.

His spirits dwindle with each passing night, until despair is the only expression his face can offer.

He moves like an automaton throughout the shoot.

Based on the reactions of the crew, he isn't delivering what they've come to expect from him.

When Éric begins packing up to leave, Gemma, the atelier's British creative director, touches his shoulder and tells him he doesn't look well.

"Just between you and I, Éric ... are you doing drugs?"

"Absolutely not!" he cries, his voice indignant. The echo of V's manner of speech reflects in his own — the sound of it takes another little chink out of his heart. "I'm just ... dealing with some stuff."

"Well, then, look after yourself. We'll be in touch." She gives him the card of a doctor and gestures to close the main entrance.

"Actually ..." Éric says, ramming his hand against the door jamb. "I really need someone to talk to. Could you just listen to me for a minute? I promise I won't unload on you. I'm just so alone in this city."

He sets all his turmoil free, resulting in a sincere downcast expression.

It isn't hard to do these days.

Gemma works her jaw a bit. The last thing she wants is to listen to yet another snivelling model. But it's her third time working with Éric, and something about his pitiful countenance touches her. She recognises the unhappiness that has settled over him like a second skin.

"Of course, Éric," she sighs. "Come into my office."

Don't cry ... don't cry ... don't fucking cry, he tells himself as he follows her. She's one of the only humans who has shown him genuine kindness since V left.

"I'm just really struggling with this whole modeling thing. I came here to build a career, and I'm from like a super small town. This lifestyle is a little overwhelming." He's astonished by the lies that roll off his tongue with such fluency.

But that last part wasn't really a lie, was it?

"Are you eating *anything?*" Gemma asks. "Your ribs show through the garments. Not that I'm complaining. That's what everyone is looking for."

"Uh ..." His eyes dart and he fidgets madly with his jacket zipper. "Sort of?"

"This is very common, Éric. It happens to many young people your age who come to Paris. Unfortunately it doesn't make you special. I have a book full of a thousand others dying to take your place. Get yourself together or you won't have a career at all. You'll be working in a café in no time, or running back to the States with your tail between your legs. You're an absolutely gorgeous young man, Éric. I don't have to tell you this. But there are many just like you who don't fuck up their lives and bodies. They take their brands seriously."

She observes his uncommon complexion, his long neck, his sharp cheekbones, the lashes that women would kill for, the arresting clavicle rising above the collar of his t-shirt.

He's never once been late ... a plus, even though he only books night shoots and insists on being paid in cash. There really is something extraordinary about him, but his once-shiny hair has lost its lustre since she first cast him, and those dark circles (oof, even the makeup artist had a hard time concealing them!). There's always post-production, but frankly she's had her fill of ravishingly beddable, troubled youth.

She shakes it off.

"Oh, trust me ... I'm *very* serious," he says, widening his kohl-smeared eyes. He hadn't removed his makeup after the last set, and the cadaverous smudges only accentuate the bluish, bruise-like darkness below — making him look even more gamin and destitute. "I'm as serious as they come about this life."

His close-lipped, lop-sided grin creeps across his face, and he stretches his skeletal arms across the front of her desk, locking her into his gaze.

Smiling during kills has kind of become his brand. The photographer and his staff, and now even Gemma, are always talking about *brand*,

and how everyone needs a fucking *brand*.

Well, this is his.

BUT — he's not going to kill her.

He only needs a little bit ...

Just enough to stave off his desperation.

Éric closes Gemma's door quietly behind him, and he's pretty sure he won't be called back to this atelier again.

He stops just outside the building and shoves his black portfolio into his backpack, hitches it over his shoulders. He tucks his ear buds in and shoves off down the Faubourg Saint Germain. He catches a glimpse of the mesmerising, sparkling animated Eiffel Tower, illuminating the night sky.

It steals the breath out of his lungs.

He had wanted to go to the top with V ... they never had the chance.

He wipes out, busting his knee wide open, and grimaces as he spits on his hand, rubbing the mangled knee with violence. A moment or two later, the knee is good as new — though the same can't be said for his jeans, which are now even more destroyed.

Back on the board, Éric sails along the streets of Paris, cutting through side streets ... some are so narrow, he can't even imagine a car passing through. He looks down at his feet on the deck, riffing across the ancient cobblestones, and wonders if V had once travelled this road in a carriage. A shudder arches his back, and as he looks up, a gargoyle leers down at him.

He shouldn't be here alone ... he should be with V.

No way you'll ever get him on a board, Éric thinks.

But the brief moment of optimism, and thoughts of being with V in the future, makes his heart hurt.

Éric sails down the street, dodging pedestrians. He carves around a wide corner on the boulevard, headed to their street, quai Malaquais, and does a kickflip. What would everyone back in L.A. think of him now?

No one would ever fucking believe it!

He stops at the corner TABAC[†] for supplies, peeling a couple of Euro notes off the thick stack Gemma had given him.

He wonders, as he loads his purchases into his backpack, if he's smoking too much ... and then he laughs at himself.

"What's it gonna do, kill me?"

« Quoi ? »[‡] the clerk asks.

Éric sucks his lower lip in. *Shit, I said that out loud.*

« Euh ... c'était rien . Merci , »[§] he mumbles.

He rolls up to the gates and takes a casual glance around him first, just like Vauquelin had taught him to do.

No one's around, so he inputs the code.

He drops his stuff in the foyer and the front gate chimes slice the thick silence of the house.

Oh ... right. It's Wednesday.

V's weekly flower delivery has arrived.

Seriously: it's enough for a fucking funeral.

But he'll never tell the shop to cancel the deliveries because he needs them. He craves them ... he craves any connection to V, no matter how seemingly small.

And so the flowers will keep coming: forever.

Éric makes three trips dragging the cartons of bouquets inside.

He'll put them in water later.

But right now he has another pressing goal, and so he marches straight upstairs to the library.

------

†- TOBACCONIST
‡- WHAT?
§- IT WAS NOTHING...THANKS

He licks the end of the quill, dips it in the ink, and, cradling his head with his right arm, absent-mindedly rubbing his scalp, drags the tip across a blank page. He's a lefty: he always smears the ink.

Fuck it ... getting the words down is all that matters, along with his hope that maybe V can hear them or sense them — wherever, whenever he is.

Night 49

I don't know why but I still haven't lost hope.

Remember the night I texted you and said I was ready? I never told you this before, but I didn't think you'd show up. I convinced myself that everything you said was bullshit. I still couldn't understand why someone like you would want a nobody like me.

But you did. You came back for me.

And you opened up the world for me.

I've been really trying hard to make you proud. I've done some more modeling. Don't worry — it's always at night, and I always make sure I'm not thirsty before I go. Well, except tonight. But it's all good. I took care of everything, I didn't leave a body.

And I haven't had to take my clothes off — from the waist down, at least. Haha. Apparently I have "the ideal figure." Whatever. That's what the clients say, anyway. I guess I've gotten a lot skinnier since we met. They really, really like that.

They're always impressed that I never seem to put on weight.

I haven't given up, V. I never will.

I love you. My eyes don't stray either, I want you to know that. After Vauquelin — well, how could anyone ever come close? But god, I miss you. I miss your voice in my ears, your mind, your body. Your blood. And I miss you bossing me around ;)

I think you'll find that I've grown a lot since you left. I'm much stronger now, because of everything you told me — but you only taught me how to protect myself and stay safe.

The one thing you forgot to teach me was how to be okay without you.

I don't think I'll ever learn that.

Fifty-five

PARIS, FRANCE | 1680

Vauquelin rushes into his house, the pamphlet tucked in an interior pocket of his *justaucorps*, barking orders to the footmen to bring the trunks into the foyer.

He is anxious to learn its secrets.

But first he takes a bath, absolving his body of the horror of the past hours.

He stinks of Yvain.

How could he move forward with that abhorrent scent on his body? There aren't enough baths in the world to help him cleanse his disgust at having Yvain's hands on his penis. He shudders, scrubbing himself with lavender soap, and dabs bergamot oil under his nose.

He must read the pamphlet with a clear mind.

Vauquelin slips naked into his ancient sheets — which only recently were very modern sheets that held Éric's beguiling body between them.

His breath catches in his throat.

Now they smell of nothing but clean linen.

His heart stutters.

What if Éric is lost to him for eternity?

Perhaps I am in hell, he thinks, *and this is my unique punishment: to be given fleeting, minuscule tastes of happiness, only to have them severed from my grasp.*

Over and over again.

Or maybe — just maybe — he has the answers now.

He should have known Yvain had some sort of instruction manual ... that he was never savvy enough to procure the miracle of time manipulation on his own.

If only he had known about this prior ... how much heartache and grief could have been prevented? Yet had he learned sooner, Éric would never have appeared in his life.

He picks up the vellum and begins reading the ancient French script.

An hour later, having read it multiple times and confirming his only option, a grief-choked scream detonates in his throat.

Fifty-six

PARIS, FRANCE | 1680

Time, as it always is for Vauquelin, is of the essence.

The moon will wane in eight nights, and Vauquelin spends those nights pacing in a daze.

He scarcely speaks a word to Olivier, who is naturally concerned by Vauquelin's peculiar behaviour. When they go out into the city to claim their blood, Vauquelin listlessly drinks down his victims with little artifice, without joy.

Olivier frets over him, repeatedly asking what is amiss, which only worsens Vauquelin's dismal mental state and makes his mood even more funereal.

On the darkest night of the month, he leads Olivier into his bedchamber, discreetly locking the doors behind them.

The fireplace is curiously unlit, rendering the room chilly despite the burgeoning late-spring temperatures. The firebox is empty and thoroughly absolved of ash and soot.

Vauquelin turned Olivier vampire over three hundred years ago in his second timeline, in this same year, in this very room.

They had grown up together in their human childhood.

Olivier was a few years older. Olivier has been, for the majority of Vauquelin's existence, his only true friend. The only one Vauquelin had ever fully trusted.

Now, after the devastating events at Évreux, he knows Olivier has a capacity for betrayal — and if he only knew how future Olivier turned his back on Éric in his desperation, his burden on this night would be that much less painful.

But he has been separated from Éric long enough.

Even one day was too much.

"I need your blood, Olivier."

"Your thirst must be heightened by your time journeys. Take all you need, my brother." Olivier tilts his chin aside.

Vauquelin frowns, his face weary with grief. "I do not need it for myself."

"I fail to understand."

"You will recall that I have returned to this time from far into the future …" Vauquelin begins.

"And you will recall that this topic remains a challenge for my sensibilities, Vauquelin."

How to tell Olivier what has transpired?

Should he even attempt it?

Yes, yes he should.

Vauquelin clears his throat.

"Of course. Well. Olivier, there I met the one who is truly meant for me. His name is Éric Castañeda de Vauquelin." His voice quivers as the name of his beloved emerges into the air. "You knew him in our future. You were there. And you had a wife. She loved Éric, and found him quite charming. *You*, on the other hand …" Vauquelin rubs his forehead. "You made things quite difficult for me. But that is neither here nor there. I need you to help me return to my proper time."

"Am I to assume you have given yourself to another man? I refuse to acknowledge this. Do you expect me to perform some magical act? This is absurd, Vauquelin. You have been unable to figure it out yourself. How can I possibly help you?"

Vauquelin swallows what he really wants to say.

His anger at Olivier's ancient ignorance is not an argument for this night. His emotions are spent, and so he pretends Olivier did not just spew hate against the most faultless, untarnished love he has ever known.

He has one aim.

One.

That is all that matters to him at this moment.

"I must reclaim the immortality I have given you, Olivier," he whispers. "You are my only progeny ... I have no other choice."

Olivier leaps from the chaise, eyes blazing.

"How dare you? After the life we have spent together? After our confidences, my devotion?" He sprints for the doors, but Vauquelin flashes ahead of him, grasping him by the shoulders and driving him toward the fireplace.

Olivier cannot match his maker's centuries of strength: he knows he is bested, and now he can see clearly — the endless future Vauquelin had promised him came with an obscure price.

In the blink of an eye Vauquelin is once again his master: no longer his brother. Olivier bows his head.

He will do anything Vauquelin asks of him ...

As it has always been.

"I remain your loyal servant, Monsieur."

At the sound of Olivier addressing him by his formal title and not Vauquelin, blood tears engorge his eyes: yet he does not loosen his grip. "Would that it were not so."

He dismounts a sword from the wall beneath his portrait, its hateful, steely rings echoing across the gilded walls, and slits Olivier's throat in one swift motion.

Vauquelin catches Olivier in his arms, gently placing his head atop the stool grate in the firebox.

"You will never know my gratitude for your sacrifice, my brother. I only wish I could repay you for your friendship and keep you alive. This is without a doubt among my greatest regrets."

Vitality is rapidly vacating Olivier's eyes, but still he whispers. "My life has always been yours, Vauquelin. It is only fitting that you should have me at my death."

Vauquelin digs his fingers into his eyes, drawing forth wretched bloody tears as he chokes back a sob.

This will remain unrivalled as the most savage act of his existence.

And then he closes Olivier's eyes.

The corruption of time, of epoch, is possible for
those who walk only in night, but the full blood
of thine own creation must be the price

On the first night of the waning moon,
merge a drachm of thy blood with
that blood of thine progeny

and burn it in a pyre, and remember on
that time in which thou wisht to visit —

If thou wisht to reunite with a beloved,
also hold that name
and realm on thy lips, and feed upon
the ashes of the blood.
Thou shalt achieve thine desire

Vauquelin takes up the sword and draws it down his cephalic artery, watching his curse coat his hand in cruel crimson, cascading into the dark pool of Olivier's martyrdom. He desperately wants to conjure an apology — but his mind is a vacuum.

He draws his fingers down his self-inflicted wound, reverting its damage.

Tilting a candle flame to the blood, Vauquelin observes as it ignites with ferocious swiftness, bubbling and popping.

The aroma sickens him.

It has the odour of meat.

He collapses supine on the floor and squeezes his eyes tight.

And suddenly the blood is spent and the flame extinguishes itself with an unceremonious poof.

He sweeps up the ash with his hands and eats it, licking his fingers clean, over and over again until every minuscule speck of it is gone.

His stomach lurches.

Nothing so close to food has entered it in over eight centuries, and it rebels with great violence, threatening to heave it up.

But he cannot allow that to happen, or Olivier's sacrifice will be in vain — and he will never see Éric again.

Vauquelin draws in all his breath, commanding his body to still, to obey him.

He places his hands over his heart, and prays.

I ask to return to my beloved, my Éric, to the time and place he is now. Wherever that may be. I offer this sacrificial blood of my blood.

Nothing happens.

What had he expected, a magical, flamboyant flourish? An automatic journey through the ether, delivering him straight into Éric's arms?

Such an undignified end to his old friend.

But the sun is due to rise, and he cannot lose hope yet.

Vauquelin descends into the belly of his house with Olivier's body cradled in his arms. He poises to feed it into his acid pit, and pauses.

He cannot decimate the remains of his friend.

Instead, he places his body in a coffin and nails the lid shut, sliding it to the back of the crypt.

At last Vauquelin succumbs to his loathsome slumber, leaning against the hard wooden shelves in the ossuary. The damp chill of the stone floor seeps into his flesh. He does not deserve comfort ... he deserves to be like these bones, picked clean and forgotten.

If nothing has changed when he wakes, he will walk into the sun.

Enough, he whispers.

Fifty-seven

When Vauquelin wakes he finds himself still lying in the catacombs.

He rises stiffly and wanders amongst the many shelves, caressing the crowns of each skull, the curves of each bone.

Perhaps this is all there is, and all he is meant for.

Death.

Not love.

Everything he touches ends in Death ... it has been so from the beginning.

He thinks of his mother.

Saverina-Maria di Caverna, the daughter of a Sicilian archduke ... her name altered to Saverine-Marie du Cavernay de Vauquelin upon her marriage to Vauquelin's French father.

He only knows how she looked from her portraits.

He cannot remember her touch, for she never held him: Vauquelin took her life the moment he took his first breath. And now her only child is wandering, wholly lost, in his own makeshift crypt.

Surely his mother and father would be anguished to know that his destiny was not to grow into a respectable man, but instead to be transformed into a preternatural abomination, foreordained to ruin human lives and spill blood across centuries.

Vauquelin's name was blackened by Yvain before his birth — he could not have altered his own fate even had he wished.

The suffocating guilt of his centuries rises to the surface, and he weeps until he is empty.

Yet even as his sanguine tears drain him, he reminds himself that the grievous act he had just committed was for Éric — an act which may very well result in naught.

Everything in Vauquelin's life — with few exceptions — has happened for a reason.

After all that has transpired, still I do not deserve him.

He stumbles toward the staircase, his body filthy and dusty, the detestable flavour of Olivier's demise spicing his tongue, his brain blunted by despair.

Peculiar noises, foreign to his ancient-again ears, erupt from the hallway off the larder and he tiptoes toward them, keeping his back close to the wall.

As he rounds a corner, the sounds increase in volume: a rolling followed by a click-click, repeated over and over.

And then a sharp stab rings into his shin bones, blinding him with searing pain, and he collides with massive force into something solid.

He reaches out to seize it, gripping with all his might.

Fifty-eight

Vauquelin's eyes focus as the pain evaporates, and in front of him stands Éric, who collapses backward, crawling across the floor and bracing himself with his wrists.

His skateboard skids and crashes into a wall.

Vauquelin clasps his hands in front of his face, biting the tips of his thumbs.

"Do you know me?" Vauquelin whispers, his voice trembling.

Éric clamours to his knees, wrapping his arms around V's waist.

"I'll always know you."

Éric rises, drawing his nose up the length of Vauquelin's body as he stands. V smells peculiar, like the inside of a museum.

They caress one another's faces, incapable of believing they are each real.

Éric moves to kiss Vauquelin and he jerks his chin aside.

"No, bien-aimé.† Not yet." Vauquelin careens up the stairs, Éric trailing him in bewildered silence.

He opens his medicine cabinet: all his modern toiletries are still there, perfectly organised, just as he had left them the night of his slip.

He scrubs his teeth relentlessly, absolving his mouth of the putrid blood ash he had consumed.

---

† - BELOVED

He scrubs them again and washes his face, dragging a soft towel across it and holding it there, still as a statue. The faucets creak behind him, and Vauquelin turns to find his beloved running him a bath.

"Now, my love."

Éric's face is written over with joy and confusion, and he hiccups a half-laugh, half-cry. He runs to Vauquelin and frames his face in his hands, drawing their foreheads together, and their lips meet at last in gentle kisses.

A shyness grows between them and they move apart.

"I'll be right back," Éric says, closing the door behind him.

Vauquelin reaches for him, whispering *don't go*, but lets his hands fall to his hips. He sheds his bedraggled, ancient garments, kicking them carelessly across the floor with a grunt, and eases into the scalding bath (Éric knows just how he likes it), drawing his knees up and resting his chin. His muscles quiver, sending miniature shockwaves rippling across the water's surface.

He sinks his head below the water, his eyes squeezed shut, his ears tuned to the frantic thrum of his weakened heartbeat, silenced by the stuttering stillness of his lungs. The creak of the doors triggers him to emerge, breathless, and water streams down his face as he gasps, reaching for a cloth.

Éric sets a glass of wine on the edge of the tub, lighting a cigarette and taking a puff before he places it between Vauquelin's lips.

Vauquelin leans back in the tub, holding the cigarette between his middle and ring fingers, and reaches out for Éric ... his fledgling sits and closes his eyes, caressing his face against Vauquelin's hand.

Éric whispers, "I didn't think I'd ever see you again. I don't know what happens to you when you slip, I —"

"Shh ... just let me look at you."

Vauquelin flicks the cigarette across the marble floor and leans his arms on the edge of the tub, stroking Éric's hair, mesmerised by the proximity of his beloved.

"How long have I been gone?" Vauquelin asks.

Éric gawps. "You mean you don't know?"

"Not precisely," Vauquelin murmurs. "Perhaps ninety days?"

An oppressive silence takes over the room as they stare at one another.

A heavy drip from the faucet breaks it, followed by a gasp from Éric.

"It's been four years, V."

The revelation knocks the air from Vauquelin's lungs, and he lurches forward, sending a wave of water over the side of the tub.

Four years.

How can that be?

The thought of Éric alone for so long fills him with rage — so much has been taken from them.

He was robbed of the joy of watching Éric come into his own.

His breath returns in ragged surges.

"I am sorry, my love, I am so sorry." The last word catches in his throat.

Éric chews his lip, and shrugs.

Don't you dare fucking cry.

But it doesn't matter anymore, does it? Because V is here now.

Then Éric completely loses it, his sobs echoing across the monstrously high walls.

Vauquelin lurches out of the tub, crouching next to Éric on the floor, taking him in his arms, unconcerned he is soaking them both. He rocks him back and forth, kissing his temples, whispering against his hair: *hush, bien-aimé, hush … I am here … we will never be parted again, I promise …*

He stands, lifting Éric by the elbow. "Come, my sweet."

He undresses his fledgling — *but no, I can no longer think of him as such, can I?* — and urges him into bed. He only wants their skins to touch, to lie beside Éric, to keep him as close as possible.

To never let him out of his sight again.

They fall asleep facing each other, all their limbs entwined, all their words hushed by their fresh unfamiliarity.

Fifty-nine

Fear wrenches Vauquelin from his rest in the middle of the day, his body frantic and shivering, his heart hammering in his chest.

But then he catches sight of Éric's shape and hurls the duvet back, finding him sleeping hard on his back, one hand in a fist over his head, opening and closing it slowly, as he frequently does in his dreams.

Vauquelin covers him again and sits on the side of the bed collecting his ravaged thoughts.

Thieves steal something much more valuable than objects or money.

The greatest theft is the victim's peace of mind.

Though he has been back in this time mere hours, Vauquelin wonders if he will ever again be able to relax, to have a life that seems somewhat ordinary.

To wake up not with a start, but with a caress, a kiss, a good evening.

To take life — and moving forward — for granted.

He has not known true peace in centuries, at least not any that ever endured … only fleeting moments of joy and happiness that he clings to as if each will be his last.

And what of Éric? How selfish Vauquelin had been, flinging him head-first into his chaotic depths.

He slips back under the duvet and onto his side, watching Éric until sunset, scarcely able to believe he is worthy of this divine sanction.

He whispers his beloved's name into the darkness, touches his curls, mindful of not disturbing his slumber.

Vauquelin's mind empties, and he warms himself in this miracle of his own making, of his own destruction, and of his own redemption — because, at long last, that is precisely what Éric is.

He reminds himself that he must heed Éric's advice about borrowing worry, that he must break that habit and fast — if he can — for both their sakes.

In the meantime, they must learn how to be together again.

Éric rolls over and opens one eye, immediately reaching out to touch Vauquelin's face.

"You're still here," he smiles.

"I will be forever, or as long as you want me to be, bien-aimé."

"For eternity," Éric whispers. "I never gave up, V ... I would've spent the rest of my life waiting, and even if you never came back it would've been worth it because you loved me once."

Vauquelin takes Éric's face in both hands.

"Not once. Until the world ends."

And it is Éric who initiates the obliteration of their shyness, now that the words have begun to flow.

Their rage at being separated manifests in passion, and their bodies slam together. All hell breaks loose, just like it did their very first night together.

"I have something to show you," Éric says, pulling on his boxers.

He looks at Vauquelin over his shoulder and they grin achingly at one another. Their lips are red and full, chapped by their reclaimed kisses — all the raw, infinite kisses they had lost.

In moments their lips will be healed, and Vauquelin wants to hold on to their sweet, short-lived sting as long as he is able.

He does not want to get out of bed ... he wants to wallow in their dirty sheets. He wants more.

His skin is not done being touched — it craves the nearness of Éric, who, much stronger now, hoists him out of the bed by his hand.

But it is pointless to refuse Éric anything.

How could he?

Instead he faux-pouts, reluctantly draping himself in a banyan.

They have all the time in the world — a concept he still must come to embrace — and so he follows Éric into the library.

Éric flips the lids off several banker's boxes and Vauquelin peers inside. "What is this? Have you been writing a book? In longhand?"

"Sort of," Éric says. "It's proof of how long you've been gone. I wrote you a letter every single night you were gone. You missed a *lot*. Do you want to read them?"

"But of course I do!" Vauquelin immediately sits on the floor, folding his long legs beneath him.

Éric hands him the first page and kisses the top of his head. "You have a lot of work to do ... I'm gonna go take a shower. I'll be right back."

Vauquelin clenches his jaw.

He tamps down the dread threatening to storm in his psyche and swallows the words rising on his tongue: do not leave me.

You wanted normal.

Putain d'enfer ![†] *Let him take his shower.*

But Éric has not waited for Vauquelin's permission or reaction — he is already closing the doors behind him.

Vauquelin turns his eyes to the first letter, reading with a fist against his mouth.

---

†- FUCKING HELL!

His heart breaks at the end, and he finds it difficult to open his eyes and continue. Pain on paper.

Éric's pain.

But he turns it face down and picks up another, and another, and by the time Éric returns, wet curls plastered on his forehead, Vauquelin is on Night 49. His eyes are red and his heart might as well have been fed through a meat grinder.

Éric sits behind Vauquelin, perching his chin on his shoulders.

"I was never okay, V. Not until last night when I crashed into you."

Vauquelin turns the page over and swerves his chin to Éric.

"My anger at Olivier refusing your calls boils over, yet I …" he looks away, unable to tell Éric that he is dead.

"He never called me back, not to this day. I guess he hates me."

Vauquelin grits his teeth, and his regret for Olivier's demise erodes away.

"Mon cœur .† Apologies are insufficient. This makes me despise my life before you … I drowned you in my own despair. I may never understand the expanse of time, but know that my grief at being parted from you equals yours."

They speak in unison: "Nothing made sense."

It makes them laugh.

Thread by delicate thread, their souls are knitting back together.

"I don't know when I'll ever stop being scared, V, or believe that you're actually here."

"Nor do I, my love, nor do I."

"Read the rest later, okay? You came back for me … literally nothing else matters."

"So, modelling, hein?‡ Do you wish to continue this?" Vauquelin is more than a little perplexed — it is so completely opposite of his own efforts to

---

†- MY HEART, MY LOVE
‡- EH?

remain hidden that he cannot empathise with it. His transcendent beloved, exposed for the world to gaze upon … it makes him nauseous.

"Please tell me you have no internet profiles."

Éric shakes his head. "No, V. No. I deleted them all before we left California."

He has no desire to add to Vauquelin's distress.

He takes V's hand, presses it to his face.

"I kept myself safe. I quit. Like three years ago. I have a ton of magazines and photos and stuff to show you. But that's all over now. You don't look well, my love. I'll go get us something."

He moves to rise, and Vauquelin firmly grasps his wrist.

"Éric, no … please. I am not ready."

Some words cannot be uttered aloud.

I do not want anyone else near.

Only us.

For now, just for now, I need our space to be sacred only to us.

Please.

Éric hears him.

He brings Vauquelin to his neck.

The protected now will protect.

Éric observes Vauquelin with a hawk's eye over the next few weeks.

Vauquelin is skittish and jumpy.

He reminds himself that V's perception of the time slip and his own are vastly different.

This isn't about what *he's* done in Vauquelin's absence.

This is about Vauquelin.

Éric has had four years to adjust.

V's slip was compressed into three months, and still he has not revealed what exactly happened to him while he was gone.

Éric was born in Generation Z: he can readily identify mental distress when he sees it. His lover is suffering, and Éric will treat him with nothing but tenderness and patience.

He refuses to pressure him: he knows V will talk when he's ready.

Vauquelin has never had anyone to dote on him, to care for him this way, and though it fills him with gratitude it heaps even more distress upon him — because his weakness is on blatant display and he is powerless to avert it. Éric's compassion humiliates him as much as it comforts him.

He is an invalid, and he is ashamed.

None of his other time-slips have debilitated his body to such a severe degree: so why this one?

He is perpetually tired and often sits staring into the distance, or wanders through the night garden.

But any moment his beloved appears in front of him his face alights, and Éric recognises V's fire behind those icy, haunted eyes.

The only time Vauquelin is himself is when they make love.

One night Éric asks him why.

Vauquelin's eyes redden and he forces the blood tears back.

"Because ... when our bodies are united, it is only then I believe you cannot be taken from me."

PARIS, FRANCE | SEPTEMBER

THIS YEAR

Vauquelin is seated on the sofa in Éric's game lair, his legs crossed like a woman as always, watching his beloved twitch and curse. He breaks out into laughter after one particular f-bomb-ridden tirade.

"What?" Éric asks, biting his lower lip in a smile but still not taking his eyes off the screen.

"This is meant to be fun, no? Is this a good expenditure of your time, being angry?"

"FUCK! I crashed." Éric sets the controller on his lap and faces Vauquelin. "It's totally fun. Trust me ... my virtual body count far outnumbers my real life one," he smirks. Then an idea strikes him, and he pushes the controller into Vauquelin's hand. "Give it a try."

Vauquelin holds it by his thumb and forefinger as if it were a filthy rag. "I think not."

"Come on ... you might like it."

"My love, perhaps another time. I am ready to let go."

Éric powers everything down without question.

When Vauquelin finishes Éric begins to pace, cradling his head in his arms, and despite the severity of the topic, Vauquelin's eyes crinkle with pleasure.

Family traits, indeed.

« Putain d'enfer ! »[†] Éric mutters repeatedly, causing Vauquelin to tilt his head in delighted curiosity at hearing his beloved curse in French.

"You killed Olivier ... your oldest friend ... in exchange for ME? Oh god, I hope you don't end up regretting this."

"Regret implies that there was a choice, Éric. Olivier was my sole existing progeny at that time and reclaiming his dark blood was my only way back to you. My greatest regret is that I did not know at the time that he turned his back to you when you needed him. Even so, I have released my guilt."

Éric collapses on the sofa next to him.

"But you knew him, what ... eight hundred years? Or more? He knew you when you were human!"

"Yes, bien-aimé ... he did." Vauquelin kneels at Éric's feet, folding his hands in his beloved's lap. "Now no one else remains alive who knew me then. But I hope this makes it quite clear that I would have done anything to return to you. Absolutely anything."

He draws Éric's lips to his.

"I am nothing without you."

Éric backs him down to the floor, and Vauquelin is thrilled by his once-fledgling's powerful strength. He groans with pleasure.

Éric grasps Vauquelin's chin in both hands, stroking his jawbone with his thumbs, looking directly into his eyes. "No regrets," he whispers, and then launches into French with an impeccable accent.

---

†- FUCKING HELL

« Je suis un fragment de coquillage brisé sans Vauquelin . Ne me laisse plus jamais seul . »[†]

Astonished, Vauquelin now understands how Éric has truly been spending his time, and he answers without hesitation, albeit breathlessly.

« Plus jamais, mon cœur . Je te jure . »[‡]

[†] I AM A FRAGMENT OF A BROKEN SEASHELL WITHOUT VAUQUELIN. NEVER LEAVE ME ALONE AGAIN.
[‡] NEVER AGAIN, MY LOVE. I SWEAR TO YOU.

Sixty-one

LOS ANGELES, CALIFORNIA | OCTOBER

Their charter plane touches down at LAX at 03:00 local time.

Vauquelin had ordered the pilot not to give any location details or arrival time over the speakers.

Éric's patience is running thin.

He's been trying really hard, but Vauquelin pulled down all the shades hours ago, and now he's being tested even further as the tires skid smoothly on the runway and V ties a blindfold across his eyes.

"Just a bit longer, my love."

"You're so fucking infuriating!" Éric isn't really mad, though ... he says this with his crooked grin in full force.

Soon, they're barrelling across the 101, and the car slows down to exit.

"These turns feel oddly familiar," Éric mutters.

The car dips as their suitcases are unloaded from the trunk, and he hears Vauquelin thanking the driver in English ... then the car door opens. A very cold hand takes his own equally cold one, and Éric entrusts V to guide him out of the car.

He reaches for the blindfold.

"Tsssst. Not yet. Almost there, *bien-aimé.*"

Vauquelin leads Éric up a steep walk, bracing him with his arm.

Éric hears a series of beeps.

"Where are we?" he whines.

The sound of a door opening, Éric trips on a threshold, and Vauquelin steadies him, whisking the blindfold off.

Éric's face illuminates and he brings a fist to his lips, jumping up and down in his elation. "Oh my GOD! Are you fucking *kidding* me right now?"

"Welcome home, my love."

That rented house on Mulholland Drive, where it all began ...

Now it belongs to them.

ACKNOWLEDGEMENTS

My most gracious thanks go to Beverley Lee — not only is she my writing
partner and dearest friend, she is the godmother of my vampires and was with
me every step of the way for *Citizens of Shadow* and beyond.
Je t'adore, ma chère !

Merci mille fois to my early readers: Alex Pearson, Tyanne Fabian,
Danielle Klassen, Paulette Kennedy, Brittany Roos, and Austrian Spencer,
all of whom gave me priceless and insightful feedback.

Last but certainly not least, my thanks to Alyssa Thorne for creating
the most beautiful and perfect vanitas for the cover of this book.
Citizens would not be the same without this magnificent visual.

ALSO BY NICOLE EIGENER

BEGUILED BY NIGHT

CRIMSON IS THE NIGHT
WITH BEVERLEY LEE

Want more? Read on.

A CONCLAVE OF CRIMSON
WITH BEVERLEY LEE

Vauquelin's and Éric's story continues in a trilogy sequel combining
the Gabriel Davenport series by Beverley Lee and
Beguiled by Night and *Citizens of Shadow* by Nicole Eigener.

Subscribe on nicoleeigener.substack.com

ABOUT THE AUTHOR

Nicole Eigener is a lifelong student of history and the macabre. Their love for haemovores became a beautiful marriage to their obsession with French history and culture, specifically of the seventeenth-century.

Citizens of Shadow is Nicole's second novel. Growing up, the words of Toni Morrison were always bubbling beneath their dark surfaces: "If there's a book that you want to read, but it hasn't been written yet, then you must write it." And so they did. Eigener is also the author, with Beverley Lee, of *Crimson is the Night*, a novelette sequel to *Beguiled by Night* and Lee's Gabriel Davenport series, parts of which appear in this book. Vauquelin's story continues in *A Conclave of Crimson: A Queer Vampire Romance Trilogy,* also with Beverley Lee.

Nicole lives in Southern California.

Instagram: @beguiledbynight

Visit *thevampire.org* to experience more of Nicole's vampire world, including French pronunciations and soundtracks.

Transcrit au bureau des Hypothèques de Rambouillet le quatorze mars mil huit cent trente quatre Vol= 205 N°= 157 Reçu sept francs quatre vingt quatre centimes

Mamotte

12 f 24 c

* 9 7 9 8 9 8 7 3 8 0 2 3 9 *